ROMANTIC TIMES PRAISES NEW YORK TIMES BESTSELLING AUTHOR MADELINE BAKER!

SPIRIT'S SONG

"Madeline Baker consistently delivers winning, heart-wrenching, passionate romances and *Spirit's Song* is no exception."

UNDER A PRAIRIE MOON

"Madeline Baker writes of a ghost, a curse, and a second chance with such power and passion readers cannot help but be mesmerized."

CHASE THE WIND

"This sequel to *Apache Runaway* is pure magic and packed with action, adventure, and passion. Madeline Baker fans, get ready to laugh and cry from the beginning to the surprising ending."

THE ANGEL & THE OUTLAW

"Readers will rave about Madeline Baker's extraordinary storytelling talents."

LAKOTA RENEGADE

"*Lakota Renegade* is as rich, passionate, and delicious as all Madeline Baker's award-winning romances!"

APACHE RUNAWAY

"Madeline Baker has done it again! This romance is poignant, adventurous, and action packed."

CHEYENNE

"This is a funny, witty, poig
Ms. Baker's fans will be mo

Other *Leisure* and *Love Spell* books by
Madeline Baker:
UNFORGETTABLE
SPIRIT'S SONG
UNDER A PRAIRIE MOON
WARRIOR'S LADY
LOVE FOREVERMORE
LOVE IN THE WIND
FEATHER IN THE WIND
CHASE THE WIND
THE ANGEL & THE OUTLAW
LAKOTA RENEGADE
APACHE RUNAWAY
BENEATH A MIDNIGHT MOON
CHEYENNE SURRENDER
WARRIOR'S LADY
THE SPIRIT PATH
MIDNIGHT FIRE
COMANCHE FLAME
PRAIRIE HEAT
A WHISPER IN THE WIND
FORBIDDEN FIRES
LACEY'S WAY
FIRST LOVE, WILD LOVE
RECKLESS DESIRE
RECKLESS LOVE
RECKLESS HEART

Other *Leisure* and *Love Spell* books by Madeline
Baker writing as Amanda Ashley:
THE CAPTIVE
SHADES OF GRAY
A DARKER DREAM
SUNLIGHT, MOONLIGHT
DEEPER THAN THE NIGHT
EMBRACE THE NIGHT

Renegade Heart

MADELINE BAKER

LOVE SPELL NEW YORK CITY

*To my husband Bill
who makes it possible
for me to stay home
and write to my heart's content.*

A LOVE SPELL BOOK®

March 2001

Published by

Dorchester Publishing Co., Inc.
276 Fifth Avenue
New York, NY 10001

If you purchased this book without a cover you should be aware that this book is stolen property. It was reported as "unsold and destroyed" to the publisher and neither the author nor the publisher has received any payment for this "stripped book."

Copyright © 1989 by Madeline Baker

All rights reserved. No part of this book may be reproduced or transmitted in any form or by any electronic or mechanical means, including photocopying, recording or by any information storage and retrieval system, without the written permission of the publisher, except where permitted by law.

ISBN 0-505-52431-7

The name "Love Spell" and its logo are trademarks of Dorchester Publishing Co., Inc.

Printed in the United States of America.

Visit us on the web at www.dorchesterpub.com.

Renegade Heart

MADELINE BAKER

Prologue

*H*is name was Logan Tyree and he was on the run. And like every other man who had ever been lucky enough to escape from the hell-hole known as Yuma Prison, he was determined never to return. Better to die of thirst beneath a blistering Arizona sun, or bleed to death from the heavy .45 caliber slug lodged low in his left side than return to a life behind bars.

Yuma Territorial Prison! A hundred and ten degrees in the shade. A miserable five-by-eight foot cell; no windows, just cold gray walls and a steel-barred door. Yuma! Eighteen months of scummy lukewarm water and putrid food not fit for a pig. Lice-infested blankets and heavy chains. Chains that hobbled his feet and curbed his long, carefree stride. Chains that rattled annoyingly with every step, loudly proclaiming the loss of his freedom. Chains that scarred his flesh and shriveled his soul.

Well, the chains were gone, he mused sourly, but the scars remained. He carried other scars, too—faint, silvery streaks that crisscrossed his broad back and shoulders like a finely spun spider web. Scars left by the whip.

Damn! Just the thought of the lash was enough to make him break out in a cold sweat. There had been one guard in whose hands the lash had come alive, until it was no longer nine feet of limp rawhide, but a sibilant twisting tongue of flame that danced endlessly over shrinking, cringing flesh.

They only had to beat him once. Other men, rebelliously proud and foolishly stubborn, died under the lash sobbing for mercy. But Tyree was no fool. There was no hope where there was no life, and there was no mercy in the Yuma pen. And so he had swallowed his pride and curbed his tongue. Outwardly, he became a model prisoner, forcing himself to say "Yes, sir" and "No, sir", obeying every command meekly and without question or complaint. And all the while he was seething inside. Seething with the need to be free, to see the stark beauty of the Arizona desert, to climb the lofty mountains of Montana, to ride across the vast rolling grasslands of the Dakotas. The love of the wild country was strong within him and he had yearned for the unfettered freedom of the plains as some inmates had yearned for whiskey or women or a deck of cards.

Prison life had not come easy to a man who had never been tied down; a man who had never in his whole adult life had to arrange his days by the rigid discipline of a clock. Always, he had done as he pleased when he pleased, and it had rankled deep inside when he was compelled to rise when he wanted to sleep, eat when he wasn't hungry or go without, meekly submitting his will to the will of others. No, it had not been easy, skulking around like a whipped cur with its tail tucked between its legs, but it had paid off.

Thinking him to be a broken man, the guards had used Tyree to run errands from one prison building to another. He had played the part of a cowed con so well the guards got careless in his presence. And their carelessness had cost two of them their lives, and earned Tyree the freedom he had so desired.

Pushing the memory aside, Tyree slapped his weary mount with the reins, demanding another burst of speed from an animal already on the brink of exhaustion. A white man would have been shocked at the brutal way he pushed the heavily lathered bay mare, but Tyree had been raised by the Apache. And it was the Apache way to ride a horse until it dropped and then, if there was time, to eat the carcass.

He swore softly as the bay stumbled, praying that the game little mare's strength would last until he reached the Mescalero stronghold high in the distant mountains, or at least until he found a decent place to make a stand against the posse that was little more than two hours behind him.

But even as the thought crossed his mind, the bay stumbled for the last time. Badly jarred, Tyree leaped from the saddle seconds before the horse rolled onto its side. There was blood dribbling from the mare's flared nostrils, the empty look of death in her liquid brown eyes.

Squinting against the blinding sun, Tyree searched his backtrail. There was no sign of the posse, but he knew Fat Ass and his henchmen were closing in on him, snuffling at his heels like buffalo wolves on the scent of a wounded calf. And so Tyree began to walk, one hand pressed hard against his wounded side. The exertion brought a fresh sheen of sweat to his face as rolling waves of pain splintered down his left side.

The desert floor dipped, dropped to a shallow bowl, angled upward once more, and now he was in a patchwork land of red-walled canyons and shallow arroyos. Pausing briefly on a narrow rocky ledge, he scanned the surrounding countryside. A wide thread of blue snaked its way southward toward Mexico, and freedom. For a moment, he was sorely tempted to head for the river. But that was exactly what the posse would expect him to do, and so he continued northward toward the sandhills, laboriously plodding through the deep sand. Each step required a concentrated effort of will, each breath caused his wound to throb with renewed vigor, but he moved forward with relentless determination, grinning crookedly as the soft sand absorbed his tracks, leaving no telltale sign of his passing.

Topping the last dune, he hunkered down on his heels in the scant shade offered by a stunted saguaro. Lifting his hand from his side, he scowled bleakly at the sticky red wetness coating his palm, quietly cursing the guard who had shot him. Grimacing, he removed the crude bandage swathed around his middle. The wound, now two days old, was festering. Bright red streaks spread fan-like from the mouth of the bullet hole like spokes on a wheel.

Replacing the sodden bandage, Tyree wished fleetingly for a cold glass of beer to chase the dust from his throat. Or, better still, for a tall glass of Kentucky bourbon to dull the searing ache in his side. But such wishes were futile and quickly forgotten as a rising cloud of dust caught his eye.

From his vantage point atop the dune, he watched the twelve-man posse ride into view. They drew rein near the bay mare's carcass, talking excitedly as they dismounted to check the ground for sign. Brody, the territorial marshal, was easily identified, even from a distance. Grossly overweight, he lumbered around like a fat, two-legged grizzly.

There wasn't a bona fide tracker in the lot, Tyree mused, and breathed a silent prayer of thanks to Usen that this posse had neither dogs nor Indians to guide them. They were stupid, Tyree thought contemptuously. So very stupid. Shuffling around like headless chickens, they were blotting out the very tracks they hoped to find.

In seconds, the few prints Tyree had left were gone, obliterated beneath the careless boot heels of a dozen men. He vented a sigh of relief as the posse remounted and rode south, toward the border. Sooner or later, Tyree knew Brody would realize his mistake and turn back. But there was no point in worrying about that now. With a grin, he rose to his feet and started down the backside of the dune.

Halfway down, he stumbled in the soft sand, tumbling head over heels to the bottom of the sandy slope. He lay there for a full five minutes, wondering if he shouldn't just curl up and die. But he had never been a quitter. Summoning what strength he had left, he gained his feet and continued walking north; a tall, dark man dressed in blue denim pants and a checked shirt stolen from a washline along the way. The clothes did not fit well. The pants were too short for his long muscular legs, the shirt too small to comfortably accommodate his broad shoulders. Though he was not a handsome man in the usual sense of the word, he possessed an aura of strength and virility that most women found irresistibly attractive. His hair, long and inky black, curled slightly at the nape of his neck. His mouth was wide, his jaw firm, hinting at stubbornness, his nose was a broad slash. His eyes were a curious shade of yellow, narrowed now to mere slits against the midday sun. A thick moustache and a coarse beard covered the lower half of his face.

The pain in his side throbbed with the steady precision of an Apache war drum, but he pressed steadily onward, his face an impassive mask that revealed none of the agony coursing through his left side. The desert was an oven, the sun was the flame, and he was the meat, cooking slowly, until all the juice had been baked from his flesh and only a dry husk remained.

His feet were like lead and it was an effort to put one foot in front of the other. Misjudging a step, he fell, jarring his wound, and he felt the blood flow warm and wet down his left flank. Bright shafts of pain danced up and down his side. It was, he reminded himself, a small price to pay for his freedom. And if the festering wound killed him, so be it. Better to die free in the desert than to live behind the high gray walls and cold iron bars of Yuma, where every day was the same as the last, and every night longer than the night before.

The air grew colder as the miles slipped by, and he shivered convulsively. Though he had not eaten for two days, his desire was not for meat, but for water. Just one sip to ease his nagging thirst. But there was no sign of water and so he plodded ever northward, bound for the lodges of the Mescalero Apache. There would be water in the rancheria, all he could drink. There would be food to fill his hungry belly, friendly faces to cheer him, gentle hands to ease his pain, a snug lodge where he could rest in peace and comfort.

Sleep. His body cried for it. And still he moved drunkenly forward, driven by sheer will alone. Slowly, so slowly, the sun slipped behind the distant mountains, turning the western sky to flame and the earth to blood.

With the coming of dusk, a chill wind began to blow across the face of the land, keening like a grieving Comanche squaw. And still he walked, doggedly placing one foot in front of the other, keeping one ear cocked for the sound of hoofbeats coming from the south. Because Brody would come. Sooner or later, he would come.

But the land remained dark and quiet save for the wail of the wind and the rasp of his own labored breathing. Overhead, the stars came alive in the sky, sparkling like a million diamonds carelessly tossed across the black blanket of the heavens, and still he walked, until his legs turned to stone and refused to move another inch. Groggy with the need for sleep, burning with fever, he sought shelter for the night in a shallow hollow that smelled strongly of skunk. Dizzy with exhaustion, weak from the loss of blood and lack of food and water, he collapsed in the hole, groaning as he landed on his injured side. Gasping with pain, he huddled in the dirt while bright lights flashed before his eyes. A sudden warmth along his left flank told him he was bleeding again, but he was too far gone in pain to care.

Death hovered over him, and with the end of life in sight, he pondered his beginnings, and the fate that had brought him to die in the desert, alone. . . .

He did not remember his father at all. And his mother was only a vague shadow, a warm memory of soft flesh and strong perfume. Later, unkind people would tell him the truth about his parents; about the half-breed Comanche who was hung for a horse thief, about the young Irish prostitute who gave him life in a bordello in a sleepy Texas town and then, three years later, abandoned him to run off with a two-bit gambler.

No one wanted a quarter-breed bastard, and so the child was sent to live with the nuns at a small Spanish convent located near the Mexican border, and there he stayed until he was eight years old. It was then the nuns decided the convent was no place for a boy, especially a boy as impudent and rebellious as Tyree. Inquiries were made and the nuns found him a foster home . . . and then another . . . and another.

He was not an easy child to love—the quiet,

sullen-faced boy with the suspicious amber eyes.

He was 12 years old and living with a bald-headed German farmer and his kindly wife when the Apaches came, killing the German couple, but sparing Tyree because there was no mistaking the Indian blood that ran in the boy's veins.

He lived with the Mescalero for thirteen years, and they were good years. He grew to manhood, became a warrior, took a wife . . . Red Leaf was her name. She came to him untouched and unafraid, fulfilling every dream he had ever hoped for. Friend, mother, sister, wife—she was all women rolled into one. Daily, he thanked all the Apache gods for the beautiful raven-haired woman who shared his lodge and made his life worthwhile. He had thought to spend the rest of his life with the Apache, but six white men came along one fine summer day and changed the course of Tyree's life.

He had been walking beside the river with Red Leaf that fateful day. They were alone, far from camp, when the white men attacked. Tyree had fought them as best he could, but his knife was no match for six rifles. A bullet grazed his arm, another pierced his shoulder. And then one of the men got behind him and buffaloed him with a rifle butt.

When he regained consciousness, Red Leaf was dead. He had stared at her mutilated corpse for a long time, unable to believe his eyes, until the vomit came and he fell to his knees.

When his stomach stopped heaving, he wrapped her body in his shirt and buried her beneath a windblown pine. And as he smoothed the dirt over her grave, all that was kind and gentle seemed to wither and die within him.

He sat by her grave all the rest of that long lonely day and night, remembering the good times they had shared, the sound of her laughter, the touch of her body against his in the quiet of the night, the way her dark eyes had glowed with love whenever he kissed her.

Slowly, the stars wheeled across the sky, and he stared, unseeing, into the darkness. A lone coyote wailed in the distance, and its melancholy cry was like the echo of his own grief.

Gradually, the horizon grew light, and when the sun rose above the mountains, Logan Tyree had shed his last tear. Relentless as a starved lobo, he prowled the river's edge, searching the ground for sign, casting about in ever-widening circles, using all the skills the Mescalero had taught him.

He was not disappointed. Hours of painstaking effort rewarded him with that which he so eagerly sought. Moments later he was tracking six iron-shod ponies headed southeast. It did not occur to him to ask the Apache for help. They would have been willing, even eager, to take a few paleface scalps, but avenging Red Leaf's death was something he needed to do alone.

The tracks separated near New Mexico: four sets going towards Colorado, two sets drifting south towards Texas. He followed the first trail because it was the biggest. And found the four men sleeping beside the dying embers of a campfire. The first four, caught while his grief was still fresh, died the hardest. Their screams had been the sweetest music he had ever heard.

Ironically, he found the last two men in the same dirty whorehouse where he had been born. He had killed them where he found them, giving them no chance to plead their innocence, no time to defend themselves, no opportunity to call for help.

And so Red Leaf's death was avenged, and now there was a terrible emptiness inside, for he had neither love to warm him nor hate to sustain him. Unable to face the thought of returning to the Apache now that she was dead, he drifted into Abilene, Kansas. And somehow, without rhyme or reason, he became a hired gun, quickly earning a reputation as a merciless, cold-blooded killer. As time passed, his reputation grew and spread, until he found himself being credited with murders he hadn't committed, accused of crimes he knew nothing about, crimes that occurred in towns where he had never been.

But they had caught him red-handed in Arizona, the gun still in his hand, the body bleeding at his feet. Perhaps, if the woman had been white, they would have rewarded him for killing the man who had been trying to beat her to death with an axe handle.

But the woman had been an Apache squaw, the white man had been her husband, and Tyree had been sentenced to 99 years in the Yuma Pen. . . .

Chapter 1

*R*achel Halloran smiled warmly at the young man sitting beside her on the front porch swing.

"I'll miss you, Clint," she said, her voice soft as honey. "You will be careful, won't you?"

Clint Wesley's grin was as bright as the six-pointed star pinned to his vest.

"Caution's my middle name, Rachel. You know that."

Rachel laughed softly. Clint *was* cautious. He never made a move that hadn't been carefully thought out in advance. She knew he loved her, wanted to marry her, yet his courtship had been slow and predictable. He had spoken to her several times in church— only after they had been formally introduced by a mutual friend, of course. After that, he had sought her out at socials and picnics. A few months later, he had asked her father if he might come to call. Now he came to see her every Saturday night and more often than not, Rachel invited him to Sunday dinner as well. Their romance was very circumspect. After they had dated for a month and a half, Clint found the courage to hold her hand. A few months later, he summoned the nerve to put his arm around her shoulders when they sat together on the porch swing. Just recently, he had found the courage to kiss her. He had asked her permission first, of course. Somehow, that had irritated her, though she was careful not to let it show. She supposed she loved Clint and would likely marry him one day in the future, but sometimes she wished he was more exciting, more spontaneous. If he wanted to kiss her, why didn't he just sweep her into his arms and kiss her?

Rachel sighed softly as Clint's arm went around her shoulders. He was a nice young man and she was terribly fond of him. People just naturally liked Clint. He was tall and handsome, with sandy blond hair and mild blue eyes. He didn't look tough enough to be a lawman and yet he had managed to keep the peace in Yellow Creek for over two years. Of course, few strangers ever came to town, and the local folk rarely violated the town laws, except for Gus Bradshaw, who got roaring drunk every Saturday night. Rachel wondered, sometimes, how Clint would react if a real bad man ever rode into town.

Clint gave Rachel's shoulders a squeeze. Then, with an audible sigh, he stood up, reaching for his hat.

"Well, I'd best be going," he said reluctantly. "I've got to get an early start in the morning."

Rachel stood up, lifting her face for his kiss. "Take care of yourself," she murmured. "I'll miss you."

Wesley nodded. "I'll see you as soon as I get back."

"I'll be waiting."

Wesley nodded again, wondering if he dared kiss her again. Instead, he gave her a last, quick hug, then went down the stairs to where his horse was hitched to the rail. He swung agilely into the saddle, tipped his hat to Rachel, and rode out of the yard.

Rachel smiled as she watched Clint ride away. He would make her a good husband, she mused as she went up to bed. If he ever got the nerve to propose! He had wanted to kiss her again; she had seen it in his eyes. Why hadn't he done it?

Climbing into bed, she drew the covers to her chin, wishing that Clint Wesley would stop worrying about propriety and sweep her off her feet. She fell asleep thinking of Clint, dreaming of all the towheaded children they would someday have.

Saturday morning dawned bright and clear and warm. Rachel's first thought was of Clint: she hoped he'd gotten off to an early start and would return safely home. Transporting a prisoner from Yellow Creek to the territorial prison at Yuma was always a dangerous assignment. You never knew when a prisoner's friends or relatives would take it into their heads to try and help a convicted man escape his fate. Patrick Murphy, the town's previous lawman, had been killed en route to Yuma, shot down in cold blood by his prisoner's brother. Fortunately, such things were rare, but they did happen.

Resolutely, Rachel put such thoughts from her mind. Slipping out of her blue flannel night rail, she dressed quickly and headed downstairs to prepare breakfast for herself and her father.

She found six year old Amy Cahill waiting for her in the kitchen. Amy was a frequent visitor at the Lazy H. Her uncle, Joe Cahill, was foreman of the Halloran ranch.

"Good morning, Amy," Rachel said cheerfully as she tousled the girl's blond curls.

"You slept late," Amy remarked. "Are we making pies today?"

"If you like." Rachel spread a clean cloth over the kitchen table and put the water on for coffee. "You'll have to pick some berries though. I'm fresh out."

"Can I pick them now?"

"Have you had breakfast yet?"

"At home," Amy said, scooping up the berry basket from a shelf in the pantry. "Mama made pancakes."

"Be careful," Rachel cautioned as Amy skipped out the back door.

"I will," Amy replied, her tone implying that was a warning she heard frequently.

The berry bushes were located behind the smokehouse. It was a long walk, but Amy didn't mind. Skipping along, she glanced at the sand hills located some miles away. She had been admonished time and again not to go there, but she promised herself that one day she would explore the forbidden mountains of sand.

But now, pies were uppermost in her mind. The bushes were heavy with fruit and Amy hummed softly as she moved from bush to bush, collecting blackberries. Her basket was nearly full when she found the man. He was lying in a shallow hole in the ground, partially covered with dead leaves.

Startled, Amy stared at the man for a long time, wondering if he were dead. He looked like he was asleep, but then, her best friend, Joe Bob Somers, said that was how dead people looked, like they were sleeping, so how was a girl to know? The man lay so still, Amy decided he had to be dead, and all the scary stories she had ever heard about ghosts and haunts made her shiver with apprehension.

She was about to turn and run for home when the man rolled over and she found herself staring into a pair of pain-glazed yellow eyes.

"Are you all right, mister?" Amy queried tremulously. Slowly, she began to back away from the man, surprised to find she was more afraid of him now that she knew he was alive than she had been when she thought he was dead.

"Need help," the man rasped. He tried to sit up, but fell back heavily. His face went white beneath its tan. "Water—"

"Sure, mister. Just lie still and I'll bring help. Honest I will!"

But the man was unconscious again and did not hear her.

Rachel held the front door open as Joe Cahill and two of the Lazy H cowhands carried the unconscious man into the house. Twenty minutes earlier, Amy had run into the kitchen shouting, "A man, Rachel! I found a man in the berry bushes. I thought he was dead, but he wasn't!"

Once Rachel had calmed the excited child down, she had learned that Amy had first gone to her uncle and that Cahill was even then bringing the man to the house.

Rachel looked at the stranger's face as he was carried inside. Who was he? Where had he come from?

"He's bad hurt," Cahill remarked.

"Take him into the spare bedroom," Rachel said. Frowning, she went down the narrow hallway ahead of the men. Turning left, she entered the spare bedroom located at the end of the hall and quickly turned back the bed-clothes.

"Don't know if he's gonna make it," Cahill muttered as the cowhands laid the injured man on the bed. "That bullet wound looks like it's festering."

"It's in God's hands," Rachel murmured. "All we can do is patch him up and hope for the best."

Logan Tyree stirred at the sound of voices but his eyes refused to open and when he tried to speak, the words would not come. Rough hands endeavored to wrest the six-gun from his grasp, but he batted them away, refusing to relinquish his hold on the .44.

"Shit, Candido, let him keep his iron," Joe Cahill growled. Then, remembering where he was, he murmured, "Sorry, Miss Rachel."

"It's all right."

"He ain't gonna turn loose of that Colt," Cahill mused, "but he ain't got the strength to cock the damn thing, neither." Color crept up the back of Cahill's bull-like neck. "'Scuse me again, Miss Rachel."

Rachel smothered a grin. When the men got excited, they often cursed in her presence. Always, they were embarrassed and quick to apologize.

"Leave the gun for now," Rachel said.

Cahill nodded as he followed the cowhands out of the room. If anyone could pull the stranger through, Rachel Halloran could. Many a man on the Lazy H owed life or limb to her nimble fingers and quick thinking.

Rachel quickly gathered several clean cloths, scissors, disinfectant and a bowl of warm water. Then, taking a deep breath, she began to undress the man lying on the bed. The wound in his side was red, swollen, and infected. Fortunately, she had been blessed with a strong stomach and steady hands and the sight of blood and torn flesh did not send her running for her smelling salts as it did so many of her friends. As the only woman on the ranch, she was often called upon to nurse the sick and tend the wounded. When times were hard and they could not afford the extra help, she often pitched in to work the cattle; occasionally she helped with the branding and the calving, sometimes she helped with the castrating, which was hard dirty work at best and usually left to the men.

With cool efficiency, Rachel began to wash the wound.

Tyree groaned as unseen hands probed for the slug lodged deep in his left side. The slightest touch caused him agony, and he clenched his teeth as the slug was pried from his flesh. Through it all, he held fast to the Colt, finding comfort in the weight and feel of a gun in his hand without remembering why.

Rachel gnawed on her lower lip, her brow knit with determination, as she removed the slug, washed the wound a second time, then swabbed the whole area with strong carbolic.

With a soft grunt of exertion, she rolled the semi-conscious man onto his side so she could remove the sodden, blood-stained linen from the bed. It was then she saw his back. It was badly scarred. She knew men in prison were often flogged for disobedience and she drew back, chilled to the bone by the thought that the man tossing restlessly on the bed might be an escaped felon.

As though hypnotized, she continued to stare in horrified fascination at the broad scarred back, feeling a surge of pity well in her heart. No human being, no matter what his crimes, should be subjected to such cruel abuse.

With tender concern, she washed the broad expanse of sun-bronzed flesh, spread a clean white sheet beneath him, then pulled the bedcovers up over his shoulders.

That done, she studied the man through boldly curious eyes. He was a big man, tall and whipcord lean. Though he was terribly thin, she could see he had once been powerfully built. A thick black moustache and bristly black beard covered the lower portion of his face, making it difficult to determine if he were young or old, handsome or plain.

His language, when he mumbled in his sleep, was coarse, filled with the kind of profanity no lady was ever permitted to hear. Even Rachel, accustomed to the curses of the men who worked the ranch, had rarely heard such foul expletives.

Abruptly, the man began to toss fitfully. His

eyelids flickered open and he stared, unseeing, at Rachel.

"You dirty sonofabitch," he growled in a voice edged with pain. "If my hands were free, I'd take that whip and give you a taste of your own medicine." He lay still, rigid, as though listening to a distant voice, and then he laughed, a deep ugly laugh laced with bitter despair. "Go ahead, you slimy bastard, do your worst!"

Rachel watched in tight-lipped silence as the man's body grew tense from head to heel. His mouth thinned to a taut line and sweat popped out on his brow as he relived the agony of the lash playing across his flesh.

It was too awful to watch. Stepping forward, Rachel placed her hand on the man's shoulder and shook him slightly.

"It's over," she murmured urgently. "Forget it. Sleep now. Hush, hush. It's over. Go to sleep."

Tyree's eyes flickered open as a soft voice murmured words of comfort. He stared at the woman hovering over him, expecting, somehow, to see the face of the woman he had loved more than his own life. But the face hovering above him was pale ivory, not copper; the hair was honey-gold instead of Indian black; the eyes the most incredible shade of sky-blue when they should have been deep chocolate brown.

Disappointed, he closed his eyes and fell into a deep black void that stretched away into infinity.

Rachel stayed at his side almost constantly during the next few days. She held him down when he began to thrash about, fearful that he would rip open the ugly wound in his side. He had already lost a great deal of blood; he could ill afford to lose more should the wound start to bleed again.

The thought that he might be a wanted man gnawed in the back of her mind. Harboring a fugitive was against the law and, though she tried to convince herself he was just a man who had run afoul of outlaws or Indians, she knew deep inside herself that he was wanted by the law. The scars on his back, the odd purple discolorations on his wrists and ankles, undoubtedly caused by shackles, the words he mumbled in his sleep, all pointed to the fact that he was an escaped prisoner.

The man was ever in Rachel's thoughts as she moved from chore to chore. Who was he? What had he done? Was it safe to have such a man in the house? When she voiced her concern to her father, he merely shrugged.

"I don't reckon he'll be much of a threat for another day or two," John Halloran said laconically, "but I'll have one of the boys take him into town to Doc Franklin if his being here bothers you."

"No," Rachel said quickly. "I don't think he should be moved just yet."

The stranger. She could think of little else. Caring for him, she was increasingly aware of the breadth of his shoulders, of the way his long black hair curled around her fingers. His moustache, though bristly to look at, was soft beneath her fingertips. She tried not to stare at his nakedness when she bathed the sweat from his body or changed the bandage swathed around his middle, but her eyes continually strayed toward his flat belly and lean flanks. He was very brown all over, and not just where the sun had touched him. His legs were long, covered with fine black hair. His hands were large and looked capable of great strength. She blushed furiously when she found herself wondering what it would be like to be touched by those hands, to be held in his arms.

He was trouble. Her instincts told her that. She knew she should pray for his speedy recovery but deep inside, she did not want him to leave and that was silly, because she didn't even know the man. She knew she should insist her father notify the proper authorities immediately, but she was too soft-hearted to have the man sent back to jail now, when he was in such obvious distress. There would be plenty of time for that later, when he was well again.

Tyree woke to pain and darkness and a raging thirst made worse by the fever burning through him. He stirred restlessly on the soft mattress, tossing aside the blankets that weighed him down like lead. His fingers tightened instinctively around the butt of the gun he still held in his right hand as a slight figure materialized out of the shadows. A soft hand rested lightly on his brow, a cool cloth gently wiped the perspiration from his face and neck. He felt the tension drain from his body as he recognized the dim outline of the woman who was constantly there to tend his needs.

"Lie still," Rachel murmured. "You're among friends." She glanced at the gun in his hand, but did not try to take it from him.

There were many questions Tyree wanted to ask, but when he tried to speak, only a choked whisper emerged from his throat.

There was the sharp smell of sulphur, a sudden burst of light as the woman touched a match to the candle on the bedside table.

"Are you in pain?" Rachel asked kindly. "Is the bandage too tight?"

"No." Tyree's voice was weak, foreign to his ears.

"Is there anyone I should notify?" Rachel asked. "A wife, perhaps?"

"No. Water." His mouth formed the words but no sound emerged.

But the woman understood and quickly poured him a glass of water from the pitcher standing on the bedside table. She lifted his head while he took a long drink. With his thirst quenched, he slept again.

The next few days passed in a kaleidoscope of pain and fever. His side throbbed mercilessly, burning as if all the fires of hell were kindled inside, and he tossed restlessly from side to side, unable to find relief from the searing pain, or from the nightmare images that haunted his dreams. Dreams of iron bars and cold gray walls, of men long dead, killed by his own hand. At times, Red Leaf's sweetly smiling face filtered into his nightmares and he heard himself babbling incoherently in guttural Apache, heard himself crying her name over and over again, like a frightened child whimpering for its mother.

In his lucid moments, he was ever aware of the woman with the lovely sky-blue eyes sitting quietly by his side. Her face was kind, her eyes sympathetic whether she was gently sponging the rivers of sweat from his brow or easing his thirst with countless cups of water. Always she was there when he needed her, her voice soft and low, as pleasant to the ear as the sound of summer rain on sunbleached prairie grass. Even when he was wandering down the dark corridors of the past, he was somehow aware of her presence lingering nearby, willing him to get well. Perversely, he resented her constant attention and concern, resented the weakness that made him dependent on another human being.

But nothing lasts forever, and a man either gets better or he dies. And Tyree was not ready to die. The day soon came when he opened his eyes and knew the worst was over. His fever was down, leaving him weak as a newborn pup. His side was stiff and sore, painfully tender to touch, but for all that, he felt better than he had in days.

How many days, he wondered, glancing

curiously at his surroundings. There wasn't much to see, just a narrow room sparsely furnished with a small oak table, a tall chest of drawers, and the bed he occupied. His clothes, neatly washed and ironed, were folded on top of the dresser. His .44 rested on the table beside the bed within easy reach of his hand. He wondered how the woman had managed to wrest it from his grasp. He was surprised to discover the Colt was still loaded, the hammer resting on an empty chamber.

He was halfheartedly thinking of trying to get up when the bedroom door swung open on well-oiled hinges and the woman with the sky-blue eyes stepped into the room, skirts swishing about her ankles. She frowned as Tyree's hand closed over the butt of the .44, one long brown finger curling automatically around the trigger.

"Surely you must realize I mean you no harm," Rachel remarked dryly, and Tyree noticed for the first time that she was hardly more than a girl, perhaps nineteen or twenty.

But what a beauty! A wealth of long honey-gold hair tied back with a white grosgrain ribbon, eyes as deep and blue as the Pacific, a small, tip-tilted nose, and a mouth made to be kissed. He had not seen a woman in a long time and his eyes lingered on her figure, admiring the way it went in and out in all the right places. A wide blue sash circled a waist so narrow, he was certain he could span it with one hand.

For a moment, he contemplated dragging her into bed with him and sampling the pouting pink lips that looked as soft as the petals of a wild rose.

"Well?" Rachel said, looking pointedly at the gun he still held in his hand.

With a wry grin, Tyree put the gun aside. "How long have I been here?"

"Nearly a week."

Tyree digested that for a moment, his face thoughtful. "The kid that found me, she yours?"

"No. She's Joe Cahill's niece."

"Cahill?"

"He's our foreman. Amy lives in town, but she comes out to visit Joe on weekends."

"Well, I'm obliged to you and the kid," Tyree said, swinging his long legs over the side of the narrow bed. "Now, if you'll excuse me, I'll get dressed and be on my way."

Rachel frowned at him. Was he kidding? He was in no condition to travel. She was about to tell him so in no uncertain terms when the sheet fell away from his body, exposing his lean torso, flat belly, and one long muscular thigh. A corner of the sheet barely covered his groin.

Rachel's eyes strayed in that direction and she felt hot color wash into her cheeks at his knowing grin. She had seen him nude, of course, when she nursed him, but that had been vastly different. He had been inert then, sick and unable to care for himself. But he was awake and alert now and even though he was still weak and pale, there was an aura of strength and vitality about him that she found both frightening and fascinating.

"Don't you dare move!" Rachel snapped, stung by his abrupt manner and his total lack of modesty. "You're in no fit condition to travel."

"I'll manage."

Rachel's smile was poisonously sweet as she gathered up Tyree's clothing and tucked it securely under one arm. Her tone was equally venomous when she spoke.

"I am sure you could manage quite well," she said, biting off each word. "But I do not intend to see my efforts in your behalf wasted. You are not to set foot out of that bed for at least another week." She gave him another cloying smile. "Now, you just lie there like a good boy and I'll bring you some breakfast. You look like you could use some solid food."

And so saying, she turned on her heel and flounced out of the room, Tyree's clothes bundled securely under one arm, her back ramrod straight with determination.

Tyree swore under his breath. What the hell! Who did she think she was, anyway, telling him what he could and couldn't do? Damned interfering female!

He grinned wryly as he settled back against the pillows. Might as well be comfortable, he mused. He sure as hell wasn't going anywhere, not in his present state of undress.

He was sitting there, his arms crossed over his chest, the sheet scandalously low on his hips, when she returned. She carried a large bowl of oatmeal mush in one hand, a delicate china cup and saucer in the other.

Rachel came to an abrupt halt as she entered the room, her eyes flaring at the sight of Tyree propped up in bed. The sheet, barely covering his loins, looked very white against his swarthy skin.

She took a deep breath, determined not to let him know how strongly the sight of his naked chest appealed to her.

"Shall I feed you?" she asked, each word dripping ice water. "Or can you manage on your own?"

"I thought you said solid food," Tyree growled, eyeing the oatmeal with obvious distaste.

"This is solid enough for a man who's had nothing but beef broth in his belly for nearly a week," Rachel retorted. "Take it or leave it."

Scowling, Tyree accepted the bowl, grimacing as he swallowed a spoonful of oatmeal.

Rachel studied him openly while he ate. His face was hard and unyielding, his eyes cold and cynical beneath straight black brows. There was a wary tenseness about him now that he was fully conscious, a kind of hunted animal alertness, as if he were waiting for a trap to be sprung.

Setting the bowl aside, Tyree met Rachel's frank gaze with one of his own. "I ate my mush like a good boy," he said with a wry grin. "But I draw the line at tea."

"Would you prefer coffee?"

"I'd prefer whiskey."

"I'm afraid you'll have to settle for coffee," Rachel said firmly. Collecting his dirty dish and the untouched cup of tea, she glided out of the room.

Tyree stared after her, his expression dark with anger and frustration.

When the woman returned, a sturdy old man accompanied her. "I'm John Halloran," the old man said, extending his left hand. "I guess you know my daughter, Rachel."

John Halloran was tall and straight, with hair the color of iron and skin that resembled old saddle leather. His right shirt sleeve, empty from the elbow down, was tucked inside his pant's pocket. His grip was firm as they shook hands.

Halloran's bright blue eyes twinkled merrily as he noticed Tyree staring at his empty shirt sleeve. "Lost my arm in a cattle stampede years ago," he remarked good-naturedly. "But I'm better now. How about you?"

"Much better. I'm obliged for your hospitality."

"Glad to help out, though Rachel, here, has to take most of the credit. I, uh, don't believe I caught your name."

"I don't believe I gave it, but you can call me Smith."

"On the run, eh?" Halloran surmised,

chuckling. "Well, rest easy, Smith. We're a long way from any real law out here." He glanced briefly at the gun lying on the table beside the bed. "You any good with that iron?"

Tyree shrugged. "I usually hit what I aim at."

John Halloran nodded slowly. "Yeah. Yeah, I reckon you do at that. Well, an extra gun might come in handy," he muttered cryptically, and ambled out of the room, his bushy white eyebrows drawn together in a thoughtful frown.

When they were alone, Rachel asked, bluntly, "Are you wanted by the law, Mr. Smith?"

"Listen, lady," Tyree answered testily, "I'm obliged to you for taking care of me, but my status with the law is none of your business."

"I don't think I like you," Rachel retorted, her sky-blue eyes flashing fire.

"Not many do."

"And you like it that way, don't you?" Rachel observed intuitively. "Ever since I came in here this morning, you've done your best to be unpleasant. Why? What are you trying to prove?"

"You're a nosey brat," Tyree muttered. "Didn't your old man teach you not to pry into other people's affairs?"

Rachel recoiled as if she had been slapped. "Pardon me," she said, the frost on her words an inch thick and rising. "I'll not pry into your personal life again." And drawing her dignity around her like a cloak, she left the room.

Tyree stared after her for a long time, mentally cursing her for taking his clothes. He couldn't very well go parading out of the place wearing nothing but his boots and a smile. Damn the woman! Why didn't she mind her own damn business and let him mind his?

He slept away the rest of the morning, dutifully accepted the thin beef broth and fresh baked bread the woman served him for lunch, and politely asked for seconds.

Mollified by Tyree's sudden appetite and subdued manner, Rachel brought him a second slice of bread still warm from the oven along with his soup. She also offered him a cup of hot black coffee modestly laced with brandy. She tidied up the room while he ate, ever aware of his eyes on her back.

"I'm sorry for this morning," Tyree said after awhile. His voice was gruff, giving Rachel the distinct impression that he was unaccustomed to apologizing for either his words or his actions.

"I'm sorry, too," Rachel said, smiling.

"You and your old man run this place alone?"

"Just about. Job Walsh and the Apaches have scared off most of our hands."

"Walsh?"

"He owns the Slash W Ranch just east of here. It's the biggest spread in this part of the territory."

"And he wants this place, too."

"Yes. How did you know?"

"It's an old story," Tyree said shrugging. "You must have a pretty good piece of land if Walsh wants it."

"Yes. Do you know Walsh?"

"I know the type."

"Then you know what we're up against."

"I know you're a fool."

"I beg your pardon."

"You heard me. You're out of your mind if you're bucking the Apaches on one hand and a land-grabber like Walsh on the other."

"That may be!" Rachel replied curtly. "But our roots are here, on the Lazy H. My mother and my little brother are buried here. We're not leaving."

"Suit yourself. It's no skin off my ass."

"No, it isn't!" Rachel snapped crossly, and stalked out of the room, slamming the door soundly behind her.

John Halloran smiled fondly at Rachel as she moved about the spacious kitchen preparing their dinner. She was a lovely young woman, every inch a lady despite the rugged life she led. He was proud of her quiet beauty, proud of the way she carried her share of the work load without complaint, proud of her inner strength and character.

We did ourselves proud, Ellen, he mused to himself. *Proud indeed*!

"He's wanted by the law, you know that, don't you?" Rachel said irritably. She was still angry with the man who called himself Smith. His language and his arrogance were beyond belief. "We've no business keeping him here any longer."

"Another day or two won't hurt," Halloran countered mildly. But Rachel was right. The man was obviously on the run. He had that hunted air about him, that wary alertness common to all hunted creatures, be they man or beast.

"I don't like him," Rachel muttered, spreading a red and white checked cloth over the table.

"He'll be moving on soon," Halloran said. Rising, he poured himself a cup of coffee from the big black pot that was always simmering on the back burner of the stove. "I wish I could—"

"Could what?" Rachel asked suspiciously.

"Nothing, nothing," Halloran answered quickly. But the thought lingered in his mind. The man calling himself Smith might be a wanted man, a dangerous man, but he could definitely be an asset to the Lazy H. He had gunman written all over him, and a good fast gun was something the Lazy H desperately needed.

John Halloran's thoughts were temporarily interrupted as Rachel put dinner on the table. She was a good cook, he mused, but then Rachel had always excelled at anything she put her mind to.

They made small talk about the ranch during dinner. It was Rachel's habit not to discus anything unpleasant during meals an Halloran obliged her. Thus, the time the spent dining together was always a time t relax and enjoy one another's company be cause, besides being father and daughter, the were good friends.

Rachel smiled at her father as he filled hi plate a second time. It amazed her that h never gained any weight, for he ate enough fc two hearty men. He was a rare and warr human being, she thought fondly. Despite th harsh land and their never-ending trouble with Job Walsh, her father remained a gentl man with a kind heart and a good soul.

Laying her fork aside, Rachel prepared plate for Smith. She dreaded the thought c seeing him again. It made her uncomfortable just being in the same room with him. He wa: she decided, the most aggravating man sh had ever met.

She felt his eyes on her face the minute sh entered the room. The force of his gaze mad her uneasy and two bright spots of colc appeared in her cheeks.

"Smells good," he drawled.

Wordlessly, Rachel placed the tray on th bedside table. Her whole attitude screame that she did not appreciate his presence in he house.

"Sorry I didn't die," Tyree muttered irrita bly. "It would have saved you a lot of extr work."

"Yes, it would have," Rachel agreed. "I'll be back later for the tray."

Tyree scowled as she swished out of the room. Never had any woman looked at him with such loathing. He attacked his food with a vengeance, admitting, grudgingly, that she was a hell of a good cook.

In the kitchen, Rachel put the last of the dinner dishes away, then joined her father in the den for a game of checkers. It was the best part of the day, a time for sharing the day's problems, a time when decisions were made, ideas exchanged.

A knock at the front door interrupted their game. John Halloran opened the door cautiously, frowned as he invited his visitors inside.

The voice of the fat territorial marshal penetrated Logan Tyree's dream, waking him instantly. Eyes closed, Tyree listened while John Halloran assured Marshal Brody that no one answering Tyree's description had been seen on the Lazy H.

"But you're welcome to search the place if you've a mind to," Halloran offered.

In the back bedroom, Tyree held his breath as he waited for the marshal's reply.

"No need," the lawman responded gruffly. "But if he comes sniffing around, you shoot first and ask questions later. He's a hired gun. A killer."

"A killer?" There was genuine alarm in Rachel's voice.

"Yes, ma'am," Brody said. "A cold-blooded murderer. Gunned down two men in a Texas whorehouse for no reason at all some years back. Never even gave 'em a chance to draw. Killed a man here in Arizona, too. And that's just three of many."

In the bedroom, Tyree had a mental picture of the worried glances passing between Halloran and his daughter, and his hand closed over the .44 lying under his pillow. Would Halloran turn him in, now that he knew he was harboring a fugitive?

Tyree's eyes probed the dusky room. The window was the only way out of the house other than the door, and while he didn't particularly relish the prospect of running off into the night stark naked, he would do it if he had to because, by damn, he wasn't going back to prison!

"He sounds quite desperate," Rachel said anxiously.

"Yes, ma'am, damn desperate," the marshal replied, warming to his subject. "And lucky to boot. We lost his trail out in the desert a couple weeks back, but we figured he'd head south for the border, so we trailed in that direction. We were circling back when a sandstorm caught us. Damned if it no sooner blew over than a handful of redskins run off with our horses. Damn savages! Took us three days to walk to the Bar J for fresh mounts. Three damn days! If I ever catch that bastard, Tyree, he'll pay for those three days."

"Well, we'll keep our eyes peeled for him," Halloran said sincerely. "You can be sure of that."

"Pa—"

"Later, Rachel," Halloran said. "You and your men are welcome to spend the night in the bunkhouse, marshal. You'll be comfortable there. It's the first building on the left."

"That's mighty kind of you," Brody said. "Evening, ma'am."

"Breakfast is at six," Rachel said. "You and your men are welcome to join us."

"We'll be there."

Rachel turned angry eyes on her father as she closed the door behind the marshal and his posse.

"Pa—"

"Hush, daughter."

"I will not hush. And I will not have that dreadful man in this house another night."

"You wanna turn a sick man over to a lawman like Elias Brody? Why, I'll bet Tyree would never make it back to Yuma alive."

"That's not our concern."

"Isn't it? He's a human being, Rachel. It's not for us to judge him."

"Oh, Pa," Rachel murmured helplessly. "You should have been a preacher."

Halloran chuckled. "Maybe. Let's go check on our patient."

Tyree was sitting up in bed when Rachel and her father entered the room. The .44 was nestled in his right hand, aimed in the general direction of the door. Rachel could not help thinking the gun looked right at home in Logan's Tyree's calloused hand.

"That's two I owe you," Tyree drawled.

"You heard?" Halloran asked, dropping down onto the foot of the bed.

"Enough. I'm obliged to you for not turning me over to the marshal. Fat Ass never takes his prisoners in alive."

"I've heard rumors to that effect," Halloran remarked, glancing pointedly at Rachel.

"I don't care," Rachel muttered defensively. "The man's an escaped convict, and we're breaking the law by having him here."

"I don't want to discuss it now, daughter," Halloran said sternly. "Why don't you go get us some coffee?"

Rachel left the room without another word, her mind in a whirl. She had heard of Logan Tyree. He was a gunslinger, a known assassin, reported to have killed at least a dozen men in cold blood. Even here, in their small town, his reputation was well-known. It was rumored that he sometimes killed for money and sometimes just for the sheer love of bloodletting and violence. Dear Lord, Logan Tyree!

Chapter 2

*T*he days passed slowly for Tyree. He chafed at lying idle day after day, but his protests fell on deaf ears. Rachel was an efficient, cool, competent nurse. She anticipated his wants, satisfied his needs, made him as comfortable as humanly possible. But she adamantly refused to let him get out of bed.

"Dammit!" Tyree fumed one afternoon, exasperated by her stubbornness. "I know you're anxious to be rid of me, so why not just give me my clothes and let me get the hell out of here?"

"Because I don't want your death on my conscience," Rachel retorted. "You're too weak to walk to the front door, let alone ride across country alone. You still have a bit of a fever, and you're not getting out of that bed for another five days.''

Another five days, hell, Tyree mused irritably. He had already spent close to two weeks in bed and that was enough for any man. Another five days would have him climbing the walls.

Later that afternoon, Tyree slipped out of bed and began pacing the floor. Rachel, damn her, had been right as rain, he thought dourly. He was weak. And his side hurt like the very devil. But he closed his mind to the pain and continued to walk up and down the length of the room, silently cursing Rachel all the while. Damn the woman for always being right!

He had never been fond of small spaces and being confined in Halloran's guest bedroom, comfortable as it was, was almost as bad as being shut up in the Yuma hotbox. . . .

He had spent ten days in that hellish contraption, and he had been naked as a newborn babe then, too, Tyree mused ruefully. You couldn't lay down in the hotbox. You could only stand erect hour after hour, or squat on your heels. Or kneel, if you had a mind to pray. But nobody had ever prayed his way out of the box. You stayed inside until the warden decided you had learned your lesson; stayed, baking in the desert heat as the temperature soared to over a hundred and ten degrees. Stayed, shivering from the cold as the mercury plummeted to below sixty in the dead of night.

Some men died in the box. Some went crazy, but Tyree had managed to cling to his sanity, though ever afterward he harbored a strong aversion to small, closed-in spaces. . . .

He paced the bedroom floor a few minutes at a time several times a day, and when he wasn't pacing, he often stood at the window, staring hungrily at the timbered hills visible beyond the western boundary of the Lazy H. And sometimes he just watched Rachel as she worked in the flower garden that bloomed alongside the house. She raked and weeded and pruned at least a couple of times a week. It was a purely pleasurable way to spend half an hour, Tyree mused, because for all her stubbornness, Rachel Halloran was a mighty pretty woman, especially when the sun danced in her golden hair, reminding him of a painting of the Madonna he had seen one time down in Santa Fe.

Damn the woman! He knew she disliked him. Knew she could not wait until he rode out of her life, and yet she refused to give him his clothes so he could go. Frowning, he fingered the heavy growth of beard on his jaw.

He was standing at the window that evening, entertaining some decidedly unpleasant thoughts about the perverse nature of some women, when the bedroom door opened and Rachel stepped into the room bearing his dinner on a tray.

She came to an abrupt halt just inside the door. Tyree had shaved off his beard and she could only stare, openmouthed, at the change the razor had wrought.

"Afternoon, ma'am," he drawled, making no effort to conceal his nakedness. "Sorry I'm not dressed for company."

She stared at him blankly for a moment, so enchanted with the change in his appearance she had not even noticed he was nude.

"Please cover yourself," Rachel said, feeling her cheeks grow hot.

"Afraid I don't have a thing to wear," Tyree said, smothering a laugh. "Somebody took all my clothes."

"Please use the sheet," Rachel implored, unable to draw her eyes from his face. He looked so different. Not handsome, exactly, but still very attractive in a rugged sort of way. His face was totally masculine, even without the beard. She was glad he had not shaved off his moustache. It drooped lazily over his upper lip, giving him the look of a Barbary pirate. His jaw was firm and square, his mouth wide, sensual. She wondered, with shame, what it would be like to press her lips to his, to have that soft moustache tickle her lip.

Tyree chuckled softly as he pulled the sheet from the bed and wrapped it around his waist.

Rachel placed the tray on the bedside table, careful not to meet Tyree's mocking gaze. Darn him! He was laughing at her because she had no one to blame for Tyree's nudity but herself. He had asked for his clothes at least a dozen times.

Hoping to hide her discomfort, Rachel snapped, "What are you doing out of that bed?"

"Getting some exercise," Tyree snapped back, annoyed by her shrewish tone. "I'm going crazy, cooped up in this room."

Something that might have been compassion flickered in Rachel's lovely blue eyes and then was quickly gone. "Candido's wife made dinner tonight," she said stiffly. "I hope you like Mexican food."

She was backing toward the door as she spoke. Coming to an abrupt halt, she squared her shoulders and lifted her chin defiantly. He wasn't going to intimidate her. Not in her own home.

"I'll be back later to pick up the tray," she announced icily, and walked out of the room feigning an outward calm that was sorely at odds with her inner turmoil.

A sudden burst of masculine laughter shattered Rachel's serene facade and she felt her cheeks flame again. Darn him! He seemed to know her every thought.

Tyree found his clothes neatly piled at the foot of his bed the following morning, and he grinned wryly, wondering if Rachel had decided he was well enough to get up and ride on, or if returning his clothing was just her way of making sure she didn't walk in and find him strutting around the way nature had made him.

He dressed slowly, careful not to make any sudden moves. His left side was stiff and a little sore and he winced as he bent over to pull on his boots, noting, as he did so, that someone had given the leather a nice shine.

He was stuffing his shirttail into his pants when he heard voices. Angry voices. Shoving the .44 into the waistband of his pants, he moved noiselessly down the hallway to the front door where he stood out of sight, listening.

"—last offer, old man. Take it or leave it."

"Be reasonable, Walsh," John Halloran replied in a conciliatory tone. "You know darn well I can't—"

"We'll leave it, Mr. Walsh." Rachel's voice cut across her father's, quick and angry. "Now kindly get off our property. And take your hired killers with you."

Tyree peered around the front door to get a look at the man called Job Walsh. He saw a tall, powerful-looking man somewhere in his late forties. Walsh sat ramrod straight in an expensive hand-tooled saddle, his work-worn hands folded negligently over the horn. His face was deeply tanned, his eyes were a hard flat brown beneath straight black brows. Eight riders flanked him. Like wolves in sheep's clothing, they were gunmen all, masquerading as cowhands.

"I'm getting almighty tired of haggling with

you people," Walsh growled impatiently. "I'd advise you to reconsider my offer while you still can."

Rachel stepped to the edge of the front porch, her head high, arms akimbo. "Is that a threat, Mr. Walsh?"

Walsh shrugged elaborately. "Take it any way you like, missy, but next time I come, I might just have to—"

"Have to what?"

John Halloran smiled broadly as Logan Tyree stepped outside, one dark-skinned hand resting lightly on the butt of the Colt jutting from the waistband of his pants.

Job Walsh swore softly. "Looks like you've gone and hired a killer of your own," he muttered, his voice heavy with sarcasm.

"I'm sure I don't know what you're talking about," Rachel replied haughtily, but there was a faint touch of guilty color in her cheeks.

"Don't play Little Miss Innocent with me," Walsh retorted crossly. He stabbed a fleshy finger in Rachel's direction. "What I want to know is, where did you get the money to hire a professional slinger like Logan Tyree?"

"You heard the lady," Tyree interjected smoothly. "Take your men and ride out of here."

"Sure, sure," Walsh said amiably. "But this ain't over yet. Not by a long shot."

Walsh was mounted on a flashy palomino stallion with a snowy mane and tail. The stud had stood quietly during the heated discussion but now, as Walsh sank his spurs into the stallion's golden flanks, the horse reared up on its hindquarters and whirled around, then pranced out of the yard. Walsh's men trailed behind him, like smoke.

All but two. Eyes hard and calculating, they measured Logan Tyree, wondering. And Tyree measured them. No words were spoken. Indeed, the three men might have been carved from granite. Taut seconds stretched into minutes. Once, Rachel started to speak, but the touch of her father's hand on her arm kept her mute.

The tension grew unbearable and Rachel glanced anxiously at her father, hoping he would do something to break the grating silence, but he was staring at Tyree and the Walsh gunmen. Rachel felt her eyes drawn in that direction, too. Once, she sent a quick glance down the road to where Job Walsh and the rest of his men sat their horses. But no help appeared to be forthcoming from that quarter, either.

Rachel could not say when it began. She heard no words, saw no signal, but suddenly three hands were streaking for three guns. The slap of flesh upon walnut and ivory gunbutts was very loud in the oppressive stillness. Two gunshots shattered the eerie silence, the second shot coming hard on the heels of the first so that the two shots blended into one long, rolling report. And both of

Walsh's gunmen went down, dead before they hit the ground.

Job Walsh did not move. His mouth thinned into a tight white line as he stared at Tyree.

The men backing Walsh reacted like a single being as six hands hovered over six revolvers.

Logan Tyree's cold yellow eyes darted swiftly from man to man, challenging each one in turn. "Anybody wanna buy into this hand?" he asked.

There were no takers.

"You killed 'em," Walsh growled, gesturing at the two bodies sprawled in the dirt. "You bury 'em."

Rachel stared after Walsh and his men as they rode out of sight. Then, eyes filled with accusation, she focused her attention on Tyree. "I thought you said you didn't know Walsh?"

Tyree shrugged. "Didn't think I did. Last time I saw him, he was calling himself Jacob Warner."

"I see. Well," she went on briskly. "You seem to be feeling much better."

"Yes, ma'am."

"I trust you'll be riding on then." She glanced at the two men lying dead in the yard. "The sooner, the better as far as I'm concerned."

"Hold on, daughter," Halloran snapped. "This is still my place, and I'll decide who stays and who goes. Tell me, Tyree, just how high do your services come?"

"Pa!" Rachel stared at her father in disbelief. Surely he didn't mean to hire Tyree!

"Depends on what you want me to do," Tyree replied, ignoring Rachel's shocked expression.

"I think you know," Halloran murmured, and his voice was suddenly old and tired.

"Walsh," Tyree said flatly.

"Yes. How much?"

"For you? Five hundred dollars, a hundred in advance, and the loan of a horse."

"Done," Halloran said quickly, as if he were afraid he might change his mind if he gave the matter any thought.

"Pa, you can't do this."

"Rachel—"

"You're hiring a killer, a man who's already wanted by the law."

"I know what I'm doing," Halloran replied. He did not sound very happy about it, only resigned.

Rachel shook her head, unable to believe he meant to go through with it. "Pa, please reconsider. No good will come of this."

"Rachel, that's enough," Halloran admonished sharply. "I know what I'm doing."

Rachel was sullenly silent at dinner that night, refusing to be drawn into the quiet conversation between her father and Logan Tyree. Job Walsh and his nightriders were the main topic of discussion, as they had been between Rachel and her father nearly every day and night for the past six months, ever since Walsh's men started riding roughshod over the Lazy H.

In the beginning, Walsh's hired guns had only roughed up the Halloran cowboys. But when that failed to scare off the hired help, Walsh's men began shooting the Lazy H riders out of the saddle. A few were killed outright. Those who recovered drew their pay and quit; the remaining cowhands refused to ride the open range. As a result, most of the Halloran herd had been run off, either by Walsh's men, or by the Apache, who were not averse to eating beef when nothing else was available. The last straw had come only a few weeks earlier when the Lazy H foreman had come home tied face down across his saddle, dead from a bullet between the eyes. That night, two thirds of the remaining cowhands quit, and Joe Cahill took over as foreman. Now there were only five men left on the payroll, and less than 300 head of cattle where there had once been thousands. Three hundred cattle that were scattered across miles of broken grassland.

"Pa, how could you hire that awful man?" Rachel demanded later, when they were alone in the house.

"Honey, what else can I do? Cahill and the others are no match for Walsh's men. And Lord knows I'm too old to strap on a gun and go after Walsh myself. Who else is there? You?''

"There's Clint."

"Clint Wesley is a fine young man, Rachel, but he's just a town marshal. Job Walsh would gobble him up and spit him out. Anyway, we've got no proof that Walsh's men are killing our cattle, or backshooting our cowhands. And Clint needs proof, not just an old man's say-so."

"Then we'll get proof."

Halloran laughed softly, hollowly. "Where are we gonna get proof that will hold up in court? Walsh and his men have got more alibis than ticks on a hound. Dammit, Rachel, we can't afford to lose any more cattle."

"But a hired killer?"

"I know, honey. It sticks in my craw, too. But I just don't know what else to do."

Rachel could not sleep that night. The clock in her room put the hour at just after midnight when she slipped out of bed, pulled on her robe, and tiptoed out of the house.

Outside, a cool breeze whispered over the face of the land, talking softly to the leaves of the trees that shaded the sunny side of the house. The sky was a cloudless indigo blue, the full moon as cold and yellow as Logan Tyree's eyes. Tyree! How she despised him!

With a sigh, she rested her elbows on the porch rail, suddenly glad that her mother, always so frail and gentle, was not alive to see what was happening. Ellen Halloran had been a wonderful, sweet, kind soul, but she had not been a fighter. She would have been appalled by the killings and the bloodshed. She would have insisted they sell the ranch to Walsh and move on rather than stay and fight it out. And perhaps, if her mother was still alive, her father would have done just that. As it was, he didn't have the heart to pick up and start over again somewhere else.

"Nice night."

Rachel whirled around, startled to find Logan Tyree sitting in the shadows at the south end of the porch, an unlit cigar dangling from the corner of his mouth. He had gone into Yellow Creek earlier in the day and had come back mounted on a rangy chestnut mare. He had bought himself a new rifle, too, and a change of clothes. Now, dressed all in black from his shirt to his boots, Rachel thought he looked like the angel of death. It was, she decided, an apt description considering his line of work.

"Care for a drink?" Tyree asked, gesturing at the bottle of Forty Rod on the floor at his feet.

"No."

"It'll help you sleep."

"I don't need anything to help me sleep, thank you," Rachel replied curtly.

Tyree grunted softly, his eyes mocking her. The fact that she was out on the porch at such a late hour was proof enough that she could not sleep.

Tyree's shirt was open and Rachel's eyes were drawn to his bare chest. The sight of his naked flesh and the dark hair curling there did odd things to the pit of her stomach. Too clearly, she remembered tending him when he had been hurt and unconscious. The memory of his flesh beneath her hands made her palms tingle and for one mad, impulsive moment she was tempted to reach out and caress the hard wall of Tyree's chest. But, of course, she did no such thing. Instead, she folded her arms across her breasts and tried to look at ease.

The rocker squeaked loudly as Tyree reached for the whiskey bottle. It was nearly empty and Rachel glanced at his face, wondering if he were drunk.

Tyree stared back at her, his face impassive, a glint of amusement dancing in his cat's eyes. She was afraid of him, and they both knew it.

"I've been puzzling over how you managed to get out of Yuma," Rachel remarked, hoping to dispel the heavy silence between them. "I've never heard of anyone escaping from there before."

"I killed two of the guards and ran like hell," Tyree replied evenly.

"Killed them?" Rachel repeated thinly. "In cold blood?"

"Yes, ma'am. And I'd have killed a hundred more to get out of that hellhole."

Rachel stared at him, unnerved by the ease with which he talked about killing, as if shooting down a man was of no more consequence than swatting a fly.

"I can't believe it," she murmured. "I simply can't believe my father hired a . . . a murderer like you."

"There isn't another like me," Tyree muttered sardonically. There was a brief flare of light as he put a match to his cigar.

"I can believe that!" Rachel retorted caustically. "Tell me, Mr. Tyree, do you always charge five hundred dollars for your . . . your services?"

"No, ma'am," Tyree snapped back. "I usually charge a hell of a lot more."

"Oh? And just what is it that makes you worth so much?"

"I'm good at what I do," Tyree answered flatly. "Damn good."

"So I've heard," Rachel said with a sneer. "They say you killed an unarmed man in Nogales. And shot one in the back over in El Paso. Even killed a widow woman in Tucson. Burned her house down while she was still inside."

A wordless sound of disgust erupted from Tyree's throat. "Where'd you hear all that?"

"It's common knowledge," Rachel answered disdainfully.

"It's a pile of shit, is what it is," Tyree countered mildly. "I'll admit I've done a lot of rotten things in my time, but gunning down an unarmed man isn't one of them. And as for that story about killing a helpless woman . . .

Oh, hell, believe what you want to believe."

"Do you expect me to believe those stories are lies?" Rachel asked incredulously. "All of them?"

"Lady, I don't give a damn what you believe."

"They say you hire your gun out to the highest bidder," Rachel mused aloud. "Regardless of who's right or who's wrong."

Tyree shrugged. "A gun doesn't know right from wrong."

"That's true," Rachel agreed, her voice thick with contempt. "But a man does. Tell me, Mr. Tyree, would you murder my father if Job Walsh topped his offer of five hundred dollars?"

She had made him genuinely angry now. His face, usually passive, was suddenly dark with unspoken fury.

"You really do have a low opinion of me, don't you?" he muttered. "You really think I'd gun down your old man after he took me in?"

"Yes. No. I don't know," Rachel stammered, and turned away from Tyree to stare out at the land that rose and fell in gentle swells, like waves upon the sea. Overhead, the moon was bright in the sky, bathing the ranch in silver-dappled shadows. The sweet scent of sage and honeysuckle filled the air as the wind shifted and she drew in a deep breath. She loved this land. Loved the wild untamed mountains that rose in lofty splendor to the east; loved the stark unfriendly desert that touched the southern border of the Lazy H; loved the ranch that was the only home she had ever known. With Walsh out of the way, the Lazy H would prosper again, and life would be good, as it had been before.

The thought of Walsh brought Logan Tyree to mind again. She did not like Tyree. She did not like him and she did not trust him. But her father was right. There was no one else they could turn to. They had to fight Job Walsh on his own terms, distasteful as that might be, or lose the ranch. It was as simple as that. Walsh was like a malignant disease, slowly eating away at the heart of everything she held dear, and Logan Tyree was the cure. Still, she could not help wondering if the cure might not prove more deadly than the disease itself. And yet, with Walsh gone, his hired guns would move on. The Slash W would go to Walsh's sister in Amarillo. Perhaps then they would have some peace.

She would be glad when it was all over and done, she thought wearily. Glad when Tyree was gone. Funny, how she just naturally assumed he would kill Walsh when the time came, when in all likelihood it would be Logan Tyree who died. Job Walsh was a cautious man, one with many enemies. He rarely left the Slash W and when he did, he always took his bodyguards with him. Walsh would know, the minute he saw Tyree, that her father had hired him. And why. Tyree would be shot on sight, and the Lazy H would be no better off than it was now. Maybe worse.

She heard the squeak of the rocker as Tyree stood up.

"Why aren't you married?" he asked.

Rachel turned to face him. "What?"

"I asked why you're not married."

"Maybe the right man hasn't asked me yet."

"Who's the right man? Wesley?"

"What do you know about Clint?"

Tyree shrugged. "Nothing. Your old man mentioned him one night is all. You sweet on him?"

"Maybe," Rachel allowed, smiling mysteriously. "It's none of your business."

"What's he like, this Wesley?"

"He's tall and handsome," Rachel said, her voice going soft and dreamy. "He's honest, kind, thoughtful. A gentleman."

"All the things I'm not," Tyree muttered sardonically.

"Yes, you could say that."

"Where is he, this paragon of virtue?"

"Out of town."

Tyree muttered a mild oath. He did not like the unexpected rush of jealousy that coiled around his insides when he thought of Rachel in the arms of another man.

Rachel swallowed hard as Tyree came to stand beside her. There was a hungry look in his deep amber eyes and she took a quick step backward, her heart pounding like a wild thing as every nerve in her body grew taut. She had never given Tyree the slightest encouragement; had never said or done anything to make him think his advances would be remotely welcome, and yet she knew he intended to kiss her.

The thought of Tyree's mouth on hers made Rachel's knees go weak, and even then he was reaching for her. Time seemed to stand still and Rachel was suddenly acutely aware of everything around her: the wind rising out of the north, the crickets singing in the trees, the scent of horse and leather and cigar smoke clinging to Tyree. Her breathing was shallow and erratic, and she felt her whole body grow warm, as if her blood had turned to flame.

Answering some inner prompting, Rachel swayed toward Tyree, all her senses urging her to surrender to the promise dancing in his eyes, to discover, once and for all, the eternal mystery of mating.

Tyree's hand was big and brown, unexpectedly gentle as it caressed her cheek and the slender curve of her throat, slipping around to cup her head in his hand to draw her closer. A killer's hand . . . the thought smothered the fire in Rachel's veins.

With a wordless cry of self-disgust for what had almost happened, she twisted away from Tyree's imprisoning hand and ran for the safety of her room. Inside, she slammed the door, but she could not shut out the sound of Tyree's sardonic laughter.

Tyree spent the rest of the week familiarizing himself with the lay of the land. He rode the borders of the Slash W ranch, acquainting himself with every hill, gully, and ravine, memorizing landmarks, determining the quickest route between the Lazy H and the Walsh spread. He noted the best places to take cover, in case going to ground became a necessity, and looked for places where he could make a stand if things got tight.

He spent several mornings on a hilltop overlooking the Walsh ranch house, taking special interest in the armed guards who patrolled the yard at odd hours. He made note of the daily routine of the cowboys, and of Job Walsh, who never left the ranch proper without several heavily armed escorts.

It was tedious work, but it had paid off for Tyree in the past. Hunting a man was a lot like hunting an animal. It was easier to bring your quarry down if you knew his tracks, his habits, and where he made his lair. Most animals tended to eat and drink and hunt at the same time each day. Likewise, most men followed a certain pattern in their daily living.

Rachel and her father never questioned Tyree about his frequent absences from the ranch. But as the days went by, both father and daughter grew noticeably more tense. It was like sitting on a powder keg, knowing the fuse had been lit, but not knowing exactly when the explosion would take place.

It was Halloran who finally broke the silence. "When?" he asked Tyree at dinner one night. "When will you do it?"

"Tomorrow morning," Tyree answered calmly. "Right around ten o'clock."

Tyree's absence went unremarked at the breakfast table the next morning. Halloran and Rachel both knew where Tyree had gone, and why. Halloran sat alone at the big wooden table, fingers drumming absently on the red checked cloth while Rachel prepared breakfast. He was usually a hearty eater, but this morning he had no appetite at all for the ham and eggs and biscuits Rachel placed before him and, after pushing the food around on his plate for several moments, he gulped down a quick cup of coffee and stomped out the back door.

With a sigh, Rachel threw her own breakfast to the dogs, then filled the kitchen sink with hot water, wondering how a man like Tyree operated. Did he just ride in and shoot his victims down in cold blood, or did he give them a fair chance?

Rachel grinned ruefully at the thought. A fair chance indeed. That was funny. Against the speed of Tyree's draw, a fair chance was really no chance at all, and though she harbored no love for Job Walsh, she shuddered to think of his being shot down as if he were of no more importance than a pesky varmint.

Leaving the kitchen, Rachel wandered aimlessly from task to task, unable to concentrate on the simplest chore until, at last, she took up a basket of mending and went to sit on the front porch. Even then, her thoughts were at the Slash W. In her mind's eye she pictured Tyree riding up to the big white house. Saw him warning Walsh to stay away from the Lazy H. Saw Walsh's gunhawks rise to the challenge. Saw them go down in a hail of lead from Tyree's Colt. Saw Walsh go down, last of all . . .

John Halloran was also finding it difficult to concentrate on the tasks at hand. Doubts and second thoughts crowded his mind as he considered the consequences of what he had done. He had bought a man's death for five hundred dollars, with no guarantee that the man who died would be Walsh. A sudden cold fear washed over Halloran with the realization that, should Tyree be killed, Walsh would come after the Lazy H with a bloody vengeance. Hiring Tyree had seemed like such a good idea at the time, but now it seemed wrong, so very wrong.

Finally, like Rachel, Halloran stopped pretending that this day was like any other and joined her on the front porch. Face drawn, he stared at the land he was trying so desperately to hang onto. Acres of good grazing land stretched away as far as the eye could see. Large, well-built corrals were situated below the house; two corrals for holding stock, a third for breaking and branding young horses and cattle. Behind the house, a large barn sheltered a half-dozen horses, including his own buckskin gelding and Rachel's dainty bloodbay mare. Adjacent to the barn was a large tack room. And beyond that, a storage shed for tools and the like. A small graveyard stood on a grassy knoll behind the smokehouse.

The ranch house itself was a fairly large, two-story structure built of wood and native stone. It featured a large parlor, a spacious, sunlit kitchen, a formal dining room—because Ellen had wanted one so very much—and three good-sized bedrooms. He remembered how thrilled Ellen had been when the house was finally finished. Nights, they had sat on the front porch, listening to the crickets and holding hands as they dreamed of filling the house with children. Strong sons and beautiful daughters. But after Rachel there had been no children for a long time. And then, when Rachel was ten, God had blessed them with a son. But Tommy had lived only a few short years. There had been no more children after Tommy, and Rachel became dearer than ever.

Lost in thought, Halloran stared at the

whitewashed crosses that marked the final resting places of his wife and son. If only Ellen were still alive. He needed to talk to her, needed to ask her advice. She had been a quiet, sensible woman, wise beyond her years, endowed with a keen insight into other people's thoughts and actions. Always, when he had needed to make a decision, he had first discussed it with Ellen.

Halloran glanced at Rachel. She was absorbed in mending one of his shirts, and he smiled at her fondly. She had Ellen's incomparable beauty, but the resemblance ended there. Ellen had been a quiet woman— serene, peace-loving. But Rachel was a fighter and could be as stubborn as an Army mule. She would never agree to sell out to Walsh, he knew that without question, and the thought gave him strength. By damn, they would hang onto the Lazy H come hell or high water, and if Logan Tyree couldn't whip Job Walsh, then, by thunder, they'd find someone who could!

It was shortly after noon when Tyree rode into the yard. Dismounting, he hitched his horse to the rack, climbed the porch steps to stand hipshot against the railing, thumbs hooked over his gunbelt. His grin was cold as glacier ice as he remarked, tonelessly, "Walsh won't be giving you any more trouble."

The words hung in the air like a death knell. For a moment, Rachel and her father stared at

each other, speechless. Then, with a small cry
of dismay, Rachel ran into the house.

"I don't think your daughter approves of
your methods," Tyree remarked dryly.

John Halloran recoiled as if he had been
slapped. Now that Walsh's death was an accomplished fact, he felt an overwhelming
sense of guilt at what he had done.

"Neither do I," Halloran muttered brokenly. "Dammit, Tyree, neither do I."

Rachel and Tyree crossed paths in the
kitchen later that day. Rachel's lovely deep
blue eyes burned with bitter contempt when
she looked at Tyree, and her mouth thinned
into a cold line of disapproval.

Walking past her to the stove, Tyree poured
himself a cup of coffee and sipped it slowly.
The tension between them was so strong, he
would not have been surprised to see sparks
dancing across the room.

Rachel's flagrant, if unspoken, contempt
annoyed Tyree more than it should have, and
he slapped his coffee cup down on the table,
ignoring the fact that the contents sloshed
over the rim, making a dark brown stain on
the freshly laundered red-checked cloth.

"All right, spit it out," he growled. "What's
eating you? The fact that I killed Walsh, or the
fact that your old man hired me to do it?"

Rachel turned on Tyree with all the fury of
a treed cougar. "Both, if you must know," she

lashed out angrily. "I cannot condone murder, not even the murder of a man like Job Walsh."

Tyree shook his head in genuine amazement. "Well, I'll be go to hell! The man was out to steal your ranch, and now you're crying because he's dead."

The contempt in Rachel's eyes turned to pity as she stared at Tyree. "You don't hold life very dear, do you, Mr. Tyree?"

"Only my own, Miss Halloran," he fired back.

"And does your life make you happy?"

"Happy?" There was a note of bewilderment in his tone.

"Yes, happy. Do you like the man you see in the mirror when you shave?"

"I don't use a mirror," Tyree muttered, frowning at her.

"You know what I mean," Rachel said crossly. "Don't be obtuse."

"Obtuse? What the hell does that mean?"

"It means thickheaded," Rachel explained in a syrupy voice. "Slow to comprehend."

"Thanks."

"You haven't answered my question," Rachel reminded him.

Tyree laughed shortly and without amusement. "What the hell difference does it make to you whether I'm happy or not?"

"None," Rachel answered with a shake of her head. "None at all. Well, I suppose you'll be moving on, now that you've earned your blood money."

"First thing in the morning," Tyree assured her, and stalked angrily out of the room.

Late afternoon found Tyree sitting on the porch steps, absently chewing on the end of a long black cigar, content, for the moment, just to sit back and stare out into the distance. It was good to be free, he mused. Good to have a belly full of food that wasn't rancid or half-raw. Good to feel the weight of a Colt .44 riding his hip. Tomorrow he would ride on, heading north. Perhaps he would spend the rest of the year with the Apache. Perhaps he would ride on to Virginia City and try his hand at the gaming tables. Perhaps not. He had never been one to plan ahead, and he saw no need to start now. The money he had earned for gunning Walsh made a comfortable bulge in his hip pocket. Blood money, Rachel had called it. And that was sure as hell what it was. But it would take him wherever he wanted to go. He glanced around the ranch yard, surprised to discover he didn't particularly want to leave the Lazy H. Or Rachel. He grinned wryly. Especially Rachel. No matter that she thought he was dirt. He did not want to leave her. What he wanted was to kiss her pouty red mouth until she admitted she wanted him as much as he wanted her. She could yell she hated him, insist she loathed his touch and despised everything he stood for, but the attraction between them was real.

He touched a match to his cigar as the screen door creaked open and John Halloran stepped out onto the porch.

"Tyree?"

"Yeah."

"Does my five hundred bucks entitle me to one more favor?"

"Depends," Tyree answered with a shrug. "Who do you want killed now?"

Halloran grimaced as though in physical pain. He would never know another peaceful night's sleep as long as he lived, he mused bitterly. Not if he lived to be a hundred.

"I don't want anyone killed," the old man answered thinly. "Rachel went riding an hour ago, and she hasn't come back yet. She hates it when I worry about her, but . . . dammit, Tyree, it'll be dark soon and she's all I've got left in the world."

"Yeah. Don't worry, Halloran, I'll find her."

Rising to his feet, Tyree sauntered down to the corral and caught up the chestnut mare he had bought in Yellow Creek. Rachel would be less than pleased when he showed up on her trail, he thought with some amusement, but what the hell. It was a nice night for a ride, and he had nothing better to do.

The mare was eager to run and she responded to the touch of Tyree's heels with a toss of her head as she broke into a comfortable lope. In moments, the ranch was left behind and they were riding across open country.

The tracks of Rachel's fine bloodbay mare were as clear as glass, and Tyree followed them with ease, frowning as her trail veered southward toward Sunset Canyon. Damn fool girl, he muttered under his breath. Didn't she realize she was heading straight into Apache country?

Three miles later he crossed a dry wash and picked up the tracks of five, maybe six, unshod ponies trailing after Rachel.

Tyree swore softly as he rolled a smoke. The land was flat here, crisscrossed by shallow draws and gullies and box canyons. The ground was soft, but not too soft to hold a print, and the tracks left by Rachel and the Indians were deep and easy to follow.

Lifting the chestnut mare into a slow trot, Tyree swore again as he passed the place where Rachel first realized she was being followed. Frightened, she had lashed her horse into a run and the Indians had quickly given chase. It had been a short flight. The Indians had swiftly overtaken her, and now one of the braves was leading her mount.

A stand of heavy timber loomed ahead, and Tyree reined the chestnut to a halt. Dismounting, he tethered the mare to a cottonwood, slipped out of his boots, and padded forward on cat feet, rifle in hand.

Pausing, he listened for some sound that would pinpoint the whereabouts of the Indians. Seconds later, a woman's frightened squeal rose in the air.

Drawing a deep breath, Tyree picked his way through the underbrush. He moved as quietly as a mountain lion stalking its prey, careful not to step on any twigs or dry leaves that would betray his presence. A clearing appeared some yards ahead, and he caught his first glimpse of Rachel and the Apaches.

Rachel was spread-eagled on the ground between four grinning Apache bucks. Her blouse was ripped, giving a tantalizing glimpse of creamy flesh. Her skirt and pantalets were bunched around her hips, revealing long, shapely legs. A fifth warrior was stripping away his clout, and the sight of his swiftly rising manhood caused Rachel to increase her struggles.

Tyree scowled as one of the warriors stuffed a dirty red kerchief into Rachel's mouth to stifle her cries.

"She has breasts like the Chiricahua Mountains," declared the brave pinning Rachel's left arm down.

"And I am going to climb them," boasted the naked warrior with a lusty chuckle. "Move over and give me some room."

Tyree mouthed a vague obscenity as he jacked a round into the breech of the rifle. The harsh metallic sound, unmistakable for what it was, quickly caught everyone's attention.

Hope flared in Rachel's red-rimmed eyes as she recognized Tyree. If anyone could get her out of this mess, Tyree could. For once she was glad he was hard and cruel and handy with a gun. He would know what to do.

The four warriors surrounding Rachel sat unmoving, their expressions slightly sheepish, like children caught playing doctor behind the barn.

The naked warrior smiled broadly as he glanced past Tyree, and Tyree felt the muscles tighten in the back of his neck as he realized there had indeed been six Indian ponies, not five, and that the sixth Indian was now standing behind him. The sudden jab of a gun barrel against his spine came as no surprise and Tyree dropped his rifle with an air of grim resignation.

The warrior behind Tyree laughed softly. "You are smart, for a white man. Drop your gunbelt, too."

"Six horses," Tyree muttered disgustedly. "I must be getting light in the head."

The Indian behind Tyree came around to face him, and Tyree swore under his breath as he recognized the broad, ugly face of Many Eagles, one of the lesser chiefs of the Mescalero Apache.

"Is this any way to treat a brother?" Tyree demanded angrily.

Many Eagles snorted derisively. "I have no white brothers," he said disdainfully. "Only enemies. Dead enemies."

"You have one white brother," Tyree retorted boldly. "I saved your life seven summers ago, in Palo Duro Canyon. And yours, too, Standing Buffalo."

A quick smile spread over the face of the naked brave. "Tyree! I did not recognize you without your face hair."

"I recognize you, Standing Buffalo," Tyree replied dryly. "Even without your clout."

The naked warrior laughed heartily, and the four warriors holding Rachel grinned as they exchanged ribald comments in soft guttural Apache.

"Go now, Tyree," Many Eagles said gruffly. "I give you back the life you once gave me."

"Not without my woman," Tyree said firmly. "Or my weapons."

"It is well-known among the Apache that you have no woman," Many Eagles countered. "She lies dead and buried along the Gila, proof of the white man's treachery."

"She has been long dead," Tyree answered tonelessly, surprised that her memory still had the power to cause him pain. "I have taken another woman."

"I do not believe you." It was evident, from the tone of the chief's voice and the look in his eye, that he wanted Rachel for himself.

"She is my woman," Tyree said again. "Ask her if you do not believe me."

Many Eagles shook his head. "Words prove nothing. She fights like a mare not yet broke to the saddle. If you are truly her man, she will let you mount her without complaint."

Tyree glared at the Indian. "It is not our

way to lie together for the amusement of others."

"You will do it," Many Eagles insisted, "or I will keep her for my own once my warriors have tired of her."

Tyree scowled blackly, his eyes intent on the face of the Apache chief. Was the Indian serious, or merely bluffing? Would Many Eagles truly take Rachel, or was he playing games to see how far Tyree would go? There was no way to be certain, and Tyree wasn't prepared to call the Indian's bluff, not when Rachel's future was at stake.

He gazed at Rachel. He could not blame Many Eagles for coveting her. Even now, begrimed with dust and sweat, her eyes swollen with tears, she was a sight to take a man's breath away.

With an effort, Tyree drew his gaze from Rachel's heaving breasts and long, shapely legs. "Hear my words, Many Eagles," Tyree growled. "I will do as you say, but I tell you now, if our paths cross again, I will cut out your heart and feed it to the coyotes!"

Without waiting for the warrior's reply, Tyree strode toward Rachel. Reaching down, he took the gag from her mouth, gestured for the Indians holding her to move aside.

Freed of the restraining grasp of the warriors, Rachel sat up, her eyes intent on Tyree's face as she drew her skirt over her legs.

"What's going on?" she queried tremulously. "What are they going to do to us?"

"That depends on you," Tyree said, hunkering down on his heels beside her. His teeth flashed in a wry grin, confusing her still more.

"On me? I don't understand."

"Well, it's like this," Tyree explained. "I told Many Eagles over there, that you're my woman. He's an old friend of mine, but he doesn't believe me. He wants proof."

"Proof?" Rachel echoed, puzzled. "What kind of proof?"

Tyree's dark amber eyes flickered over Rachel's comely form, causing a slow flush to spread from the roots of her hair to the tips of her toes as she read the answer to her question in Tyree's gaze.

"No, never," she whispered, vigorously shaking her head. "I'd rather die!"

"Suit yourself," Tyree replied with a shrug. "Only dyin' ain't in the cards, at least not for you." His voice went suddenly hard and flat. He did not like the idea any more than she did, but it was the only way for both of them to survive, and the sooner he could make her understand that, the better. "You'd better face facts, honey. You've only got two choices: me or them."

"What kind of choice is that?"

"Not much, I reckon. But if you refuse me, Many Eagles is gonna kill me for lyin' to him. And when his bucks are through with you, you'll probably wish you were dead, too."

"No," Rachel whimpered plaintively. "No, no, no."

"Well, like I said, it's up to you."

"But I hardly know you," Rachel wailed inanely, and Tyree chuckled.

"You don't know them, either," he reminded her with a rueful grin. "But you will. Intimately."

It was like a nightmare, Rachel thought in despair. Worse than a nightmare. And whether she was ravaged by six leering savages or one cool-eyed gunslinger didn't really matter. The results would be the same. Her reputation would be ruined, her virginity gone.

"Will they let us go, after?" she asked.

"I don't know," Tyree answered honestly. "But there's only one way to find out."

"But I've never . . . I mean, I'm still—"

Tyree swore irritably. "You tryin' to tell me you're still a virgin?"

It sounded like a sin, the way he said it.

"Well, you won't be much longer," Tyree drawled matter-of-factly, and a faint hint of amusement danced in his amber eyes as he stood up and unbuckled his belt.

"This can't be happening," Rachel thought numbly. But it was. As though hypnotized, she watched Tyree undress. His hands were big and brown and they moved purposefully and without haste as he removed his pants. He didn't wear longjohns like most men and she gasped aloud as he stood partially naked before her, his skin as dark as the skin of the leering Apaches.

"Lie down," Tyree said curtly.

Sucking in a deep breath, Rachel did as bidden. The dirt was hard beneath her, the sky above a brilliant blue. She stared at the setting sun, trying to separate her mind from what was happening to her body.

Tyree threw Many Eagles a venomous glance; then, feeling like some sort of damned sideshow freak, he lifted Rachel's skirt and removed her pantalets. Muttering an oath, he lowered himself over her, acutely aware of six pairs of ebony eyes watching his every move.

Rachel's body jerked and went rigid as Tyree's bare legs touched her own. With a small cry, she closed her eyes, her hands tightly clenched at her sides.

"Relax," Tyree whispered.

"I can't," Rachel retorted. "I'm too scared."

"Yeah. Well, this is going to hurt you a hell of a lot more than it does me, but whatever you do, don't fight me. This has got to look like just another roll in the hay between old married folks."

Rachel's eyes snapped open, anger and indignation blazing in their depths. "Must you be so crude?"

"Sorry, honey," Tyree said lightly. "Now, put your arms around me like a loving little wife and let's get this stupid charade over with."

Reluctantly, Rachel placed her arms around Tyree's neck. His dark hair was soft against her hands, the muscles in the back of his neck taut with anger and desire as he drew her close.

She was frightened, more frightened than she had ever been in her life. Of the Indians. Of Tyree. He was stroking her arms lightly, kissing her eyes, her cheeks, the tip of her nose. Every instinct urged her to fight him, to preserve her chastity, but her fear of the Indians was stronger than her desire to remain chaste and she closed her eyes again, praying it would soon be over.

Tyree felt his desire rise swift and hot as he caressed Rachel's arms. She was sweet, so sweet, and he had wanted to make love to her for so long. But not like this.

He heard the Indians ride away as he kissed Rachel, felt the tension drain from his body as his lips slid over Rachel's closed eyelids. So, Many Eagles had been bluffing after all. Reluctantly, he drew away from Rachel. Letting her go was the hardest thing he had ever done, and he regretted it immediately. But violating virgins was something he'd never done, and he didn't intend to start now.

Rachel's eyes flew open as Tyree took his mouth from hers. "What's wrong?" she whispered.

"They've gone."

She glanced around, her eyes wide with fear, her body shaking visibly. She was so scared, and so cold. She looked at Tyree. He was so brave. And his arms looked so strong and warm. Without conscious thought, she reached out for him, needing to be held. He had come to her rescue. He would protect her, shelter her from harm. In the face of fear and danger, he was all that was solid and familiar.

Tyree let out a long sigh as Rachel's arms slid around his neck. She was shivering violently and he held her close, his arms wrapped around her, his lips moving in her hair as he whispered words of comfort.

In that moment, she forgot that she hated him, forgot everything but the security of his arms and the consoling warmth of his body pressed to her own. She lifted her head, her lips seeking his. He hesitated for a moment, and then he was kissing her, his mouth moving over hers slowly, languorously, his tongue darting out to savor her lower lip. It was a wondrously heady sensation, and totally unexpected. She tried to remind herself that he was an outlaw, but even that didn't seem to matter, not now, with his mouth on hers and her blood turning to fire. Tyree caressed her and she responded in kind, her hands slipping under his shirt to roam over his broad back and shoulders, reveling in the feel of his scarred flesh beneath her fingertips.

All her fears fled as Tyree made love to her, answering a need she had not known she possessed. She had been cold and afraid; now she was warm and alive, every nerve-end tingling, every inch of her skin attuned to his touch.

Tyree tried to hold back, tried to resist, but her lips were so sweet, her arms so welcome. He vowed each kiss would be the last. Just this one, and he would let her go before it was too late, before he could never let her go. Just one more . . .

His tongue slid into her mouth, kindling new fires between them. Rachel groaned with pleasure, her arms drawing Tyree closer, her body pressing against his. Not realizing how she was affecting him, she knew only that she wanted to be closer. Her tongue caressed his, then slid shyly into his mouth, and it was too late to turn back.

His yellow eyes were ablaze with desire when he thrust into her. Rachel uttered a little cry of pleasure and pain as his body melded with her own, making her forget everything but the wonder of his touch as wave after wave of ecstasy flooded her being, filling her with delight, until she lay sated and spent in his arms.

Later, she lay silent and ashamed beside him, wracked with guilt. What had she done? Always, in the back of her mind, she had imagined it would be Clint who would initiate her in the ways of love. They would be married, of course, sheltered within the cosy darkness of their own little house. She would be shy, hesitant, and yet eager to explore the intimate secrets shared by a man and a woman. Clint would be strong and tender, pleased with her inexperience, proud that she had saved herself for her husband . . .

She shook her head and the idyllic images faded. She had ruined all that now, ruined any chance she might have had for a life with a decent man. How could she have given herself to Tyree? How could she have let him make love to her out in the open like some kind of primitive savage? Shame flooded her cheeks with color. She was ruined now, soiled. Moments before, the loss of her virginity had seemed a small price to pay for the security and pleasure of Tyree's touch. Now, as harsh reality set in, she realized the cost. No respectable man would want her now. Damaged goods, they would say, and turn away in disgust.

Abruptly, she burst into tears.

Tyree drew a long breath and blew it out slowly. He had wanted to make love to Rachel ever since the day he had first seen her bending over him, her vibrant blue eyes filled with concern, and he was a man who generally got what he wanted, one way or another. Nonetheless, he was aware of a sudden wave of remorse for what he had done. No matter that she had practically asked for it, no matter that she had been scared and in need of comfort. Rachel Halloran was a nice girl, much too nice for the likes of a drifting gunhawk like Logan Tyree. He had not bedded a decent woman since he left the lodges of the

Mescalero. He had taken his pleasure in cheap cribs and cantinas, slaking his carnal desires with whores who didn't need sweet words and gentle wooing to satisfy a man's hunger. Rachel was not a harlot to be used and forgotten, no street girl to be paid a few dollars and cast aside.

He slid a glance in her direction, wanting to apologize, to say something that would ease the pain in her heart, but words would not come. If only she had not put her arms around him. If only she had not kissed him back. He might have been able to let her go but for that. And yet, he should have held back anyway. Difficult as it would have been, he should have stopped.

Cursing softly, he stood up and pulled on his pants. The Indians had taken Rachel's mare, he noted with a shake of his head. But better the horse than the woman.

Rachel sat up as her tears subsided. Reaching for her pantalets, she drew them on, then stood up, drawing her skirts down over her thighs, brushing the dust from her dress. The sun had gone down and the darkening sky was stained with brilliant slashes of crimson, like the faint smears of blood that stained her thighs.

She flinched as Tyree laid a hand on her shoulder. "Don't touch me," she said. "Don't you ever touch me again."

Tyree cocked an eyebrow at her, surprised by the venom in her voice.

"You cad!" she hissed. "I never want to see you again."

"Now just a damn minute," Tyree growled angrily. "You wanted it as much as I did."

"That's a lie!" Rachel cried, her cheeks flooding with color. "It was all your fault. You knew I'd never had a man before. You took advantage of me."

Tyree swore under his breath. "I took advantage of you? I think you might have that just a little bit backwards."

"I do not!" She stamped her foot, hating him because he was right and she was wrong. But she simply couldn't admit she had wanted him. It was so much easier to blame him than admit the truth.

"Like hell. You were hotter than a July firecracker and now you're too damn gutless to admit it."

"I hate you." She spoke the words through clenched teeth, meaning them. And then all the anger went out of her as she thought of going home again, of facing the people she knew and loved.

Lowering her eyes, she said, "Promise me you won't tell my father about this. Not my father, or anyone else."

"You mean Wesley, I guess," Tyree muttered irritably.

"I mean anyone!" Rachel snapped crossly.

But she did mean Clint. What would he think of her if he found out what she had done, and with whom? Would he still look at her as if she were the sweetest, most wonderful girl in the world, or would he turn from her in disgust, his mild blue eyes filling with revulsion?

As if reading her thoughts, Tyree muttered, "No one's ever gonna know what happened here today, so quit worrying about it."

"I'll know," Rachel replied quietly. Indeed, it was something she would never forget.

John Halloran was waiting for them on the front porch, a worried expression on his weathered face.

"Everything all right?" he asked anxiously. His eyes sought Tyree's. "Where's Rachel's mare?"

"Your daughter had a little run-in with the Apache," Tyree answered, stepping down and lifting Rachel from the saddle. "They took her horse."

"Apaches!" Halloran exclaimed. "Rachel, are you all right?"

Rachel moved away from Tyree, her eyes not meeting her father's. "I'm fine, Pa," she said flatly. "Just fine."

Halloran's glance skittered back and forth between his daughter's wan face and Tyree's grim expression. There was something they weren't telling him, something they were both holding back, but what? He watched Rachel as she slowly climbed the steps and disappeared into the house.

"Are you sure she's all right, Tyree?"

Halloran asked dubiously. "She looks . . . upset."

"She's got a right to be upset. She had a bad scare, but she'll be fine after a good night's sleep."

"You're a handy man to have around," Halloran remarked, somewhat relieved by Tyree's assurance that Rachel was unhurt. "Think you could stay on for a few more days, just to make sure we've had our last run-in with the Slash W bunch?"

"Sure," Tyree said, though he knew Rachel would be less than pleased to have him underfoot. "I've got no place to go, and no one waiting for me when I get there."

Chapter 3

*W*ith Walsh's death, life on the Lazy H soon returned to normal. Cahill and two of the cowhands rode out into the hills to round up what strays they could find, leaving the remaining two men to mend the fences Walsh's men had torn down and patch up the outbuildings that had fallen into disrepair.

Three days later, Cahill and his men returned with better than sixty head of cattle. These were driven into the holding pens behind the barn and for the next couple of days, the stench of scorched cowhide and the bawling of unhappy cattle filled the air as calves long overdue for branding were cut out of the herd and marked with the Halloran brand.

From his place on the front porch, Tyree

took it all in, marveling that Halloran's hired hands would work so hard for so little pay. Why, he had made more money in two weeks killing rustlers down in the Panhandle than these men would make in a year of range work. And he had made it with far less effort, Tyree mused as he watched a bowlegged cowboy throw a bawling calf to the ground while a second wrangler laid a hot iron against the animal's flank.

Off in the distance, Joe Cahill and a freckle-faced cowboy were perched on the top rail of a fence, taking a break while they watched Candido try to break a flashy gray stallion to the saddle. From the way the men were hollering and carrying on, Tyree figured the bronc was winning.

Yeah, the place was jumping all right, no doubt about that. Inside the house, he could hear Rachel singing softly as she swept the parlor floor. She had a pleasant voice, Tyree thought. But then, everything about Rachel was pleasant. Everything except her attitude toward him.

She did not like the fact that he sat idle while everyone else worked, and she said so, openly, bluntly, and often.

"You could at least help water the stock," she had remarked earlier in the day. "Or feed the chickens."

"I could," Tyree had replied easily. "But your old man ain't paying me to tend his stock."

That remark had unleashed a tirade that had gone on for several minutes and had ended only when Tyree dropped a hand over Rachel's mouth, cutting her off in mid-sentence.

"Why don't you just calm down and admit what's really bothering you?" Tyree had suggested.

"I don't know what you mean," Rachel had replied stiffly.

"The hell you don't! You're still in a lather about what happened at Sunset Canyon, and we both know it."

Rachel had thrown Tyree a withering look. Then, head high as a spooked filly, she had turned on her heel and flounced angrily into the house, her cheeks awash with color.

That had been better than an hour ago, and though she had been in and out several times since then, she had never acknowledged Tyree's presence on the porch by so much as a glance. Oh, she was mad all right, he mused. No doubt about that.

Tyree spent the whole day loafing on the porch, content to sit in the shade with his hat tilted over his eyes, his long legs stretched negligently in front of him, his arms folded over his chest.

Rachel burned every time she saw him sitting there, catnapping or smoking a thin black cigar while everyone else toiled in the sun. There was so much to be done, and so few hands to do it. There were still stray cattle to be rounded up, calves that needed branding, fields to plow, hay to cut, fences that needed mending, stock to be fed and watered, harness that needed repairing, wood to cut. And there was a large hole in the kitchen roof that simply had to be patched before the rains came.

Oh, there were a hundred things that needed doing and one more pair of hands would be welcome, even the hands of a gunslinger like Logan Tyree. But no, he could not be bothered with anything as mundane as manual labor.

"Too bad we don't have another landgrabber for him to kill," she muttered crossly. "I'm sure he wouldn't mind adding another notch to his gun."

His gun. That was another area of contention. He never took it off, not even at the dinner table, and that irritated Rachel more than anything else. She had asked him, politely, to please remove his gunbelt during dinner, but he had refused with a curt, "Sorry, no."

He had usurped her father's place at the head of the table, too, offering no apology or explanation. Later, her father had pointed out that Tyree insisted on sitting at the head of the table because it put his back to the only wall in the room that didn't have a window in it, and afforded a clear view of the door.

"Self-preservation, honey, that's all it is," Halloran had explained. "You can't blame a man for being careful. Especially a man in Tyree's line of work."

Tyree. He stayed up long after everyone else had retired for the night. Often, from her window upstairs, Rachel saw the faint glow of his cigar as he took a last turn around the house, or paced the length of the front yard. Dressed all in black, with his cigar casting eerie shadows across his swarthy face, she often thought he looked like Satan prowling the bowels of Hell. Not a pleasant comparison, she admitted, but then, Logan Tyree was not a particularly nice person. Arrogant, yes. Self-assured, yes. But pleasant? Definitely not!

But what bothered Rachel the most was her father's attitude toward Tyree. Somehow, her father had resolved his feelings of guilt regarding his part in Walsh's death and seemed to have thrust the matter behind him. He never mentioned the incident and seemed to have forgotten it ever happened.

Not only that, but her father seemed to have developed a genuine fondness for Tyree's company and the two of them spent many an evening discussing the ranch, debating whether it would be wiser to take their small herd to market this year, or wait until the following spring.

Rachel was bewildered by Tyree's attitude, as well. She knew he cared little for the ranch, or for the problems facing them, yet he listened patiently while her father waxed long and loud about his hopes for the Lazy H. On occasion, Tyree even offered worthwhile suggestions. Men! There was no understanding any of them.

As time went on, there was considerable speculation about what would become of the Slash W ranch now that Walsh was dead. There was talk in town that an eastern syndicate was thinking of buying the place. Another rumor concerned a Scotsman and a flock of sheep. There was even mention of some English lord coming out to look the place over, but Rachel dismissed such talk as idle gossip. Most likely, Walsh's sister, who lived in Amarillo, would sell the Slash W to some nice family man with a dozen kids and that would put an end to the trouble in the valley once and for all.

Sunday found Tyree slouched in his usual place on the front porch, an unlit cigar clamped between his teeth, his hat pulled low. Rachel was inside singing "Nearer, My God, to Thee" while she dressed for church. Halloran was down at the barn, talking to Cahill while one of the hands hitched a pair of spirited bay geldings to a shiny black buggy.

The ranch was quiet today. Candido had already left for town, bound for mass. The freckle-faced wrangler was going courting. You could always spot a cowhand with romance on his mind. They were squeaky clean and usually smelled heavily of lilac water.

Tyree pushed his hat back on his head as Rachel opened the front door and stepped out onto the porch. She looked lovely, as always; her face was lightly powdered and a few tendrils of golden hair peeked out from beneath the brim of a perky straw bonnet. Her slender figure was modestly clad in a dress of some dark blue material trimmed in delicate white lace. The dress outlined every luscious curve. Just looking at her made his mouth water.

Rachel frowned as she stood on the edge of the porch, waiting for her father to bring the buggy up from the barn. Why did Tyree have to be sitting on the porch just now, she wondered dourly. It was a beautiful morning and she didn't want anything, or anyone, to spoil it. She was reluctant to acknowledge his presence. The sight of his lip curling down in that hateful way made her angry; but it was his amused silence that goaded her into speaking.

"Good morning, Mr. Tyree," she said coldly, formally. She glanced toward the barn, wishing her father would hurry.

"Mornin', ma'am," Tyree drawled. As usual, she was ill at ease in his presence. Her face mirrored her relief when Halloran drove up in the buggy.

"Morning, Tyree," Halloran called cheerfully. "Care to come to church with us?"

"Now what would I do in church?" Tyree asked, flashing a sardonic grin.

"Well, now—" Halloran began, only to be cut off in mid-sentence by his daughter.

"You could pray for the souls of all the poor

unfortunate men you've gunned down," Rachel suggested sweetly.

"You must have a hell of a long service," Tyree replied easily. "I've killed a lot of men."

Rachel stared at Tyree, her face pale, her eyes filled with condemnation. What kind of monster was he, to talk so casually about the men he had killed? Didn't he feel any remorse, any guilt or regret, at taking a human life?

The horrified look on Rachel's face sparked Tyree's anger. Who was she, to sit in judgement on him? When had she ever known anything but love and security? What did she know about him, or his past? What did she know about pain?

"A lot of men," Tyree repeated, some perverse quirk of nature urging him on. "Widows and orphans, too," he added sourly. He was kidding, of course, but Rachel took him seriously, and that angered him still more.

"Maybe you should say a prayer or two for your own soul," Rachel murmured quietly, her voice filled with pity. "Though I doubt it would do much good at this late date."

John Halloran cleared his throat as the tone of their conversation grew heavy. "Rachel, that's enough."

"I'm sorry, Pa. Mr. Tyree." Lifting her skirts, she hurried down the steps to the side of the buggy.

She was about to step in when two strong

hands closed around her waist. "Allow me, ma'am," Tyree said with exaggerated politeness, and before Rachel could protest, he had lifted her onto the high front seat as though she weighed no more than a sack of feathers.

"Thank you," Rachel said through tight lips.

"Sure you won't join us?" Halloran asked. "We've plenty of room."

Tyree was about to refuse when he glanced at Rachel. She was sitting stiff as a board beside her father, her cheeks suffused with color, her hands folded primly in her lap. She refused to meet his eyes.

Tyree grinned roguishly, knowing his company was the last thing she wanted on this bright sunny morning.

"I think maybe I will join you after all," Tyree decided, and climbing into the rig, he took a place next to Rachel.

It was a lovely morning for a ride, but Rachel found no pleasure in it. The flowers growing alongside the road might have been weeds, the sky overhead black with clouds instead of a clear sapphire blue. Trapped between her father and Tyree, she stared straight ahead, furious with them both. Men! Whatever had possessed her father to invite a man like Logan Tyree to church? And what in the name of all that was holy had prompted Tyree to accept?

As the miles slipped by, she grew increasingly aware of Tyree's hard thigh pressed against her own, of the touch of his arm jostling hers whenever the buggy bounced over a rut in the road. Almost as tangible as the pressure of his arm and thigh was the bold way his eyes caressed her, making her blush with embarrassment. His holster was a hard lump against her hip, a constant reminder of who and what he was. How she hated him! He was the most arrogant, insufferable man she had ever known.

"It's good to have things back to normal," her father mused as they pulled onto the main road that led to town. "Cahill thinks we might have enough cattle to make a decent herd come spring."

"He's a good man," Tyree remarked. "Handy with a rope."

John Halloran ran a nervous finger around the inside of his shirt collar, knowing Rachel would not take kindly to what he was about to suggest. "Tyree, I'd, uh, like to have you stay on with us. Permanent."

"Pa!" Rachel exclaimed in horror. "You can't be serious."

"Don't worry, ma'am," Tyree said smoothly, his voice quietly mocking the despair in her eyes. "I've no intention of settling down and becoming a farmer. But I'm obliged for the offer, Halloran."

They rode the rest of the way in silence. Rachel glanced at her father out of the corner of her eye. What was he thinking of, to ask Tyree to stay on at the ranch? Dear Lord, what would she have done if Tyree had accepted? There was no way she could face him every day. His presence was a constant reminder of something she longed to forget, and only the fact that he would soon be riding on made his presence bearable. Every time she looked at him, she knew he was remembering Sunset Canyon. The knowledge of what had happened between them was always lurking in the back of his eyes, tormenting her, taunting her. She could hardly bear to look at him.

The Yellow Creek Methodist Church was a small square flat-topped building crowned with a large wooden cross. Saguaro, ocotillo, Spanish bayonet and palo verde grew around the church, their leaves and flowers making bright splashes of color against the white-washed walls. Buggies, wagons, and riding horses were tethered to the long hitch rail in front of the building.

Hat in hand, Tyree followed Rachel and John Halloran into the church and down the narrow aisle to their pew, which was located near the front of the chapel. He should not have come, Tyree mused glumly. He had only agreed to accompany them to annoy Rachel, after all, and not because of any deep burning need to hear the gospel preached by some whey-faced minister who had probably never seen sin close-up, or known how satisfying a bottle of good whiskey and a bad woman could be.

Several heavily corseted dowagers dressed

in somber hues turned to stare at Tyree, making him feel as welcome in their midst as a bottle of rotgut at a temperance meeting. One stout, gray-haired matron whispered, loudly, that the Lord's house was not the proper place for guns. Or gunmen.

Tyree could not have agreed more.

A hush fell over the congregation as the Reverend made his way to the pulpit to offer the invocation. It was a long prayer, filled with praise and thanksgiving for the Lord's benevolence. Tyree glanced furtively at the people sitting nearby, bemused by the rapt expressions on their faces. The nuns who had raised him had worn similar expressions of love and devotion during worship services at the convent.

Tyree grimaced as he lowered his gaze and studied the raw plank flooring at his feet. Personally, he had never found much comfort in the stilted rites and rituals of the Catholic church, or any solace in the cold pattern of their prayers, only a wondering curiosity that God did not get tired of hearing the same rehearsed prayers day after day, year after year.

The religion of the Apache had been more to his liking. Usen was the All-Father, the supreme being; Child of the Waters was His son. The Apache was one with nature, believing that every rock, every animal, every blade of grass, had a spirit of its own. Nothing was ever wantonly killed or wasted, lest its spirit become angry. Only the white man killed for sport. He had even killed his God.

The opening strains of an unfamiliar hymn put an end to Tyree's reverie, and he listened with real pleasure as Rachel's voice joined with the congregation, the notes sweet and clear as she praised the Lord in song.

There followed several announcements relating to recent births, deaths and marriages in the community, and then the preacher began his sermon.

The clergyman was a nice enough looking fellow, with close-cropped curly brown hair, expressive brown eyes, and hands that looked as soft as a baby's bottom. There was, in fact, nothing remarkable about the man, until he began to speak. His voice was deep and rich, with a resonance that carried past the last pew. The minute the pastor began to speak, Logan Tyree knew he should have stayed at the ranch.

"My text for this morning concerns the sixth commandment," the minister said in his best hell-and-damnation voice, "thou shalt not kill—"

For the first time since leaving the Lazy H, Rachel glanced directly at Tyree. "Are you listening?" her lovely blue eyes seemed to say. "This one is for you."

Scowling, Tyree settled deeper into his seat, wondering how Rachel had managed to write the preacher's sermon.

"He who lives by the sword shall perish by

the sword," the Reverend went on, warming to his subject. "Man was not placed upon the earth to contend with his brother, but to love him, to help him in times of trouble, to comfort him in times of sorrow—"

Face dark with annoyance, Tyree managed to sit through forty-five minutes of pious mutterings before the good reverend said "Amen" and sat down.

There was another hymn, and another prayer, before the service was finally over. Stepping outside, Tyree took a deep breath. Never again would he willingly enter a church. Not even to annoy Rachel. Better to fry in hell than sit through another long-winded lecture on the evils and consequences of sin.

After church, the congregation went outside to socialize. A long gateleg table held cookies and punch. Tyree stood near the Halloran buggy, his arms folded across his chest, while John Halloran and Rachel mingled with their friends. Several young men went out of their way to speak to Rachel.

Tyree scowled as a pair of young boys clad in dark blue suits ventured in his direction, their eyes round as saucers as they stared at the gun slung low on his thigh.

"Told ya it was a Colt," bragged the older of the two.

"Jeff Barnes, you come away from there this instant!" called a female voice. "And you, too, Jimmy Norris!"

The two boys didn't move, but continued to stare at Tyree and at the tied-down gun that marked him as a gunman.

"Jeff! Jim!" The voice was shrill now with anger.

Tyree grinned. "Best run along, boys," he suggested. "She sounds mad."

Jeff Barnes shrugged. "She's always mad."

"Yeah," Tyree said, thinking of Rachel. "Some women are like that."

"Jeff! Jim!" The voice was masculine this time, and the two boys turned and ran back to the churchyard.

A short time later, John Halloran and Rachel made their way to the buggy. Rachel was careful to let her father sit in the middle on the ride home. It was a move that did not go unnoticed by Tyree.

"Fine sermon," Halloran remarked on the trip back to the Lazy H. "Preacher's got a good head on his shoulders for such a young sprout."

"Yes, indeed," Rachel agreed. "Tell me, Mr. Tyree, did you agree with what the Reverend Jenkins had to say?"

Tyree quirked a knowing eyebrow in Rachel's direction. "You mean that part about dying by the sword, I reckon?"

"Why, yes, I did," Rachel acknowledged sweetly. "How did you know?"

"Just a wild guess," Tyree answered dryly.

"Well, do you agree with him?" she persisted.

Tyree shrugged. "I suppose what he says is true. But then, everybody dies sooner or later, and a bullet's as good a way to check out as any. Better than most." He threw Rachel a lazy grin. "And it sure beats hanging."

"You talk very casually about death," Rachel remarked. "Doesn't the thought bother you? I mean, in your line of work, it could happen anytime."

"I guess I've seen death up close too many times to be afraid of it," Tyree murmured, his tone no longer light and teasing.

"What are you afraid of?" Rachel asked.

She waited intently for his answer, feeling that if she could discover what he feared, she would discover something meaningful about the enigma known as Logan Tyree. But he did not answer her. Instead, he stared into the distance, his eyes guarded, his mouth a tight line.

"Well?" Rachel urged.

"I think I can answer that one, daughter," Halloran remarked quietly. He glanced in Tyree's direction. "Some men ain't afraid of life or death. They're afraid of other things, like growing old, or being helpless. Ain't that right, Tyree?"

"Yeah," Tyree admitted slowly. "Something like that."

Rachel stared at her father, puzzled that he should have such insight into the character of a man like Tyree.

"You have a very strange outlook on life,

Mr. Tyree," Rachel mused aloud. "Very strange indeed."

"We weren't talking about life," Tyree reminded her with a rueful grin. "We were talking about death. When the time comes, I want to go out to meet it. I don't want to be too old or too stove up to put up a fight."

"Amen," John Halloran murmured fervently. "But tell me, Tyree, until the old man with the scythe shows up, what's a feller like you want out of life?"

"Not much," Tyree said, chuckling. "A good horse. A good gun. A bad woman."

"Amen again," Halloran chortled, slapping his thigh. "Amen and amen."

Rachel looked at her father, openly astonished. "Pa!"

"Don't get riled, daughter," Halloran chided, winking at Tyree. "I was only funnin'."

Funning, indeed, Rachel thought sourly. Her father's whole attitude had changed in the last few months, and she could trace the change directly to Logan Tyree!

Chapter 4

*I*n the days that followed, Rachel avoided Tyree whenever possible, and when they were together, she was cold and distant. Halloran spent most of his time with his nose buried in his account books, his brow puckered in a worried frown as he pored over his ledgers. Tyree loafed on the front porch, apparently indifferent to anything that did not concern him personally.

On Saturday morning, Cahill's niece, Amy, made her weekly visit to the ranch. She was a winsome child, full of energy, and Cahill loved the child dearly, but after three hours of "what?" and "why?", he sent her down to the barn to find Candido. One of the mares had recently dropped a foal and Cahill hoped Amy would pester the head wrangler with questions about the filly for awhile, thereby giving his own ears a much-needed rest.

But Amy could not find Candido, and so she wandered into the barn alone, excited by the prospect of playing with the baby horse.

She had to stand on a feed bucket to see over the stall door, and her eyes grew wide as saucers when she spied the long-legged buckskin filly nuzzling its dam's teat.

Amy's hand fairly itched to touch the darling foal, but both horses ignored her. The mare was content to nibble at the hay in the manger; the filly continued to suck greedily at its mother's milk.

With an exasperated sigh, Amy jumped off the bucket and kicked it aside. It took several minutes of concentrated effort before she managed to unlatch the stall door. Then, totally unaware of any danger, she stepped into the stall, smiling as her eager hands reached out to stroke the filly's neck.

Tyree was catnapping on the front porch when the mare's scream of rage shattered the afternoon stillness. Hard upon the mare's angry whinny came the terrified shriek of a frightened child. It was the girl's cry of terror that galvanized Tyree into action and he raced down the porch stairs and across the yard toward the barn, hoping he wasn't too late to save the child from whatever trouble she had stirred up.

Amy was pressed hard against a corner of the stall when Tyree arrived. Her blue eyes were round with fear, her rosebud mouth open in a soundless cry for help.

The mare was blocking the stall door, and she was mad as hell. The filly was her first foal, and the mare was as jealous and protective of her offspring as only a new mother can be. Ears flat, she snapped at the child, her big yellow teeth missing Amy's right shoulder by mere inches.

"Easy, mama," Tyree murmured. "Easy, girl."

The mare whirled around to face the new threat, her sides heaving, her teeth bared. The filly pressed close against her mother's side, frightened by the confusion in the stall.

"Easy, mama," Tyree murmured again. "Easy now. No one's gonna hurt you or that pretty baby. Easy, mama. Easy now."

The mare stared at him, ears twitching, nostrils flared.

Still speaking softly, Tyree reached out and laid one big brown hand on the mare's shoulder. Ever so slowly, he slipped a rope around the mare's neck. "Come on, mama," he coaxed in a quiet voice. "Let's go outside."

For a moment, it was uncertain whether the mare would respond to the tug of the rope and the quiet words. Snorting softly, the mare swung her head around to stare balefully at the small human creature huddled in the corner, and then the mare reached out to sniff

Tyree, who was murmuring to her in soft Apache as he gently stroked her neck.

"Mr. Tyree—"

"Be quiet, kid," Tyree admonished. Then, to the mare, "Come on, mama. Everything's all right."

With a toss of her head, the mare followed Tyree out of the stall, whickering to the foal dancing nervously at her heels.

Candido, Cahill, and Rachel were waiting outside the barn. Cahill looked hard at Tyree, his face pale, his eyes worried.

"The kid's all right," Tyree assured Cahill. "Just scared."

"Thank God!" the foreman said fervently, and ran into the barn. He reappeared a moment later with Amy cradled in his arms. "Tyree," Joe Cahill murmured sincerely. "How can I ever repay you?"

"No need," Tyree said, grinning at Amy. "I was just returning a favor. Right, kid?"

"Right," Amy said tremulously, and burst into tears.

"Tyree, if there's ever anything I can do for you," Cahill said, "anything at all—"

"Sure," Tyree answered, handing the mare's lead rope to Candido. "I'll let you know." With a smile at Amy's tear-stained face, Tyree started back toward the house.

Rachel was grinning broadly as she followed Tyree. His concern for Amy's safety was the first decent human emotion he had shown, and for some reason she did not care to examine too closely, it pleased her immensely.

"What the hell are you grinning at?" Tyree asked sourly. "My face turning blue?"

"Better be careful," Rachel teased, "or you'll ruin your tough-guy image."

"What?"

"People might think you've got a heart under that thorny exterior if you start rescuing children in danger."

"I'll keep that in mind," Tyree retorted dryly.

Rachel laughed out loud. "Just kills you to think you were caught doing a good deed, doesn't it?" Rachel crowed. "Well, I shall remind you of it at least once a day."

"You do, and I'll knock your teeth down your lovely throat," Tyree threatened, only half kidding.

"I'm not afraid of you any more, Logan Tyree," Rachel declared boldly.

She was beautiful when her spirits were up, Tyree mused. Her cheeks were flushed a becoming shade of pink, and her sky blue eyes twinkled merrily as she walked beside him, taking long steps to keep up. Oh, she was having a high old time, needling him about his so-called good deed. There was no doubt about that.

"So you're not afraid of me any more," Tyree drawled lazily.

"That's right," Rachel answered saucily. "I used to think you were all cold steel and ice, but now I know you're really soft as melted butter."

They were standing on the front porch now. Rachel had her back against one of the uprights, her head tilted up so she could see Tyree's face. A curious light danced in his eyes as he took a step toward her.

"Come closer," he said, "and I'll show you just how soft I can be."

Suddenly Rachel didn't feel like smiling any more. The husky wanting in Tyree's voice sent a cold shiver down her spine and that, coupled with the hungry look in his catlike eyes, started her heart pounding like an Indian war drum.

"Never mind," she said briskly. "I believe you."

Tyree took another step forward, placing his hands on either side of Rachel's head so that she was trapped between his arms. His eyes lingered on the warm curve of her mouth, then dropped suggestively to her breasts before he returned his gaze to her face. She looked scared and very vulnerable.

"I thought you weren't afraid of me any-more," he challenged.

Rachel swallowed hard, all her bravado gone now that he was standing so near. The scent of cigar smoke and leather tickled her nostrils, reminding her of Sunset Canyon. She could not hold his inquiring gaze and she glanced at the arms that imprisoned her. His sleeves were rolled up, exposing his forearms, and the sight of his bare flesh started a little thrill of excitement in her stomach. His black shirt was the perfect foil for his swarthy skin and ebony hair. His eyes, so intent on her face, burned with a deep amber fire.

"I'm not afraid," Rachel stammered nervously. "It's just that I . . . I have something in the oven, and I think it's burning."

"That right? I don't smell anything." He was laughing at her now, his mouth turned down in that mocking grin she hated, his eyes alight with mischief.

"Well, I do!" Rachel shrieked. Ducking under his arms, she bolted for the front door and the safety of the house.

Once inside, Rachel glanced over her shoulder, then sighed with relief. Thank goodness, he hadn't followed her. Damn the man! Why didn't he go away and leave her alone? She hated the way he looked at her whenever they were alone together, his amber eyes hungry, his mouth curled down in that mocking way she despised. She knew all too well what he was thinking when he looked at her like that; knew, beyond a shadow of a doubt that he was remembering Sunset Canyon.

The memory of that day was indelibly burned into Rachel's memory, too, and she felt her blood grow cold as she recalled the heart-stopping fear that had taken hold of her when she realized the Indians were following her. Her flight had been in vain, and all her struggles futile. Vividly, she remembered how frightened and humiliated she had been when they threw her to the ground and lifted her skirts, their deep-set black eyes leering at her as they held her down. She remembered how relieved she had been to see Tyree. Thank God, she had thought, help was on the way.

As always, she burned with shame at the memory of what she had done. She could not blame Tyree for what had happened between them. He had been ready to let her go as soon as he realized the Indians were gone, but no, she had put her arms around his neck and practically begged him to take her.

Oh, if only he would go away! Maybe then she could forget the whole thing. And yet, she didn't really want to forget. She had thrilled to his touch, to the feel of his arms around her. She had marveled at the way his body felt pressed against her own, had thrilled to the crush of his lips, to the sound of his voice whispering in her ear, telling her she was beautiful, desirable.

She was glad when Amy came in, clamoring for milk and cookies.

Chapter 5

*E*arly Monday morning, Tyree saddled his horse and rode into town. He had been cooped up at the Lazy H for too long, he mused, and he felt the need for a drink and a few hours of solitude at the local watering hole.

Riding down the main street, he stopped at the first saloon he came to. *Bowsher's*, the sign said, and Tyree grinned. Flat-Nose Beverly Bowsher was a name known on both sides of the Missouri. Flat-Nose had been a notorious madam in a swanky Denver saloon until she fell in love with a half-breed Apache scout. The Indian had no understanding of a woman who sold herself to men and sliced off the end of her nose. Beverly had fled Denver and taken up residence in the quiet town of Yellow Creek. She was old now and kept to her rooms above the saloon. But her name remained a legend.

Dismounting, Tyree looped the chestnut's reins over the hitchrack, slipped the cinch, and gave the animal a pat on the neck before stepping inside the saloon. Ordering a bottle of rye whiskey from the bar dog, he carried the bottle to a rear table. Sitting there, with his back against the wall, he slowly and methodically worked his way to the bottom of the bottle, feeling his muscles relax as the pale amber liquid warmed his belly.

The saloon grew crowded as noontime approached. Shopkeepers drifted in for a quick drink after lunch. Unemployed cowhands ambled in, hoping to get a lead on a job at one of the local ranches.

Tyree studied each man that entered the saloon, sizing them up with a practiced eye. Toward evening, a pair of hardcases swaggered in, and Tyree felt himself grow tense as he recognized two of Walsh's hired guns. The Slash W riders spotted Tyree at the same time. Frowning, they stood with their heads together for a few moments before they hurried out of the saloon.

It was late when Tyree returned to the Lazy H. Only one light burned in the house and Tyree went inside expecting to find Rachel's old man asleep over his account books. Instead, he found Rachel curled up in a chair, reading a volume of Shakespeare.

Damned if she didn't look like some kind of golden temptress sitting there, Tyree mused, what with her tawny hair spilling over her shoulders and the lamplight softly caressing the curve of her cheek.

Rachel looked up, startled by his sudden appearance. "Mr. Tyree. We thought you had left."

"Sorry to disappoint you, ma'am, but I just took the day off."

Rachel wrinkled her nose with distaste as she caught a whiff of his breath. "And spent it at the local saloon," she muttered with obvious disapproval.

"Yeah. You got any coffee?"

"There's some left from dinner," she said grudgingly.

"That'll do. Think you could warm it up for me?"

"I suppose so." Her tone implied she was less than pleased with the thought of his prolonged presence.

"Thanks."

Tyree followed her into the kitchen, admiring her tiny waist and the supple sway of her hips.

"Would you care for something to eat?" Rachel asked, coolly polite and impersonal.

"Just coffee."

"Will you be staying with us much longer, Mr. Tyree?"

He chuckled softly. "Just can't wait to get rid of me, can you?"

"No," Rachel answered bluntly. "My father may be charmed with your presence here, but I am not. I'd like to know how much longer you plan to stay with us."

"Until your old man tells me to leave," Tyree snapped, annoyed as always by her too-obvious disaffection. "That coffee ready?"

"Yes."

Tyree took the cup Rachel offered him, swallowed the hot bitter brew. Too bad it wasn't poison, he mused wryly. That would put a smile on her face.

"Got enough for another cup?" he asked, more to irritate her than anything else.

Rachel refilled Tyree's cup without speaking, not liking the way his eyes moved over her, or the way he had maneuvered her into a corner, so that he stood between her and the door. He drained the cup, his eyes never leaving her face. She wished suddenly that she was wearing more than just a cotton nightgown and a flannel robe. Unconsciously, she drew the robe tighter around her waist.

Setting the empty cup on the table, Tyree reached out and ran his hand through the heavy mass of Rachel's hair. It was soft as cornsilk, smooth as satin beneath his fingertips. Stepping closer, he caught the faint fragrance of lavender-scented soap, the aroma of fresh-baked bread. And over all was Rachel's own scent, warm and womanly.

Muttering a soft oath, Tyree took Rachel in his arms and kissed her, his mouth hard and demanding, his lean body pressed suggestively against hers.

For a moment, Rachel stood limp in his arms, her knees suddenly weak, as if his kiss had drained all the strength from her limbs. A slow fire started in the pit of her stomach and spread downward as his hands caressed her back. She felt bereft when he took his lips from hers and she swayed against him, her face upturned, her mouth strangely eager for his kiss.

Tyree chuckled softly as he covered her mouth with his own. "Sweet," he murmured, nibbling her lower lip. "So sweet."

His breath tickled her ear as his mouth moved up her neck and against her hair. Rachel sagged against him, shuddering with pleasure as his hands kneaded her lower back and buttocks, grinding her hips against his groin, leaving her breathless and yearning for more. Her arms went around his waist, her hands roaming over his muscled back and shoulders. He was so big, so tall, so very male. All her senses responded to his touch as her questing hands moved up and down his arms, excited by the play of powerful muscles beneath the black cotton shirt he wore.

"Sweet," Tyree said again, and his hand was warm on her bare flesh as he loosened her bathrobe and dropped his hand inside her gown.

The touch of Tyree's calloused hand on her breast shocked Rachel into a sudden awareness of what she was doing, and with whom. With a squeal of alarm, she twisted out of Tyree's grasp. Two bright spots of color stained her cheeks, and her eyes blazed with anger and indignation as she slapped him with all the strength at her command.

The print of her hand stood out clearly on Tyree's cheek, as livid as the rage that flickered and died in his eyes. With a muffled cry, Rachel pushed past Tyree and headed for the door, but before she could escape, Tyree grabbed her by the shoulders and yanked her backward. Trapping her within the hard prison of his arms, he turned her toward him and kissed her a third time, his tongue boldly raping the soft inner recesses of her mouth.

Rachel struggled in vain, and the more she fought him, the harder Tyree kissed her until, at last, she stood passive in his embrace. There was a dull roaring in her ears, a peculiar quivering in her limbs, and a growing desire to stand there forever, with Tyree's arms tight around her and his mouth pressed to hers, evoking wave after wave of delightfully wicked longings deep in the core of her being.

She was almost sorry when Tyree finally released her.

"Go on, slap me again," he invited impudently. "It's worth it."

The next morning, Rachel's mouth was still bruised from the force of Logan Tyree's kisses. What an arrogant, insufferable man he was! And how readily she had responded to the touch of his mouth and hands.

She was decidedly cool and aloof at breakfast, refusing to meet Tyree's smugly knowing gaze, or to be drawn into any conversation with him.

John Halloran frowned at his daughter. He knew she heartily disapproved of Tyree but, in his opinion, there was no reason to be rude to the man. Tyree was, after all, a hired hand and deserving of at least a modicum of polite attention.

Rachel was relieved when breakfast was over and the men left the house. She quickly did the dishes and tidied up the kitchen, then returned to her bedroom, intending to put the finishing touches on a new dress she was making. But as she passed the window overlooking the yard, she spied a familiar figure lounging against one of the breaking pens watching Candido throw a saddle on a bronc. Candido was a top hand with horses, and she was somewhat surprised to see he was still attempting to break the big gray stallion that had recently been brought in off the range. The stud, once king of all he surveyed, was a fighter and his ears went flat the minute he felt the weight of the saddle on his back.

With a last jerk, Candido pulled the cinch

tight and stepped into the saddle. And all hell broke loose. Ears flat, back humped, nose to the ground, the maddened stallion began bucking. Amazingly, Candido rode the pitching bronc as if glued to the saddle. The mustang bucked like a rodeo bronc, now sunfishing, now swapping ends. And when bucking failed to dislodge the unwelcome rider, the stallion reared straight up and crashed over backward. But Candido was out of the saddle before the gray hit the ground, and nimbly remounted as the angry horse scrambled to its feet.

With a shrill scream of rage, the stud grabbed the bit between its teeth and lined out in a dead run. Thinking the stallion meant to jump the corral fence, the wiry Mexican wrangler settled deeper into the saddle. But the mustang did not launch himself over the corral. Instead, he swung sideways at the last minute, slamming Candido against the stout wooden rail.

The sound of breaking bone was sharp, punctuated by a high-pitched cry of pain as Candido's right leg snapped. Sensing victory, the gray bucked again and Candido toppled out of the saddle and hit the ground, hard.

With the quickness of a mountain cat, Tyree vaulted over the fence and grabbed the mustang's bridle while a pair of cowhands slipped between the rails and dragged the luckless waddie out of harm's way.

Tyree paid no attention to the commotion

outside the corral. He had eyes only for the horse as he stood at the stallion's head, patting the animal's lathered neck and shoulder, gently scratching its ears. And all the while he was talking to the horse, and the horse was listening.

Still speaking to the horse, Tyree removed the saddle and sweat-dampened blanket, then led the skittish stud out of the corral toward the barn.

Rachel stared after Tyree, her dress forgotten. How could a man be so gentle and patient with a wild animal and callously kill a human being?

Early the following morning, Rachel saw Tyree working with the stud. From her bedroom window, she watched Tyree ease a halter over the gray's head, then pick up a light saddle blanket and let the horse sniff it. That done, Tyree rubbed the blanket over the stud's neck and withers, along its back, over its muscled rump and down each leg. Sacking out, the cowboys called it, though it wasn't a common practice. Most cowhands just saddled a bronc and rode it out, breaking the horse by sheer force. But not Tyree. Again and again, Tyree dragged the blanket over the animal, showing the nervous horse there was nothing to fear.

The saddle came next: on, off, on, off. And all the while she could see he was talking to the horse.

Fascinated, Rachel left her room and took a

place behind a tree, hoping to hear what Tyree was saying to the skittish mustang. But the words were harsh, foreign to her ears.

Tossing the saddle and blanket aside, Tyree stroked the gray's neck. And then, still speaking gently to the stud, he swung aboard the animal's bare back. There was a moment when the stallion's ears went flat, when its nostrils flared with suspicion and confusion, but Tyree was speaking to the horse again, soothing its nervousness with quiet words and gentle hands, and after a few halfhearted crowhops around the corral, the stallion stood quiet, ears twitching back and forth.

Dismounting, Tyree led the horse around the corral, first one way, then the other. A second time he swung effortlessly onto the animal's back. Dismounted once again. Then, as if he had been doing it every day for years, he saddled the gray and stepped aboard. And the mustang stood there like it had been carrying a man all its life.

"Care to try him, ma'am?"

Startled, Rachel stepped out from her hiding place. "How did you know I was here?"

"Smelled you. Wanna try him?"

"That outlaw? No, thank you!"

"He's no outlaw," Tyree said, patting the gray's neck. "He's just been mistreated, but he'll come around. You'll see. Some kind words, a light hand on the reins, and he'll be as gentle and law-abiding as your own mare was."

"Too bad those methods don't work with people," Rachel muttered dourly.

"Meaning me, I suppose," Tyree said testily.

"Exactly you."

Dismounting, Tyree led the stallion out of the corral. He grinned wickedly as he came to stand beside Rachel.

"Maybe it would work," he suggested. "Why don't you try being nice to me for a few days and see what happens?"

"I am nice!" Rachel snapped.

"Yeah," Tyree agreed, laughing softly. "Real nice. And soft-spoken, too."

Rachel felt her cheeks grow hot. He was baiting her again, trying to make her angry. And he was succeeding, damn him. Hands clenched at her sides, she took a deep breath, determined not to bandy words with Tyree this time. Smiling sweetly, she inclined her head toward the stallion. "What were you saying to him?"

"I'm not sure," Tyree answered with a shrug. "It's Apache horse talk."

"It's certainly effective."

"Yeah, works every time." His eyes searched hers, then dropped suggestively to the swell of her breasts beneath her yellow shirtwaist, and the curve of her hips. "Too bad it doesn't work as well with women."

"Meaning me, I suppose?" Rachel replied. The words, meant to sound light and teasing, emerged as a choked whisper. The look in

Tyree's cool amber eyes were doing odd things to her heart and a sudden heat, like liquid fire, ignited deep in the core of her belly as a slow smile spread over his face. Why did he have to be so disgustingly handsome, she lamented. And why did her heart behave so queerly whenever he was near? Clint's smiles didn't make her toes curl with pleasure, nor did Clint's kisses leave her breathless and longing for more.

"Exactly you," Tyree drawled softly, intimately.

For a timeless moment, they faced each other, a vibrant heat pulsing between them. Rachel stared at the man standing beside the gray stallion. He was arrogant, full of self-confidence, always so damnably sure of himself. He reminded her of the Indians that roamed the mountains. Like them, he was as wild as the wind, free as the air, deadly as a sidewinder. But there was something about Tyree that attracted her, that made her want to delve into his heart and soul and discover who he really was. Her mind told her he was exactly what he appeared to be: a ruthless killer, a man who could snuff out a human life without turning a hair. And yet, in her heart, Rachel knew he had a gentler side. She had seen the softer side of Tyree when he suspected no one was watching. She had seen his hands, so big and brown and strong, softly caress Amy's hair. Had seen him rescue a baby bird from the jaws of a hungry cat. And she herself had felt his tenderness at Sunset Canyon.

Tyree cocked his head to one side, one black brow rising inquisitively under Rachel's prolonged gaze. What was she thinking? he wondered. What mischievous thoughts were running around inside her pretty little head? What would she do if he reached out and grabbed her trim waist and planted a kiss on that delectable mouth? Would she scream? Slap him? Run back to the shelter of the house? Or admit that she found him desirable and kiss him back?

As if reading his mind, Rachel took a step backward and crossed her arms over her breasts.

"Apache horse talk?" she said, breaking the spell between them. "Where did you ever learn such a thing?"

"From the Mescalero. I lived with them awhile back."

There was something in his tone that warned her not to ask any more questions, but they popped into her mind willy-nilly, one after the other. How long ago had he lived with the Indians? Why had he lived with them? Was that where he had learned to walk with that cat-footed grace that was so rare in big men? Was that why he was so secretive about his past? Had he ridden the war trail with the Apache? Rachel shivered in the sunlight. It was all too easy to imagine Tyree looting and killing and scalping. And liking it.

The sound of approaching hoofbeats drew Tyree's attention and he glanced over his shoulder to see a tall, blond young man ride up to the house, dismount, and look around. A smile spread over the stranger's face when he saw Rachel and he started toward her at a brisk walk.

Rachel was smiling too, her vibrant blue eyes sparkling with pleasure as she took the man's hands in her own.

"Clint," she said warmly. "I'm glad you're back."

Bending, Clint Wesley kissed Rachel on the cheek. "Did you really miss me?" he asked huskily.

"You know I did."

"How much?"

"More than I can say," Rachel answered with mock gravity, and then they both laughed, as though sharing a private joke.

Tyree studied the blond young Adonis, taking special note of the shiny six-pointed tin star pinned to the man's black leather vest, and of the .45 Colt holstered on his right hip. The gun didn't look as if it had seen much action, but it was well cared for.

Tyree glanced at the Marshal again, annoyed to see the man was still holding Rachel's hands.

"Say, Rachel," Wesley was saying, "you're still going to the box social with me, aren't you?"

"Of course," Rachel answered, dimpling prettily. "I wouldn't miss it. Can you come for dinner tonight? I know Pa would love to see you."

"Sure." Wesley seemed to notice Tyree for the first time. "Who's your friend?"

"Oh, I'm sorry," Rachel said, some of the enthusiasm draining from her voice. "Clint Wesley, this is Logan—"

"Matt Logan," Tyree interjected smoothly.

The Marshal nodded, a faint look of suspicion clouding his mild blue eyes. It was a look Tyree had seen countless times before. It was a look that went with the badge.

"You a friend of the family, Mr. Logan?" Wesley asked.

"Just a hired hand."

Wesley rubbed a hand across his jaw, his eyes thoughtful. "You been in these parts before?"

"Not lately."

"Hmmmm. Your face looks familiar. Mind if I ask where you're from?"

That was another thing about lawmen, Tyree thought sourly. They were nosey as hell. "Yeah, I do mind," he said curtly. "If you'll excuse me, I'll be getting back to work."

And before Wesley could object, Tyree vaulted into the saddle and gigged the gray toward the barn.

"Not a very friendly cuss, is he?" Clint muttered.

"No. I hate him. When did you get back?"

"Just now. I haven't even been to my office yet."

"You were gone so long, I was beginning to worry about you."

Clint shrugged. "I got tied up with a bunch of red tape at the territorial prison."

Rachel nodded. If Clint hadn't been to town, then he probably hadn't heard about Walsh. But he would. And if he turned up proof that Tyree killed Job Walsh, what then? It was true that Tyree had pulled the trigger, but her father would be equally culpable before the law.

"Well, I'd better be going," Clint said reluctantly. "I've got a lot of paperwork to catch up on. Dinner at six?"

"Yes," Rachel answered absently, and lifted her face for his kiss.

Rachel prepared Clint's favorite dinner that night: roast beef, mashed potatoes, gravy, corn-on-the-cob, green beans, biscuits dripping butter and honey, and deep-dish apple pie for dessert.

"Lordy, John, I'm surprised you're not as fat as old man Emerson's hogs," Wesley laughingly remarked as he helped himself to a second slice of apple pie. "I know I would be if I ate this good every night."

"Well, it could be arranged," Halloran said, winking broadly.

"Pa, stop it," Rachel admonished. But she

slid a shy smile in Clint's direction. He looked wonderfully handsome, all decked out in a bright red shirt and brown whipcord britches. Unconsciously, she compared Clint to Tyree, who was dressed all in black, as usual. Clint was the more handsome of the two, she decided, and yet there was something earthy and sensual about Tyree that appealed to her, though she was loath to admit it, even to herself. And Tyree *was* handsome, ruggedly so.

"Did you get Curly Bob delivered to Yuma all safe and sound?" Halloran asked Wesley. "There was some talk that his gang might try to spring him."

"Never saw hide nor hair of any of them," Clint replied, chuckling. "I put the word out that I'd blow Curly Bob's head clean off at the first hint of trouble."

"Hot damn!" Halloran chortled in amusement. "I guess they knew you'd do it, too."

"I reckon. Say, I saw Walsh's sister in town this afternoon. She's a mighty pretty woman."

"She planning to sell the ranch?"

"I don't know, John. I didn't get a chance to talk to her. But judging by the amount of baggage she brought along, I'd say she's planning to stay on for quite a spell."

Halloran nodded, his face thoughtful.

"Funny thing about Walsh being bushwhacked," Clint mused aloud. "Nobody seems to have any idea who did it, or why."

Rachel glanced sideways at her father, waiting for him to reply, but he was staring into his coffee cup, his mind apparently on something else.

"It was a dreadful thing," Rachel said quickly. "Tell me, Clint, did you stop to see the O'Brians on your way to Yuma? Has Molly had her baby yet?"

Tyree grinned to himself as Rachel adroitly steered the conversation to safer ground.

With dinner over, the three men retired to the parlor for brandy and cigars while Rachel cleared the table and washed the dishes.

If the Marshal thought it peculiar that Matt Logan was the only hired hand to take his dinner at the main house with the boss and to linger for brandy afterwards, he did not remark on it, though he had treated Tyree to several long speculative glances during dinner. Now, as John Halloran filled their glasses, Wesley said,

"I saw a couple of Slash W riders in town this afternoon. They seem to think somebody paid to have Walsh disposed of."

"That so?" Tyree asked disinterestedly.

"Do they have any idea who was behind it?" Halloran asked bleakly.

Tyree's face remained impassive, but John Halloran's guilt was etched across his weathered face as clearly as print on a page. But Clint Wesley did not see it. He was staring at the man called Matt Logan. Wesley's eyes gave him away even before his hand started toward his gun.

"I wouldn't," Tyree warned flatly. "Not if you expect to walk out of here."

Clint Wesley swallowed hard as he stared into the yawning maw of the .44 that had magically appeared in Tyree's hand.

"Tyree," Wesley muttered sheepishly. "Logan Tyree."

"Took you long enough," Tyree chided in a mild tone.

"It was you, wasn't it?" Wesley accused. "You gunned Walsh."

"Did I?"

"You just rode in and shot him down in cold blood."

"Anybody see me do it?"

"No."

"Too bad."

"Yeah. Well, what now? You gonna gun me down the way you killed Job Walsh?"

Tyree laughed shortly and without amusement. "You hopin' I'll make a slip and say yes? Well, forget it. I didn't bushwhack Walsh and I'm not aimin' to kill you unless you do something stupid."

Halloran had been nervously silent during the exchange between the two younger men. Now, he cleared his throat and said, curtly, "Tyree, put that gun away. I'll not have any gunplay in my home. And you, Clint, you just forget that badge for a minute and remember you're a guest in this house."

"I don't feel very welcome just now," Clint replied, rising stiffly to his feet. "If it's all the same to you, I think I'll go bid Rachel good-night and take my leave."

Halloran and Wesley shook hands and then Clint left the room, his back rigid, as if he expected a bullet to follow him out the door.

"Damn!" The word whispered past Halloran's lips and his face was suddenly drained of color. "He knows," the old man murmured, shaking his head in dismay. "He knows."

"He doesn't know a damn thing," Tyree stated flatly. He drained his glass in a single swallow. Striding to the table where Halloran kept his liquor, Tyree poured himself another drink. "Don't worry, old man," he said calmly. "I didn't backshoot Walsh. And even if I had, there weren't any witnesses."

"I never should have hired you," Halloran said wearily. "I haven't had a peaceful night's sleep since Walsh died. Dammit, I wish I had given him the ranch!"

"Would you feel better if I told you I shot Walsh in a fair fight?"

"Did you?" Halloran asked hopefully.

Tyree grinned at the eager expression on the old man's face. "Sure I did," he lied smoothly. "Sleep easy tonight, Halloran, you've got nothing to worry about."

Halloran didn't believe him, not for a minute. But he wanted to . . . needed to, and so he nodded. "Thanks, Tyree. See you in the morning."

Stepping outside, Tyree sat on the porch

rail and rolled and smoked a cigarette. It was a cool clear night, fragrant with the scent of sage and honeysuckle. Overhead, countless stars shimmered against a black velvet sky.

Grinding out his cigarette, Tyree ambled down to the corral, smiled faintly as the gray stallion came up to him.

"Hi, fella," Tyree murmured, scratching the stud's ears. Abruptly, he whirled around, hand flashing for his gun as he heard footsteps behind him. But it was only Rachel.

"Awfully fast with that, aren't you?" Rachel remarked caustically.

"Middling. Just middling." He returned the .44 to his holster in a swift, unconscious movement that was not lost on Rachel. "The Marshal gone?"

"Yes."

"You want something Rachel?"

It was the first time he had called her by her given name. She could not explain the rush of pleasure it gave her, to hear her name on his lips.

"You want something?" he asked again.

"Yes. Your promise that you won't hurt Clint."

Tyree snorted. "I can't make a promise like that."

"Why not?"

"Because sooner or later he's gonna feel like it's his duty to come after me. And I'm not going back to prison. I spent eighteen months in that hell-hole and I'm not going back. Not for you. Not for anybody. And if Clint Wesley tries to take me in, I'll kill him. You tell him that. As for Walsh, I called him out and I killed him. Anything else you'd like to know?"

Wordlessly, Rachel shook her head, thinking she had never seen such a hard cold expression in a man's eyes before.

Abruptly, the look on Tyree's face changed and Rachel knew he was going to reach for her. The memory of his last kiss made her knees tremble, and she turned on her heel and ran for the safety of the house, running as though all the hounds of hell were barking at her heels.

Tyree did not follow her.

Chapter 6

*T*he day of the box social bloomed bright and clear. Tyree was sitting on the front porch chewing on a cigar when Clint Wesley came to call for Rachel. The Marshal, damn his hide, looked handsome as hell in a blue plaid shirt, black denim pants, and a black leather vest. And Rachel, bless her, looked good enough to eat, all gussied up in a pink and white polka-dot dress. A large white sunbonnet trimmed with long pink and blue streamers was perched atop her honey-colored hair.

Tyree scowled as the young couple went off in a rented hack, laughing and smiling at each other like a couple of carefree school kids.

Tyree had scoffed at the idea of anything as

frivolous as a box social. No one else on the ranch seemed to share his opinion, however, and soon he was the only one left at the Lazy H. Even old man Halloran had ridden off to town earlier that morning.

Tyree sat on the porch for over an hour, enjoying the solitude, content to be alone with his thoughts.

It was nearing noon when hunger tugged at Tyree's belly. The idea of cooking left him cold and he decided to ride into town and grab a bite at the saloon. Ten minutes later, he was swinging into the saddle and riding toward Yellow Creek at a good fast trot.

He heard the noise of a fiddle and the shrieks of kids having a good time long before he rode into the town itself. Entering the town proper, he saw a dozen couples dancing on a clearing in front of the schoolhouse. Rachel and Wesley were among them, holding hands and laughing as they sashayed back and forth.

Farther down the road, several tables were set up. They were covered with gaily colored cloths and piled high with cakes and pies and cookies. Another table, covered with a white linen cloth, stood off by itself, loaded with box suppers all done up in ribbons and bows and fancy paper. The sale of those boxes would be the highlight of the day's festivities.

Leaving the gray stallion at the livery stable, Tyree sauntered down the main street, his left thumb hooked over his gunbelt, his right hand brushing the butt of the .44 strapped to his right thigh. He could feel the curious stares and disapproving glances of the townspeople directed at his back as he moved toward the schoolhouse, his hunger forgotten.

Yellow Creek wasn't much of a town, compared to Dodge or Wichita or El Paso. There was a church to please the ladies, a school to educate the kids, a small hotel. Thorngood's General Store was sandwiched between Bowsher's Saloon and a Chinese laundry. The newspaper office stood next to the marshal's office. A half-dozen small stores catered to the needs of the local farmers and their families.

Tyree took a place against the schoolhouse wall, his hooded amber eyes watching Rachel's every move. She was by far the prettiest girl in town and though Tyree hated to admit it, she was the real reason for his presence at what he considered a foolish waste of time and energy. Men of all ages vied for Rachel's attention, willingly waiting in line just to dance with her, telling her jokes and clowning around like schoolboys in hopes of making her smile.

No one ventured near Tyree.

The dancing went on for another quarter of an hour, and then the fiddler put his fiddle away and the contests began. Clint Wesley entered the pie-eating contest and won first place. Overcome with the thrill of victory, Wesley grabbed Rachel and kissed her soundly on the mouth, smearing her face with cherry pie as several of the local gents cheered him on. The blacksmith won the wrestling match, which came as no surprise to anyone. He had arms like oak trees and a chest like a beer keg. A young, freckle-faced boy of about fifteen won the foot race, while a fairly attractive young woman won the archery contest.

Tyree watched it all with a curious sense of scorn and envy. It was all such nonsense, stuffing pie down your throat, or chasing a greased pig, or engaging in a tug-of-war across a mud puddle. And yet, for all that, everyone appeared to be having a good time.

It was nearing two o'clock when the Mayor called for quiet. "Ladies," he began, bowing formally to the group of women clustered around the table bearing the box suppers. "Gentlemen. It's time for the bidding to start. As you know, any man who buys a basket will not only buy a delicious lunch, but will be entitled to share the meal with the charming young lady who prepared it. The proceeds will, of course, go toward building a new parsonage for the Reverend Jenkins and his lovely family."

The Mayor inclined his head toward the minister and his family as he picked up the first basket. "This one smells like fried chicken and apple pie," he said jovially. "What am I bid?"

Rachel's basket was the fifth one offered. Clint Wesley made the first bid, at a dollar, and in a matter of minutes the bidding had gone up to ten dollars as every eligible young man in town bid on Rachel's lunch, and a chance to be alone with her.

"Ten dollars," the Mayor was saying. "Going once, going twice—"

"Fifteen dollars."

Heads turned. A few of the older women gasped out loud, a few of the younger ones stared enviously at Rachel. Fifteen dollars!

Clint Wesley threw a hard look at Tyree. Very quietly, the Marshal raised his bid to sixteen dollars.

"Twenty dollars," Tyree called.

"Twenty-one," Wesley said, answering the challenge.

Tyree glanced at Rachel, who stood blushing furiously beside the Mayor. Then, throwing Wesley a wry grin, Tyree bid fifty dollars, knowing the Marshal could not afford to match such an outrageous bid, not on a lawman's pay.

The Mayor looked at Wesley askance. Slowly, Clint shook his head.

"Sold to the stranger in black for fifty dollars!" the Mayor declared with a broad grin. "Hope you enjoy it."

With the basket paid for, Tyree followed Rachel to a shady spot near the schoolhouse, dropped down beside her on the blanket she spread on the ground.

"You must be awfully hungry," Rachel muttered, "to spend fifty dollars on a lunch you could buy for fifty cents at the restaurant down the street."

"It's your company I'm buying," Tyree replied candidly. "And we both know it."

Rachel's cheeks flushed at that. Wordlessly, she opened the basket, filled a plate with baked ham, potato salad, a slice of fresh-baked bread, salad, and strawberries. She handed the plate to Tyree, poured him a glass of cold cider.

Rachel ate without tasting her food, conscious of Tyree's predatory gaze, and of Clint's presence only a few yards away. Millie Cloward sat beside Wesley, her basket between them. Millie was a plump young woman with mousy brown hair and placid brown eyes. She was not popular with the young men, and at the moment she looked mighty pleased to have a handsome young man like the Marshal all to herself. Clint Wesley responded to her ceaseless chatter automatically, more interested in keeping an eye on Tyree and Rachel than listening to Millie ramble on about her sister's wedding.

After a few moments, Rachel put her plate aside and regarded Tyree with frankly curious eyes. "Why did you come here today? I thought you said this kind of thing was silly, and no fit way for a grown man to spend his time."

Tyree shrugged. "So I changed my mind.

You gonna sit there and glare at me all afternoon just because I outbid Wesley for your lunch?"

"No. But you must have known Clint and I planned to eat together."

"Then he should have topped my offer."

"He can't afford to spend fifty dollars on a box lunch and you know it."

"Lucky for me, his being so poor," Tyree said, grinning at her. "Come on, cheer up. What's in that tent, yonder?"

"A fortune-teller. I hear she's quite remarkable."

"That right? What say we go take a look? I've never seen a gypsy before."

Rachel smiled at Tyree, suddenly pleased with the thought of spending some time with him. He had obviously bought her supper because he wanted to be with her, or maybe just to irritate Clint. Whatever the reason, she didn't care. She knew only that she was suddenly, unaccountably happy.

"I'm game if you are," she said agreeably. "But it's just a lot of hocus-pocus."

The interior of the tent was stark and dim, the only furnishings a small round table made of dark wood and a pair of straight-backed chairs that had seen better days. A fat white candle sputtered in the center of the table, casting eerie shadows on the canvas walls.

The fortune-teller was seated behind the table, facing the doorway. She was not a gypsy, after all, but an old Apache squaw with iron-gray hair and sunken cheeks. A shapeless red dress hung loose on her frail frame.

A full minute went by before she acknowledged their presence with a faint nod. Then, staring at them through fathomless black eyes, she spoke in a raspy, faraway voice.

"Sit, my children. Give me your hand. Lady first."

Feeling suddenly apprehensive, Rachel took a seat and placed her right hand into the claw-like palm of the old woman.

A moment passed by, and the tent was silent save for the sputtering flame.

"There has been trouble in your life," the old woman said tonelessly. "You think it is over, but it will rise again when you least expect it."

Nodding to herself, the Apache woman turned Rachel's hand over and ran a gnarled, bony finger across Rachel's palm. "You are not married, though two men desire to have you. One loves you with his whole heart and will make a good husband and provider. There will be little excitement in your life if you marry this man, yet you will live in peace and want for nothing. The other man also loves you, though he does not yet know it. Life with this man will be turbulent at times, but if you marry him, you will never regret it."

Rachel leaned forward. Despite her earlier skepticism, she felt herself drawn into the hypnotic web of the old woman's eyes and voice. "How shall I know which man to choose?"

The Indian woman cocked her head to one side, as though listening to a distant voice that only she could hear. "When the time comes, you will know which man is right."

Rachel gazed intently at the fortune-teller, believing the woman's words inspite of herself. She waited for the old woman to go on and was disappointed when the seer dropped her hand and turned to Tyree.

"You now."

For a moment, a strange stillness hung over the dingy little tent. The Apache woman's depthless black eyes looked hard at Tyree, as if seeking to penetrate his soul.

"You are of the blood," she murmured, taking Tyree's hand in hers. "It has brought sorrow into your life, but it has also made you strong. Perhaps too strong." There was a long silence as she stared past Tyree.

Was she gazing down the long corridor of Tyree's past, Rachel wondered, or peering into the murky darkness that was the future?

The candle sputtered, the soft hiss sounding overly loud in the taut stillness that shrouded the tent. Rachel glanced sideways at Tyree. His eyes were intent upon the face of the old woman, his expression almost frightening in its intensity. He believes her, Rachel mused incredulously. He believes every word.

The old woman took a deep breath, and her hand tightened around Tyree's. "I see great turmoil in your future," she predicted in a voice heavy with sadness. "And great pain. But you will triumph, and in the end you will find that which you thought forever gone out of your life."

The gray head drooped. The withered hands withdrew. The ancient eyes closed. The reading was over.

Tyree pressed a twenty dollar gold piece into the Apache woman's hand before following Rachel outside. The sun seemed extraordinarily bright after the tent's gloomy darkness, and Rachel took a deep breath, feeling as if she had just escaped from some sorcerer's dungeon. Here, in the sunlight, it was hard to remember how convincing the old woman had been.

"Well, that was certainly interesting," Rachel said, laughing.

"Yes," Tyree agreed.

"Her predictions for you were a little gloomy, don't you think? I thought fortunetellers were supposed to foretell happy things."

"I thought she was very perceptive," Tyree remarked.

"Perceptive, indeed," Rachel said disdainfully. Now that they were away from the old woman, the whole incident seemed ridiculous. "She said there had been trouble in my life, and that two men desire me." Rachel laughed again. "Everyone has trouble in their life, and most girls have more than one beau."

"She knew I was part Indian," Tyree pointed out. "She wasn't guessing about that."

"Be serious, Tyree! Anyone can tell that just by looking at you."

"Yeah," Tyree agreed softly. "But she was blind."

Rachel digested that bit of information for a moment. Was it possible the old woman was really gifted, and not just some charlatan? Rachel glanced at Tyree. It was easy to see from his expression that he had been deeply impressed with the old Indian woman's predictions.

"You don't believe all that stuff, do you?" Rachel asked, hoping he would say no and dispel the uneasiness that was settling over her. "Not really?"

"I don't know," Tyree answered slowly. "When I lived with the Mescalero, there was an old medicine man who could foretell the future with uncanny accuracy."

"Coincidence, perhaps?"

"Perhaps, but—"

A sudden burst of gunfire near the Blackjack Saloon stifled Tyree's reply and he immediately turned in that direction, his hand poised over the butt of his .44, his eyes narrowed against the sun.

But there was no danger, and he relaxed when he saw that the commotion was being caused by a half-dozen men shooting at empty whiskey and beer bottles. In minutes, a crowd had gathered around the sharpshooters and money began to change hands as bets were made and paid off.

Tyree watched with interest as a gangly young man with limp brown hair and washed-out green eyes calmly proceeded to outshoot five competitors.

The boy was good, Tyree allowed. Damn good. Fast as lightning. But, even more important, he had a sharp eye and the kind of eye-and-hand coordination that could not be taught. It was a gift, an innate quality few men possessed, one that allowed a man to place his shots exactly where he wanted them.

"That's Pauley Norquist," Rachel remarked. "He's the best shot in town. He's won the Thanksgiving turkey shoot every year for the last five years."

Tyree grunted as Norquist shattered another bottle.

"He is good, isn't he?" Rachel mused as Pauley drew his gun and fired at three bottles thrown into the air in rapid succession.

"How many men has he killed?" Tyree asked flatly. "Anybody can shoot bottles out of the air."

"Is that all you ever think about?" Rachel exclaimed, exasperated. "Killing?"

"I think about other things occasionally," Tyree drawled, and his amber eyes moved over her in a long lustful glance that brought a shiver to Rachel's spine and made her heart flutter in a most peculiar fashion.

"He hasn't killed anybody," Rachel answered, wishing Tyree would stop looking at her as if he could see through her clothing. "He's a shopkeeper, not a hired gun."

There was a sudden cessation in the contests as a swarthy-faced man in a flowered brocade vest and striped pants stepped out of the crowd and put his arm around Pauley's shoulders.

"Gents," he said in a loud voice. "I'm prepared to back Norquist, here, against all comers. Anybody got the guts to shoot against my boy for twenty dollars?"

Several men stepped forward, and Tyree watched with real admiration as Norquist beat them one by one.

When the last man walked away in defeat, Norquist's backer raised up a chubby hand stuffed with greenbacks. "I've got two hundred dollars here," he called out jovially. "And Pauley's still rarin' to go!"

"I'll take that bet," Tyree said, walking to where Norquist and the gambler stood. "Pick a target."

"How much of this do you want?" the gambler asked, rifling the bills in his hand.

"All of it," Tyree said, pulling a wad of greenbacks out of his hip pocket.

There followed an extraordinary contest as Pauley Norquist and Logan Tyree matched each other shot for shot, until there were no more empty bottles left. It was a contest the likes of which Rachel had never seen and she looked at the two men with awe. Truly, they were amazing.

"Looks like we'll have to call it a draw," Norquist said good-naturedly. He holstered his gun, ready to call it quits.

"Or try a different kind of target," the gambler suggested.

"We're just wasting ammunition," Tyree said, reloading his Colt. "The kid, here, is a fine shot. I'm satisfied with a draw."

"Well, I'm not," the gambler said curtly. "We made a bet, and it has to be decided, one way or the other."

"Mr. Brockton, let him have the money," Pauley Norquist said. "It isn't important."

"Brockton!" Tyree whistled under his breath. "I thought you cashed in down on the Panhandle."

"Not hardly," Brockton said impudently.

"You killed a friend of mine down there, Newt Ralston."

"Ralston! I didn't know that squaw lover *had* any friends."

"He had one. You as fast with that iron as they say?"

"Only one way to find out," Brockton said. Very slowly, his hand lifted to hover over his gun butt.

Tyree swore under his breath. He had not meant to goad the man into a fight, not with Rachel standing behind him, her eyes wide and frightened.

"Make your move," Brockton challenged.

"Forget it."

Brockton laughed. "I might have known any friend of Ralston's would be a coward. Go for your gun, squawman, or I'll shoot you down where you stand."

"If you think you can do it, go ahead."

Rachel's gasp sounded like thunder in the sudden silence that surrounded the two men. Brockton reached for his gun, his eyes shining with confidence. But Tyree's draw was quicker, smoother. The bullet slammed into Brockton's right shoulder, numbing his arm so that he dropped his gun into the dirt.

"Get out of here," Tyree said in a hard voice.

Brockton nodded, his face white as he turned away from the crowd and made his way down the street.

Tyree stared after him. Once he would have killed the man without a qualm, but not now. Not with Rachel watching his every move.

The crowd parted like soft butter as Tyree took Rachel's arm and headed for the school-yard.

"Damn!" murmured Wesley, who had watched the whole thing from the sidelines. "One of these days he's gonna kill someone, and I'm gonna have to take him in."

Chapter 7

It was John Halloran's sixtieth birthday and Rachel was planning a party. She spent several days organizing the menu, and then spent another full day trying to decide how to get rid of Tyree on the night of the party.

As it turned out, Tyree solved the problem for her. One look at the guest list was all it took. Rachel had invited Essie O'Shay, who was the Yellow Creek schoolmarm; Olaf Johnson, the blacksmith; Mr. and Mrs. Thorngood, who owned the General Store; Gus Kibbee, who doubled as barber and dentist; Vincent Myers, editor of the local newspaper; and her best friend, Carol Ann McKee. The Reverend and Mrs. Jenkins were also on the list, as well as Clint Wesley, and several other, equally dreary people.

It was the thought of making polite conversation with the likes of the minister and the marshal that persuaded Tyree to spend the evening in town.

He left the Lazy H just before dark.

Rachel's party was a big success. The food was excellent, the guests congenial, the conversation intelligent, interspersed with witticisms and laughter. They ate and danced and played a few parlor games before Rachel served the cake.

By midnight, everyone had gone home except for Clint Wesley, who lingered on the front porch with Rachel, reluctant to bid her goodnight.

"It's pretty out," Rachel commented. "The stars are beautiful."

"You're prettier than any star," Clint murmured, taking her in his arms. "You're the prettiest, sweetest, most wonderful girl I've ever known."

"You probably say that to all the girls," Rachel teased, though she was flattered by his kind words.

"You know you're the only girl for me," Clint said earnestly.

"Am I?" Rachel was boldly flirting now. "Millie Cloward couldn't keep her eyes off you in church last Sunday."

"Millie Cloward!" Clint exclaimed in a

pained tone. "She looks like a pregnant heifer."

"She does not. She has a lovely figure. And I overheard Mrs. Cloward say she'd be happy as a clam to have a lawman in the family."

Clint looked genuinely shocked. "You're not serious?"

"Yes, indeed," Rachel assured him with mock gravity. "Mrs. Cloward is going to invite you to Sunday dinner next week. And Millie is making a new dress for the occasion. I saw her in Thorngood's picking out material and she was all aflutter."

Wesley groaned. "Whatever made her think that I . . . I never did anything to . . . Why, I've hardly spoken ten words to the girl."

"Well, you did buy her lunch at the box social," Rachel pointed out, laughing impishly. "And you did look like you were enjoying yourself."

"Don't be silly. I only bought that awful box because I felt sorry for her. And so I could keep an eye on you and that gunslinger."

"Well, Millie seems to think there was much more to it than that. And I'm sure she would make you a truly fine wife."

"Wife!" Clint choked on the word. "Rachel, you've got to get me out of this. Invite me to dinner next Sunday."

"Coward."

"Guilty as charged," Wesley allowed. "Can I come for dinner?"

"Of course." Rachel's laughter was as light

and musical as the tinkling of Christmas bells. "You know you're always welcome here. Listen! Candido is playing his guitar."

Wesley nodded as the faint strains of a Spanish love song drifted up from the bunkhouse. Wordlessly, he held out his arms and Rachel moved into his embrace, their feet moving to the melody as they danced across the porch.

Tyree watched them from the shadows beside the house, feeling a sharp twinge of jealousy as Clint Wesley kissed Rachel. They stayed in each other's arms a long time, now dancing, now kissing, now just standing quietly close. The moonlight touched Rachel's hair, turning the gold to silver. Her expression was soft, warm, beautiful.

Rachel sighed as she laid her head on Clint's shoulder. They had been courting for over a year now, and still Clint had not asked her to marry him. But he would. And she was content to wait. She felt safe with Clint, secure. He would always be there, dependable as the sun. There were no high mountains in their relationship, but there were no dark valleys, either.

"I guess I'd better be going," Clint said with regret. "I've got a meeting with Judge Thackery in the morning. Eight o'clock sharp."

"Will I see you Saturday?"

"You bet. And Sunday, too," Clint reminded

her. "And every Sunday until old lady Cloward gets the message."

Rachel laughed softly as she took Clint's arm and walked with him down the stairs to where his horse was tethered. Still smiling, she lifted her face for one last kiss.

Dreamy-eyed, she stared after Clint as he rode out of the yard. She was picturing herself as Clint's wife when she became aware of someone standing behind her. Startled, she whirled around to find Tyree at her shoulder. With a curt nod of her head, Rachel acknowledged his presence, then started toward the front steps.

"Seems a shame to let that music go to waste," Tyree drawled, pulling her into his arms, and before Rachel could protest, he was waltzing her around the moon-dappled yard.

"I never thought of you as a dancing man," Rachel remarked, hoping a little lighthearted conversation would cover the nervousness she felt at his nearness.

"Oh, I've got a lot of talents you've never dreamed of," Tyree assured her. "Shall I whisper sweet nothings in your ear, and tell you you're prettier than all the stars in the sky?"

Anger flared deep in Rachel's eyes as she twisted out of Tyree's arms. "How dare you spy on us!"

"I wasn't spying. I just happened to get back while the two of you were on the front porch."

"You should have made your presence known," Rachel accused.

"Maybe," Tyree allowed with a shrug. "But it seemed a shame to intrude on such a romantic moment."

Rachel glared at him, irritated by the sardonic laughter dancing in the depths of his amber eyes. Oh, but he was incorrigible!

"Come here," Tyree whispered.

Rachel shook her head, confused by the conflicting emotions that warred within her breast. She knew she should go inside the house, knew that it was wrong to be alone in the moonlight with a man like Tyree. He wanted only one thing from her, and she had vowed it would never happen again. And yet, knowing all those things, she did not resist when he drew her into his arms a second time.

The music from Candido's guitar filled the air with a haunting melody that spoke of lost love and bitter tears shed in the darkness of a long and lonely night. Tyree's arms were strong around her as they danced under the stars, and Rachel's body molded to his as if they had danced together for years. He was incredibly light on his feet, and she thought again how catlike Tyree was, his movements always quick and sure with a smooth masculine grace, his eyes yellow-gold, like a tiger's.

Tyree was intensely aware of the woman in his arms. The scent of her perfume filled his nostrils, her nearness filled his senses and his arms tightened around her waist, drawing her closer, closer.

His eyes met hers, then dropped downward to linger on her mouth. He felt the sudden intake of her breath and he knew she was remembering Sunset Canyon, just as he was.

Rachel flushed under his probing gaze, but could not draw her eyes from his. Tyree's kiss came unexpectedly, catching her off-guard. One moment he was gazing into her face, and the next his mouth was slanting over hers, sending sparks to every part of her body. For a time, she remained placid in his embrace, caught up in the magic of the music and the moonlight and the waves of pleasure his merest touch sent spiraling through her.

"You really are lovely," Tyree murmured in her ear. "Your eyes are as blue as cornflowers, and your hair is as soft as new grass." His lips moved to her neck, nibbling softly. "Sweet," he whispered huskily. "So sweet."

"Tyree, you mustn't—" Rachel protested weakly.

"Mustn't what?"

Confused, Rachel shook her head. "I don't know. You make me feel so strange."

"There's nothing strange about this," Tyree said. His hands caressed her back while his mouth traveled up her neck toward her left earlobe. "It's all perfectly natural. Kiss me, Rachel."

"No. Go away and leave me alone."

"You don't like me very much, do you?" he asked, but there was no anger in his voice, no reproach, only a husky yearning.

"No," Rachel replied quickly. "I like men who are gentlemen."

"I can be a gentle man," Tyree purred in a low tone. "Kiss me and see."

Feeling as though she were in a trance, Rachel stood on tiptoe and pressed her mouth to Tyree's, bewildered by the tremors that shook her from head to foot as his mouth met hers. She did not even like Logan Tyree, she thought absently, and yet his kisses left her weak and wanting, sparking a hunger deep in her insides the likes of which she had never known. Clint's kisses never aroused her in such a way, never left her longing for more than just kisses. But Tyree had only to touch her and every nerve ending in her body sprang to life, straining toward him, eager to be touched and caressed. It was most peculiar.

"You're beautiful," Tyree said, his voice low and husky, mesmerizing. He stroked her hair, bent to breathe in the scent of it. "So damn beautiful."

"Tyree, don't—"

"I want to make love to you. Now. Tonight."

Rachel shook her head. She had vowed never to surrender to Logan Tyree again. One mistake was enough.

"Rachel." His voice was warm and coaxing, sweeter than honey.

He kissed her again. Unbidden, unwanted, came the memory of his body pressing against hers, possessing her. As though reading her thoughts, he pulled her close. His tongue slid over her lips, teasing the soft inner flesh of her lower lip like a darting finger of flame, spreading a delicious warmth to every fiber of her being. His hands moved lazily over her shoulders and back and hips, gentling her to his touch, arousing her to fever pitch, letting her feel his rising desire, until she stood trembling in his arms, her eyes half-closed, her heart fluttering wildly, her face lifted for his kisses.

Mesmerized by his touch, she sagged against him while he continued to murmur soft words in her ear. It felt so good to be in his arms, to feel his hard length pressed against her. His voice was soft, husky, entreating.

It was only when she found herself being carried swiftly toward the barn that sanity returned. Alarmed, she slapped Tyree's face with all the force at her command. Who did he think he was, that he could woo her so easily! Did he think a few sweet words would render her completely senseless, so that he could have his way with her?

Tyree stared down at Rachel, anger and surprise reflected in his hot yellow eyes.

"Logan Tyree, you put me down this instant," Rachel demanded indignantly.

"Change your mind?" Tyree asked dryly. But he did not put her down.

"No! Yes! Oh, I never intended for you to . . . to . . . and you know it!"

"You seemed pretty willing a minute ago."

"I was not. I . . . you tricked me."

One black eyebrow arched upward like a question mark. "Tricked you?" Tyree mused. "Don't be silly. Why don't you just admit you're as eager for it as I am?"

Rachel's cheeks flushed crimson as words failed her completely. A sudden guilt brought tears to her eyes and she lowered her head, refusing to look at Tyree because what he said was true. All too true. She did want him. Desperately. No matter that she constantly professed to hate him. No matter that she continually professed to despise his touch and all he stood for. The truth was that she *liked* Logan Tyree and that thought frightened her almost as much as the way her body responded to the desire in his eyes and the slightest touch of his hands. Even now, she longed to let him carry her to the barn and satisfy the need he had aroused in her. But it was wrong, so very wrong.

Tyree held her in his arms for what seemed like forever and then, gently, he set her on her feet and walked away, leaving Rachel standing alone in the moonlight, feeling suddenly empty and very alone.

Rachel was trying to understand her feelings for Tyree the next morning when she slipped on the back stairs and sprained her ankle. It was Tyree who found her lying in a heap at the bottom of the steps, her face white with pain.

Wordlessly, he carried her into the house and up the stairs to her bedroom, where he deposited her gently on the bed. Panic took hold of Rachel as Tyree stood looking down at her. Only the night before he had tried to seduce her, and now she was helpless, and quite alone in the house.

"Tyree—"

"Just sit tight," he said, ignoring the anxiety that was evident in her voice and eyes. "I don't think anything's broken."

"It hurts like blazes."

"You want me to send for your old man?"

Rachel considered that for a moment, then shook her head. Her father had left before dawn to visit an old friend who had been in a bad accident, and now that her initial panic had subsided, she saw no reason to summon him home. There was nothing he could do. And surely even a man as callous as Tyree wouldn't try to take advantage of her now.

Tyree's hands were surprisingly gentle as he wrapped her ankle in a towel he had soaked in cold water.

"You'll be all right," he assured her. "Lie back and take it easy. I'll send for the sawbones."

To Rachel's distress, the doctor prescribed two weeks in bed.

"Two weeks!" Rachel complained to Tyree later. "Who'll look after the house while I'm stuck in bed?"

"I think I can handle things around here until you're back on your feet," Tyree said with a shrug.

"You?" Rachel laughed out loud. "Who's going to do the washing and ironing and the cooking and—"

Tyree dropped a hand over Rachel's mouth, effectively stifling her tirade. "Nothing to it," he drawled, and proved it later that night by serving Rachel a dinner of roast beef, potatoes with brown gravy, peas, and hot biscuits only a little less light and fluffy than her own.

Tyree grinned at her as she ate with obvious enjoyment. "Well?"

"It's delicious," Rachel admitted.

"But?"

"But I just can't believe you made all this yourself."

"Why not? Who do you think cooks for me when I'm drifting?"

"I don't know," Rachel said with a shrug. "I guess I never gave it any thought."

"Yeah. Well, you be a good girl and tomorrow I'll fix you some fried chicken and dumplings that will melt in your mouth. And if you're real good, I might bake you a chocolate cake."

"I had no idea you were so domestic," Rachel muttered dryly.

"Just another of my hidden talents," Tyree retorted.

"Yes. Well, I'm sure you'll make some lucky girl a wonderful wife."

Tyree looked momentarily taken aback, then he quirked one black eyebrow at her. "That a proposal?"

"Of course not," Rachel answered quickly.

"Another hope crushed," Tyree lamented with mock sorrow. "Get some rest now."

Rachel's convalescence proved to be one surprise after another as Tyree took over the running of the house. Rachel had been born and raised on the ranch and she was used to the never-ending hard work that was a part of every ranch woman's life. To stay in bed and be waited on was a rare treat. For once, she had time to linger over a romantic novel, or browse through her father's mail order catalogs. She could even sit back and enjoy being idle without feeling guilty. She had time to think and dream and ponder, and most of her thoughts were of Tyree. When had she stopped hating him? When had she stopped thinking of him as a heartless murderer and begun to see him as a strong, virile, desirable man?

As promised, he took over the domestic chores and Rachel saw a side of him she had never dreamed existed. He waited on her as if she were a princess. He cooked her meals, changed the linen on her bed, laundered her clothing, including her underwear and stockings, changed the bandage on her ankle, swept the floors, and washed the dishes.

Some nights he rubbed her back, his hands

gently kneading her shoulders and back and neck. She reveled in the touch of his hands, warm and soothing through the material of her nightgown. Other nights he brushed her hair until it glistened like spun gold. His nearness thrilled her, filling her with excited tremors as he drew the brush through her hair, his breath warm upon her neck. Sometimes she wished he would take her in his arms and kiss her, but he never did.

Each morning there was a gift on her bedside table when she woke up: a bouquet of brightly colored flowers, a book of poetry, a box of candy, a bottle of fragrant perfume. When she tried to thank Tyree for his thoughtful gestures, he denied having anything to do with the gifts.

"Where did all these things come from then?" Rachel asked. "There's no one in the house except you and me."

But Tyree just shrugged. "Maybe you've got a secret admirer," he suggested, and refused to discuss the matter further.

One afternoon, he surprised her by carrying her outside and serving her an elaborate lunch under the shade of the old oak tree that grew alongside the house. Another time he served dinner on a blanket spread in front of the fireplace.

Rachel looked at Tyree through eyes filled with wonder, unable to believe that this was the same man who had cold-bloodedly gunned down Job Walsh, the same man who had been willing to steal her virginity to humor six Apache warriors. She remembered how, when he had first arrived at the Lazy H, he had refused to do any work at all. He wouldn't mend a fence or help with the cattle. Still wouldn't, Rachel thought, confused. And yet he didn't seem to mind playing nursemaid for her and that was really odd, because most men, especially a man as virile and untamed as Tyree, would have handled housework awkwardly at best. Even Clint, who was a gentleman through and through, was self-conscious around ailing women, and totally out of his element where even the simplest domestic chores were concerned.

But what surprised Rachel the most about Tyree was the fact that he made no advances toward her and she could not help wondering if, deep down, some latent sense of chivalry prevented him from taking advantage of her while she was unable to defend herself.

She recalled how, late one night, they had talked to each other, really talked to each for, without malice or sarcasm. She had hoped to learn something about Tyree that would unlock the mystery of his past, but he had adroitly sidestepped all her questions. Looking back, Rachel could not remember how they got on the subject, but before she quite knew what was happening, she was telling Tyree of her hopes and dreams, how she longed to marry and raise a big family. Strong boys and beautiful accomplished girls who would marry and raise families of their own, children who would subdue the land and bring civilization to the wilderness.

"It's all I've ever really wanted," Rachel had admitted shyly. "To be a wife and a mother, to have what my parents had before my mother died. But what about you, Tyree? What do you want out of life?"

Tyree had stared into the fireplace, his eyes intent on the dancing flames, his brow furrowed and thoughtful. Slowly, he shook his head. "I don't have any dreams," he had said quietly. "Not anymore."

Rachel had stared at him, bemused. No dreams? How could anyone, man or woman, live without dreams or hopes for the future? She thought about the Lazy H. If not for the hopes and dreams of her father and mother, the ranch would still be an empty stretch of uncultivated ground, untouched and unloved.

"Surely there must be something you want out of life?" Rachel had insisted. "Some goal that sustains you, some vision of the future that gives you hope and a reason for living?" She shook her head, not understanding. "Some dream to strive for?"

"Dreams are for fools," Tyree had retorted bitterly. "Or for the very young." He had been that young once, he thought, not wanting to remember. Red Leaf had been his dream, his hope for the future.

"Dreams are not for fools!" Rachel had

exclaimed. "My father is neither a fool nor a child, but he still dreams of the day when the Halloran name will stand for something in this part of the country."

Tyree's grin was melancholy as he muttered, "Sometimes I think I'm older than you and your old man put together. Hell, the best thing a man in my line of work can hope for is to grow a little older every day."

Rachel had wanted to argue with him further. Somehow, it had seemed important to make Tyree fight back, to make him admit that somewhere under that practical, hard-headed exterior there lurked a vision for the future.

But she never got the chance to probe further, for Tyree suddenly picked her up and carried her, protesting, to her room, putting an abrupt end to their conversation.

Rachel had stayed awake a long time that night, thoughts of Tyree crowding her mind. He was such a strange man. Not that she was an expert on men by any means. Far from that. But even in her limited experience with the opposite sex, she had learned that most men retained a boyish quality deep down inside. Her best friend's father loved practical jokes. Candido loved to wrestle or play tug-of-war. Even her own father was still a boy at heart. But there were no boyish qualities in the man known as Logan Tyree and she wondered if he had ever played or danced or sung, or laughed out loud just because he was glad to be alive.

Carefully, she slid out of bed and hobbled to the window overlooking the front yard. As she had suspected, Tyree was there, pacing up and down, a cigar clamped between his teeth. What did he think about as he walked restlessly back and forth? What was there in his past that weighed him down so heavily?

She watched Tyree until her eyelids grew heavy and she went back to bed to sleep, and dream of a tall dark man with brooding amber eyes and a cynical grin.

Rachel had been in bed a little over a week when her best friend, Carol Ann McKee, came to call. Carol Ann was a pretty girl with curly auburn hair, mild brown eyes, a quick smile, and a smattering of freckles across the bridge of her turned-up nose. They had been close friends ever since Carol Ann's family moved to Yellow Creek eleven years ago.

The minute their hellos were over, Carol Ann dragged a chair close to the bed and blurted, with very real concern, "Rachel, my dear girl, how can you stay in this house alone with that dreadful man?"

"What dreadful man?" Rachel asked, forgetting that she, too, had once thought of Tyree as some kind of ogre.

"Why, Logan Tyree, of course. I insist you come and stay with me until your ankle is better."

"Carol Ann, I'm fine."

"Don't you know who he is?" Carol Ann asked in a hushed voice. *"What* he is?"

"Of course I know. But he's all right. Really. He's taking very good care of me."

Carol Ann looked doubtful. She had heard stories about Logan Tyree, about the men he had killed, the women he had abused. She had been in the crowd the day he had winged Brockton. People were still talking about that. Brockton hadn't been very well liked, but he had been a resident of Yellow Creek, and the townspeople didn't take kindly to strangers riding in and taking shots at the local citizens. For all that, no one had been sorry when Brockton left town.

"Carol Ann, I'm fine. Really," Rachel insisted. "He cooks for me and everything. Even cleans the house."

"He cooks!" Carol Ann exclaimed, practically choking on the words. "And cleans house? Mercy," she laughed. "Who would believe it?"

"Well, it's true, though I wouldn't spread it around town if I were you. But he can be very nice when it suits him."

"He doesn't look nice to me. In fact, he scares me to death. He hasn't tried to . . . you know?"

"No," Rachel answered firmly. "He hasn't."

"Well, personally, I'd be afraid to be in the same room with him," Carol Ann said, shivering at the mere thought. "He has the coldest eyes I've ever seen."

Everything Carol Ann had said about Tyree was true, Rachel mused when she was alone again. Tyree didn't look very nice. And he did have cold eyes. But he continued to treat her as if she were made of glass.

She was almost sorry when the doctor pronounced her well enough to get out of bed.

Chapter 8

The list in Rachel's hand grew longer and longer as she went from cupboard to cupboard, absently jotting down the things she needed from the store in town: sugar, salt, flour, pepper, a case of peaches, some hard candy for her father, a horn of cheese, a bolt of cotton cloth, thread, dried apples, coffee. She added other items as they occurred to her, yet all the while it was Logan Tyree who filled her thoughts.

More and more he was on her mind. Why was he a gunfighter? What events in his past had shaped him into the kind of man he was now? What an enigma he was, changeable as the wind. Now cold as ice, now considerate and kind. She wondered if he had ever been head-over-heels in love with a woman, or tasted the bitter tears of sorrow.

Nights, while she waited for sleep to come, his swarthy face danced before her eyes: the mouth cynical, the eyes cold, almost cruel. It was a strong face, one that revealed little warmth, little emotion. There seemed to be no softness in him, no place for tenderness or compassion. And yet she knew that to be untrue, for he displayed infinite patience with the gray mustang, and he had certainly been considerate of her own wants and needs during her recent convalescence.

Rachel grinned as she thought of the gray stud. Her father had ordered the horse put down as soon as he learned about Candido's broken leg, declaring he would not have a rank stallion on the place, but Tyree had asked if he could work with the bronc for a few days, and her father had reluctantly agreed.

Rachel had spent several hours watching Tyree work with the wild stallion. He was a beautiful horse. Predominantly gray in color, with three black stockings, a black mane and tail, and the spotted hindquarters that denoted Appaloosa blood.

While admiring the stud, Rachel could not help but notice that, in his own way, Logan Tyree was also a beautiful animal. He often worked without a shirt, exposing skin as brown as an Apache's, and powerful muscles that rippled in the sunlight. The sight of his

naked torso did peculiar things to the pit of
her stomach. Sometimes, watching Tyree, she
suddenly felt warm all over. So many muscles,
she mused and could not help remembering
the unyielding strength of his arms around
her the night of her father's birthday party.
Occasionally, as now, she thought how nice it
would be to feel those arms around her again.
Sometimes she could not help wondering
what it would have been like if she had surrendered to the longing in his eyes.

Tyree and the stud—they drew her eyes like
a magnet, making her heart pound and her
blood race. They were a perfect match, both
headstrong and wild, both wary and distrustful of people. But, little by little, the man was
winning the mustang's trust and affection.

In the days that followed, Tyree discarded
the harsh curb bit in favor of a light hackamore, and Rachel noticed that he never wore
spurs when working the stallion. Tyree
seemed blessed with endless patience, never
raising his voice, never striking out at the
horse when it failed to respond, never resort-
ing to force or fear.

Rachel watched, fascinated, as Tyree taught
the gray to rein right and left, to slide stop, to
back on cue, to break into a full gallop from a
standing start, patiently coaxing the skittish
stallion to respond to hand and heel and
voice. And always he spoke to the horse in that
strange, soft tongue.

Once the gray had learned the basics, Tyree

taught the horse to go to its knees on command, to come at his call, to cut a cow from a herd, to stand ground-tied for as long as necessary.

It was hard to believe that a drifting gunslinger could succeed with the horse where a top hand like Candido had failed, but it was true, nonetheless. Within a matter of weeks, Tyree had turned a rank bronc into a well-mannered saddle horse that anyone on the ranch could ride, though Rachel thought the gray worked a little better and stepped a little higher when Tyree was in the saddle.

Scowling, Rachel pushed Tyree from her mind and settled her thoughts on Clint Wesley. Almost as tall and broad as Tyree, Clint reminded Rachel of the prince in a fairy tale, with his sunbleached blond hair and mild blue eyes. Clint's mouth was wide and honest and never curled down in that mocking way that Tyree's did. His face was open and honest, hiding nothing, not an impassive facade that shut out his thoughts and kept the world at bay.

Going to her room, Rachel stood before the mirror, brushing her hair until it was soft and shimmering. Tying the heavy golden mass away from her face with a crisp white linen ribbon, she slipped out of her work garb and donned a light blue cotton dress that had a scoop neck and short sleeves. It was Clint's favorite, and if luck was with her, she just might run into him while shopping in town.

She was humming softly as she skipped down to the barn. Her father was waiting for her there.

"Mornin', Pa," Rachel said cheerfully.

"Mornin', daughter."

"Isn't it a lovely day?"

"Yeah, lovely," Halloran replied absently. "Listen, Rachel, I don't want you driving into town alone this morning."

"Why not?"

"I saw smoke in the hills awhile ago. Could be nothing. Could be the 'Paches are on the prod again."

Apaches! Rachel's face paled a trifle as she recalled her last encounter with Indians. Perhaps she shouldn't go into town after all.

"You can take Tyree with you," Halloran decided. "You'll be safe with him."

"Tyree!" Rachel wailed in dismay. "Can't I take Candido? Or Cahill?"

"No. Tyree's the only man on the place who isn't doing anything just now."

"He hasn't done anything in weeks," Rachel pointed out sourly. "Why is he still hanging around here anyway? We could hire two wranglers for what it's costing us to keep him here."

"Rachel—"

"All right, Pa, I'm sorry. Where is he? I'm ready to go."

"Right here," Tyree said, materializing out of the barn's shadowy interior. "Nice to know you're so happy to have me along."

"Oh, shut up."

"Want me to drive?"

"I can do it," Rachel said curtly, and scrambled into the buggy.

"Suit yourself," Tyree drawled, unperturbed by her obvious annoyance. Climbing into the buggy, he stretched his long legs out in front of him and hooked his thumbs in his gunbelt.

They drove in silence for several miles. Tyree seemed totally relaxed and at ease, and yet Rachel could not help feeling that he was aware of every rock and tree and rabbit they passed. Glancing his way, she noticed his eyes were continually moving over the countryside and she supposed, correctly, that it was his constant awareness of everything around him that had kept him alive so long.

"You gonna marry that badge-toter?" Tyree asked after awhile.

"Maybe."

"Has he asked you yet?"

"No."

"He will. He looks at you like a love-sick bull calf."

"He's a fine man!" Rachel cried defensively. "And I'd be proud to be his wife. He's kind and honest and loyal, and not just a . . . a—"

"No good saddle tramp like me?"

"That's not what I was going to say," Rachel replied sullenly.

"It's exactly what you wanted to say," Tyree

said with a grin. "Wesley's the knight in shining armor and I'm the dragon."

"Oh? And what does that make me? The wicked witch?"

"Of course not," Tyree said smoothly. "You're the beautiful princess."

"Oh, good!" Rachel exclaimed enthusiastically. "That means I get to marry the handsome knight."

"Not in my fairy tale," Tyree objected gruffly.

"How does your story end?" Rachel asked, wondering why it was suddenly so hard to speak.

"The dragon slays the handsome knight and carries the princess off to his lair in the mountains."

Grimacing, Rachel said, "I think I like happy endings better."

"My ending is happy."

"Yes, but only for the dragon."

Tyree's hard amber eyes pierced Rachel's like twin daggers. "Maybe for the princess, too."

"I doubt it. There can be happiness only when like marries like."

"How do you know we're not alike?"

Tyree's soft reply sent shivers down Rachel's spine. Flustered, she stammered, "Because . . . because I . . . we could never—" Unable to think of a suitable answer, she stared ahead at the road. Her stomach was doing crazy flip-flops, and her mouth was dry as dust. Imagine, being married to Tyree . . .

She sighed with relief as the town came into view, but her hands were still shaking minutes later when she drew the team to a halt at the General Store. She hopped out of the buggy before Tyree could assist her.

Tyree followed Rachel into Thorngood's where he stood against one wall, arms folded across his chest like a cigar store Indian while Rachel made her purchases. Rachel willed him to go away and let her shop in peace, but he seemed quite content just to stand there, watching her, like a cat at a mousehole.

The other customers in the store made a wide berth around Tyree. His reputation was well-known, and his shoot-out with Brockton was still being talked about from one end of town to the other. Rufus Thorngood kept a wary eye on Tyree, as if he feared the gunman might draw his weapon and rob the cashbox.

Rachel's smile was weak as she thanked the Thorngoods and stepped outside, Tyree close on her heels. They were standing at the buggy, waiting for their supplies to be loaded, when Clint Wesley joined them. Tyree frowned. The Marshal looked properly official in black Levi's, crisp white shirt, and shiny tin star.

While Rachel and the Marshal exchanged pleasantries, Tyree's eyes swept the main street. Satisfied there was no posse tagging along in the badge-toter's footsteps, he shifted his position so that his back was toward the sun. It was a move that did not go unnoticed by Wesley, and Clint stepped away from Rachel, not wanting her to be caught in the line of fire if Tyree decided to take a shot at him.

"Afternoon, Tyree," Clint said quietly.

"Marshal."

"I was looking through some old flyers last night."

"Good for you."

"I found a couple that might interest you," Wesley remarked, reaching inside his vest.

"I wouldn't do that," Tyree warned, and though his words were softly spoken and without menace, Clint quickly dropped his hand to his side, away from his gun.

"I guess you've seen those flyers before," Wesley said. "There's one from the Dakotas, and another from El Paso."

"Keep looking. You'll find one from Ellsworth, too. So what?"

Wesley took a deep breath. "So I'm gonna have to take you in."

"That right?" Tyree drawled, looking a-mused.

"Dammit, Tyree, it's my job."

"You do what you have to do, Marshal, but I'm not going back to Yuma."

"But it's my job," Wesley sputtered.

"So you said. Rachel, get in the buggy."

She quickly did as bidden, afraid that Clint would actually try to arrest Tyree, and that Tyree would kill him without a qualm.

The two men stared at each other for a full

minute; Tyree, cool and aloof, Clint nervous and showing it, eager to do his job, yet intimidated by Tyree's reputation and by his own lack of experience.

For a moment, it looked like there would be gunplay, but then Tyree swung up on the seat beside Rachel, and Clint stomped off toward the jailhouse, his face flushed with anger.

Rachel stared after Clint, confused by the chaotic thoughts tumbling through her mind. On the one hand, she was glad Clint had sense enough not to tangle with a scoundrel like Logan Tyree. Clint was a fine man, a good town marshal, but he was no match for a professional gunman. And yet, perversely, she could not help being ashamed of Clint for not standing up to Tyree.

"The Marshal's got more sense than I gave him credit for," Tyree drawled, slapping the reins across the lead horse's rump. "Most law dogs would have felt duty-bound to try and take me in."

"I guess you think he's a coward!" Rachel snapped, hating herself for thinking the same thing.

Tyree stared at her, one dark eyebrow raised quizzically. "Did I say he was a coward?"

"No," Rachel admitted sullenly. "But that's what you're thinking, isn't it?"

"No," Tyree answered, shaking his head. "It's what you're thinking."

They rode in silence for several miles, the

animosity between them like a third person in the rig.

If only Tyree would go away, Rachel thought crossly. She had never felt angry and confused like this until Tyree entered her life. She had always been content, sure of who she was and what she wanted out of life, proud of Clint, certain he was the only man in the world for her. Even when they were having trouble with Walsh, she had been at peace within herself. But no more.

"It's going to rain," Tyree remarked, breaking into her thoughts.

Surprised, Rachel looked up to find the sky was dark with clouds. Moments later, a jagged bolt of lightning split the darkened skies. And then the thunder came, reverberating across the plains like the echo of distant drums.

They were still five miles from the ranch when the rain came, driven by a fierce wind that flattened the tall yellow grass and sent tumbleweeds spinning crazily down the road. In seconds, Rachel and Tyree were soaked to the skin.

"Any place where we can hole up until this blows over?" Tyree asked, shouting to be heard above the raging storm.

"There's a cabin just over that ridge," Rachel hollered back, pointing to a low rise. "It used to belong to a family named Jorgensen until Walsh drove them out."

With a grunt of acknowledgement, Tyree reined the team off the road and urged them up the rain-slick slope. It was slow going. The horses slipped constantly in the heavy mud, and only Tyree's firm hand on the reins kept them going.

The cabin was located at the foot of the ridge in a small grove of aspens. It was small, dark, and blessedly dry. It was also well furnished, giving Tyree the impression that the Jorgensen family must have lit out with little more than the clothes on their backs. Except for a thick layer of dust on the furniture and the cobwebs hanging in lacy strands from the ceiling, the cabin looked as if it were expecting the former inhabitants to return at any moment.

Shortly, Rachel and Tyree were huddled side by side before a cheery blaze, wrapped in dry blankets pulled from one of the beds. Outside, the rain came down in icy sheets, accompanied by a howling wind that rattled the cabin door and shook the glass in the windows.

Rachel cast an apprehensive glance at Tyree, who was sitting hunched beside her. He was staring into the flames, a dark, brooding expression on his swarthy countenance as he took long swallows from a flask pulled from his hip pocket.

Rachel huddled deeper into the blanket draped around her shoulders, acutely conscious of the man sitting beside her. Unbidden came the memory of Logan Tyree lying unconscious in bed, his long lean body naked beneath the sheets. She remembered how shocked she had been the day she caught herself staring at his nakedness, unabashedly admiring the muscles corded in his arms and legs. She had never dreamed a man's body could be beautiful, but Tyree's was magnificent. His belly was flat as a tabletop, ridged with muscle, his chest was broad and lightly furred with curly black hair, his shoulders were as wide as a barn door. Even lying helpless in bed, he had radiated a kind of latent strength and power that she had found both frightening and intriguing.

He had not been so helpless that day in Sunset Canyon. He had taken her boldly. And he had enjoyed it, apparently feeling no shame at taking her maidenhead, no remorse for what he had done.

Rachel swallowed hard as she sensed Tyree's eyes moving over her, felt herself caught in the web of his gaze.

Rachel felt her cheeks grow hot. "If he mentions Sunset Canyon, I shall die of embarrassment," she mused, genuinely distressed, and frantically searched her mind for some safe topic of conversation that would take Tyree's attention away from her and away from the fact that they were alone. Quite definitely alone.

"The gray stallion," Rachel said quickly. "I hear you bought him."

Tyree's knowing grin assured Rachel that he was well aware of what she was trying to do. "Yeah," he said, willing to go along with her, for the moment. "I gave your old man fifty bucks for him."

"Fifty dollars for a mustang!" Rachel exclaimed. "Why so much?"

"He's worth it," Tyree answered succinctly.

With a sly grin, he offered her the flask and chuckled aloud when she refused to sample the contents.

Another silence fell between them. Rachel fidgeted nervously for a moment, then took a deep breath. "Why are you so secretive about your past?" she queried, determined to make Tyree talk to her, if not about his past, then about something else, because she was afraid if she didn't keep him talking, he would keep drinking until he was drunk. And she was afraid of drunken men. And of the hungry, waiting look that lurked in the back of Logan Tyree's glittering yellow eyes.

"I'm not secretive about it," Tyree countered. He took another long pull from the bottle, wiped his mouth with the back of his hand. "It's just not particularly pleasant."

"I'd like to hear about it," Rachel coaxed prettily. "Please?"

Tyree gave her a long probing glance; then, with a shrug, he stared at the flames again, his swarthy face wiped clean of expression.

"My old man was a half-breed Comanche," he began in a voice gone cold and flat. "He was hung for horse stealing before I was born. My mother was a slut. She ran off with a faro dealer when I was three. Left me with some nuns. They kept me until I was eight or so, and then sent me off to live with a widow lady who needed help running her farm. We didn't get along at all, me and that old lady, and she threw me out. The nuns sent me to live with a rich Yankee family next. Made 'em feel like real Christians, taking in a poor little orphan. But the old man caught me stealing a dollar, and he sent me packing.

"My next home was with a preacher and his wife. I lasted there about six months, then it was back to the nuns. I guess I was about ten when an old German couple took me in. They were really just looking for some cheap help, but they were pretty decent people, and I might have stayed with them and turned into a dirt farmer if the Apaches hadn't raided their place when I was twelve. The Indians killed the old couple and took me back to their village."

"Goodness!" Rachel exclaimed. "Weren't you scared?"

"No. I liked living with the Indians." His voice grew less harsh. "They were supposed to be savages, but they were the only people who ever gave a damn about me. The only ones who ever cared about what I wanted, or what I thought."

"If you were happy with the Indians, why didn't you stay?"

"Things happen," Tyree said curtly.

"What things? Why did you leave?"

"I don't want to talk about it, Rachel." Scowling, he took a quick drink, and then another. His fingers were white around the flask.

"What is it?" Rachel asked curiously. "You look like you're about to explode!"

"Dammit, I said I don't want to talk about it!"

"I'm sorry," Rachel murmured contritely. "I just thought it might help if you got it off your chest."

For a moment, Tyree looked at her as if she were completely insane. Help? Nothing had ever helped. In the beginning, he had looked for solace in whorehouses and saloon brawls and when that didn't ease the pain caused by Red Leaf's death, he had turned to drink. But that hadn't helped either.

Abruptly, Tyree began to laugh, a harsh bitter laugh filled with pain. Too late, Rachel wished she had not pried into something that was none of her business.

"So you think talking might help," Tyree drawled gruffly. "Let's talk about it then! I lived with the Indians for thirteen years. Learned their language. Prayed to their gods. Fought their enemies. Married one of their women. It was a damn good life. And then one day I took her hunting with me."

He paused, as if seeing it all in his mind. "We were on our way home when six white men attacked us. One of them decked me with a rifle butt. Knocked me out cold. When I came to, she was dead. They hadn't killed her right away, though. They raped her first. And when they were through, they mutilated her body, hacked off her fine black scalp, and rode away."

"Tyree, I'm so sorry," Rachel whispered, stricken by the grotesque images his words had evoked. "So very sorry."

"So were they, when I caught up with them."

"You killed them." It was not a question.

"Damn right. And they died hard." Tyree stared at her, his eyes glittering like shards of bright yellow glass. "Shall I tell you how they died?"

Rachel shook her head. She was not surprised to learn Tyree had killed those six men. It was no less than she had expected. No less than they deserved.

With a shrug, Tyree raised the flask, draining it in a single swallow. For a moment, he stared at the empty container as if it had betrayed him. Then, muttering a vile oath, he hurled the bottle across the room where it struck a wall and shattered into a thousand sparkling pieces.

"You loved her," Rachel murmured, her voice tinged with wonder. It was hard to imagine Tyree loving anyone. He seemed so hard, so self-sufficient.

"More than my life," Tyree said flatly.

"Was she beautiful?"

"Yeah." Tyree's voice grew soft, almost

wistful. "Her hair was long and thick, black as sin. Her eyes were dark, dark brown and always filled with laughter. She was just a kid, no more than fifteen or sixteen when I married her. All the young bucks wanted her, but she loved me." Tyree laughed softly. "That was the miracle, you know. She loved me."

Tyree's eyes were naked with pain when he faced Rachel again. It was the first time she had seen the real Logan Tyree. Not the arrogant gunman who was a law unto himself, but the man who had experienced a terrible loss and was still hurting deep inside. It was an awful thing, Rachel thought compassionately, to see a man's soul laid bare.

"You were wrong, Rachel," Tyree muttered brokenly. "Talking doesn't help."

Tyree laughed bitterly and Rachel realized he was more than a little drunk.

"Drinking doesn't help, either," Tyree mumbled. "Nothing helps."

"I'm sorry, Tyree. I never knew. I never dreamed—"

"It's been ten years," Tyree said, staring into the dancing flames. "Ten long years. You'd think it would stop hurting after ten years."

Pity and compassion welled in Rachel's breast. How tragic, to love someone as dearly as Tyree had loved his Indian wife, and then lose her in such a dreadful way. No wonder he was bitter.

Thinking only to comfort him, Rachel drew

Tyree close, cradling his dark head against her breast as if he were a small child in need of solace. But Tyree was not a child, and his hands were sure and strong as they slid around Rachel's waist, drawing her against him. His mouth closed over hers, stifling her surprised gasp. She had not meant to encourage him, only to let him know she cared.

Tyree's kiss was not gentle. Rather it was filled with raw primal passion and a deep yearning hunger. Rachel's first thought was to resist, but she sensed that Tyree needed her, needed to feel the strength of her love, to know she understood. With a little sigh, she surrendered to his lips, giving herself over to the exquisite thrill of being in his arms again.

Tyree drew back, a little surprised by her quick capitulation. He had expected her to resist. Perhaps he had hoped she would struggle so that he could hurt her and by hurting her, ease a little of his own pain. But what he saw in her eyes drove all thought of hurting her from his mind.

Rachel whispered his name as she put her hand at the back of his neck and pulled his head down, her mouth seeking his. With a shock, she realized she had been waiting, hoping, for this very thing to happen. It was a bitter thing to admit, but true nonetheless. No matter how she had scorned his attention in the past, no matter how loudly she professed to despise Logan Tyree and everything he stood for, she had secretly yearned for the wonder of his touch, burned for the taste of his kisses.

Now, as his hands caressed her flesh and his tongue tickled her ear, she was filled with an urgent sense of need. It was a frightening sensation, and yet, strangely satisfying at the same time. He kissed her ardently, his hands lazily exploring the smooth curves and contours of her body, and Rachel moaned low in her throat as wave after wave of sensual pleasure washed over her. His hands and mouth, the merest touch of his naked flesh against her own, aroused her to fever pitch. This was what she wanted. This was where she belonged.

And then Tyree was removing her dress and petticoat, shrugging out of his pants and shirt, and Rachel realized he was not going to settle for a few kisses and a quick caress.

The sight of Tyree's fully aroused male body smothered the fire in Rachel's blood. What was she doing?

Tyree felt the change in her and he drew back. "Change your mind?" he asked thickly.

"Yes. No. I don't know."

"Rachel, I . . ."

She laughed softly, warmed by the desire in his eyes, and by his willingness, however reluctant, to let her go if that was what she wanted. She gazed into his face, so strong, so handsome, and now so vulnerable. Had he been about to confess that he needed her? The thought filled her with tenderness. He *did* need her, whether he knew it or not. And she needed him.

"Make love to me, Tyree," she whispered, and sighed with pleasure as he made them one, carrying her higher, higher until there was only layer upon layer of ecstasy. His breath was hot upon her skin, his eyes intense, burning with a clear amber flame. He growled her name as his teeth nibbled her neck, her shoulder, her breast, and each touch was more wonderful, more thrilling, than the last.

Rachel cried his name, begging him to satisfy the need he had created and he obliged her willingly, smiling down at her as she let out a whimper of wonder and fulfillment.

Moments later, with a long shuddering sigh, Tyree rolled off her, though he continued to hold her body close against his own.

Outside, the rain continued to fall, its steady roar drowning out all other sound save for the crackling of the flames.

It was dark when Tyree made love to her again. Rachel gloried in his touch, reveling in the wondrous waves of ecstasy that crested and broke and crested again. She was fascinated by his hands—strong brown hands that could so masterfully tame a wild stallion. Angry hands that could callously snuff out a human life. Warm, gentle hands that knew how to arouse the sensuous hunger sleeping in a woman's soul.

Later, with Tyree's arm lying heavily across her stomach, Rachel stared thoughtfully into the darkness. So this is love, she mused, this wonderful sense of peace and contentment. She glanced fondly at the man sleeping beside her. He had made no mention of loving her, had said nothing of marriage, but surely no man could possess a woman as completely and thoroughly as Tyree had just possessed her without loving her deeply. And she loved him. Perhaps she had loved him all along.

Through eyes warm with affection, Rachel studied the man who had brought her such pleasure. He was lying on his stomach, his face turned toward her. Once, on a picnic, Clint had fallen asleep, and Rachel had studied him in much the same way. She had thought how innocent Clint looked lying there on the grass, almost like a little boy.

But there was no such hint of innocence in Tyree. Even when he was asleep, there lurked about him an air of violence ready to explode at the slightest provocation and Rachel felt that, should she waken him suddenly, he would pounce on her like a tiger roused from its nap.

She touched the scars on his broad back, her fingertips lightly tracing the faint silvery lines. She imagined how he must have looked in prison, his long hair unkempt, his face a hard mask of impotent anger. In her mind's eye, she could see the whip slice through the air, hear the sibilant hiss as the rawhide cut into his flesh. She knew, somehow, that Tyree had endured the pain without uttering a sound.

At her touch, Tyree stirred and drew her closer. Rachel nestled against him, to be lulled to sleep by the steady rhythm of his heart and the soft tattoo of the rain on the roof.

When she woke, it was morning and Tyree was scattering the coals in the fireplace to make sure the ashes were cold. Rachel smiled up at him uncertainly, feeling all the joy and happiness of the night before shrivel in her breast as Tyree scowled at her. It was obvious he had a whale of a hangover.

"Let's go," he said tersely. "Your old man will be wondering what happened to you."

Rachel dressed quickly, blushing when Tyree happened to glance in her direction. Bewildered, she wondered where all the magic had gone. She still felt the same. Why didn't he? Her mind whirling with confusion, she followed Tyree outside.

The world was fresh and clean and beautiful. Raindrops sparkled on the emerald leaves, shining like tears on a sun-kissed cheek. The sky was a hard bright blue, so dazzling it almost hurt Rachel's eyes just to look at it.

With exaggerated politeness, Tyree handed her into the buggy, took the seat beside her, and shook out the reins.

"Sorry about last night," he apologized gruffly. "I was more than a little drunk and, well . . . things happen."

Rachel felt a cold hand knot around her heart as Tyree casually shrugged off all that had happened between them the night before. The sweet words he had murmured, the intimacies they had shared, it had all been a lie and she had swallowed it whole. What a fool she had been, thinking he cared for her, when any woman would have done as well. She meant nothing to him, nothing at all other than an outlet for his drunken lust.

Suddenly she felt like crying. Instead, she lifted her chin and squared her shoulders. He would never know how deeply his lovemaking had touched her heart.

Staring straight ahead, she said, icily, "When we get back to the ranch, I think you'd better pack up and ride on."

For a long moment, Tyree didn't say anything. Rachel held her breath, hating herself for hoping that he would admit he loved her, that last night had been as wonderful for him as it had been for her, that it hadn't been just a casual encounter in the rain.

But the words she yearned to hear did not come.

"Whatever you want," Tyree drawled. "Giddap, horse."

Ten minutes after they arrived at the Lazy H, he was gone, leaving Rachel to explain his sudden departure to her father.

Chapter 9

The streets of Yellow Creek were pretty much deserted when Tyree rode into town. After settling the gray into the livery stable, Tyree took a room at the Imperial Hotel. It was a small room, cheaply furnished considering the exorbitant price, smelling faintly of stale sweat and old cigar smoke. But the bed was reasonably firm and free of lumps and vermin, and the sheets were clean.

After a quick look around, Tyree dumped his gear on the bed and headed for Bowsher's Saloon. Ordering a bottle of rye whiskey, he carried it to a table in the far corner of the room where he slowly and methodically worked his way to the bottom of the bottle.

The barkeep, a red-headed Irishman named Kelly, had a pot belly and a florid face. He had been a bar dog long enough to know trouble looking for a place to happen when he saw it, and Tyree looked like trouble with a capital T. Periodically, Kelly let his gaze wander in Tyree's direction, but the explosion he anticipated never came. The liquor seemed to have no effect at all on the taciturn gunman, and he was still steady on his feet some hours later when he bought another bottle and left the saloon.

In the weeks that followed, Tyree spent a good part of every day in Bowsher's Saloon, always sitting at the same table with his back to the wall, his right hand never far from the butt of his Colt. Customers came and went, but no one ever approached the grim-faced gunman. There was something about the way he sat there, calmly downing one drink after another; something about the chill look in his eyes that warned others to steer clear of his table. Even the saloon girls lacked the courage to get too close.

Late one night, Flat-Nose Bowsher made one of her rare appearances in the saloon. Despite her years and the disfigurement to her nose, she was still an attractive woman. Her hair was snow-white, her face, though lined by years of hard living, managed to retain a ghost of its former beauty. Like a queen, she glided down the staircase, aware of the whispers and glances her presence elicited from the customers. Her narrowed eyes swept the room in a long glance, then came to rest on Tyree. She was not put off by his stern visage, or by the unfriendly look in his eye.

She gave Tyree a wisp of a smile as she pulled out a chair and sat down.

"Evening, Tyree," she said in a raspy voice. "I heard you were in town."

Tyree nodded. He was not in the mood for talk or company, but Flat-Nose was in the mood for both. Calling for a bottle of bourbon, she settled back in her chair.

"Was Yuma as bad as everyone says?" she asked.

Tyree nodded again as he poured her a drink of bourbon.

"I knew they wouldn't keep you there long," Flat-Nose said. "So, you left the Halloran spread. Too tame for you?"

"Flat-Nose, mind your own business," Tyree said mildly.

She laughed at that, a big booming laugh. Still smiling, she emptied her glass and poured herself another drink. The two of them sat there, drinking steadily, until the saloon closed five hours later.

Riders from the Walsh spread drifted into Bowsher's now and then, always in groups of two or three, never alone. Arrogant and impudent, they strutted around the saloon as if they owned the place, bullying the other patrons, harassing the barkeep, making lewd suggestions to the saloon girls.

But they never bothered Tyree.

The Marshal made his rounds twice each night, but Clint Wesley also avoided Tyree, never acknowledging the gunman's presence by so much as a glance.

Which suited Tyree just fine.

Tyree overheard a lot of idle talk as he sat in Bowsher's Saloon, most of it about Annabelle Walsh. Apparently, she had no intention of selling the Slash W, as Rachel had supposed. Indeed, Annabelle seemed to be every bit as land-hungry as her brother had been. Rumors were flying hot and heavy that the Walsh nightriders were operating again, and that one of their victims had been a homesteader who had the audacity to settle on a corner of property claimed by the Slash W. Not only that, but there were a lot of new men hiring on for Annabelle, and they weren't all cowhands.

But over and above all the gossip, the men talked excitedly about Annabelle Walsh herself. She was some looker, they said, with a mane of thick red hair and eyes the color of polished jade. She had a hell of a figure, too, if they were to be believed, and flaunted it by wearing low-cut peasant blouses and tight-fitting pants.

But the news that really made Tyree sit up and take notice was the five thousand dollar bounty Annabelle was offering for the name of the man who had killed her brother.

There was a lot of speculation on the subject of who had gunned Walsh, and Logan

Tyree was the prime suspect. But it was just talk. There were no facts, no evidence, no witnesses. Nevertheless, Tyree could not help wondering if Annabelle would regard the hearsay as idle gossip, or accept it as gospel.

He was thinking about pulling up and leaving Yellow Creek the night he stepped out of Bowsher's Saloon and found himself surrounded by five men armed with rifles and shotguns. Tyree was reaching for his Colt when a rifle barrel slammed into his right side.

"I wouldn't," warned the rifleman, and Tyree slowly raised his hands over his head.

One man, dressed in a fancy shirt with pearl buttons and a sheepskin vest, stepped forward and relieved Tyree of his hardware. Another man, younger than the others, tied Tyree's hands behind his back. That done, the men hustled Tyree down a dark alley that dead-ended against a two-story brick building.

A big bull of a man stepped out of the pack, a half smile on his thick lips. "We've got a message for ya from Miz Walsh," the man drawled in a voice as deep as six feet down. "She don't want any gunmen running around Yellow Creek that ain't on the payroll, so we're here to make ya an offer."

Tyree glanced with wry amusement at the man who stood before him like a solid wall of flesh. "Say your piece," Tyree muttered sardonically. "Doesn't look like I'm going anywhere for awhile."

The big man grinned, showing crooked yellow teeth. "You're smarter than I thought, 'breed. Well, here's the deal. Either you ride for the Slash W, or you ride outta town now, tonight."

"That's your offer?"

"That's it."

Tyree let out a slow sigh. He had been planning to ride on, but all that was changed now. To ride on would look like he'd been run off, and he couldn't live with that.

"Well, you can tell your boss lady that I'm obliged for her offer," Tyree said evenly, "but I'm not looking for work just now."

"That your final say on the matter?"

"That's it."

The big man shook his head sadly. "I guess you ain't so smart after all."

Tyree felt all his muscles tense as the big man handed his rifle to the youngster who had lashed Tyree's hands together.

There was a moment of silence, then Annabelle's men began to move. The man in the sheepskin vest grabbed Tyree's bound arms so he couldn't make a break for it. Another man went to stand watch at the mouth of the alley. The big man and a dark-skinned Mexican sporting a black eye patch stood before Tyree, flexing their muscles and cracking their knuckles, the lust for blood showing clearly in their eyes.

And then it began. One blow following hard on the heels of the last, pounding into Tyree's flesh with smooth, steady precision, smashing into his face and throat, driving deep into his belly. A knee sent sharp slivers of pain racing through his genitals. A hard right cross sliced his cheek to the bone. There was blood in his mouth, his nose.

The faces of his attackers rushed toward him, then receded, like waves breaking on the sand. His vision blurred and there was a loud roaring in his ears. Vaguely, he wondered if Rachel would brand him a coward for not trying to defend himself. But only a fool tried to buck insurmountable odds, and Tyree had known from the beginning that Annabelle's men did not intend to kill him. Not this time.

And so he took the awful beating, carefully imprinting the face of each man in his memory—making special note of the two men whose fists were brutally punishing his flesh. Sooner or later, they would meet again.

After what seemed like hours but was, in reality, no more than ten minutes, the big man hissed, "That's enough, Rafe," and the blows came to a merciful halt.

The young kid cut Tyree's hands free and Tyree fell to his knees, panting for breath, his whole body throbbing with pain.

But they were not through with him yet. The big man knocked Tyree flat, while the man called Rafe pinned Tyree's right hand to the ground, palm down.

"Miz Walsh had a feeling you wouldn't cooperate," the big man said. "But if you've got any sense at all, you'll hightail it outta town while you can still walk, 'cause if we see your ass in town again, we'll drop you cold."

The man at the mouth of the alley called, "Hey, Larkin, what the hell's taking so long?"

"Shut up, Harris," the big man snarled. Then, to Tyree, "Just in case you ain't got the sense to skedaddle, me and Rafe, here, decided to put your gun hand outta commission. Permanent-like."

Larkin was moving as he spoke. Grabbing his rifle from the youngster, he brought the butt crashing down on Tyree's pinioned right hand. There was a sickening crunch as skin and bone splintered beneath solid wood. Tyree's body shuddered convulsively; a low groan rumbled in his throat as waves of excruciating pain shot through his hand and arm.

As if from far away, he heard the sound of footsteps as Annabelle's men left the alley. The man in the sheepskin vest kicked Tyree in the ribs as he passed by.

The big man, Larkin, was the last to leave and he chuckled maliciously as he stepped on Tyree's shattered hand, grinding his boot heel into the torn flesh. The pain was unbearable and Tyree uttered a hoarse cry of agony as darkness closed in on him, mercifully dragging him down, down, into nothingness . . .

When he regained consciousness, it was after midnight. For a long time, he remained inert, trying to pretend that the pain radiating from his right hand belonged to some other poor bastard.

Larkin. Rafe. Harris. The names pounded in his skull, throbbing to the relentless beat of the pain hammering in his right hand. The ground was hard and cold beneath him, the air chill.

"Damn, you can't stay here all night," Tyree muttered through clenched teeth, and forced himself to his knees, and then to his feet. There was a sharp stabbing pain in his side and he quietly cursed the man who had kicked him while he was down.

Hanging onto the wall for support, he made his way down the alley. The broken rib tortured him with each breath, and he was panting like a blown mustang by the time he reached the street.

The gray stood hipshot at the rail of Bowsher's Saloon some ten yards away. Ten yards that looked like ten miles—and damn near felt like it as he staggered across the moonlit street. A quiet word to the stud sent the animal to its knees and Tyree congratulated himself on having had the foresight to teach the horse such a valuable trick.

Gritting his teeth, he stepped into the saddle. Every muscle in his body shrieked in protest as the gray lurched to its feet. For a moment, the world reeled drunkenly; when it stopped, he took a good look at his right hand. Swollen, caked with dirt and blood, it looked more like a slab of chewed-up meat than a human hand.

Indecision held Tyree motionless for a long moment. Unarmed, his gun hand useless, he was as vulnerable as a newborn babe. It was a new and decidedly uncomfortable feeling.

He grinned wryly as he wheeled the gray around and headed for the Lazy H. He would not be welcome at the Halloran spread, he mused ruefully, but he had no place else to go.

Rachel sat before her dressing table, absently brushing her hair. Tyree had been gone for almost five weeks. It seemed a lifetime. Funny, how all the joy of life seemed to have ridden away with him. She missed his sardonic laughter, his occasional ribald remarks, the sight of his lean, hawk-like face grinning at her from behind a long black cigar, an expectant look dancing in his amber eyes. She had often complained about his laziness, but now she missed seeing him lounging on the front porch steps, his hat pulled low, his legs stretched negligently before him. She remembered how considerate he had been when she sprained her ankle, how tenderly he had cared for her, the intimate dinners they had shared. She remembered dancing with him in the moonlight, his arms tight around her waist, his eyes caressing her. She remembered the night at the Jorgensen cabin . . . felt her cheeks grow hot with the memory. What a fool she had been, to think Logan Tyree had actually cared for her, that he could care for anybody. It had all been a monstrous joke, a cruel, cruel joke. How he must have laughed at her . . . silly country girl, to be so easily wooed and won. If only she could stop remembering. If only it didn't hurt so much. If only she didn't care.

She had filled her days with work, cleaning and polishing and waxing, as if her very life depended on spotless floors, shiny furniture, and gleaming windows. She sought out Carol Ann's company, forcing herself to laugh and gossip and flirt as if she didn't have a care in the world. She went out of her way to be nice to Clint. She volunteered to teach a Sunday School class, insisted on helping out at the Watkins place when Mabel Watkins broke her leg.

But endless chores and the company of other people failed to ease the ache in her heart. Night after night she lay awake, staring at the ceiling, remembering.

She dropped the hairbrush onto the dressing table and stared at her reflection in the mirror. How had it happened? How had a man she had once despised managed to work his way so deeply into her heart? Did she really love him, or was it just lust?

She frowned at her image. It wasn't just base desire, she mused. She wanted to comfort him, to make him forget the Indian woman who had been killed so savagely. She wanted to blot out the horrors of prison, to wipe out all the unhappiness of his past and replace the misery with joy. She wanted to erase the hard lines of pain and hurt from his face, to see him smile, hear him laugh, bear his children. Tyree, Tyree. If only she could forget him . . .

A faint noise interrupted her melancholy thoughts and she cocked her head toward the door, listening. And then it came again, a faint knock on the front door. She felt a mild twinge of apprehension as she stood up, drawing her blue cotton wrapper around her. Cahill and her father were spending the night out on the range, and she was alone in the house.

Belting her robe snugly around her waist, Rachel padded barefoot down the carpeted stairway, paused to light the lamp on the table beside the front door before calling, "Who's there?"

"Tyree."

Tyree! Rachel felt her pulse quicken at the thought of seeing him again, felt her cheeks flame as the memory of the night they had shared at the Jorgensen place leaped to the forefront of her mind. Anger followed hard on the heels of that memory. He had used her to satisfy his drunken lust, letting her believe what they shared had been something beautiful when it had been sordid and ugly. How dare he come back to the Lazy H. She would send him packing, and right quick!

Hot words rose in her throat as she opened the door, but she never uttered them. One look at Tyree stilled her tongue and cooled her anger.

"Good Lord," she gasped. "What happened to you?"

"Annabelle Walsh set her dogs on me. Can I come in?"

"Yes, of course. Here, sit down."

She hovered over him as he eased into one of the big overstuffed chairs in the parlor, her sky-blue eyes reflecting the horror of what she saw. Tyree's face was swollen, pale as death beneath the multicolored bruises and drying blood. Both of his eyes were puffy and turning black; his mouth was cut in several places, there was a jagged gash in his left cheek. His shirt hung in tatters, exposing his lean torso and she saw that his chest, too, was a mass of bruises and angry red welts. And his right hand . . . she turned away, fighting the urge to vomit.

"Not a pretty sight, is it?" Tyree muttered. "Damn, it hurts like hell. You got any whiskey?"

"I'll get it. Just sit tight."

Tyree leaned back in the chair and closed his eyes. Every breath was an effort, but the pain caused by his broken rib was nothing compared to the constant pulsing pain in his hand and he swore under his breath, cursing Annabelle Walsh and her sadistic night riders.

Rachel returned shortly, carrying a tray

laden with salve, bandages, scissors, and a tall bottle of scotch whiskey.

Tyree reached for the bottle and took a lengthy swallow as Rachel began working on his hand. He flinched involuntarily each time she touched him, swore aloud as she cleaned the wound with a disinfectant that stung like hell.

Going to the kitchen again, she returned with a bowl of warm water, and one of cold. Tyree grimaced as she placed his injured hand in the cold water in hopes of reducing the swelling. While his hand soaked, she began sponging the blood from his face and chest with a soft cloth dipped in warm water.

"Tyree, I can clean up the blood and bandage the cuts on your face and chest, but your hand . . . I don't know anything about setting bones that badly crushed." There was a tremor in her voice, and her eyes were dark with worry when she met his gaze. "I think I can splint your fingers," she went on uncertainly, "but I don't know what to do about the rest. You need a doctor."

"What about the sawbones in Yellow Creek?"

"He's gone back east to visit his daughter. She had a baby last month."

"Damn."

"The only other doctor is over fifty miles away. I . . . I can take you in the buggy, if you like."

Tyree loosed a long sigh. Riding fifty miles

across rough, unbroken country with a busted rib and a ruined gun hand was out of the question.

"Shit, Rachel," he murmured wearily, "just do the best you can, but do it the hell now."

With a nod, Rachel removed what was left of Tyree's shirt and began to dab disinfectant on the wounds on his chest and face. The gash in his cheek was deep and he swore aloud as she bandaged it. Another scar, she mused, when he had so many. His side was badly bruised and discolored.

It was nearing two a.m. when Rachel taped the last bandage in place. Tyree was quite a sight. A wide strip of cloth was swathed around his middle to support his broken rib, a square of gauze covered the gash in his cheek. His face was swollen and purple, one eye was nearly swollen shut. His right hand was splinted and loosely wrapped.

With a sigh, Rachel stood up, one hand pressed against her aching back. She had done her best to mend the damage to Tyree's hand, and she knew, with real regret, that her best had not been good enough. With luck, he would eventually regain the use of his right hand, but only for the simplest tasks. He would never fast-draw a gun with that hand again. She knew it as surely as she knew her own name. And so did Tyree. The knowledge was clear in his eyes, and in the bitter twist of his mouth.

Tyree got slowly to his feet, each movement

an effort. "Thanks, Rachel," he murmured. "I wouldn't have come here if I'd had anywhere else to go."

"It's all right." She lowered her eyes, suddenly shy in his presence. So much had passed between them and yet, for all that, he seemed like a stranger. "The spare bedroom is still empty," she said in a low voice. "You're welcome to stay until you're feeling better."

"No."

She had not expected him to refuse, nor had she thought to feel such regret when he spoke of leaving.

"You're welcome to stay," she repeated. "Really."

"I can't," Tyree said wearily. "I need a place to hole up, someplace where no one will think to come looking for me."

"But you just said you had nowhere else to go. Besides, you're in no fit condition to ride. Not tonight, anyway."

"Oh? How the hell do you think I got here?"

"But where will you go?" Her concern was evident in her voice, but Tyree did not seem to notice.

"Out to the Jorgensen place," Tyree answered as if the idea had just occurred to him. "I'd be obliged if you'd keep my whereabouts to yourself."

Rachel nodded. Once word got out that Tyree's gunhand was ruined, he would be a sitting duck for any bounty hunter in the territory. Anyone catching him off-guard would have no trouble getting the drop on him. She thought fleetingly of Clint.

"You'll need a gun," she said, thinking aloud. "Pa's got an extra one in his room. You'll need some food, too, and a clean shirt."

Before he could argue or agree, she began gathering the items she had mentioned. With a sigh, Tyree sat down again. Closing his eyes, he rested his head on the back of the chair. Damn, but he was tired. It would be so pleasant to stay at the Lazy H and let Rachel take care of him. He had missed her more than he cared to admit. But he could not stay. Annabelle's men would not waste any time bragging about how they had whipped Logan Tyree, smashed his gunhand, and sent him running. Once word got around that he was hurt, he would be fair game for anyone who felt like hauling him into the nearest lawman.

And he was not going back to jail. Not now. Not ever.

"Tyree?"

"Yeah?" It was an effort to open his eyes.

Rachel was standing before him, a burlap bag in one hand, a shirt and an old Walker Colt in the other. With a low groan, he stood up, reaching for the shirt with his good hand.

"Here, let me help you," Rachel said quickly.

Halloran's shirt was a trifle snug through the shoulders and the sleeves were a couple of inches too short, but it was better than nothing. Tyree accepted Rachel's help because he had no choice, but it galled him nevertheless. She could see that. He was a man who did not take kindly to depending on others.

Wordlessly, she handed him the gun. The barrel of the old Colt was too long to fit into his holster, so he shoved the gun into the waistband of his pants.

"Thanks," he said gruffly. Brushing her cheek with his left hand, he picked up the sack of food and left the house.

Peering out the front window, Rachel watched Tyree hang the sack over the saddle horn. Saw his face go gray with pain when he accidentally jarred his right hand as he pulled himself into the saddle. Once mounted, he sat there for several moments before he reined the stallion north toward the old Jorgensen place.

Rachel watched him ride away into the darkness, bewildered by her feelings. He had used her and abused her. He had taken her as callously as he would have taken some cheap saloon girl. And yet, inexplicably, it grieved her to see him in pain, to know he was alone and hurting.

She stayed at the window, staring down the empty road long after Tyree was out of sight.

Chapter 10

*T*he cabin was cold and dark, empty of life save for an owl perched on one of the overhead beams, its bright yellow eyes blinking in the sudden light as Tyree lit a lamp. With a faint rustle of wings, the owl flew out into the night. Tyree stared after the bird, frowning. The Apache believed an owl was a bad omen, a forerunner of death.

Moving sluggishly, Tyree went outside, slipped the rigging from the gray before turning him loose in one of the pole corrals located behind the shack.

Inside again, he dropped his warbag on the floor, barring the door behind him. Pain slashed through him with every move, and he cussed long and loud as he eased down on the lumpy mattress, his left arm thrown across his forehead, his right hand pillowed on his chest.

Outside, the wind came up, whispering mournfully as it blew across the valley. Tyree stared out the curtainless window, his thoughts grim as he watched the clouds drift across the inky sky. It would be weeks before his right hand healed, and even then it would likely be as useful as teats on a boar. And until then, what? He had money, but didn't dare show his face in Yellow Creek to buy supplies as long as he was crippled up. He could ride on, he mused grimly, but the next town was over fifty miles away, and he was too damn sore to travel that far. And too damn mad!

Unconsciously, he stroked the smooth walnut butt of the Walker Colt jutting from his waistband. There were five men who had a debt to pay and by damn, he meant to see they paid it. In full.

Courting thoughts of vengeance, Tyree fell into a troubled sleep . . . and sleeping, began to dream—dark dreams peopled with the skeletal images of men he had killed. The ghost of Job Walsh materialized in the midst of the others, his eyes burning like twin coals plucked from the bowels of hell. With a death's-head grin, Walsh drew his gun, cocked the hammer, sighted down the barrel. Tyree saw himself grinning confidently as he reached for his own gun. But his hand refused to obey his mind's command. Puzzled, he glanced down at his right hand, screamed in horror at the gnarled and distorted claw growing from the end of his arm and screamed yet again as his left hand withered before his eyes. Helpless now, he looked up to find Walsh laughing at him, laughing like a crazy man as he pulled the trigger again and again . . .

Tyree woke in a cold sweat. The bandages on his right hand made a white blur in the shadowy darkness. He stared at his ruined hand for a long time before sleep claimed him again.

He woke the following morning feeling ill-tempered and sore as hell. Scowling blackly, he touched a match to the wood stacked in the fireplace, dumped some coffee into the battered coffeepot, and put it on the fire to boil. Rummaging in his warbag, he pulled out a slab of bacon, sliced it awkwardly with his left hand, dropped the pieces in a cast-iron skillet. There were a half-dozen biscuits in the sack, and he ate them with the bacon, washing it all down with gulps of hot black coffee.

With breakfast over, he pulled a set of hobbles from his pack and went out to check on the gray. The clear morning air was blue with the sound of Tyree's angry curses by the time he had the hobbles in place. That done, he turned the stud out to graze on the sparse yellow grass growing around the cabin.

He spent the day drowsing in the sun, letting its warmth bake the ache from his battered body. Sitting there, he found himself thinking of Rachel and wishing she didn't have such a low opinion of him. He frowned as he recalled how she had flung his past in his face, taunting him with the men he had killed, like the supposedly unarmed man he had shot in Amarillo. True, the man hadn't been armed in the usual sense of the word, but he had been swinging a double-bitted axe that was every bit as lethal as a six-gun. And then there was that helpless woman. Rita Lacey, her name had been, wife of Tom Lacey, one of the fastest gunmen this side of the Missouri. Tyree had killed Lacey in a saloon brawl, and Rita had come looking for her husband's killer, shotgun in hand. And Tyree had killed her. He hadn't liked killing a woman, especially a woman as attractive as Rita Lacey had been, but what the hell. It had been him or her. And it wasn't her house that had burned down, but an El Paso crib where Rita worked part-time.

And as for the man he had reportedly shot in the back without even a call, shit, the man had never existed except in the mind of whoever set the story in motion. Of course, there were dozens of other men he *had* killed. A sheriff in Texas. A Pinkerton man in Abilene. A drunken cowhand in Dodge. A double-dealing gambler in Tombstone who tried to palm a fifth ace. The list was endless, but he had never regretted killing any of them. He had chosen the path he rode, and he would ride it to the end.

Tyree frowned as he pulled his thoughts back to the present, and Rachel. His only regret in life was taking her virginity. She was a lovely young woman, much too good for the

216

likes of a washed-up gunfighter. And too good for a man like Clint Wesley, too.

Wesley. Tyree spat into the dirt. Wesley wasn't a bad kid, but unless he got rid of that badge, or got a lot better with his gun, he wasn't going to live long enough to marry Rachel, or anyone else. A green kid packing a gun was just asking for trouble.

The days passed with annoying slowness. Inactivity made Tyree restless and irritable; his inability to use his left hand with the same sureness and dexterity as he had used his right hand made him angry and bad-tempered. Cooking, eating, shaving, bathing, dressing, looking after the stallion, even combing his hair—all the simple everyday tasks he had once performed with ease now took twice the time and required twice the effort and concentration.

Thoughts of vengeance crowded his mind every time he looked at his ruined hand, and he spent long hours plotting the demise of the five men responsible.

As his strength increased, he took long walks to pass the time. Sometimes he took the gray stud along for company. The horse trailed at his heels like an overgrown puppy.

He played countless games of solitaire, cussing mightily every time he tried to shuffle the cards.

He was about out of food, cigars and patience when Rachel showed up at the cabin door.

"I hope you don't mind a little company," she said by way of greeting. She was glad to see he was looking much better. His face was no longer swollen, though it was still slightly discolored. The gash in his cheek had scabbed over; it would leave a ragged scar. She noticed he had not shaved in several days.

"Come on in," Tyree invited. "Sit down. What brings you clear out here? Come to gloat?"

"Of course not. I . . . I just thought you might be a little lonesome."

"Did you?"

Rachel lowered her lashes, unwilling to meet his probing gaze. Regaining her composure, she looked up and smiled. "You look like you could use a shave," she remarked, resisting the temptation to reach out and stroke his beard.

"Reckon so," Tyree agreed, rubbing his left hand across the dark stubble sprouting on his jaw.

"This place could use some cleaning up, too," Rachel observed, glancing with distaste at the dirty dishes stacked in the sink, and at the empty bottles and papers piled in one corner.

"Yeah," Tyree muttered glumly. "And the window is dirty and the blankets need washing, and the floor needs sweeping. And, dammit, I need a drink."

Rachel's laugh was soft and musical, like the purling of spring water over a mound of mossy stones. "Poor baby," she crooned, "got a broken hand and can't go into town."

Tyree's deep amber eyes glittered angrily. "Dammit, Rachel, it's not funny!"

"I know," she said, instantly contrite. "Everyone is wondering what happened to you. Larkin and his bunch are bragging about how they whipped you and ran you out of town."

"I'll bet they are."

"Yes." Rachel smiled up at him, her eyes twinkling merrily. "The way they tell it, you were tougher than Hickock and Cody rolled into one."

Tyree snorted derisively. "But not too tough for Larkin and his thugs, right?"

"Right. They're boasting, modestly, of course, that they went through you like a hot knife through butter."

"They'll pay dearly for that bit of bravado," Tyree vowed quietly. "Damn, I wish I had a drink."

"Would you like me to ride into Yellow Creek and buy you a bottle?"

"Yeah. And some ammunition. And a holster for a left-handed draw. And a box of the best long nines the town has to offer."

"Are you going to live on cartridges and cigars?" Rachel asked dryly.

"If I have to."

"Be serious. How's your food supply holding up?"

"Cupboard's about bare. Here." He pressed

a wad of bills into Rachel's hand. "Buy whatever you think looks good."

"I'll see what I can do. Tyree?"

"You need more money?"

"No, this is plenty. Can I ask you something?"

"You can ask."

"Why did you become a gunfighter?"

Tyree regarded her for a long moment while he considered and discarded several answers, and then he shrugged. "A man has to do something for a living."

"I'm sure you could have found another line of work if you had tried."

"Sure. I could have swamped out saloons for two bits a day."

"Can't you ever be serious!" Rachel snapped.

"I am being serious. Take a good look at me, honey. I'm a 'breed. Nobody's gonna give me a job that amounts to anything. Besides, I like what I do."

"I can't imagine why. Just look at you. You can't even ride into town for fear of being shot at, or arrested. Why don't you quit?"

"I can't," he retorted, somewhat bitterly. "No matter where I go, there's always someone who knows me, some young punk who thinks he's faster than I am, and won't rest until he takes a stab at proving it."

"Have you ever tried to quit?"

"Once. I went to California. Cut my hair. Changed my name. Grew a beard. But it didn't work. I'd only been there a week or so when somebody recognized me. Next thing I knew, I'd killed two men and I was on the move again. So I figured, what the hell. Might as well cash in on it. And I have."

"You could try again. To quit, I mean."

"Maybe."

Tyree's eyes probed Rachel's, wondering what lay behind her questions, and her sudden silence.

"I'd better be going," Rachel announced abruptly. "I'll be back tomorrow with your supplies."

"Rachel—"

"Yes?" She looked up at him, her heart aching to hold him, to mother him, to feel his mouth on hers. She did not like to think of him staying in such a dreary place alone, with no one to care for him, to love him.

"I seem to be thanking you for something every time I turn around."

"There's no need," she said quickly, and hurried out of the cabin before she did something foolish, like throw herself into his arms.

Rachel rode into Yellow Creek early the following morning. Mrs. Thorngood eyed her with open curiosity as she ordered a box of long nines and four boxes of ammunition. She was ordering flour, bacon, sugar, salt and canned goods when Clint entered the store. He smiled warmly when he saw Rachel standing at the counter.

"Morning, Rachel," Wesley said, coming to stand beside her. He glanced at the cigars and cartridges stacked on the counter, then turned an inquiring eye on Rachel. "Your old man take up smoking cigars?"

"No," Rachel said, not meeting his eyes. "They're for Candido."

Wesley nodded, though he could not remember ever having seen the Mexican wrangler smoke anything but a pipe. "Everything okay out at the ranch?"

"Yes, fine," Rachel answered quickly. "Are you coming for dinner Sunday?"

"You bet. There's going to be a dance at the Grange on Saturday night."

"Sounds like fun."

"Pick you up at seven?"

"I'll be ready. I've got to go now, Clint," Rachel said, picking up her order and placing it in a burlap bag. She paid Mrs. Thorngood, smiled at Clint, and left the store.

Wesley stared after her, a bemused expression on his face. Something was wrong, but what?

Tyree shoved the heavy old Colt into the waistband of his pants and left the cabin. After a quick look around to make sure he was alone, he unloaded the Colt and replaced the weapon in his belt. Then, drawing a deep breath, he palmed the gun.

Like most gunfighters, he could shoot with his left hand, though his aim was only fair and his draw was nothing to brag about. True, there were gunmen who made a big deal about wearing two guns, and a couple of them were as fast with one hand as the other. But for a man who was good, one gun was usually enough to get the job done, because if you couldn't hit your target with six shots, you weren't likely to get six more, not if you were shooting at something that was shooting back.

Tyree drew the Colt with his left hand again and again, getting the feel of it, getting used to the weight and the balance. He practiced all morning. It was good to hold a gun again, good to feel the smooth walnut butt cradled against his palm.

He was still working on his draw when Rachel rode up. Tyree had taken off his shirt and she stared at his well-muscled torso, feeling a sudden stab of desire at the sight of so much masculine flesh. He was a big man, yet he moved with the silky grace of a tiger, his muscles rippling in the late morning sun as he turned to face her. His chest was still livid where Annabelle's men had beaten him, his ribs were still tightly bound. His coarse black beard made him look like a pirate, but for all that, he appealed to something raw and earthy deep within her.

"I brought the things you asked for," she said, and blushed under his frank gaze, wondering if he could read the unladylike thoughts tumbling through her mind. "I'll go and put this stuff away. You go on with what you're doing."

It was suppertime when Tyree returned to the cabin. Stepping inside, he could see that Rachel had been hard at work. The cabin's single window sparkled. The floor was dust-free. The cobwebs were gone from the corners. His blankets had been washed, the bed was freshly made. A red-checked cloth covered the table. He quirked an eyebrow inquiringly when he saw it was set for two. A clean shirt was laid out on the bed, together with a bar of yellow soap and a clean white towel. A basin of hot water was waiting on the counter, his razor beside it. There was a pot of stew simmering on top of the stove, a pan of biscuits warming in the oven.

Tyree whistled softly. "Nothing like a woman's touch."

"You might as well live like a civilized human being while you're here," Rachel retorted sharply, mistaking his compliment for sarcasm.

"Hey, calm down," Tyree admonished. "I like it. It looks . . . nice."

Mollified, Rachel said, "Dinner is almost ready." She looked pointedly at the whiskers sprouting on Tyree's chin. "You have time to shave first."

"Shaving left handed's more trouble than it's worth," Tyree muttered, dragging a hand across his jaw.

"Would you like me to do it?"

"You?" Tyree chuckled. "Hell, I'm game if you are."

Tyree sat in one of the cabin's rickety chairs while Rachel lathered his face and then, very carefully, began to shave him. Her touch was light, her fingers warm on his cheek, and a sudden tension sprang up between them as she continued to draw the razor across his jaw. Somehow, what had started out as a routine chore suddenly became much, much more, leaving Rachel to wonder how it had happened. She was acutely conscious of Tyree's face only inches from her breast, of his thigh brushing hers as she moved from side to side.

Tyree was thinking about picking her up and carrying her to bed when Rachel wiped the last of the lather from his face and took a step back, head cocked to one side as she admired her handiwork. Seeing the look in Tyree's eyes, she took another step back, putting herself out of his reach.

"Not bad," she declared, offering him a hand mirror she had found in a drawer of the highboy. "What do you think?"

"Better than a barber," Tyree decided. "Maybe I should set you up in business."

"No, thanks. Dinner is ready."

They ate in silence. Darkness came swiftly, enveloping the cabin and its occupants, shutting them off from the rest of the world. Rachel avoided Tyree's eyes as she cleared the table, glad to have something to do with her hands, glad that she could turn her back to Tyree while she washed and dried the dishes. But even then she was aware of his presence only a few feet away.

Leaning back in his chair, Tyree chewed on the end of a cigar, openly admiring the way the lamplight played in Rachel's hair, turning the honey-blond to gold, finding pleasure in the graceful way she moved as she wiped the dishes and stacked them in the cupboard.

Removing her apron, Rachel ran a slender hand through her hair and coughed nervously. "It's getting late. I've got to go."

"You shouldn't be riding home alone in the dark."

"I'll be all right."

Tyree was about to argue with her when the shrill scream of an aroused stallion cut across the stillness of the night.

"The gray," Tyree remarked. "Your mare must be in season."

Rachel nodded, and then they were running for the corrals behind the cabin.

In the light of the full moon they could see the stud pacing the rail that separated him from Rachel's mare. He had been pacing back and forth for some time as evidenced by the path cut into the soft dirt on his side of the fence. As Rachel and Tyree rounded the corner of the cabin, the stallion sailed over the six-foot fence.

"Tyree, stop him!" Rachel shouted. "I don't want my mare to drop a late foal."

"It's too late. Look!"

Rachel's mare was a maiden mare. Too frightened to run, she stood in one corner of the corral, her dainty head high, her eyes showing white as the stud pranced back and forth in front of her, his neck arched, his tail high. His organ dropped, swelled.

Rachel gasped. "No wonder Morgana's

afraid," she murmured, unaware she had spoken the words aloud.

The gray herded the mare into the center of the corral, nipped her viciously on the right flank when she seemed unwilling to cooperate. Then, with a squeal that sent shivers down Rachel's spine, the gray reared up and mounted the quivering mare.

"Damn!" Tyree breathed. "He's magnificent."

Rachel had to agree. The stallion was magnificent. And though she had seen mares covered before, there was something special about this occasion, and not just because her mare was involved. The other breedings she had seen had been at the ranch under controlled conditions, not like this, with the mare cowed into submission by a stallion that had run wild and free only a few short months ago.

Rachel licked her lips, suddenly conscious of the man standing close beside her, and she sent a furtive glance in his direction. He was like the gray, she thought, blushing furiously. Half-wild and totally unpredictable.

A shuddering sigh wracked the stud as, with a shake of his massive head, he withdrew from the mare to stand with his nose almost touching the ground, his sides heaving mightily.

"Come on, you old reprobate," Tyree called softly, and the stallion followed him docilely into the adjoining corral.

"Lets have some coffee while your mare settles down," Tyree suggested.

"Might as well," Rachel agreed. "The damage is done."

"I'll bet she throws a fine foal," Tyree predicted. "She's a good-looking mare, and the gray has good conformation for a range-bred stallion. I'll bet he's got some Thoroughbred somewhere in his background."

"Could be," Rachel agreed, stepping into the cabin. "He's much too tall for a mustang."

The minute Tyree shut the cabin door, Rachel knew returning to the cabin with him had been a mistake. The mating between the horses had affected Tyree, too. There was a hungry look in his eye, a telltale bulge rising in the crotch of his Levi's.

"I'll put some water on," Rachel said with forced lightness, but Tyree shook his head.

"Well, if you've changed your mind about that coffee, I'll be running along. It's a long way home, and I'm tired." She was babbling, and she laughed self-consciously. "Morgana's probably tired too," she said, and could have bitten her tongue. "So long, Tyree."

"Rachel."

His voice stopped her as she reached for the door latch. Slowly, she turned to face him. "No, Tyree," she whispered. "Please don't."

But she made no move to avoid the hand that reached out to stroke the curve of her cheek. Nor did she turn away when he bent to kiss her.

Hating herself, Rachel let Tyree lead her to the bed and willingly sank down beside him on the lumpy mattress. Later, she would be ashamed of the brazen way she responded to his touch, would be embarrassed to recall the love words she had whispered in his ear. But not now.

With provocative deliberation, Tyree began to undress her. Slowly, using his good hand alone, he unfastened her shirt and slipped it off her shoulders, then began to remove her jeans. For a moment, his fingers stroked her naked belly and thighs. Rachel stared up at him, her whole body quivering under his burning gaze. He did not take his eyes from hers as he stood up and began to undress. In moments, he stood naked before her and Rachel marveled anew at the span of his shoulders, the spread of his black-furred chest, the length of his legs, the strength in his arms.

With a little cry, Rachel reached for Tyree, pulling him down beside her on the narrow bed, loving the touch of his skin against hers as she explored his scarred body with shameless abandon. She was surprised to find that his lean nakedness did not repel her. Surprised to learn his nakedness excited her, that she thought his body beautiful to behold.

Lying beside Tyree, feeling his hand caress her flesh, tasting his kisses, she felt loved and protected and terribly female. He was so completely masculine, so virile, it made her more glad than ever to be a woman. Oh, but it was wonderful to know that Tyree found her desirable, wonderful to glory in the easy strength of the arms enfolding her, wonderful the way their bodies came together, as if they had been born to share this one glorious moment . . .

When Tyree woke in the morning, Rachel was gone. The cabin seemed empty without her gentle presence.

Rising, he dressed, ate, and then got to work filing the front sight off the barrel of the Walker Colt so that it wouldn't catch on the holster. That done, he began working on the holster Rachel had brought him, softening it, rubbing it inside and out with oil, shaping it so that the leather fit the gun like a second skin.

When both gun and holster suited him, he blocked everything from his mind and concentrated on drawing the weapon. Ten times, twenty, fifty, a hundred times he drew the heavy Colt until he was satisfied with the way the gun felt in his hand, satisfied that his draw was flawless. Only then did he load the gun.

Long hours of target practice followed. He fired at his target from all angles: with the sun at his back, with the sun in his face, standing, kneeling, prone on the ground. He practiced in full daylight, in the changing shadows of twilight, in moonlit darkness.

Days passed, and he thought of nothing but the Colt, touching it, handling it, until it was like an extension of his hand.

But the nights . . . ah, at night, when he stretched out on the bed, he thought only of Rachel, wondering if she would come to him again, remembering her warm softness beneath him and the sweet taste of her lips. She had left in the pre-dawn hours, after their lovemaking, no doubt embarrassed by what had passed between them. She had made no mention of returning. Grudgingly, he admitted he missed her, but there was no time to fret over her absence. There was only time to practice with the Colt and he did so from dawn til dark, hoping, in a far corner of his mind, that the long hours of practice would prove to be unnecessary and that, when healed, his right hand would be as good as ever even though he knew that such a miracle was virtually impossible.

Draw and fire. Draw and fire. At a leaf, a rock, a bottle, a tin can. Draw and fire. At a twig, a squirrel, a jar tossed into the air. Remembering, always remembering, the man who had crushed his hand. Always remembering the pain, the anger.

So the days passed, each one the same as the last. Practice with the Colt during the day; dream of Rachel at night.

Eventually, Tyree was satisfied that he could draw and fire the Colt with his left hand as proficiently as he had with his right. Then and only then did he remove the bandages from his right hand.

Face impassive as stone, he studied his hand as if it belonged to someone else. He watched the fingers move, stiff as old leather. Noted that the first three fingers were permanently deformed; that the skin on the back of his hand was fishbelly white, and badly scarred.

A muscle worked in his jaw when he discovered that he could not make a tight fist. He was standing there, staring at his ruined hand and remembering the face of each man responsible, when Rachel entered the cabin. One look at his face, at the hard set of his jaw and the angry look in his eye, told her clearly that his hand had not healed the way they had hoped it would, the way she had prayed it would.

"Tyree?"

He looked up slowly, surprised to find her there.

"I'm sorry, Tyree. I did the best I could. I . . . I feel like it's my fault."

"Well, it isn't," he said curtly. "Go on home."

"Is there anything I can do before I go?"

"No."

"Please let me help."

"Dammit, Rachel, I don't need your help, and I don't want your pity. Just get the hell out of here and leave me alone!"

Arms akimbo, Rachel glared up at him, a challenge rising in her vivid blue eyes. "Why don't you stop feeling sorry for yourself then?" she demanded crossly. "Just because you can't hold a gun in that hand doesn't mean your life is over."

"A gun!" Tyree snarled. "Shit, I can hardly hang onto a cup of coffee. You ever try saddling a bronc with one hand? Or tying a knot? Or shuffling a deck of cards?"

"My father can do all those things," Rachel replied quietly. "And he lost half an arm."

"You're right," Tyree admitted ruefully. "I am feeling sorry for myself. I guess I was hoping for a miracle." He laughed bitterly. "Imagine me, hoping for a miracle. I can't think of anyone who deserves one less."

"Let me fix you some lunch," Rachel coaxed. "I brought some roast beef and potato salad with me."

"You win. Let's eat."

Tyree sat down at the table while Rachel served him, staring glumly at his right hand while she sliced the meat and dished up the potato salad.

"Tyree?"

"Yeah?"

"Are you going to eat, or just sit there, brooding?"

"Sorry."

She tried not to stare at him as he endeavored to cut the thick slice of roast beef on his plate with a fork, wondering why she hadn't thought to slice it thin, like she did for her father. As it was, it had to be cut with a knife. And Tyree could not manage both knife and fork with one hand.

Thinking only to help, Rachel reached across the table to cut the meat for him.

It was a mistake. Growling an oath, Tyree hurled his fork against the far wall.

"You gonna feed me, too?" he rasped. And pushing away from the table, he unleashed his pent-up anger and frustration in a string of the most foul epithets Rachel had ever heard.

When he finished, he went to the window where he stood looking out, his hands shoved deep in his pockets.

"Tyree—"

"Dammit, Rachel, stop treating me like a kid."

"Then stop acting like one."

"Oh, hell, I'm not used to being waited on. I'm not used to having people do for me. I don't like it. Never have."

"I don't mind."

"I do."

"Tyree, why haven't you ever remarried?"

Tyree swung around to face her, his eyes mirroring his astonishment. "What?"

"You heard me. Why haven't you ever re-married?"

"Are you crazy? What girl in her right mind would marry a gunfighter?"

"I would," Rachel said, and it was a toss-up as to who was more surprised by her unexpected reply, Logan Tyree, or Rachel herself.

Tyree stared at her for several seconds, too stunned to speak. Marriage! Good Lord.

"You can't be serious?" he said, shaking his head.

"But I am."

The corner of Tyree's mouth twitched in a wry grin. "You think the love of a good

A Special Offer For Love Spell Romance Readers Only!

Get Two Free Romance Novels

An $11.48 Value!

Travel to exotic worlds
filled with passion and adventure—
without leaving your home!

**Plus, you'll save $5.00
every time you buy!**

Thrill to the most sensual, adventure-filled Romances on the market today...

FROM 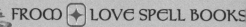 LOVE SPELL BOOKS

As a home subscriber to the Love Spell Romance Book Club, you'll enjoy the best in today's BRAND-NEW Time Travel, Futuristic, Legendary Lovers, Perfect Heroes and other genre romance fiction. For five years, Love Spell has brought you the award-winning, high-quality authors you know and love to read. Each Love Spell romance will sweep you away to a world of high adventure...and intimate romance. Discover for yourself all the passion and excitement millions of readers thrill to each and every month.

Save $5.00 Each Time You Buy!

Every other month, the Love Spell Romance Book Club brings you four brand-new titles from Love Spell Books. EACH PACKAGE WILL SAVE YOU AT LEAST $5.00 FROM THE BOOK-STORE PRICE! And you'll never miss a new title with our convenient home delivery service.

Here's how we do it: Each package will carry a FREE 10-DAY EXAMINATION privilege. At the end of that time, if you decide to keep your books, simply pay the low invoice price of $17.96, no shipping or handling charges added. HOME DELIVERY IS ALWAYS FREE. With today's top romance novels selling for $5.99 and higher, our price SAVES YOU AT LEAST $5.00 with each shipment.

AND YOUR FIRST TWO-BOOK SHIP-MENT IS TOTALLY FREE!

IT'S A BARGAIN YOU CAN'T BEAT! A SUPER $11.48 Value!

Love Spell ✦ A Division of Dorchester Publishing Co., Inc.

GET YOUR 2 FREE BOOKS NOW—AN $11.48 VALUE!

Mail the Free Book Certificate Today!

TWO FREE BOOKS

Free Books Certificate

YES! I want to subscribe to the Love Spell Romance Book Club. Please send me my 2 FREE BOOKS. Then every other month I'll receive the four newest Love Spell selections to Preview FREE for 10 days. If I decide to keep them, I will pay the Special Member's Only discounted price of just $4.49 each, a total of $17.96. This is a SAVINGS of at least $5.00 off the bookstore price. There are no shipping, handling, or other charges. There is no minimum number of books I must buy and I may cancel the program at any time. In any case, the 2 FREE BOOKS are mine to keep—A BIG $11.48 Value!

Offer valid only in the U.S.A.

Name _____

Address _____

City _____

State _____ Zip _____

Telephone _____

Signature _____

If under 18, Parent or Guardian must sign. Terms, prices and conditions subject to change. Subscription subject to acceptance. Leisure Books reserves the right to reject any order or cancel any subscription.

A $11.48 VALUE

Get Two Books Totally
F R E E —
An $11.48 Value!

▼ Tear Here and Mail Your FREE Book Card Today! ▼

PLEASE RUSH
MY TWO FREE
BOOKS TO ME
RIGHT AWAY!

Love Spell Romance Book Club
P.O. Box 6613
Edison, NJ 08818-6613

AFFIX
STAMP
HERE

woman will make me mend my evil ways?" he asked, amused.

"Don't make fun of me, Tyree."

"I'm not. I just can't believe you mean it. I thought you hated me. You've certainly said so often enough."

"I know, but it isn't you I hate. It's what you stand for."

"It's pretty much the same thing, don't you think?"

"No," Rachel argued softly. "It's not the same thing at all."

For once, Tyree had no quick retort and Rachel could not help smiling. It was the only time she had ever seen him at a loss for words.

Then his face closed against her and he said, flatly, "Go home, Rachel. You'll only get hurt if you stay."

"Why? Don't you care for me at all?"

"That's got nothing to do with it."

"That has everything to do with everything."

"Shit, Rachel, life's not that simple. In the next day or two, I'm gonna kill five men. And sooner or later, I'll probably have to kill Clint Wesley, too. How are you gonna feel about me then? And what about Wesley? I thought you were sweet on him."

"I thought so, too." Rachel dismissed the Marshal with a wave of her hand. "Tyree, come back to the ranch and stay with us. We need you. I need you."

"Dammit, honey, I'm no farmer."

The hand Rachel placed on Tyree's arm was soft and warm and trembling visibly. "Will you come home with me, Tyree?"

"Do you know what you're saying?" Tyree asked gently. "Do you know what you'd be getting? And what you'll be giving up?"

Rachel nodded slowly. Tyree would never be the kind of husband she had dreamed of when she was a young girl. He would never be completely content to live in a small town like Yellow Creek. He would never completely settle down. And though she did not like to think about it, she knew there was a strong possibility that he would tire of her in a year or two and ride out of her life. And yet . . .

She looked at the man standing before her. He was tall and dark. His face was hard, his amber eyes unfathomable. She knew, logically, that Clint would make a far better husband. He was honest, even-tempered, well-liked and respected in the community, a hard worker, a man with ambition and roots. He would make an excellent husband, a good father, a reliable provider. But it was Logan Tyree who made her blood sing with longing, Tyree who made her feel vibrant and alive, Tyree who had captured her heart and soul.

"Will you come with me, Tyree?" she asked again.

Tyree looked at Rachel, and knew he should refuse. He would never make her happy, never in a million years. He could never be the kind of man she wanted, the kind of man she deserved. And yet he could not resist the love shining bright and clear in her eyes, could not shatter the hope he read in her expression. Or deny that he wanted her.

"I'll come," he agreed. "But only after I've squared a few debts with the Slash W. Does that suit you?"

"Can't you let them go?"

"No."

Tears sparkled in Rachel's eyes as she begged, "Please let them go, Tyree. I can't abide the thought of any more killing."

"It's something I've got to do."

The closeness she had felt with him suddenly shattered, and she took her hand from his arm. "Why can't you just forget it?" she cried out, frustrated by his stubbornness. "Killing them won't make your hand whole again. Nothing will."

Anger flared deep in Tyree's amber eyes. There was hate there, too, and an implacable desire for revenge. And suddenly Rachel thought she knew what was driving him so relentlessly.

"It's your pride, isn't it?" she exclaimed incredulously. "That's why those five men have got to be killed."

"Shut up, Rachel."

But now she was angry, too, and she shouted, "I will not shut up! You're going after those men because they got the best of the great Logan Tyree in a dark alley!"

Tyree did not deny it, only said, stonily, "It's something I've got to do. If you can't live with it, I'll ride on."

"That's not fair and you know it."

"Fair!" Tyree held out his ruined hand and his expression turned ugly. "How can you look at what those bastards did and still talk to me about what's fair?"

"I suppose you'll have to kill Annabelle, too, seeing as how those men work for the Slash W."

"No. The beating was her idea and I could have lived with that. Hell, I've been whipped by experts. But breaking my hand, that was Larkin's idea. And he's going to pay for it."

The fight went out of Rachel then, leaving her drained and empty. "Will you come to me when it's over?"

"You still talkin' marriage?" Tyree asked gruffly.

"Yes."

Tyree stared at her for a full minute, his face inscrutable. Hell, maybe he could change. Maybe, with Rachel's help, he could settle down and become a respectable citizen. And maybe hell would freeze over, he mused wryly. But she was so lovely, so sweet, and perhaps she was his last chance for a decent life. He was almost tempted to forget about the Walsh riders, but he knew he would never rest until they were dead.

"I'll come," he said at last. "When it's over."

"I'll be waiting," Rachel murmured, and left the cabin without a backward glance.

Chapter 11

*J*ohn Halloran studied his daughter carefully as she prepared breakfast the following morning. Her eyes seemed red, puffy, as if she had spent the night crying. She was unusually quiet, preoccupied, her thoughts obviously worrisome.

"Rachel. Rachel?"

"Yes, Pa?"

"Is anything wrong?"

"No. Pa, I . . . I might be getting married soon."

"Oh?"

"Yes."

"You don't seem very happy about it," Halloran remarked.

"I am. Really."

Halloran grinned broadly. "So! Clint finally proposed. Well, I'll be damned."

"No, I . . . Pa, I asked Tyree to marry me."

"Tyree!"

Rachel nodded. "Would you mind? Having him for a son-in-law, I mean."

Halloran shook his head slowly. "No, not if it's what you want. Is that where you've—" Halloran coughed, not knowing exactly how to ask what he wanted to know.

"Yes. I've been meeting him out at the old Jorgensen place."

"So that's where he went to ground," Halloran mused. "I didn't think he'd run far. Not Tyree." Halloran chuckled. "Won't Larkin and his bunch be surprised when they learn they didn't scare him off after all."

Rachel nodded, tears welling in her eyes.

"What is it, honey?" Halloran asked. Reaching out, he laid his hand over hers and gave it a squeeze. "You can tell me."

"Tyree's planning to kill Larkin and the other men responsible for breaking his hand. I tried to talk him out of it, Pa, but he wouldn't listen. He's determined to make them pay for what they did."

Halloran nodded. "Can't say as I blame Tyree, daughter. It was an awful thing they did to him."

"I know, but . . . Oh, Pa, he's killed so many men. I can't stand the thought of more killing. When will it end?"

"Do you love Tyree?"

"Yes," Rachel answered fervently.

"You knew what he was when you asked him to marry you."

"Yes."

"You can't change him, Rachel. You'll either have to learn to live with what he is and hope he'll change on his own, or spend the rest of your life together being miserable. That, or give him up."

"I can't give him up, Pa. I love him so very much."

"I think he's a good man, honey. I think, deep inside, he's everything you want. Everything you need. If I didn't think so, I'd try to talk you out of marrying him." Halloran gave Rachel's hand another squeeze. "When's the big day?"

Rachel smiled through her tears. "I'm not sure. Tyree said he'd come for me when it was over."

Father and daughter looked at each other, neither voicing the thought that lurked in the backs of their minds. Five to one, the odds were. And no matter how good Tyree was, there was always a chance that he couldn't beat the odds.

The next few days were hard on Rachel. She didn't know when Tyree planned to make his move, didn't know how much longer he would practice with the Colt before he felt ready to take on Larkin and the others.

She filled her days with work, dusting, washing, ironing, mending, sweeping, rearranging the furniture, cleaning closets and cupboards, tidying up the attic, waxing and polishing. She pulled an old cookbook out and tried a dozen new recipes. She baked pies and cakes and cookies and bread until her father begged her to stop. She bought several yards of dress goods and began making herself a new wardrobe to please Tyree: a Sunday go-to-meeting dress of soft blue wool because Tyree liked her in blue; a day dress of green-sprigged muslin with a square neck and a wide white sash.

When chores and sewing and baking grew tiresome, she began to take long rides on Morgana. Often, she was tempted to ride out to the Jorgensen place to visit Tyree, but she never did. She had gone to him, offering her love, begging him to marry her. Now he must come to her.

The nights were the worst of all. Lying alone in her bed in the dark, she went over every word, every touch and warm embrace they had shared, remembering the strength of his arms, the magic of his kiss, the sound of his voice. Doubts crowded her mind. What if Tyree had changed his mind? What if he killed Larkin and the other Slash W men and then rode out of Yellow Creek, never to return? What if he were killed?

Doubts and dreams warred within her, but through it all she held fast to her love for

Tyree. She loved him and he loved her. She knew he did even if he had never said the words. She believed it with her whole heart. She had to believe it, or drown in despair.

Each day, as she combed out her hair before the mirror, she whispered, "Today. He'll come today."

And each night, she whispered, with a little less conviction, "Tomorrow. He'll come tomorrow for sure."

And then she cried herself to sleep.

Dawn, and the air was frosty cold. Tyree's breath produced a cloud of white vapor as he saddled the gray. He cussed mightily as he fumbled with the cinch, wondering, ruefully, if he would ever get the hang of doing things one-handed.

Swinging up into the saddle, he reined the stallion toward the Slash W, his face impassive, his mind closed to everything but the five men he intended to kill before the sun went down.

Willie McCoy left the Walsh ranch shortly after breakfast. Gigging his spotted pony into a lively trot, he headed for Yellow Creek. There was a girl in town, a very expensive girl, and he grinned with anticipation as he patted the roll of greenbacks in his jeans. Today he could afford to buy all Ginny's time, and that was just what he intended to do, even if it cost him every cent of the five hundred dollars he had earned for his part in roughing up Logan Tyree.

Willie frowned as he mulled over that particular job. Annabelle Walsh had promised equal shares for working over the gunman, but Larkin had doled out the money, taking the lion's share for himself and his sidekick, Rafe Hobbs. The others, Harris and Tolman, were good guns, but neither had the guts to argue with Larkin about the split. And neither did Willie McCoy. Better a live coward with a pocket full of money than a dead hero.

Lifting his paint pony to a lope, Willie put Gus Larkin and the others out of his mind and turned his thoughts back to Ginny, and the endless hours of pleasure he would find in her arms.

Tyree reached the Walsh spread just as the sun topped the distant mountains. White-faced cattle stirred at his passing, staring at him out of wild, suspicious eyes. A covey of quail burst from a clump of sagebrush, spooking the gray stallion. Tyree grinned as the stud tossed its head and danced sideways. Damn, but it was good to be alive.

Tyree covered ten miles before he spotted a lone rider off in the distance. Reining the gray to a halt, he dismounted in the cover of a low rise, waiting patiently for the rider to come within range.

Tyree grinned coldly as he recognized the youngest of the Walsh gunnies. Muttering,

"This must be my lucky day," he palmed the Colt, thumbed back the hammer, and stepped into the open.

"Hold it, cowboy," he called, and Willie McCoy pulled his horse to a sharp halt. The young gunman's face went white as he recognized the man behind the gun.

"Hi, kid," Tyree drawled. "Remember me?"

Willie McCoy was scared. Too scared to speak. His Adam's apple bobbed up and down, and then he nodded vigorously.

"Good," Tyree said flatly. "Get those hands up."

McCoy looked at his hands as if he had never seen them before.

"Get 'em up!" Tyree snapped.

Slowly, as if they weighed a great deal, Willie McCoy raised his hands above his head. He screamed with sudden pain as Tyree fired two quick shots, sending a bullet through each of the youngster's palms.

"Tell your friends I'll be waiting for them at Bowsher's," Tyree said to the sobbing youth. Holstering his Colt, he stepped into the saddle and rode toward Yellow Creek.

Tyree left the gray tethered at the rail of Bowsher's Saloon. Inside, he ordered a bottle of rye, carried it to his usual table in the back of the room where he could keep one eye on the door and his back to the wall.

Thoughts of Rachel crowded his mind.

Whatever had possessed him to agree to marry her? Did she really think he could give up drifting and settle down? Did he? Tyree stared at the pale amber whiskey in his glass as, unbidden, came the memory of the life he had shared with Red Leaf. Theirs had been a good marriage, filled with laughter and harmony. He had liked the feeling of belonging to someone, of having someone who belonged only to him. But that had been long ago. He was not the same man now that he had been then.

He emptied the glass in a single swallow, absently poured another drink. He had not shared his life with anyone else since Red Leaf's death. He had shut out the world, and the people in it. Perhaps, with Rachel, he could recapture the magic he and Red Leaf had shared . . .

His melancholy thoughts were interrupted as Flat-Nose Beverly glided over to his table. She looked truly elegant this day, with her silver-white hair piled atop her head and her thin figure clad in a blood-red gown.

"Afternoon, Tyree," she murmured.

"Flat-Nose."

She gave him a ghost of a smile. "Be careful."

Tyree nodded. A moment later, Gus Larkin and his men pushed their way into the saloon.

Tyree stood up, all thoughts of Rachel forgotten. There was no past now, and no future. There was only this moment. Hand hovering over the butt of his gun, he called to Annabelle's men.

Three wranglers standing at the bar scrambled for cover at Tyree's warning call, tripping over each other and their own feet in their haste to get out of the line of fire.

Kelly swore softly as the trouble he had been expecting ever since the tall gunman first entered his place finally arrived. The barkeep crossed himself as he ducked behind the safety of the solid mahogany bar.

The four Walsh gunmen whirled around as if pulled by the same string. Gus Larkin was fast. His gun was in his hand and seeking a target when Tyree's bullet found him. The heavy .45 caliber slug smashed into the side of Larkin's head and exited amid a red tide of blood and brain tissue.

Tyree's second shot took out the man called Rafe.

Satisfied he had killed the two men he wanted most, Tyree dropped to the floor, rolling to the left and then to the right as he hosed off the remaining rounds in his gun, oblivious to the bullets whizzing around his head like angry hornets.

He swore softly as a chunk of flying lead nicked his arm, gouging a deep furrow in his right shoulder.

In less than a minute, four men were dead.

Rising to his feet, Tyree reloaded the Colt and walked out of the saloon. Swinging into the saddle, he reined the gray out of town toward the Slash W Ranch.

The Walsh spread was built around a court-yard, Spanish-style. Flowers bloomed in colorful clay pots and hanging baskets. A dozen cages housed twice that many canaries and their cheerful trilling filled the air. A wide veranda circled the house, offering shade from the fierce desert sun.

It was a nice-looking spread. The outbuildings gleamed with a fresh coat of whitewash; the corrals were snug and well-built, filled with blooded horses and a pair of Texas longhorns.

A fat Mexican woman clad in a severe black bombazine dress answered Tyree's knock.

"Where's your mistress?" Tyree demanded brusquely.

"Taking a siesta," the woman replied in stilted English. "Go away."

"You go get her, pronto, or I will," Tyree said firmly. "You savvy?"

"Si, si," the woman answered quickly, and scurried toward the back of the house.

Stepping inside, Tyree closed the door behind him, stood in the entry hall examining his surroundings. The hallway was dark, hung with several paintings of the desert and a sunset. The parlor beyond was a large, high-ceilinged room. Colorful rugs covered the floor, a few smaller ones, Navajo in design, decorated the walls. A sofa and two large chairs upholstered in dark leather were grouped around a huge stone fireplace. Several oil lamps hung from the ceiling. A life-sized statue of St. Francis stood in one corner, surrounded by lacy ferns and flowering plants. A large mirror hung over the fireplace. A shelf housed a small display of Indian pottery.

Annabelle Walsh entered the room on silent feet. She was tall for a woman, dressed in a simple blue cotton skirt and an off-the-shoulder white blouse which was decorated with tiny blue and yellow flowers. Her hair was rich and red and fell in soft waves around her face and over her shoulders.

She halted six feet away from Tyree, her bright green eyes running over him, appraising him in much the same way a man judged a horse he was thinking of trying.

"You must be Logan Tyree." Her voice was deep, husky, with a sensual quality that kindled a quick desire in Tyree's loins.

He nodded curtly. "And you must be Annabelle Walsh."

"Yes. Would you care for a drink? Food?" She glanced pointedly at the blood caked on his shoulder. "Bandages, perhaps?"

Tyree shook his head. Annabelle Walsh was the most blatantly beautiful woman he had ever seen. Her skin was the color of rich cream, her mouth pouting and red. Full breasts pushed impudently against the thin fabric of her blouse, and he had a crazy urge to tear away the flimsy material that covered her voluptuous breasts and see if they were real.

A smile of amusement played across Annabelle's lips as she read Tyree's thoughts —thoughts she had seen reflected in the eyes of every man she had ever met.

"Why have you come here?" Annabelle asked.

"To tell you not to send any more of your men after me. And to lay off the Lazy H."

"I'm sure I don't know what you're talking about," she replied coolly.

"Then I'll spell it out for you. I killed four of your gunmen less than an hour ago. And if one more cow turns up missing or dead on the Lazy H, I'll come after you."

"The way you came after my brother?"

"Now I don't know what you're talking about," Tyree lied smoothly. "Just remember what I said. If anything suspicious happens out at the Lazy H after today, if one cow gets sick or dies, I'll come after you. And I never miss."

It was not an idle threat, Annabelle was sure of that. He had severely wounded Willie McCoy, now he admitted to killing four of her best men. No doubt he had killed Job, too. Yes, she mused, Logan Tyree was an accomplished killer. He would not hesitate to kill a woman.

Giving her head an impatient toss,

Annabelle smiled a secret smile. Perhaps, instead of fighting against Tyree, she should make him an ally. If she could hire his gun, Halloran's remaining few men would desert the Lazy H like rats fleeing a sinking ship. And if he would not succumb to the lure of money, there were always other enticements. He was interested in her body. Even now he was having trouble keeping his eyes from her breasts and hips. Always, men had looked at her as if she were a melon ripe for the harvest. She had offered herself to other men when they possessed something she desired. And they had always yielded to her charms. Logan Tyree would be no different. For all his arrogance, she was certain he would do as she wished if she made him the right offer.

"Is that all you have to say?" Annabelle inquired coldly.

"I reckon that covers it."

"Very well. Good day, Mr. Tyree."

With some amusement, Tyree realized he had been dismissed. But he made no move to leave the room, and neither did Annabelle Walsh.

Tyree stared openly at the lush figure clad in the blue skirt and virginal white blouse. But there was nothing virginal about Annabelle, he mused. She was a woman who had known many men. The knowledge was bright in her taunting green eyes, and in the pouting smile that curved her full red lips.

But more than that, it rose from her like the musky scent of a mare in heat, alerting any stallion within range.

Unruffled by his steady gaze, Annabelle gestured at Tyree's wounded shoulder. "You really should have that taken care of."

"Yeah."

"I have some salve and bandages in my room."

"Fine."

Annabelle turned on her heel and led the way through the parlor and down a long hall to her bedroom, secure in the knowledge that Tyree would follow her. She smiled smugly as she heard his footsteps start after her. It was always so easy.

Annabelle's room was large and smelled of powder and perfume. A four-poster bed dominated the room. Heavy red velvet draperies were drawn across the windows, shutting out the late afternoon sunlight. A tall rosewood chest of drawers took up most of one wall. A small commode held a pitcher of water and a basin. There was a rosewood armoire, a full-length mirror, a painting of a wild stallion chasing a herd of mustangs hung on one wall.

Tyree removed his shirt and sat on the edge of the bed, his hand idly toying with the soft red velvet spread while Annabelle bandaged his shoulder. He eyed her expectantly, waiting for her to make the next move.

He did not have long to wait.

"I want you to work for me, Tyree," she

murmured. Her fingers stroked his bare arm, caressing the muscles bulging there.

"I already said 'no' once, remember? It cost me a good right hand."

"Change your mind." Annabelle's fingers trailed suggestively down his arm to rest on his thigh. "I'll pay you whatever you ask, within reason."

"Anything?" His hungry eyes traveled to the twin mounds of her breasts, and then to her inviting red lips, which were moist and slightly parted.

Annabelle laughed softly as Tyree's amber eyes devoured her. Men! They were all alike. Always wanting just one thing from a woman.

"I was thinking of a thousand dollars a month," Annabelle said.

"That's a lot of money. What do you want in return?"

"Just your name, really. Once Halloran's men find out you're riding for the Slash W, they'll hightail it out of the country. No one in his right mind will work for the old man once they know your gun is siding me. Halloran will be forced to sell out and when he does, I'll give you a five thousand dollar bonus and you'll be free to go." The tone of her voice, the fire smouldering in her vibrant emerald eyes, assured Tyree he would not want to leave her. Ever.

Tyree whistled softly. "Five grand. That's a hefty sum."

"Yes." She looked up at him through the

dark fringe of her lashes, her eyes bright, her mouth forming a smile because it had been so easy.

"A hefty sum," Tyree repeated. "But I don't need the money. Thanks, anyway."

Annabelle sucked in a deep breath that caused her ample breasts to strain against the thin cotton cloth that held them bound. Her eyes glowed like green fire as she purred, "Perhaps I could offer you something else?"

"Yeah?" Tyree asked, suppressing a knowing grin. "What did you have in mind?"

Annabelle pressed herself against Tyree. "Do I have to say it?"

Tyree's mouth turned down, and his voice was cruelly mocking as he said, "You worth five grand? Most whores don't come that high."

He had expected her to get angry, but she only smiled up at him. "I'm worth much, much more, cowboy," she boasted. "But you'll never know unless you agree to work for me, starting today."

Tyree's laugh was humorless. "That right? What's to stop me from taking you here and now?"

"Nothing," Annabelle said with a small shrug of her creamy shoulders. "But a gift freely given is much more satisfying than one taken by force."

"You think so? I've always found the victory sweeter when the battle is hard fought."

Annabelle was sitting beside him, her leg

pressed against his, her hand gently kneading the muscle in his thigh. At his words, she flounced over onto her stomach, leaving him to study her smooth back and softly rounded buttocks.

Too late, Tyree realized it was a ruse. In a quick pantherish movement, Annabelle delved under the nearest bed pillow and withdrew a silver-plated derringer. With a triumphant smirk, she thrust the cocked weapon into Tyree's groin.

"No man takes me against my will," she hissed, all ice where she had once been fire. "No man! We do things my way, or not at all."

"Suits me," Tyree said easily. "Now put that gun away before I break your arm."

Annabelle swallowed a triumphant smile as she slipped the gun back into its hiding place beneath the pillow. Men. They were so pliable, so easily led. Even Tyree, for all his rough talk, was willing to bend to her will just for the promise of bedding her.

His slap came as a shock, doubly so because she had been so certain of another easy victory. The blow brought quick tears of pain to her eyes, and a string of vituperative words to her lips as she reached for the derringer again, but Tyree knew what to expect this time and his long arm slid under the pillow first. With lazy grace, he unloaded the deadly little pistol and tossed the shells on the floor.

"Next time you try that, I'll kill you," he remarked, his tone easy and calm, as if he were commenting on something trivial, like the weather or the price of wool.

"How dare you strike me!" Annabelle shouted angrily. "Leave my house at once!"

"I'll be going all right," Tyree assured her. "But not until I've had a taste of what you've been offering ever since I walked through the door."

"You wouldn't dare!"

Tyree's insolent smile assured her that he would.

Grabbing a handful of her hair, he forced her back on the bed, his mouth closing over hers, his teeth bruising her lips. It was a brutal kiss, and Annabelle kicked and bucked beneath him, her fists pummeling his back in useless fury.

He did not release her, only caught her hands in his, rendering her helpless. He kissed her long and hard, until it was difficult for her to breathe, until she stopped struggling and lay passive beneath him.

Abruptly, she changed tactics and began to arch against him, pressing her breasts against his chest, twining her long legs around his waist, urging him to possess her fully. Her pulse began to race as Tyree's kiss became more intimate. He was a big man, so much more masculine than the Kansas City railroad man she had conned out of several thousand dollars. So much more handsome than the rotund Chicago banker who had wined her and dined her and offered to buy her a fur coat for just an hour of her favors.

Annabelle smiled smugly as Tyree's hand slid along her breast. She would have to be careful in her handling of Logan Tyree. He was a dangerous man and not one to be trifled with. She had underestimated him, she mused, but she would not make that mistake again. No man had ever bested her. And Logan Tyree would soon learn to toe the mark, just like all the others.

Watching her, Tyree thought Annabelle looked like a spoiled kitten plotting mischief. He grinned wryly as he stood up.

Annabelle frowned. "Where are you going?"

"I'm leaving."

"Leaving?"

"You're not worth five grand," he said with a shrug. "Sorry."

Her angry screams followed him out of the house and into the dusk.

Chapter 12

Clint Wesley sat in his office, a sour expression on his handsome young face. Word of Tyree's shoot-out with the four Walsh riders was the talk of the town. Tyree's reputation, which was already formidable, was growing with each retelling of the tale. Everyone in Yellow Creek was yammering for Tyree's scalp, but there wasn't one man in the whole damn town willing to pin on a deputy's badge and share the risk in bringing him in. And Clint did not have the guts to take him on alone. It was as simple as that. None of the townspeople really blamed the Marshal for his reluctance, but they rode him hard just the same. After all, he was the law. It was his job, not theirs.

Clint ran a hand over his eyes, dragged it across his jaw and down his neck. It had always been such an easy job, keeping the peace in Yellow Creek. At least until Logan Tyree rode into town. Sure, there had been some trouble between the Lazy H and the Slash W. Halloran's men had been killed, cattle stolen. John Halloran had sworn that Job Walsh was responsible for everything, but there had never been any real proof that Walsh's men were gunning the Halloran cowhands. Not any proof that would stand up in a court of law. Of course, none of that mattered now that Walsh was dead and buried. But Tyree . . . damn! The man had killed four men in Bowsher's Saloon in front of a score of witnesses. Everyone said Tyree had bushwhacked Walsh, too, but once again, there was no proof.

What a mess! Fingering his badge, Clint considered quitting and riding on. Let someone else tackle Logan Tyree. Let someone else try and bring the gunfighter in. The town wasn't paying him enough to take on a professional killer like Tyree.

With his mind made up, Wesley unpinned the badge from his vest. The star felt heavy in his hand. Staring at it, he thought of Rachel. He would never see her again if he rode out of town with his tail tucked between his legs. Thirty bucks a month wasn't worth getting killed over, but Rachel . . . that was a different story. She was every man's ideal: beautiful, soft-spoken, with a promise of heaven in her sky-blue eyes and a radiant smile on her sweet red lips. Rachel. He would never be able to face her again if he backed down from doing a job that was rightly his.

Frowning thoughtfully, Clint unholstered his gun and laid it on the desk. Tyree hadn't been born with a gun in his hand. He had to learn to draw and fire just like everybody else. No doubt it had taken hours of practice. Anybody could quick-draw a Colt if he practiced hard enough.

Face grim with determination, Clint pinned his badge to his vest where it belonged. Then, with a sigh of determination, he picked up his gun and went out behind the jailhouse to begin practicing his draw . . .

Chapter 13

*T*yree rose with the sun. Dressing, he gathered his gear together and stowed it in his warbag. Outside, he paused briefly on the front porch of the old Jorgensen place to watch the sun climb over the distant mountains. It was a sight he never tired of, though few people who knew him would have thought him capable of appreciating anything as ordinary as a sunrise.

Settling his hat on his head, he walked down to the corral. Minutes later, he was riding toward the Lazy H. He passed several bunches of cattle, all wearing brands that wouldn't bear close inspection, and he wondered how many of the cattle wearing the Walsh brand belonged to the Lazy H. It seemed Annabelle was as big a crook as her brother had been.

Annabelle. Tyree grinned ruefully. Once, he would have taken what she had offered without a qualm. But Rachel's sweet lovemaking had ruined him for all other women. Annabelle was beautiful in face and form, and yet she had left him cold and unmoved. Her kisses had been empty, her promises hollow.

Lifting the stallion into an easy lope, Tyree put everything from his mind, losing himself in the smooth rocking motion of the gray, and in the pastoral beauty of the wild land, savoring the wondrous sense of freedom and well-being he always experienced when riding alone across the open prairie.

He rode for a long time, stopping once to watch a handful of Indians on the move. They were heading south to spend the coming winter in Mexico. They were a sorry sight, the warriors mounted on scrawny, slat-sided ponies, the women walking behind the men, their long cotton skirts dragging in the dust. A sorry sight, indeed. Even the dogs looked beat. And yet, for all that, Tyree felt a sudden urge to ride after them, to forget the complicated ways of the white man and go back to the blanket.

The urge to follow them was strong, but he had promised Rachel he would return to her, and his word was about the only honorable thing he had left. It would not be easy, settling down, living summer and winter under the same roof, loving only one woman, but what the hell, Rachel wanted him, and it was for sure no one else did. He thought briefly of Annabelle, but she did not want Tyree, the man. Just his gun.

Turning north, the land changed as the flat unbroken ground gradually gave way to gently rolling hills and thick stands of timber. A tall sandstone spire loomed in the distance, pointing like a finger toward heaven. A lone eagle soared overhead, wheeling and diving in an endless search for prey.

Riding on, Tyree passed a line shack, long unused judging by the broken windows and the sagging front door.

And then he was on Halloran ground. As he rode toward the ranch, he could readily understand why Job Walsh had coveted the Lazy H, and why Annabelle was trying to get her hands on it now. There was plenty of good grass, water all year round.

The sun was high in the sky when he drew the gray to a halt beside a quiet stream that flowed in the valley between two low hills. Dismounting, he stripped the rigging from the stallion; then, placing his gun within easy reach, he shucked his clothing and stepped into the chill water. Squatting on his heels in the shallow stream, he rinsed away the dust of the trail. Later, feeling relaxed and refreshed, he stretched out under a leafy cottonwood and took a nap.

The sky was aflame with color when he

rode into the Halloran yard. He spent twenty minutes currying the gray before going up to the house. Tossing his hat on the rack inside the front door, he headed for the kitchen, expecting to find Rachel stirring up some supper.

Instead, he found John Halloran hunched over the kitchen table, staring bleakly into a cup of cold black coffee.

"What's going on?" Tyree asked, standing hipshot in the doorway. "Where's Rachel?"

Halloran did not look up. "I don't know," he said heavily. "She rode out early this morning. Her horse came back three hours ago. Candido and the men are out looking for her now—"

Tyree did not wait for any further explanations. Grabbing his hat, he ran down to the corral, whistled for the gray. He did not waste time with a saddle, merely threw a hackamore over the stud's head and vaulted onto its bare back. A sharp kick sent the mustang thundering out of the yard, hellbent for the Slash W.

Annabelle was waiting for him in the parlor, coolly sipping a glass of red wine. Two mean-looking Yaqui cowboys stood off to one side, their arms crossed over their chests. A third vaquero stood behind Annabelle's chair, a shotgun cradled in his burly arms.

"Why, Mr. Tyree," Annabelle purred as he stomped into the room. "How nice of you to drop by so soon after your last . . . visit."

"Cut the crap!" Tyree said tersely. "Where's Rachel?"

"Quite safe, for now." Annabelle gestured at the chair beside her. "Won't you sit down?"

"Where is she?" Tyree repeated through clenched teeth.

"Keeping company with a few of my men. As I said, she's quite safe. For now. Whether she stays that way depends entirely on you."

"I'm listening."

"Rachel and I had a rather interesting little talk this afternoon," Annabelle remarked in a conspiratorial tone. "As you know, I've been rather curious to know who killed my brother, and after a little, ah, persuasion, Miss Halloran was kind enough to tell me what I wanted to know."

Tyree's face remained expressionless, but he felt his muscles begin to grow tense. His left hand curled into a tight fist. "That so?"

"Yes." Annabelle leaned forward, her eyes bright. "Can you guess who she named as Job's murderer?"

"No. Who?"

"You, Mr. Tyree?"

He did not have to turn around to know that the two Yaqui cowboys had drawn their guns. "Oh yeah?"

"Yes. I would like to hear it from your own mouth, if you don't mind."

"Okay, I killed him." Tyree felt the hair raise along the back of his neck as he waited for Annabelle's men to cut him down.

"Why did you kill my brother?" Annabelle's eyes bored into Tyree's, hard and cold and ruthless.

"What the hell difference does it make now?" Tyree asked impatiently. He heard one of the Yaquis take a step forward and his back grew rigid as he waited for a bullet to smash into him.

"I want to know," Annabelle said.

"I did it as a favor to Halloran for saving my life."

"Hogwash! You've never done anybody a favor in your whole life." Annabelle looked at him shrewdly. "Halloran paid you, didn't he?" she demanded. "He paid you to kill my brother!" She stamped her foot angrily when Tyree did not answer. "Tell me, Tyree, or you'll never see Rachel Halloran alive again."

"She's nothing to me," Tyree said with a shrug. But his insides were coiled tight as bedsprings. If anything happened to Rachel, Annabelle Walsh would pay, and pay dearly.

"My men will be glad to hear that," Annabelle remarked, smiling smugly. "All twelve of them."

The implication was all too clear, Tyree mused. Either he told Annabelle what she wanted to know, or Annabelle would turn her men loose on Rachel.

"You win," Tyree conceded gruffly. "Old man Halloran paid me five hundred dollars to get your brother off his back. I did it the only way I know."

Annabelle nodded as she sat back in her chair. "Yes, I thought as much."

"What now?" Tyree asked dispassionately. "A quick bullet in the back?"

"Of course not," Annabelle said, laughing softly. "I made you an offer last night. One that you rudely refused." She pulled a piece of paper from her skirt pocket. "I still want you to work for me, Tyree. And I always get what I want."

Tyree eyed the paper suspiciously. "That so?"

"Yes. This is a confession stating that you killed my brother. I would advise you to sign it."

"And if I refuse?"

"Miss Halloran will wind up in the river. Dead, of course."

"Of course," Tyree repeated dryly. "And if I sign?"

"I'll lock this up in a safe place. You'll come to work for me, and we'll forget all this unpleasantness ever happened." Rising, she placed her wineglass on a low table. Moving toward Tyree, she placed her hand on his shoulder, let it slide suggestively down his arm, secretly reveling in the taut muscles coiled beneath her fingertips. "Don't be stubborn, Tyree," she crooned. "We'll be good together. And if it will make you happy, I'll even let Halloran keep his ranch. All but the southeast section that borders on my back pasture. That's fair, isn't it?"

"It's blackmail, is what it is," Tyree muttered.

"Surely working for me would be better than seeing that poor old man wind up in jail as an accessory to murder? And infinitely better than hanging."

It was in Tyree's mind to tell Annabelle Walsh to go to hell. But John Halloran had done him a favor, and he couldn't ride out of Yellow Creek and leave the old man to face Annabelle's ruthless greed alone. And then there was Rachel. The thought of Annabelle's men, of any man, touching her made his blood run cold.

And what the hell, he mused. He was better suited to hiring out his gun to a woman like Annabelle Walsh than trying to settle down. A little voice in the back of his mind chided that he was taking the coward's way out, but he refused to listen. He had known all along he was making a mistake by promising to marry Rachel. He would never make her happy, never in a million years.

And so he said, "Okay, Annabelle, you win. I'll sign your confession. But only if you draft a new one that leaves Halloran's name out of it completely."

"All right," Annabelle said agreeably. "I don't see any reason to tell Rachel or her father about our bargain, do you?"

"No."

"Good. Then it's all settled."

"Just one more thing. If anything happens

to Rachel or her old man, I'll come after you, confession or no confession. You remember that."

"I'll remember. Nacho, bring more wine. This is an occasion for celebrating."

Rachel's tears had long since dried up, but the fear remained, tying her stomach in knots, making it difficult to swallow, to think clearly.

Hours had passed since Annabelle's men had brought her to this run-down cabin. Hours that seemed like days. She kept her eyes closed, not wanting to see the faces of the men leering at her. They had stripped her down to her chemise and petticoat, and she could feel their eyes on her breasts, barely concealed beneath her lacy chemise. Occasionally, a man ran his hand over her leg or through her hair, sometimes they made crude remarks about her anatomy.

She had never known such paralyzing fear, had never felt so helpless and alone. Somehow, the Indians at Sunset Canyon had not seemed so threatening. They had been savages and had acted as such. But these were white men, most of them, civilized men. Men she had seen in town.

She shivered, her fear making her cold. Dared she ask for a blanket? She opened her eyes and quickly closed them again. It was eerie, the way the men just sat there, staring at her.

She jumped as the cabin door swung open,

gave a small cry of joy when she saw Tyree outlined against the darkening sky. She had never been so glad to see anybody in her life.

Tyree swore softly as he stepped into the dingy cabin and closed the door behind him. Rachel was lying on a filthy mattress, her wrists and ankles tied to the rusty bed frame. A grimy red kerchief was tied over her mouth. Her left eye was swollen and discolored; her right cheek was badly bruised, as if someone had hit her, hard.

He swore again. Seeing Rachel bound and gagged stirred him in a way he did not like. Scowling blackly, he tore his gaze from Rachel's violently trembling body and glanced around the room. Annabelle had not been bluffing. There were twelve men present, and a more disreputable-looking bunch would have been hard to find. Any one of them looked capable of raping Rachel until she was unconscious, and then slitting her throat without a qualm.

Annabelle's men expressed no surprise at seeing Tyree, and he felt a quick surge of anger. She had been very sure of him, damn her.

He said the password Annabelle had given him and the Slash W riders filed out of the shack, grousing a little because Tyree had arrived and spoiled their fun.

When the last Walsh gunman was gone, Tyree cut the ropes binding Rachel's hands and feet and removed the gag from her mouth.

Embarrassed by her scant attire, Rachel crossed her arms over her breasts. "Tyree—" It was a plea and a prayer combined, the way she whispered his name.

"You all right?" he asked.

Rachel nodded wordlessly, flushing scarlet as Tyree's eyes moved over her exposed flesh.

"Good," he said curtly. "Get dressed."

"She knows," Rachel said, reaching for her dress. "Annabelle knows you killed her brother."

"It's all right."

"I had to tell her," Rachel said in a small voice. Her brilliant blue eyes pleaded for Tyree's understanding and forgiveness. "She said she would let her men amuse themselves with me if I didn't tell her what she wanted to know. At first, I thought she was just trying to scare me. But then she brought me out here." Rachel's words came faster and faster as she relived the horror of the past few hours. "Her men passed me back and forth, kissing me, making remarks about . . . about . . . Oh, Tyree, it was awful! And then, when I still wouldn't tell her anything, she told one of the men to tie me to the bed. When he started to take off his pants, I knew she wasn't bluffing. Tyree, she said she would let all twelve of her men have me, and I believed her. I had to tell her. I was so afraid!"

"It's all right, Rachel," Tyree assured her. With a sigh, he took her in his arms and held her while she cried, thinking all the while that a good hiding with a bullwhip would benefit Annabelle Walsh immensely, though it would be a sin to permanently mar that exquisitely sculpted alabaster body.

"Come on," Tyree coaxed when Rachel's tears subsided. "We'd better get you home. Your old man is worried sick."

Something in his tone made Rachel's heart go cold. "You're not coming with me, are you, Tyree?"

"No."

"Why not? What's happened to change your mind?"

"Annabelle made me a better offer," Tyree said flatly. He winced at the hurt rising in Rachel's eyes. Damn! He had never meant to hurt her, never meant to get so deeply involved. He knew now it had been a mistake to promise to marry her. He was too old to hang up his gun, too set in his ways to start a new life. "Let's go."

Rachel followed Tyree meekly out of the shack, climbed stiffly into the saddle of the horse he had brought for her to ride. She stared straight ahead as they made their way through the dark night, her mind in turmoil. Tyree, too, was staring into the darkness and Rachel felt her heart melt with longing as she studied his swarthy profile. *What happened,* she wanted to cry. *Why have you changed your mind?* But her pride kept her tongue mute and the silence between them grew thick and impenetrable.

Tyree reined the gray to a halt under the high double arch that marked the beginning of the Halloran ranch yard. "Tell your old man the Walsh riders won't be bothering him any more."

Rachel looked at Tyree askance, one delicate brow rising like a butterfly in flight.

"And tell him I'll be over one day soon to get his signature on a bill of sale deeding your southeast section to Annabelle."

"So that's the way it is," Rachel said dully. "You're working for her now."

"Yeah."

It was too much for Rachel to absorb: the kidnapping, the awful hours in the shack with Annabelle's men, and now Tyree talking to her in a cold, impersonal tone, as if she were a stranger.

With a curt nod, Rachel slammed her heels into her mount's flanks and galloped down the tree-lined road toward home and the solid comfort of her father's arms.

Chapter 14

Life was easy on the Walsh spread. Two dozen Mexican vaqueros handled all the ranch work, while a handful of house servants waited on Annabelle and her hired guns.

As was his wont, Tyree kept to himself, ignoring the other gunmen whenever possible. But Annabelle could not be ignored. She was as bold and beautiful as a crimson flower in a patch of dry weeds.

She appointed Tyree as her personal bodyguard and insisted he sleep in the main house in the bedroom that adjoined her own. She dressed always in rich vibrant colors that accentuated her flawless complexion and complimented her luxurious red hair and emerald eyes. She rarely wore dresses, preferring tight pants and low-cut silk blouses that outlined the generous curve of her hips and the proud thrust of her breasts. Tyree often thought she was wasting her time on a ranch when her true talents could be put to better use in the rooms above Bowsher's Saloon.

Annabelle ruled the Slash W like a queen, granting favors when she was pleased, meting out quick and severe punishment when she was offended. And she was easily offended. The servants were quick to obey her slightest wish, wary of arousing her fiery temper.

She was riding high, Tyree thought sardonically. Mistress of all she surveyed and loving every minute of it. She certainly enjoyed bossing him around, there was no doubt about that. And Tyree let her get away with it because it amused him, for the moment, to let Annabelle think she held the upper hand.

She made no secret of the fact that she found Tyree tremendously desirable. Time and again she came to his bedroom, her voluptuous form barely concealed in some flimsy gown that accentuated every curve. Often, she sat on the edge of his bed, her hand boldly stroking his thigh.

Some nights, when he was lying alone in the dark and Annabelle came to him, he was tempted. Sorely tempted. Annabelle was beautiful, and she was more than willing to ease the ache in his loins, but he could not bring himself to make love to Annabelle

Walsh, not with the memory of Rachel's sweetness so fresh in his mind.

Rachel. He missed her more than he cared to admit. She was always in his thoughts. He missed seeing her every day, missed the sound of her voice, the warmth of her smile.

As the days passed, it grew harder and harder to put Annabelle off. She was a comely wench when she was getting her own way, all seductive smiles and tempting softness. So filled with pride and arrogance she never realized Tyree was humoring her because it suited him at the moment. Tyree had never thought of himself as a coward, but the truth was, the idea of marrying Rachel scared him to death. It had seemed easier to give in to Annabelle's demands, to let Rachel believe he found Annabelle more enticing, than to admit he had cold feet. For now, it amused him to placate Annabelle, to let her think he was cowed by her threat to turn him in for killing her brother. Hell, he was already wanted for murder in Kansas and Texas, and they could only hang him once. For now, he would play Annabelle's game and when he tired of her tricks, he would move on.

Annabelle wielded all her charms the night Joaquin Montoya came to call. Montoya was an outlaw who traded in human flesh, kidnapping men, women, and children and selling them into slavery south of the border. The women were sold to brothels, the men and children were sold to the mines. No one was safe from Montoya's grasping hand, and he sold those of his own blood as quickly as gringos.

Annabelle introduced Tyree to Montoya, and the two men shook hands. They disliked each other immediately.

Somehow, Tyree was not surprised to find that Annabelle and Montoya were well-acquainted. They talked amiably all through dinner about people and places they had known in the past. Annabelle smiled at Montoya often, frequently finding an excuse to touch his arm, his shoulder, his hand. Montoya paid her several compliments, his dark eyes praising her beauty.

Tyree remained silent through most of the meal, amused by the whole thing. He was not surprised, or jealous, when Montoya followed Annabelle to bed. Only relieved that she would not be pestering him.

Montoya left early the following morning, and Tyree was glad to see him go.

As the days passed, the other gunslicks in Annabelle's employ became increasingly jealous of Tyree's relationship with the boss, but that was their problem, not his, and Tyree went his own way, unperturbed by their envious glances and snide remarks. If they wanted to believe he was sleeping with Annabelle, it was no skin off his ass.

During those first few weeks in Annabelle's employ, the hardest thing Tyree had to do was face Rachel. He had hurt her deeply, and he was sorry. But far better to cause her a little heartache now than marry her and subject her to a lifetime of regret.

Rachel was sitting on the front porch darning a pair of her old man's socks the morning Tyree rode over to get Halloran's signature on a Bill of Sale. She looked as fresh as a spring flower, what with her hair shining like liquid gold and her skin glowing soft and smooth. Looking at her, he wondered how he had ever thought Annabelle Walsh remotely attractive.

Tyree reined the gray to a halt near the porch steps. "Mornin', Rachel," he said quietly. "Is your old man home?"

"He's inside," Rachel answered coldly. She rose to her feet, her fingers digging into her palms. Why did her heart lurch with such longing at the mere sight of him? She yearned to run to him, to throw her arms around his neck and pour out her heart, to beg him to love her as she loved him. But pride stilled her tongue and stiffened her spine. "I'll get him."

She did not invite Tyree into the house, and he did not dismount.

John Halloran came out of the house alone. Pen in hand, he took the deed from Tyree, quickly signed his name to the paper that gave Annabelle Walsh title to a section of land long coveted by the Slash W.

"How long before she takes the rest of the place?" Halloran asked bitterly.

"She won't."

Halloran laughed hollowly as he thrust the deed at Tyree. "No? Who's gonna stop her? You?"

"If I have to," Tyree replied calmly. "So long, Halloran."

From inside the house, Rachel watched Tyree ride out of the yard. For a moment, she tried to fight back the tears welling in her eyes. Then, with a sob, she sank down in a chair and let the tears flow. It felt good to cry, good to release the hurt she had been carrying within her heart.

How foolish she had been to think Tyree would change; to think he would hang up his gun and become a rancher. She had been kidding herself all along. Maybe he was too old to change. Maybe he had never cared for her at all. The thought made the tears come faster, blurring her vision, making her eyes red and swollen, her throat sore.

She cried until she was empty inside, but the heartache remained and she knew she would love Logan Tyree as long as she lived.

Tyree had been in Annabelle's employ about a month when she decided it was time he earned his keep.

"There's a squatter out near Coyote Butte," she remarked one night after dinner. "Get rid of him for me, will you, Tyree?"

It was not a request, Tyree mused, but a command wrapped in velvet.

He left the Slash W early the following

morning. It was a beautiful day, blessed by a brilliant blue sky that reminded him of the color of Rachel's eyes, and a soft summer breeze that held the heat at bay.

The squatter had chosen a wooded section of land watered by a narrow, gurgling stream. It was a pretty spot, perfect for a homestead. A good place to put down roots, raise kids and crops and cattle.

The man was sawing the branches off a newly fallen tree when Tyree rode up and stepped easily from the saddle.

"Folks usually wait to be asked to step down back where I come from," the squatter remarked, shading his eyes so he could see Tyree's face.

"That so? Around here, folks don't take up residence on somebody else's land without permission."

"This is free range," the squatter protested belligerently. "I checked it out before I came."

"You made a mistake," Tyree said flatly. "Pack your gear and move on."

"I got no place else to go," the man argued. "I'll have my floor in by tomorrow. I plan to have the walls up before the month is out."

"You'd best change your plans," Tyree warned, "or I'll change them for you."

The squatter was a young man, perhaps twenty-five years old. He was square-built, as solid as oak. He had dark brown hair and blue eyes that were looking scared.

"You've got five minutes to pack up and be on your way," Tyree said curtly.

"And if I refuse?"

Tyree jerked a thumb at the man's gunbelt, lying atop a flat rock some six feet away. "You can try your luck with that."

"I'm no gunfighter," the man protested, backing away from Tyree.

Tyree's smile was deadly. "I am."

"You'd shoot me down, in cold blood?" the young man asked incredulously.

"No. You'll have your chance. Buckle on that gunbelt."

"No."

"Then ride on."

The squatter stared at Tyree, his emotions as transparent as the water gurgling in the nearby stream. He did not want to leave. He had sold everything he owned to make the move West. He did not want to draw against a professional gunman, and he did not want to run.

"It's your move," Tyree drawled softly.

"Damn!" The man whispered the oath as he sidled toward his gunbelt. His eyes never left Tyree's face. Almost in slow motion, he picked up his gunbelt. Then, flinging himself to the ground, he jerked the .44 out of the holster and pulled the trigger.

The slug went wide, missing Tyree by a good two feet. Without conscious thought, Tyree drew his gun and sighted down the barrel.

The squatter stared up at him, helpless as a rabbit in a trap, too scared to pull the trigger a second time.

Tyree's finger was steady on the trigger and taking up the slack when Rachel's voice sounded in the back of his mind: "A gun may not know right from wrong," her voice accused, "but a man does."

Abruptly, Tyree holstered the Colt and rode on, leaving the squatter to stare after him in open-mouthed astonishment.

Two weeks later, Annabelle sent Tyree out again, commanding him to finish the job this time. It was dusk when he left the hacienda, a rifle across his saddle, his Colt riding heavy on his hip.

The squatters he sought were huddled around a cheery campfire when he arrived. There were four kids under twelve, a man and a woman. The family's lively chatter came to an abrupt halt as Tyree rode into the firelight. The woman was plump in a pleasing sort of way, with a mass of russet-colored hair, brown eyes, and rough workworn hands. Her face paled visibly when she saw the rifle nestled in Tyree's capable hands.

Her husband rose slowly to his feet, his arms dangling harmlessly at his sides. He was short and thin, with sandy brown hair, gray eyes, and a full beard. He wore a knife sheathed on his belt. An old Colt's Dragoon was shoved into the waistband of his trousers.

"Hi, mister," piped one of the kids, a girl about five years old. "That sure is a pretty horse."

"Tessie, hush!" her mother scolded.

"They told me in town that you'd show up," the man said dispiritedly. "I was hoping they'd be wrong."

"You're not wanted here," Tyree said.

"We're staying."

"No."

Slowly, the man shook his head. "I don't hold with killing," he said sadly. "But you do what you have to do."

"Suit yourself," Tyree murmured. He jacked a round into the breech of the Winchester, swung the barrel in the direction of the squatter's heart.

And couldn't pull the trigger.

With a heavy sigh, he lowered the rifle. "You're on Slash W range," he said tersely. "Don't be here tomorrow."

Wheeling the gray around, he galloped into the darkness without giving the man a chance to reply.

He was in a foul mood when he returned to the Slash W ranch house. Annabelle was waiting for him in the parlor, a question in her green eyes.

"It's done," Tyree said curtly.

"They're dead?"

"No."

The green eyes narrowed ominously. "Why didn't you kill them?"

"Because there was no need. The man doesn't have the guts to stay and make a fight of it. They'll be gone by tomorrow."

"What's the matter, Tyree?" Annabelle taunted. "Lost your nerve?"

Lazily, Tyree reached out and grabbed her arm in a grip of iron. "Is that what you think?" he challenged. He gave her arm a cruel twist, but Annabelle only laughed up at him, delighting in his easy strength.

But later, alone, her words came back to haunt him. Had he lost his nerve? Once, he would have gunned the squatter without a second thought. But that was before Rachel, he mused. Somehow, her values, her ideals of right and wrong had become his.

The following Saturday morning Tyree rode into town. He spent the early hours of the day loafing on the porch of the Palace Hotel, watching the townspeople go about their business, amused by the surreptitious glances they slanted in his direction. Everyone knew he was working for the Slash W and there was a lot of lively speculation about his unexpected change of employers.

Clint Wesley rode by the hotel on his way out of town shortly after noon, and Tyree felt a mild sense of relief. Sooner or later, Wesley's devotion to duty would overcome his good sense and when that day came, Tyree would have to kill him. He was glad it would not be today.

Moments later, Tyree saw Rachel. She was alone, standing on the boardwalk in front of the doctor's office. She looked good enough to eat, all dolled up in a pale yellow muslin day dress, and a white straw hat bedecked with long yellow streamers. It had been over two months since the night he seduced her at the Jorgensen place, and his eyes lingered hungrily on her trim form. He frowned thoughtfully as he glanced from Rachel's face to the doctor's office. With a grunt, he gained his feet and moved down the street.

Rachel frowned when she saw Tyree striding purposefully toward her. Turning on her heel, she headed in the opposite direction, but she wasn't fast enough to elude Tyree. His hand closed firmly over her arm, halting her flight.

"Take your hand off me!" Rachel demanded, her voice pitched low so as not to attract any undue attention.

"Afternoon, Miss Halloran," Tyree said with exaggerated politeness. "Sorry I'm late for our appointment."

"Appointment?" Rachel exclaimed angrily. "What are you talking about?"

"The one we have now," Tyree said. "Come on, take a walk with me."

"No."

"You're coming with me whether you like it or not," Tyree growled. "I'll carry you if I have to."

Rachel scowled irritably. He was just insolent enough to do such a scandalous thing.

"Oh, very well," she relented. "But take your hand off my arm."

"So you can run away? Not a chance."

"I won't run," Rachel promised sullenly. "Now unhand me."

Reluctantly, Tyree released his grip on Rachel's arm. Side by side, they walked down the street toward the end of town.

Rachel stared straight ahead, acutely conscious of the man walking beside her. Her skin was still warm and tingled faintly where his hand had grasped her arm. As they strolled silently down the street, Tyree's hand brushed hers and she pulled away, not wanting him to touch her, even though all her senses screamed for the pressure of his body next to her own. Night after night she had lain wide awake, yearning for his touch, hating him because he had dumped her for Annabelle Walsh. The thought of Tyree kissing Annabelle made her sick at heart. Oh, it wasn't fair, Rachel wailed in silent rage. His face haunted her dreams. Her mouth hungered for the taste of his kisses. No matter how hard she tried to convince herself that she hated and despised Logan Tyree, her body continued to yearn for his touch. She missed the sound of his laughter, his sardonic smile, the way his eyes lingered on her face as soft as a caress.

They were at the outskirts of town before Tyree broke the silence between them. "How are things at the ranch?" he asked gruffly. "Everything okay?"

"Yes." Rachel's eyes were cold when she looked at him.

"Your old man all right?"

"Yes."

"Are the Walsh riders giving you any more trouble?"

"No."

Tyree muttered a mild oath, annoyed by her curt monosyllabic replies. He scowled blackly, his narrowed eyes moving slowly over her full breasts and tiny waist.

"How about you?" he rasped. "Are you fine, too?"

For a moment, Rachel frowned at him. And then her cheeks flamed with embarrassment as she perceived the real meaning of his concern for her health.

"I'm not pregnant, if that's what you're thinking," she snapped. "And if I were, I'd kill myself before I gave birth to a child sired by a varmint like you!"

Anger flared deep in Tyree's yellow eyes, shining bright as summer lightning before it died away. A cynical smile curved his mouthline. "Death to dishonor," he drawled lazily.

"Honor!" Rachel's laugh was cold. "What would you know about honor, you . . . you—" She stamped her foot in frustration as words failed her.

"Murderer?" Tyree supplied the word, his

tone hard as flint. "Despoiler of fair damsels?"

"Yes," Rachel lashed out scathingly. "You're all those things and worse." She lifted her head, her clear blue eyes burning into his. "A man was found dead near Coyote Butte last month. You killed him, didn't you?"

"If I said no, would you believe me?"

"If you didn't kill him, who did?"

"Yarnell."

"Why?"

"The man was on Slash W land," Tyree answered tersely. "Annabelle wanted him off."

"That's open range and you know it," Rachel retorted.

"The Slash W has been grazing cattle there for years. Annabelle considers it a part of the ranch."

"And Annabelle always gets what she wants, doesn't she?" The words "including you" hung unspoken in the air between them. "Tell me, Tyree, how much did Annabelle pay you to gun that man down in cold blood?"

"I didn't kill him."

"I don't believe you. Everyone knows that's why Annabelle hired you. Did you give that man the same chance you gave Job Walsh?"

"Dammit, Rachel, back off!"

"What's the matter? Don't tell me you've developed a conscience at this late date?"

That was the trouble, Tyree thought bitterly. He *had* developed a conscience.

He glared at Rachel, confused by the anger

he felt. His hands were balled into tight fists at his sides, and a muscle worked in his jaw. For a moment, Rachel feared she had pushed him too far and that he might strike her. Instead, he turned on his heel and strode away, leaving her standing in the hot sun feeling alone and strangely sad.

Tyree was in a foul mood the rest of the day. Maybe a leopard couldn't change his spots. Maybe it was too late to try. He had never thought of himself as a murderer before, not really. Sure, he'd gunned down more than a dozen men, but never without a call. Never in cold blood. Damn her! Who was she to judge him? If it hadn't been for his gun, her old man would be dead by now, and Job Walsh would be running his cattle on the Lazy H.

Annabelle looked at Tyree with a question in her eyes more than once as the day wore on, but he remained stubbornly silent, refusing to be drawn into any conversation, answering her questions in as few words as possible. He drank several glasses of wine with dinner and later, sitting alone on the veranda, he emptied a bottle of tequila.

Wisely, Annabelle left Tyree alone. There was little about men she feared, but the look in Tyree's eye carried a warning she was loath to challenge.

It was late when Annabelle went to bed. Lying there alone, she stared out the window at the stars. For weeks, she had been trying to seduce Tyree, but to no avail. No matter how she teased, no matter how brazenly she coaxed, he never touched her. No other man had ever been able to resist her charms. No other man had ever filled her with such desire.

Unable to sleep, she drew on a thin cotton wrapper and went outside.

Tyree was there, standing in the yard, his profile dark and unfathomable. He was shirtless and the sight of his lean bronze torso stirred Annabelle as never before, making her blood sing with desire.

Tyree turned at the sound of her footsteps. It took but one look at Annabelle's face to know what she wanted and he expelled a deep shuddering sigh as he took her in his arms and kissed her. Why not make love to Annabelle? She wanted him. She didn't care how many men he had killed. She didn't care about a damn thing.

And that was what was wrong with her.

With a vile oath, he pushed her away. He did not want Annabelle Walsh. He wanted a girl with flaxen hair and eyes as blue as a summer sky. He wanted Rachel, blushing and modest in his arms.

"Tyree?"

He shook his head. "Forget it," he muttered, and stalked out of the yard, leaving Annabelle to stare after him, a puzzled expression on her lovely face.

Chapter 15

Autumn came in a colorful panorama of changing leaves, of warm, sun-kissed days and crisp, cool nights. And now, at last, there was peace between the Slash W and the Lazy H.

John Halloran hired three new cowhands. They hailed from Montana and they were young and strong and eager to work. Halloran was pleased with their enthusiasm and he began making plans for a cattle drive the following spring.

In late October, he began courting Claire Whiting, the seamstress in Yellow Creek, and he went around the house whistling cheerfully, his steps lighter than they had been in years. Claire made him feel young, carefree, and life was suddenly good again.

Rachel was happy to see her father in such high spirits, but she could not shake the gloomy feelings that permeated her days and nights. In an effort to dispel the lassitude that gripped her, she threw herself into a fit of housecleaning, dusting furniture and waxing floors as if her very life depended on shiny tabletops and slick parquet. Windows sparkled, wood surfaces gleamed. Curtains and bedspreads and tablecloths were washed and ironed until they looked like new. Cupboards and closets were duly put in order, rugs were aired, pillows were fluffed. A fresh coat of paint covered the walls in the kitchen.

Rachel worked unceasingly as if, by keeping herself constantly busy, she could keep all thought of Logan Tyree at bay; hoping, perhaps, that she could sweep Tyree's memory from her heart as easily as she swept the dust from the floors.

Why, of all men, did she have to fall in love with a man like Tyree? And now that he was out of her life, why couldn't she forget him?

When the house was so clean there was nothing left to do, she turned her attention to the bunkhouse, putting up curtains, waxing the plank floor, airing the mattresses, refurbishing the beds. John Halloran grinned and shook his head helplessly when the men began to complain that Rachel was turning their world upside down.

"If this keeps up, she's gonna have us in ruffled shirts and patent-leather boots,"

Candido grumbled. "Hell, this is a bunk-house, not the White House!"

When Rachel ran out of chores to keep her busy at the ranch, she began to spend time in town with her friend, Carol Ann. Together, they shopped for material and patterns and began sewing new dresses for church. Carol Ann was like a breath of fresh air, her idle gossip about the townspeople humorous and harmless. Betty Miller was pregnant with number six. Lydia Foreman was engaged. One of the blacksmith's sons had run away with a saloon girl, shaming his family and friends.

Spending so much time in town, Rachel could not help seeing Clint Wesley. His attention was like a healing balm to her aching heart. Clint was everything Tyree was not, everything a woman could want in a man. He was kind, polite, attentive, eager to please her. He brought her flowers and candy, took her for long walks, escorted her to church and to parties. He was tolerant of her quicksilver mood changes. He complimented her beauty, admired her new dress, was never crude or demanding or unkind. If only she could love him, Rachel lamented. If only his shy kisses had the power to make her heart beat with excitement the way Tyree's did. Clint was so unfailingly sweet, why couldn't she love him as he deserved? Why did her heart continue to yearn for a scoundrel like Logan Tyree?

It was late one blustery afternoon when Rachel drove into town, bent on a visit to Lulu

Mae's Millinery Shoppe, her heart set on a darling bonnet she had seen in the window the day before.

Stepping from the buggy, she was halfway across the street when she saw Annabelle Walsh walking down the boardwalk, one gloved hand laid possessively over Tyree's arm.

A sharp pain tore through Rachel's heart when Tyree looked down into Annabelle's face, laughing softly at something Annabelle had said. Why did Tyree have to be in town today, of all days? And why did he have to look so devilishly handsome? As usual, he was dressed all in black except for a red silk scarf that was loosely knotted at his throat. Rachel tried not to notice how the black silk shirt clung to his broad shoulders, or the way the tight whipcord britches outlined his long muscular legs. He wore expensive black kid boots and a black stetson hat, and she wondered, peevishly, if Annabelle had paid for his clothing.

Quivering with jealousy, Rachel tried not to stare at Annabelle Walsh. She had to admit, if grudgingly, that the woman was beautiful. Her hair was a glorious shade of red, her eyes as green as new grass, her smooth skin flawless. Her figure, clad in a gaudy blue and yellow stripped dress, could not be faulted.

Lifting her chin and squaring her shoulders, Rachel walked past the couple, her eyes riveted on the rectangular red and white sign that hung over the doorway to Lulu Mae's salon.

Annabelle's hand tightened on Tyree's arm as Rachel Halloran glided swiftly past, her skirts held to one side, as if she were too good to associate with anyone from the Slash W.

"Little snit," Annabelle thought sourly. What had Tyree ever seen in John Halloran's old maid daughter? Rachel's face was as cold as stone. Little wonder she was still unmarried. Bedding her would probably be as exciting as bedding a dead fish.

Tyree's mouth thinned in an angry line as Rachel hurried past him without so much as a glance. For a brief moment, he was tempted to reach out and grab her arm, to pull her to him and kiss the blank expression from her face. But he could not do that. He had lost all right to Rachel when he consented to work for the Slash W. Mouthing an obscenity, he tore his gaze from Rachel's back and pretended to be interested in what Annabelle was saying.

Inside Lulu Mae's Millinery Shoppe, Rachel leaned against the door frame, fighting the urge to cry. Damn him, damn him, damn him! Why did seeing Tyree with Annabelle have to hurt so much? Foolishly, she felt betrayed, almost as if she had seen her husband with another woman. She was being ridiculous, and she knew it. Tyree was nothing to her.

Nothing at all. She had no claim on him. And yet, they had once been as close as a man and woman could be. Once, he had bared his soul to her. Then, apparently without even a smidgen of regret, he had turned to another woman.

With a sigh, Rachel closed her eyes, and for a moment a horrible picture danced across her mind, a vivid image of Tyree bending over Annabelle, caressing her long red hair, whispering tender words of love in her ear. . . .

The image was too awful, and she opened her eyes to find Lulu Mae Harding staring at her curiously.

"Aren't you feeling well, Miss Halloran?" the pudgy shopkeeper inquired solicitously. "You look . . . upset."

"I'm fine," Rachel said, forcing a wan smile. "I just felt a little faint for a moment."

"Too much sun, perhaps?" Lulu Mae murmured sympathetically.

"Yes, I suppose so," Rachel agreed quickly. "Could I see the hat in the window? The blue one?"

Distracted by the prospect of a sale, Lulu Mae hurried to the display in the front window and carefully removed the hat Rachel had mentioned.

"This is perfect for you," Lulu Mae gushed. She placed the bonnet on Rachel's head, tied the wide blue ribbon under Rachel's chin. "My dear, this hat was made for you. Why, it makes your eyes glow!"

"I'll take it," Rachel said. "Put it on my account, will you?"

Without waiting for Lulu Mae's reply, Rachel hurried out of the shop. She had to get away, to be alone with her thoughts.

Rachel wore the blue hat to church the following Sunday, graciously accepted Clint's compliment on how becoming it was. She got little out of the meeting, however, for engraved in her mind was the picture of Tyree walking beside Annabelle. His face, lean and brown and maddeningly attractive, seemed to mock her heartache. She had been right about him all along, she thought morosely. He was no good, nothing but a drifter, a man completely without morals or scruples. Once, she had been certain there was some good hidden beneath his gruff exterior. She had convinced herself of that the day he rescued Amy from harm's way. She had even convinced herself that his words and kisses were sincere, that he had truly cared for her. Now she knew she had only been kidding herself. The nights they had spent in each other's arms, those nights she cherished even now, had meant nothing to him. Nothing at all. Even his promise to marry her had proved to be nothing but a lie.

"Annabelle made me a better offer," he had said, and had ridden out of her life without a backward glance.

Clint took her for a buggy ride after church.

They stopped for a while beside a lazy stream, content to sit in the shade while the horse munched on the sparse yellow grass.

"Dinner tonight?" Clint asked.

"Of course," Rachel replied. "You know how my father enjoys your company."

"And you?" Clint asked in a low voice. "Do you still enjoy my company?"

"Of course," Rachel said quickly. "Did you really arrest Mr. Pedersen for beating his wife last night? Carol Ann said he spent the night in jail."

Distracted, Clint launched into the story of Pedersen's arrest.

Returning home later that afternoon, Rachel removed the becoming blue bonnet. Placing it carefully in a hat box, she placed it on a shelf in her closet, knowing she would never wear it again. Knowing that every time she saw that hat, she would remember Tyree walking with Annabelle.

Chapter 16

*W*inter settled over the land. The rain, long overdue, came with a vengeance, flooding the gullies and arroyos, filling the natural granite tanks in the mountains to overflowing. The roads were treacherous, and people left their homes only when absolutely necessary. The Slash W lost a hundred head of cattle in the season's first big snowstorm.

For the time being, the fighting between the Slash W and the squatters was over. The settlers migrating westward would not be a problem again until after spring, and Tyree looked forward to a quiet, peaceful winter. He spent most of his time sprawled on the couch in the parlor, staring into the fire that burned night and day in the big stone fireplace, his thoughts obviously far away.

Annabelle fretted over Tyree's brooding silence, but he turned a deaf ear to her tantrums and tirades. He ignored her sultry looks, shrugged off her eager caresses.

But Annabelle was a hot-blooded woman, one who could not go long without a man. And when Tyree continued to shun her favors, she salved her humiliation by taking a young gunman known as Morgan Yarnell under her wing. But even that failed to provoke a response from Tyree. And after awhile, Annabelle stopped trying to make Tyree jealous. Whatever was bothering him would pass. And until then, there was always Yarnell.

Tyree was faintly amused by Annabelle's behavior, but he had other things on his mind and when being cooped up in the house got to be more than he could stand, he saddled the gray and rode out across the vast Slash W range. Riding became a daily ritual, but no matter in which direction he started out, he invariably wound up on the outskirts of the Lazy H. He went there hoping to catch a glimpse of Rachel, though he would not admit such a thing even to himself. Sometimes he caught sight of her in the window of the Halloran house as she stared out at the blanket of snow that covered the land, but she never left the protection of the house, and he never rode into the yard.

Christmas Eve came, and the Slash W ranch house glittered with shiny decorations and candles. Annabelle bought lavish gifts for everyone in her employ: hired hands, household servants, the boy who gathered the eggs, no one was left out. Her gift to Tyree was a new Winchester rifle. It was a handsome weapon, beautifully wrought, with his name intricately worked into the smooth rosewood stock.

Tyree gave Annabelle a delicate ruby teardrop on a fine gold chain.

The new year came amid a raging storm that dropped three feet of snow in two days. The cowhands worked doubly hard now, loading hay onto a great flatbed wagon and hauling it out to the range to feed the hungry cattle that bawled for food. Tyree smiled ruefully as he watched the wagon plough through the drifts of snow. Buffalo and horses would paw through the snow to search for food, but not a cow.

And still the elements raged. Snow had to be shoveled from the roof of the house, pathways had to be shoveled between the buildings. Ice had to be removed from the water troughs. Cattle died, and their carcasses lay like fallen statues in the deep snow. The river froze solid. The trees stood naked and forlorn in the howling wind, their branches sagging beneath a blanket of white.

Tyree grew increasingly restless. He paced the parlor floor until Annabelle feared he would wear a rut in the carpet. He grew quick-tempered and even more sullen until the servants refused to be in the same room with him, and even the other gunmen began to give him a wide berth.

The first day there was a break in the weather, Tyree threw a saddle on the gray and rode out across the stark white wilderness. Everyone on the Slash W was glad to see him go.

Tyree drew in a deep breath as he left the Walsh hacienda behind. Nothing moved on the face of the land save for the gray stud plodding laboriously through the deep drifts.

Tyree had gone a good ten miles when black clouds scudded across the sky like angry waves, completely blotting out the sun. Thunder echoed in the distance as fat drops of rain began to fall. The stallion tossed its head and rolled its eyes as a jagged streak of yellow lightning slashed the lowering skies.

"Easy, boy," Tyree murmured, patting the stallion's neck.

The rain came in earnest then, soaking Tyree and his mount in a matter of seconds. Reining the gray to a halt, Tyree checked his bearings. He was about halfway between the Slash W and the Lazy H, and for a moment he remained undecided. Then, clucking to the stud, he urged the animal toward the Halloran spread, feeling good for the first time in weeks.

John Halloran's eyes widened when he opened the door and saw Logan Tyree standing on the porch, hat in hand.

"Something wrong?" the old man asked.

"No. Mind if I come in?"

"I guess not," Halloran said warily. "You

look like you could use a drink, and a few minutes before the fire."

"Obliged," Tyree replied. He shook the water from his hat before stepping into the hallway.

"What brings you out on a day like this?" Halloran inquired, leading the way into the parlor. He poured two drinks, handed one to Tyree. "Sit," he invited. "Make yourself at home."

Taking a place on the sofa, Tyree stretched his long legs out in front of him. The whiskey was prime, and the fire and the smooth liquor quickly chased the chill from his bones.

The parlor was a comfortable room, done in rich mahogany and native stone. A gun rack held several Henry repeaters and an old Sharps buffalo gun. There was a bearskin rug on the floor, a rack of antlers over the mantle. It was definitely a man's room, and Tyree wondered how long Ellen Halloran had been dead. The only evidence he could find to indicate a woman's touch was a vase of dried desert flowers on one of the tables.

"I hear Annabelle lost some stock," Halloran remarked after a lengthy silence.

"Yeah, a couple hundred head or so. How about you?"

Halloran made a vague gesture of defeat. "All dead. Somebody burned my winter hay awhile back. The cows that didn't freeze to death died hungry." He laughed bitterly. "I guess we're broke for sure."

The old man stared vacantly into the fire-place. "I had to let Candido and the others go. I guess, come spring, Annabelle will run me out." There was a thinly veiled look of accusation in Halloran's eyes when he glanced at his guest.

"You think I'll come gunning for you?" Tyree asked flatly.

"I don't know," Halloran answered honestly. "I'd like to think not."

"But . . ."

Halloran raised his shoulders, then let them drop. "I keep remembering Job Walsh. I paid you five hundred dollars and you gunned him down without a second thought. And now . . ."

"And now I'm working for Annabelle," Tyree muttered with a sigh. "And she can afford to pay more than five hundred dollars."

"Yeah."

"Stop worrying, Halloran. If she wants this place, come spring, she'll buy you out."

"Annabelle seems to have a great deal of money," Rachel said from the doorway. "And yet, I hear she's paying you more than just cash for your services." There was contempt in her tone and in her eyes as she stepped into the room.

A muscle worked in Tyree's jaw. "Where'd you hear that?"

"It's all over town. Are you going to deny it?"

"Would you believe me if I did?"

"No, I wouldn't."

Tyree scowled at her as she took a seat in one of the big brown leather chairs that flanked the fireplace, trying to ignore the way the blue wool dress she was wearing outlined her figure, and the way the flames danced in her hair, highlighting the thick golden mass with streaks of red. Looking at her stirred a familiar ache in his loins.

"Just what are you doing here, Mr. Tyree?" Rachel asked bluntly.

"I came by to see how you and your old man were making out," Tyree replied curtly, angered by her rude tone of voice, and by the disdain shining in her eyes.

"Why?"

"Rachel!"

"Oh, Pa, how can you sit here and talk to him like he's a long lost friend? You know he's only here because Annabelle sent him to spy on us."

"Dammit, that's not true!" Tyree hurled the words at Rachel. "*I* came because . . ." The sentence died unfinished. "I'd better be going."

"Don't be a fool," Halloran chided gruffly. "You can't ride in this weather. You'll freeze before you get out of the yard."

"Good riddance," Rachel muttered under her breath, then flushed guiltily when she realized Tyree had heard her.

"I don't think I'm welcome here," Tyree said dryly. "But thanks for the drink and the fire."

"I'm still the boss in this house," Halloran declared, silencing Rachel with a sharp glance. "And I won't have you riding out in this storm. Supper's about ready. And there's enough for one more. Isn't there, daughter?"

"Yes, Pa," Rachel answered sullenly.

"Good. It's settled then. You'll stay the night, Tyree. And tomorrow, too, if the weather doesn't clear."

When dinner was over they gathered in the parlor again, around the fireplace. Outside, the wind howled and the elements raged, but inside it was warm and comfortable, save for the strained atmosphere between Rachel and Tyree.

John Halloran rambled on about crops and cattle and the advantages of barn feeding as opposed to pasture feeding until he ran out of small talk. Lighting his pipe, he stared at the flames, letting his thoughts wander back to the nights when Ellen had sat beside him, her small hand in his, her face warm with love as they dreamed and planned for the future. He remembered how beautiful she had been when she sat with Tommy at her breast, her face glowing like the Virgin Mary's.

Feeling a sudden tightness in his throat, Halloran rose abruptly to his feet and left the room.

"I'll be saying goodnight, too," Rachel said,

after her father left the parlor. "You can sleep in here, on the sofa, if you like. It'll be warmer than the spare bedroom."

"What's the matter, Rachel?" Tyree challenged. "Afraid to be alone with me?"

Rachel's chin went up defiantly. "Afraid? Why should I be afraid?"

"I don't know," Tyree responded softly. "You tell me."

He was standing in front of her, so close she could smell the heady male scent of him. She had forgotten how tall he was, how overwhelmingly masculine. His nearness dwarfed the memory of every other man she had ever known, making them all seem pale and insignificant by comparison. A slow fire started in the core of her being, rising hotter and faster with every moment that passed, and it was all she could do to keep from reaching out to touch the dark hair brushing against his shirt collar.

Tyree's eyes danced with amusement and with the sure knowledge of what Rachel was thinking and feeling. The current between them was like a live wire, humming with shared longing, and Tyree whispered her name as he reached out to caress the curve of her cheek.

Rachel stood like one hypnotized as Tyree's long brown fingers touched her skin. Slowly, he tilted her face up. Slowly, he bent down to cover her mouth with his own. Her eyelids flickered down and she swayed toward him, her arms stealing around his neck, her body molding itself to his. She had dreamed of being in his arms for so long, so long, and now he was here.

She breathed in the scent of him, let her fingers curl in his hair. Slowly, her hands dropped to his shoulders, marveling anew at the strength there before letting her fingers trail down his back, under his shirt to caress his skin. She heard Tyree groan softly, felt the tangible proof of his rising desire, and exulted in the knowledge that he wanted her.

It was like a dream, she thought, gazing up into Tyree's eyes. The rain hissing against the windows, the fire filling the room with primitive warmth. It never occurred to her to refuse him. She had waited for him, wanted him, for far too long to resist now and she remained passive while he undressed her, felt her cheeks blossom with color as his eyes openly admired her bare flesh. She watched through eyes dark with passion as Tyree shed his own clothing, revealing a body of bronze perfection, and then he was stretching out beside her on the couch. She turned readily in his arms, hungry for his kiss, sighing with pleasure as he made her his at last.

Rachel woke in her own bed the following morning with no recollection of how she had gotten there. But she had no trouble recalling what had happened in the parlor the night before, and her cheeks burned with shame.

How would she ever face Tyree again after her wanton behavior of the night before?

Oh, but she would do it all again, she mused. It had been heavenly to be in his arms, to feel his touch, hear his voice. No matter that he did not love her, no matter if he looked at her in that dreadful mocking way, it had been worth it. She was all aflutter as she wondered how to behave when she went downstairs and then a terrible thought crossed her mind. What if he had already gone?

Jumping out of bed, she dressed quickly, brushed her hair, and flew down the stairs, her heart pounding with the need to see him again, dreading the thought that he might already be gone.

Tyree and her father were sitting in the parlor, talking about the weather, when Rachel rushed in.

"Mornin', Rachel," Tyree said pleasantly, and for once there was no mockery in his voice or his eyes.

"Something wrong, daughter?" Halloran asked. "You came running in here like the devil was at your heels."

"No, Pa. I was afraid . . . I mean, I overslept. I'll get breakfast."

Cheeks red with embarrassment, Rachel fled to the kitchen. Glancing out the window, she saw that the world was still swathed in white. A light rain began to fall while she scrambled eggs and fried up a mess of bacon.

She was grinning as she set the table. The rain would turn the roads to slush, making travel dangerous, and that meant Tyree would have to stay another day. The thought filled her with joy and dread at the same time.

Breakfast seemed to last longer than usual. Rachel was thrilled that Tyree was sitting across from her at the table, that he was really here, at last. She could not keep her eyes from his face, could not keep her heart from racing each time he looked in her direction. And yet, she felt uncomfortable when their eyes met. She kept waiting for him to make some veiled remark about the night before. What did he think of her? She professed to hate him, and yet she had fallen into his arms without so much as a verbal protest, her lips eager for his kiss, her body all too ready for his.

When the meal was over, Tyree and her father returned to the parlor, leaving Rachel to tidy up the kitchen. She cleared the table and washed and dried the dishes, hardly conscious of what she was doing. Instead, she was haunted by the memory of Tyree bending over her, his amber eyes alight with desire, his hands gliding over her flesh, arousing her, pleasing her. . . .

Thrusting the image aside, she began to sweep the kitchen floor, but Tyree's swarthy countenance kept intruding on her thoughts. All too clearly, she could picture his dark handsome face and recall the way his body felt pressed against her own. He had a handsome physique, as well, all hard muscle and bronzed flesh. True, he carried a multitude of scars on his back and chest from old wounds, but somehow they did not repulse her or mar his appearance in the least.

She spent the rest of the morning baking bread and doing a few chores, always conscious of Tyree's presence in the house.

After lunch, Tyree and her father got involved in a game of five card stud while Rachel sat in a chair near the fireplace, a pile of mending in her lap. A fire blazed cheerfully in the hearth, and only the sound of the men's voices and the sharp crackle of the flames disturbed the companionable silence of the room. Somehow, it seemed right for Tyree to be in the house, and Rachel felt strangely content each time she glanced up and saw him comfortably slouched in the chair across from her father.

Dinner passed peacefully, with the men talking amiably about politics and the rising price of beef. Rachel said little, but she did not feel left out of their conversation. Indeed, she felt warm and secure, seated between the two men she loved best in all the world. For she did love him, in spite of everything.

About ten o'clock, Rachel and her father bid Tyree goodnight, leaving him alone in the parlor. Alone for the first time that day, Tyree pulled off his boots and rolled a cigarette. Staring into the fireplace, he tried to remember when he had spent a more pleasant day.

Halloran was good company and he had enjoyed talking to the old man. But it was Rachel who had made the day special, even though they hadn't exchanged more than a dozen words. Nevertheless, he had been acutely aware of her presence in the house, even when she was in another room. Once or twice, it had taken every ounce of his willpower to keep from reaching out to touch her, and it was only the fact that her father slept in the room next to hers that kept him from going to her now.

Stripping off his shirt, Tyree stretched out on the rug in front of the hearth and closed his eyes, only to snap to attention as someone tiptoed into the room and closed the door.

"Rachel!" Tyree murmured, surprised. "What are you doing here?"

"I . . . I forgot something."

Tyree lifted one black brow. "That so?" he asked, his voice suddenly husky.

Rachel nodded. She looked beguilingly beautiful standing there in a lacy white nightgown embroidered with dainty pink rosebuds. Her long honey-gold hair fell over her shoulders in wild abandon. Her deep blue eyes were wide and scared.

Afraid he would frighten her off, Tyree made no move toward her, though he wanted desperately to go to her, to take her in his arms.

Rachel coughed nervously. Coming here had seemed like such a good idea when she had been safe in her own room. She wanted Tyree. She admitted it freely, and so she had padded down the hallway, her heart pounding with excitement and anticipation. But now, with his eyes on her face, she felt shy and uncertain.

"I left my . . . my book in here and I . . . please don't make this hard for me, Tyree," she whispered plaintively. "We both know why I'm here."

"Yeah," he said softly, and held out his arms.

Rachel let out a breathy sigh as she moved into Tyree's arms. She spread her hands across his bare back, her face burrowing into the hollow of his shoulder. For long seconds he held her close, his hand moving soft as a whisper over her back and shoulders. She could hear the faint beating of his heart, feel her own heart pounding a quick tattoo as his fingers threaded through her hair. She drew a deep breath and the scent of cigar smoke and leather and man filled her nostrils, stirring her desire.

Gently, he tipped her face up, his head descending toward hers, blocking everything else from her sight. His eyes were like a deep yellow flame, and when his mouth closed over hers, she felt the fire of his kiss all the way to her toes. His lips played across her face, as gentle as rain, nourishing her desire. Her limbs felt suddenly weak, her pulse was racing, her stomach fluttering wildly.

"Tyree." She breathed his name, her voice shaky, her eyes clouded with passion.

"I know," he murmured huskily. "I know."

Carefully, he stretched out on the rug, drawing her down beside him. His hands and lips were gentle, unhurried, as though she were a rare treasure that must not be handled roughly, a fine wine that must be sipped to be appreciated.

Sensations and emotions swirled through her, wrapping her in a cocoon that knew nothing but Tyree's touch, nothing but the pleasure of his kisses.

He caressed the nightgown from her shoulders, his mouth savoring each inch of her skin, his amber eyes telling her she was beautiful, desirable. She ran her fingertips over his back and shoulders, across his broad chest, over his hard flat belly. She uttered a wordless cry of protest when she encountered his trousers and he shrugged them off, grinning at her impatience, then gasped with pleasure as she stroked his thigh.

At last, when she could stand the sweet pain of wanting no more, she drew him close, her arms and legs wrapping around him, certain she would die if he did not satisfy the desire he had aroused.

They came together with a rush, mouths fused together, bodies joined in passion's embrace, as wave after wave of pleasure broke over them. There was no past, no future, only their love, as old as time, as new as the dawn.

For the second time in as many days, Rachel woke in her own bed with no recollection of how she had arrived there. But this morning she felt no shame for what had gone on the night before, no regret, only a warm sense of fulfillment.

Stretching languidly, she gazed out the window, and sighed heavily as her joy turned to ashes. The storm was over and a brilliant sun was rising in the east. Flouncing over onto her stomach, she punched her fist into her pillow. Tyree would be going home now. The words, "Home to Annabelle" whispered in the back of her mind, filling her with bitter despair. How could she have forgotten Annabelle?

She dressed slowly, putting off going downstairs because she didn't want to know if Tyree had already gone. So long as she was in her room, she could pretend he was downstairs in the kitchen, drinking coffee with her father.

She brushed her hair carefully, just in case Tyree was still in the house, applied a bit of color to her mouth. Squaring her shoulders, she started down the stairs. If he was gone, he was gone, and if he wasn't, she was wasting precious time.

Happiness bubbled inside her when she entered the kitchen and found Tyree sitting at the table. He seemed to be in no hurry to return to the Slash W, but spent the morning in the kitchen, chatting with her father as he drank one cup of black coffee after another.

Rachel left them there while she moved

through the house doing her regular morning chores. For some reason, she found herself singing as she worked and she realized with a start that she hadn't felt like singing since Tyree left the Lazy H months ago.

Damn Logan Tyree! Why was it that he was the only man who had the power to stir the passion in her soul? Why didn't she feel the same quivering excitement in her flesh when Clint held her tight? Why was it that Tyree had only to look at her to make her blood sing and her heart beat like a wild thing caught in a trap?

She puzzled over her feelings while she made the beds and dusted the furniture. Tyree was going back to the Slash W. Back to Annabelle's voluptuous charms. The Lazy H was on the verge of being wiped out. They had no livestock left except their saddle horses, a few pigs and chickens; no cash money to speak of, no prospects for the future. But she was singing, and all because Logan Tyree was in the house!

She had missed Tyree. She had worked hard at hating him ever since he had gone to work for Annabelle Walsh, reminding herself time and again that he was a killer, a hired gun with no scruples and no conscience to speak of. He had promised to marry her and then changed his mind, never telling her the reason except to say that Annabelle had made him a better offer. He had ridden out of her life without so much as a backward glance, offering no explanation for his behavior, no apology. Now, without rhyme or reason, he was back, threatening to steal her heart a second time. Oh, it wasn't fair!

Still, for the first time in months, her heart was light and she was happy, and she knew it was all because Logan Tyree was sitting in the kitchen. Just knowing he was nearby made her feel vibrant and alive, and she hurried through her chores, anxious to return to the kitchen, always afraid he would leave without saying goodbye.

Breathless, she almost ran into the kitchen. Tyree was still there, his long legs crossed negligently in front of him, his hat pushed back on his head.

Tyree's hand reached out to brush hers as she moved to the countertop and began slicing apples for a pie. His touch went through her like an electric shock.

"I don't know what we'll do, come spring," her father was saying. "I owe Mort Walker a sizeable debt. I'd planned to pay him out of next year's calf crop, but now . . ." Halloran shrugged and stared out the window, his brow furrowed. If Lew Harris over at the Cattleman's Bank wouldn't give him an extension on their loan, they would have to sell the ranch to pay the mortgage. The thought rankled. Ellen was buried here. And Tommy. Rachel's roots were here. It was the only home she had ever known. He could not let the place go. He just couldn't.

Discouraged, Halloran muttered something to Tyree about going out to check on the horses and left the house, his steps heavy with defeat.

Rachel concentrated mightily on the ingredients she was measuring into a bowl, keenly aware of Tyree's eyes on her back, and of the fact that they were alone in the house. Where only moments before she had been glad that Tyree was still here, she now wished he would just go and get it over with.

She heard the scrape of a chair as he pushed away from the table and her hands began to tremble. He was standing behind her. She could feel his presence there and she grew suddenly tense as she waited for him to take her in his arms. She knew a moment of swift disappointment when nothing happened.

Abruptly, she whirled around. His yellow cat's eyes trapped hers in a long lingering gaze filled with desire and Rachel felt her knees go weak as he reached for her. She experienced a moment of panic, not because he was going to take her in his arms, but because she was so helpless to resist him. Her feet felt rooted to the floor and she swayed against him, powerless to stem the powerful urgings of her own heart.

Tyree's kiss was gentle, his hands light on her shoulders as he drew her close. Time seemed to stand still and Rachel wished that she could stay thus in his arms forever.

With a muffled oath, Tyree turned away and

strode out the back door, leaving Rachel to stare after him. For a moment, she was speechless, and then she ran out the door after him, calling his name.

Tyree stopped, waiting for her to catch up. His expression was cold when he turned to face her.

"I love you," Rachel said in a rush. "Please don't go back to Annabelle."

"Don't waste your love on me, Rachel," Tyree said in a rough tone. "I'm not worth it."

"You are!"

"No. I'm all the things you accused me of being when I first came here."

"I don't believe that. Not any more."

"You believed it well enough then."

"Please stay, Tyree. I'll make you happy. I'll live and die for you. Please don't go."

"Rachel, I . . ." He swore under his breath. The love shining in her eyes reached out to him, warmer than the summer sun, trusting as a young child who believed wanting something bad enough could make it so.

Tyree gazed into Rachel's eager, upturned face. He had never intended to make love to her. He had only wanted to see her, make certain she and her father were doing all right. Even when he had kissed her that first night, he had expected nothing more, but she had been on fire for him, her arms stealing around his neck, her body pressing against his, arousing his own. What had happened that night and the next had seemed so right at the time. But now, when he was about to return to the Slash W and Annabelle, it all seemed so wrong.

Feeling like the worst kind of heel, Tyree turned and walked quickly toward the barn.

Rachel did not follow him.

Annabelle was furious when she found out where Tyree had weathered the storm. She ranted and raved for three days, calling him all manner of names: names no decent woman should even know, let alone speak aloud. Tyree let her carry on until, at last, she ran out of steam.

"I'm going into town," he said the morning of the fourth day. "You want anything?"

"Town?" Annabelle queried suspiciously. "What for?"

"I don't think it's any of your business how I spend my free time," Tyree drawled, grinning at her in a way that made her eyes flare with anger.

"Well, you're wrong!" Annabelle shrieked. "You don't have any free time. I bought your time, gunfighter. And paid for it. *All* of it. And don't you forget it."

"Whatever you say," Tyree muttered, unruffled by her outburst. "I'll be back early."

Mort Walker was a short, florid-faced individual with round blue eyes and chin whiskers the color of tobacco. He looked askance at Tyree as the gunman pressed a wad of currrency into his fat little hand, admonishing him to mark John Halloran's debt paid in full, and to keep quiet about where the money came from.

"Yessir, Mr. Tyree," Walker agreed in a cowed tone. "I don't want any trouble with you."

"And you won't get any so long as you keep your mouth shut about this."

Lew Harris was a tall, dignified gentleman with a mane of silver hair and eyes the color of pewter. He readily accepted Tyree's money in payment on the Halloran loan, but protested at having to keep Tyree's name out of the transaction.

"I'll have to tell Mr. Halloran something when he asks where the money came from," Harris protested briskly.

"Tell him anything you want," Tyree replied with a wry grin. "Anything but the truth."

"You don't expect me to lie?" Harris gasped, horrified.

"I don't care what you do," Tyree warned. "But Halloran is not to know where that money came from. And if he finds out, I'll be back."

Tyree's threat to return produced the desired results. "Very well," Harris agreed meekly. "I'll think of something."

Satisfied with the day's events, Tyree went to Bowsher's Saloon to while away the rest of the afternoon. There would be hell to pay if Annabelle found out who had settled

Halloran's debts, he mused, but he didn't really care. Annabelle was at her best when she was mad. Perhaps that was why she got mad so often.

It was after midnight when he returned to the Slash W. There was a light burning in Annabelle's room and he stepped inside without knocking, intending to tell her he had picked up her mail while he was in town. He grinned as Morgan Yarnell's curly red head popped up from under the covers, his expression sheepish and smug at the same time.

"Sorry," Tyree murmured. Stifling the urge to laugh, he backed out of the room and closed the door.

Yarnell accosted Tyree early the next morning, a satisfied smirk on his handsome young face, a challenge lurking in the back of his deep-set brown eyes.

"Knock first, next time," Yarnell said curtly.

"What makes you think you'll have a next time?" Tyree retorted.

"Because she's through with you," Yarnell said insolently. "From now on, it's me and Annabelle. You're out of it."

"That so?"

Yarnell swelled up like a turkey gobbler. "You heard me say so, didn't you?"

Tyree shrugged indifferently. "I've heard you say you're the fastest man with a gun, too, but that doesn't make it so."

"Just name the time and the place, old man," Yarnell said daringly. "I'll be there."

The next day was Sunday. Tyree slept late and woke to the sound of gunfire. His first thought was that someone was attacking the ranch, but then he realized some of the hands were indulging in a little target practice to while away the time.

Rising, Tyree pulled on his pants and boots and made his way to the kitchen where he poured himself a cup of coffee before going out onto the back veranda.

In the yard, Yarnell and three other men were shooting at bottles lined up along the top rail of the nearest corral.

Tyree watched with professional interest as Morgan Yarnell drew and fired. The man was fast, and he never missed. The other slingers were good, too. They hit their targets nine times out of ten, and they unleathered their weapons with little wasted motion, but they lacked the inbred eye-and-hand coordination that came naturally to men like Yarnell. And men like Tyree.

Yarnell turned around, expecting to see Annabelle on the veranda. The welcome in his eyes turned to contempt when he saw Tyree.

"Like to try a few, gunfighter?" Yarnell said with a sneer.

"Only kids waste their time showing off," Tyree retorted disdainfully.

"What's the matter, old man?" Yarnell

taunted maliciously. "Afraid to find out I'm faster than you are? Or afraid you'll miss?"

Tyree snorted. "You've got the fastest mouth, that's for sure. What do you do, talk your opponents to death?"

Yarnell turned red around the ears as the other men began to laugh. Yarnell had a quick temper, Tyree mused, and that could be dangerous.

"I'll take you on, any time, any place," Yarnell shouted. "Just name it!"

"That so?"

"Damn right!" Yarnell took a step forward, his hands poised over his guns, a gleam of anticipation in his coffee-colored eyes. "I can outdraw you any day of the week, old man," he boasted. "And I'm ready to prove it here and now."

They might have settled it then and there if Annabelle hadn't appeared on the scene.

"Quit it, you two!" she snapped, annoyed by their childish bickering. "There's a squatter setting up housekeeping out near Tabletop Mesa. I don't know how he made it here through the snow, but I want him out." Annabelle's green eyes settled on Tyree. "And I want them dead this time."

Thirty minutes later, the two gunmen rode out of the yard. Yarnell rode his horse like a knight going to battle, his eyes alert and eager, a lethal smile on his thin lips.

Tyree rode easy in the saddle, conscious of Yarnell's eagerness to use the pair of matched

.44's he wore in cross-draw holsters. He was like a wolf on the scent of blood, Tyree thought sourly.

The man they had come to roust had a handsome wife and six sandy-haired kids. They were living out of an old Conestoga wagon that had seen better days. The woman was stirring up a big pot of stew when Tyree and Yarnell rode into their camp. The man was cutting timber. Slash W timber, Tyree mused absently, because this time the intruders really were on Slash W property.

The kids were helping their father, chattering happily while they trimmed the branches off the felled trees. A boy of about three was making a pile out of wood chips.

The man was the first to notice the two riders. His eyes were light brown and they reflected a quick apprehension as the strangers drew rein beside the wagon. He sent a glance at his rifle, propped against a log some fifteen feet away, hopelessly out of reach if there was trouble.

The woman threw her husband an anxious look. Fear was plainly etched on her face, and in her clear blue eyes. Her hair was long and reddish-brown, the figure beneath the worn calico dress still firm and trim in spite of bearing a half-dozen children.

"This is Slash W land," Yarnell said brusquely. "You're not wanted here."

"I was told this is open range," the man said affably, "and I intend to homestead it."

"And I intend to bury you on it," Yarnell threatened. Lazily, his hand moved toward the gun riding on his left hip.

There was a sudden explosion as the woman pulled a little over-and-under derringer from her apron pocket and fired at Yarnell. The slug creased the young gunman's cheek, and he hollered with pained surprise as he glared at the woman.

The man was moving now, his face white with horror as he lunged for his rifle.

With an oath, Tyree slapped leather and fired a round into the squatter's shoulder. As the man fell to the ground, barely conscious, the oldest boy, a gangly youth of about sixteen, made a wild dive for his father's rifle. Rolling to his feet, the boy leveled the gun at Tyree.

"Don't do it, kid," Tyree warned.

Shaking his head, the boy pulled back the hammer of the old Spencer rifle. His finger was white around the trigger, his face streaked with tears.

Tyree swore softly as he lined his Colt on the boy's right shoulder. It was a dirty business, shooting at kids, even when you weren't shooting to kill.

He was squeezing the trigger of the Colt when a bright red stain blossomed on the boy's chest. A look of surprise spread over the boy's face as the slug from Yarnell's gun slammed him to the ground. A convulsive tremor shook his slight frame, and then he was still, his pale blue eyes wide and staring.

Tyree's yellow eyes drilled into Yarnell. "Don't ever do that again," he warned in a voice heavy with menace.

Yarnell looked surprised. "I just saved your life!" he exclaimed, punching the spent cartridges from the cylinder of his gun.

"I've been killing my own snakes since you were in three-corner pants," Tyree said coldly. "I think I can manage just a little longer." His mouth curved down in a disdainful smile. "Or maybe that's how you got that big rep you're always bragging about, killing kids."

"Anybody with a gun in his hand is fair game," Yarnell said brashly.

"That right?" Tyree's voice was cool, soft as silk. "There's a gun in my hand."

Yarnell accepted the challenge without hesitation. He was thumbing back the hammer of his Navy Colt when Tyree shot him out of the saddle.

"Fair game," Tyree muttered under his breath. "C'mon, ma'am," he said, holstering his gun and swinging out of the saddle. "Let's look after your old man."

Annabelle was not happy with the news of Yarnell's death. She had grown rather fond of the young gunman in the past few weeks, as fond as she ever grew of anyone. Yarnell had been an accomplished lover and while she would have preferred to have Tyree in her bed, she knew instinctively that Yarnell had proved easier to handle.

She was giving Tyree the rough side of her tongue in the parlor later that day when he reached out and slapped her, hard, across the face.

"Consider that my resignation," he drawled impudently.

Stunned by the blow, Annabelle raised a hand to her throbbing cheek. No man had ever dared strike her. "You'll be sorry for that," she hissed.

"I've been sorry for a lot of things lately," Tyree replied with a shrug. "Just remember, if anything happens to Rachel or her old man, anything at all, I'll be back to take it out of your pretty hide."

"Come back here!" Annabelle shrieked as he walked purposefully toward the door. "No one walks out on me. No one! Damn you, Logan Tyree, I'll make you sorry you were ever born!"

Chapter 17

*T*yree was feeling good as he rode out of the Slash W yard. At last, he was his own man again, unhindered by ties of any kind, free as the wind.

Putting his heels to the gray's flanks, he headed east, toward Sunset Canyon and the Mescalero. Perhaps he would hole up there for awhile until he decided what his next move would be. It would be good to see the People again, to live in the old way, hear the old songs.

He had gone about three miles when he drew the stallion to a halt in the shade of a yellow bluff. Rachel. He swore softly as the memory of the nights they had spent together came to mind. The fragrance of her hair, the way she felt in his arms, the touch and the taste and the smell of her, all were fresh in his mind, and he knew he had to see her again. Perhaps, if she still wanted him, they would get married after all, even have some kids before it was too late . . . .

Tyree frowned as he urged the gray to a walk. He had never thought much about getting old before, but it came to him suddenly that he was almost thirty-five. Not a vast age, by any means, but mighty old for a man in his line of work. He grunted softly as he considered getting married again. He had never really thought of it seriously, not even that night at the Jorgensen place when Rachel had begged him not to go after Larkin and the others.

But now, somehow, the idea of settling down with Rachel didn't sound so bad, and he smiled faintly as he reined the gray toward the Lazy H. Imagine, Logan Tyree, drifter, gunman, escaped con, a family man!

Rachel came to the front door looking as fresh and lovely as a spring day and Tyree felt a peculiar catch in his throat. Damn, but it made him feel good just looking at her.

"Tyree," Rachel murmured, looking confused. "Is anything wrong?"

"No. Can I come in?"

Rachel hesitated for just a moment, her heart beating wildly, then she opened the door. "Come on in. I was just making a cake. Would you like a cup of coffee?"

"Sure." He followed her into the kitchen,

dropped into a chair while she took a cup from the shelf and poured him a cup of steaming black coffee.

Rachel was flustered by Tyree's unexpected appearance. She could feel his eyes on her back as she poured the cake batter into the pan. Sliding the pan into the oven, she turned to face him.

"What . . . why are you here?" she asked anxiously. "Did Annabelle send you?"

"I'm through with Annabelle," Tyree said quietly. "I quit today."

Rachel's smile was radiant. At last, her prayers had been answered. Secretly, she was dying to know why Tyree had quit the Slash W, but her intuition warned her not to pry. He would tell her why he had quit in his own good time, and if not, well, it didn't really matter. He was here and that was all that mattered.

She went willingly into his arms when he reached for her, lifted her face eagerly for his kiss, sighed as he crushed her close.

Tyree grinned as he pressed his lips to Rachel's hair. Once, he had asked her if she thought the love of a good woman would make him mend his evil ways. He wasn't quite sure how she had done it, but it had worked.

"You still want to get married?" Tyree asked gruffly.

"Yes," Rachel answered happily. "Oh, yes!"

"Well, set the date. I'll talk to your old man about it tonight, after dinner."

* * *

John Halloran did not seem surprised to find Tyree sitting at the dinner table that night, nor was he taken aback by the gunman's desire to marry Rachel. He gladly gave the pair his blessing, and Rachel set the date for May 25, just three months away.

In the days that followed, Rachel could not stop smiling. Her spirits soared, her feet flew from task to task, her eyes sparkled with happiness. A kiss from Tyree sent her smiling off to bed, a kiss in the morning set the tone for the day. She watched, pleased, as he followed her father around the Lazy H, learning the ins and outs of running a cattle ranch.

Nights, after dinner, Tyree sat in the parlor with her father, going over the books, debating the necessity of hiring on some help for the summer.

It was during one of their nightly sessions that Halloran remarked, "Funny thing. Somebody paid off my loan at the Cattleman's Bank. Squared my debt at the general store, too."

"That right?" Tyree murmured.

"Yeah. Wasn't for that, we'd be out in the cold. I don't suppose you have any idea who might have settled my accounts in town?"

"Beats me," Tyree muttered. "Going around doing good deeds ain't exactly my style."

"Yeah," Halloran agreed. He looked the tall gunman square in the eye. "Still, if I knew who it was, I'd sure be beholdin' to him. He really saved my neck."

"Some do-gooder in town, no doubt," Tyree suggested.

"Okay, okay," Halloran conceded amiably. "Have it your way. But if you ever find out who it was, you tell him thanks from the Lazy H."

Sunday morning, they all went to church. Tyree had gone into town earlier in the week and bought a pair of brown slacks and a cream colored coat, as well as a couple of shirts, a new pair of boots, and a new Frontier Colt. He donned the brown pants, a tan shirt and the coat for church, and Rachel thought he looked terribly handsome in his new duds. A thrill of excitement danced along her spine as she laid her hand on his arm. And then she frowned.

"Do you have to wear your gun to church?" she asked.

Tyree nodded, his eyes warning her not to argue.

"All right," she said softly. "I understand."

Tyree smiled at her. "I'll hang it up one day," he promised. "But not just yet."

"Okay," Rachel said, smiling back at him. "But I'll hold you to it."

"I'm sure you will."

The good ladies of the town treated Tyree to the same disapproving stares as before, but Tyree just tipped his hat and smiled pleasantly as he followed Rachel and her father into the pew. Tyree's smile, when it was not cold and cruel or mocking, could charm the spots off a leopard, and several of the town dowagers began to think maybe they had misjudged the man. After all, how bad could he be if Rachel approved of him? And she quite obviously approved. A blind man could see that. Why, she hardly took her eyes off the man for a moment, and the open adoration in her eyes caused the good ladies of the town to take a second look at Logan Tyree. And they saw that, besides being something of a gentleman, after all, he was quite handsome to boot. Not in the usual, clean-cut way, to be sure, but extremely handsome nevertheless.

"You'll have the women eating out of your hand in no time at all if you keep smiling at them like that," Rachel teased, squeezing Tyree's hand. "Just remember, I saw you first."

Tyree was all charm and sweet talk after the meeting, too. He tipped his hat to the ladies again, shook hands with several of the men, complimented the Reverend Jenkins on a fine sermon, smiled winningly at Carol Ann.

Carol Ann returned Tyree's smile hesitantly, then gave Rachel a friendly hug.

"Carol Ann!" Rachel exclaimed. "I've been looking everywhere for you. Guess what? Tyree and I are going to be married in May!"

Tyree grinned good-naturedly as Carol Ann blurted, "Oh, no!"

"I thought you would be happy for me," Rachel said coolly, stung by her best friend's blatant shock and disapproval.

"I'm sorry, Rachel," Carol Ann murmured

contritely. "Truly, I am. It's just such a surprise. I . . . congratulations to you both."

Mollified, Rachel said, "You'll be my maid of honor, won't you?"

"Of course." Carol Ann glanced at Tyree. What did Rachel see in him? The man was a murderer, a hired killer. He had shot down four men in Bowsher's Saloon not very long ago, and everyone said he had killed Job Walsh in cold blood. She flushed guiltily as Tyree's eyes met hers, quickly looked away.

"Can you come over Friday?" Rachel asked, excited once more. "We'll have to decide on colors and I want you to help me with a pattern and, oh, there's so much to do. You will help me?"

"Of course I will. See you Friday. Good day, Mr. Halloran. Mr. Tyree."

Tyree was frowning as he handed Rachel into the buggy. "You're not going to turn our wedding into a big shindig, are you?"

"Not too big," Rachel promised, smoothing her skirt over her hips. "But I do want a nice one. After all, a lovely wedding is something every girl dreams of from the minute she realizes boys and girls are different."

"Girls are different, all right," Tyree muttered, climbing in beside Rachel.

Heads turned as the Halloran buggy made its way out of town, and more than a few of the single young women wondered why they had ever thought Logan Tyree a boorish clod and not worthy of their notice. He was really quite a gentleman. And so very, very handsome, especially when he smiled.

John Halloran slapped his thigh with glee when they reached the road that led to the Lazy H. "Damn, Tyree," he chuckled, "I never knew you had so much charm. I think Rachel's right. I think you'll have old Mrs. Fairchild and Dorothy Monahan and all the other old cats inviting you over to Sunday supper before you're through."

Halloran's words proved to be prophetic. The redoubtable Mrs. Fairchild cornered Rachel in Thorngood's General Store the next day and invited her and her young man to dinner the following Sunday after church.

Rachel accepted politely, then fretted the entire week, fearing the evening would turn out to be a disaster. She dressed carefully that night, choosing a light blue muslin with puffy sleeves, a square neck, and a full skirt. Tyree looked wonderful in a pair of black whipcord britches and a wine-red shirt.

Rachel's fears for the evening were quickly put to rest. Tyree played the country gentleman to the hilt. It was all Rachel could do to keep from laughing out loud when he gallantly kissed Mrs. Fairchild's pudgy pink hand.

Selma Fairchild blushed to the roots of her carefully coiffed gray hair as Tyree made a courtly bow over her hand, but from that night on, Logan Tyree could do no wrong in her sight.

Rachel listened in astonishment as Tyree

politely answered Mrs. Fairchild's none-too-subtle questions about his past. Of course, many of Tyree's answers were lies. His past was painful and was not something to be discussed over dinner. But he freely admitted to being an orphan and to being raised by Catholic nuns. He did not mention the fact that his father was a half-breed horse thief, or that his mother had been a whore. Nor did he mention that he had lived with the Indians, though he did admit to having some Indian blood in his background.

The following Sunday, they went through the same thing again, at Dorothy Monahan's house. Indeed, for the next five Sundays, they ate out at a different home as the town dowagers took turns entertaining Rachel and her beau. The consensus was that, despite his unsavory past, Logan Tyree was a gentleman and a good catch.

Carol Ann spent many days at the Lazy H in the weeks that followed, helping Rachel make plans for the wedding. Secluded in Rachel's bedroom, the two girls spent hours sewing their dresses. Carol Ann's dress was pale pink silk, with a high ruffled collar, long sleeves edged in lace, and a full skirt. Rachel's wedding gown was a study in simple elegance. Made of white taffeta, it was uncluttered by frills or bows, save for the dainty white lace that was gathered along the throat and cuffs. Her veil trailed to the ground in a cloud of soft white.

"Remember how we used to dream about the men we would marry," Carol Ann mused one sultry afternoon. "I always planned to marry a banker or a lawyer; somebody with brown hair and brown eyes, who would think I was the most wonderful girl in the world. And you always wanted to marry a man with blond hair and blue eyes, like Clint."

"Things don't always turn out the way we plan," Rachel remarked, threading her needle. "I certainly never planned to fall in love with Tyree. I always thought I'd marry Clint, but the magic just isn't there. I love him, but I'm not in love with him. Do you know what I mean? He'll never be more to me than just a good friend."

"That's all he's ever been to me, too," Carol Ann said wistfully. "And I would so like to be more than just a friend."

Rachel glanced at her friend in surprise. "Why, you're in love with Clint, aren't you? I never dreamed. Why haven't you ever told me?"

Carol Ann shrugged. "Clint has always been in love with you. Everybody knows that. And I always thought you cared for him, too, so . . . golly, Rachel, you're my best friend. How could I even think about Clint when he was supposed to be your beau?"

"Well, he's not my beau any longer," Rachel said, giving Carol Ann a hug. "Have you ever told Clint how you feel?"

"Of course not!" Carol Ann exclaimed, mortified at the very idea. "And don't you dare say a word, promise?"

"I promise, but I think you're making a big mistake. You've got to let him know you're interested."

"I couldn't," Carol Ann said, shaking her head. "I just couldn't. He has to make the first move. And I know he never will."

With a sigh, Rachel turned her attention back to her dress. Carol Ann was a pretty girl, but she was so shy, most men never paid any notice to her. She would be perfect for Clint, Rachel mused. They were very much alike, both warm, friendly souls who loved to read and listen to music.

Pulling her thoughts from Carol Ann and Clint, Rachel thought about Tyree. They had very little in common, she mused. There was nothing similar in their backgrounds, or in their interests. In truth, she did not know what Tyree's interests were, other than the fact that he liked poker and whiskey and long black cigars. He had never mentioned wanting a place of his own, or wanting children. She didn't know if he liked to read, or if he liked to travel, or if he'd ever had any ambition to be anything but what he was.

Pausing to set in a sleeve, Rachel vowed to learn more about the man she planned to marry. She would learn what he liked, and then strive diligently to give him those things.

Surely, if she delved deep enough, she would find they shared more in common than the fierce passion that burned between them.

News of Rachel's engagement did not sit well with everyone. Annabelle Walsh was furious with Tyree, and swore publicly and privately that she hated him. But she did not want Rachel Halloran to have him.

Sitting alone in the Slash W ranch house, she stared into the cold stone fireplace, her lovely brow creased and thoughtful. Her bargain with Tyree was off now, and that meant Halloran was fair game as far as she was concerned. But before she could move against the Lazy H, she had to dispose of Tyree. His threat to come after her had been a warning she could not ignore. She did not doubt for a moment that he would make her pay if anything happened to Rachel or Halloran or the Lazy H.

Eyes narrowed, Annabelle rubbed her cheek, remembering the pain and humiliation Tyree had inflicted upon her the day he walked out. He would pay for that slap, she vowed, and pay dearly . . . .

Clint Wesley viewed Rachel's engagement with anger and jealousy. He had been calling on Rachel regularly for more than two years, courting her in his own shy style, hoping that one day she would agree to be his wife. He had been taking her to church, and to socials, to parties and dances. They had gone walking together in the moonlight. He had dinner at the Lazy H at least once a week, but somehow their relationship had never gotten past the hand-holding stage. And then Tyree had appeared on the scene. Damn the man!

Wesley scowled darkly as he glanced out the jailhouse window. Unconsciously, his hand stroked the butt of his holstered Colt. He had been practicing his draw for several months, and it was smooth and fast.

But was it fast enough?

Chapter 18

The spring social was one of the most looked forward to events of the year. Everyone in the valley was invited, and everyone attended. For this one night, old grudges were forgotten or forgiven, petty quarrels were put aside, debts were not mentioned, and having a good time was top priority.

Rachel hummed softly as she dressed for the big dance. It was good to be alive, good to be in love. She laughed with exuberance as she slipped her dress over her head and smoothed it over her hips. Twirling before the mirror, she was pleased to see that the color was very becoming. The dark lavender made her skin glow like rich cream, and turned her eyes to violet.

Wrapping a light wool shawl around her bare shoulders, she floated down the stairway. Tyree was waiting for her at the foot of the stairs. Dark brown trousers hugged his long muscular legs, a rich maroon broadcloth coat complemented his dark complexion. He smiled at her and Rachel felt a little thrill of excitement dance in the pit of her stomach as she lifted her face for his kiss.

Moments later, John Halloran stepped into the room. "Ready?" he asked cheerfully, and the three of them left the house, chatting amiably.

When they arrived at the schoolhouse, the dance had already started. The desks had been removed, and the ceiling was hung with colored streamers and lamps. Long tables were set up along the edge of the dance floor, laden with coffee and punch and cakes and cookies. Couples whirled around the floor, talking and laughing, as the musicians played a waltz, a polka, a fast-paced reel. On this one night, the men did not leave their ladies to argue about cattle and crops and the rising price of land. Instead, they gallantly courted their women, plying them with compliments and attention, and the women responded by laughing and flirting outrageously with their husbands or beaux.

The next hour passed pleasantly. There was an abundance of food and drink. The fiddler played tirelessly, now something fast, now something slow, now fast again. Rachel was constantly amazed at the wide variety of numbers that he played throughout the night.

During a brief lull, Annabelle Walsh made her entrance on the arm of a tall, dark-haired man. Annabelle looked exquisite. Her gown, a brilliant green silk, had been imported from France. The bodice clung to her ample bosom like a second skin, leaving little to the imagination. The full skirt swished softly as she walked. Her hair was piled high atop her head, save for one long red curl that fell over her left shoulder. Green satin slippers hugged her feet.

Tyree frowned as he noticed Annabelle's only adornment was the ruby teardrop he had given her for Christmas.

Moments later, Clint Wesley strode into the room, his badge shining brightly on the pocket of his dark blue coat. It was, Tyree mused sourly, shaping up to be one hell of a night.

The single men, both young and old, flocked around Annabelle, vying for her attention, arguing back and forth over who had the next dance, and the next. Wesley stood with his back against the east wall, his blue eyes moody as he watched Rachel dance by with Tyree.

Damn, the Marshal mused to himself. Why hadn't he proposed sooner? Why had he thought he had to wait until he had more money? Why hadn't he grabbed her and hauled her off to the preacher's before it was too late? But then, like everyone else, he had taken it for granted that Rachel would marry him. And now he had lost her. Maybe it wasn't too late. Maybe, if he told her how he felt, she would change her mind. It was a slim chance, but one he had to take.

Squaring his shoulders, Clint marched boldly onto the dance floor and tapped Tyree on the shoulder.

Tyree's eyebrows went up in surprise as he surrendered Rachel. It would have been pleasant to tell Wesley to go to hell, but Tyree knew such a thing would have made Rachel angry. And he had no desire to make her mad.

"Evening, Clint," Rachel said, smiling warmly. "Isn't it a lovely night?"

"Lovely," Clint agreed. "Rachel, I love you more than anything in the world. I want you to marry me. I know I've been a fool not to speak up sooner, but I wanted to have enough money put away to buy you a house of your own. I wanted to be able to give you everything you wanted, to spoil you. I love you. I . . . you must know how I feel, how I've always felt. I thought, I hoped, you felt the same."

Rachel stared at him, her mouth slightly open, completely surprised at his outburst. Why had he chosen this particular moment to bare his soul? And what could she possibly say?

"Rachel?" Clint whispered her name, his heart in his eyes.

"Clint, I . . . I love you, but I'm not in love

with you. I . . . it wouldn't have made any difference if you had a lot of money, or if you had asked me to marry you months ago. I love Tyree. I don't know how it happened, I can't explain it, but I love him with all my heart."

Clint nodded. There was nothing more to say.

Standing at the makeshift bar located at the back of the room, Tyree ordered a beer. From the corner of his eye, he saw Annabelle swishing toward him, and he muttered a mild oath under his breath.

"Good evening, Tyree," Annabelle purred.

"Miss Walsh," he replied formally.

"That's a lovely tune they're playing," Annabelle remarked. "It's always been one of my favorites."

"If you want to dance, just say so," Tyree growled, annoyed by her coy attitude.

"I want to dance."

With a scowl, Tyree led her onto the dance floor, gingerly took her in his arms. He would as soon hold a snake, he mused. Certainly a rattler could not be more dangerous than the green-eyed vixen gazing up at him through the dark veil of her lashes.

"How have you been, Tyree?" Annabelle asked, her fingers kneading his left shoulder.

"Fine. You?"

"Fine. My new man, Ricardo, is very pleasant. So much more agreeable than you ever were."

"Then why aren't you dancing with him?"

"He dances like an elephant," Annabelle replied, laughing coquettishly. "Few big men are as light on their feet as you are."

"Save the flattery."

"Rachel looks well with the Marshal, don't you think? Such an attractive young couple."

"Yeah. Thanks for the dance."

Tyree left Annabelle as soon as the music ended, swiftly crossed the floor to where Rachel and Wesley were standing. Without a word, Tyree took Rachel by the arm and guided her, none too gently, toward the punch bowl.

"Tyree, you're hurting me," Rachel protested, pulling away. "What's the matter with you, anyway? You look ready to explode."

"Just jealous, I guess," Tyree admitted somewhat sheepishly.

"*You're* jealous!" Rachel exclaimed. "How do you think it makes me feel to see you with Annabelle, knowing the two of you used to be . . . friends."

"Rachel, I never made love to Annabelle."

"Never?" Could it be true? Oh, please let it be true.

"Never." Tyree grinned at Rachel, his good humor restored. "Let's go home," he suggested, throwing her a wicked glance, "and be friends."

"Tyree, you know we agreed to wait until after the wedding before we . . . you know."

"Change your mind," he whispered.

"Tyree, behave yourself," Rachel scolded, but inwardly she was pleased. It was a heady feeling, knowing he found her desirable. Almost, she was sorry they had decided not to be intimate again until after the wedding.

Unmindful of the eyes watching them, Tyree pulled Rachel into his arms and gave her a kiss that took her breath away.

"Sure you won't change your mind?" he asked.

"I'm sure," Rachel said with regret. "Anyway, we can't just go off and leave my father here with no way home."

"I don't think he'd even miss us," Tyree said, jerking a thumb in Halloran's direction. "He hasn't left his lady love's side all night. She'd probably be glad for an excuse to put him up for the night so they could be 'friends'."

"Tyree!" Rachel gasped, shocked at the very idea of her father and Claire Whiting doing anything so scandalous.

"Okay, okay. Come on, let's dance."

From across the room, Clint Wesley felt a sharp stab of jealousy tear at his heart. Somehow, some way, he would get rid of Logan Tyree and win Rachel's love.

Annabelle's eyes burned with a dark and fierce rage of their own as Tyree and a blushing Rachel whirled around the dance floor, oblivious to everyone else. Rachel's face was radiant, her eyes warm with devotion as she gazed up at Tyree. And Tyree! When had he ever smiled at her like that! His amber eyes were ablaze with desire and, yes, Annabelle thought angrily, with love. Love for that snit in his arms. Abruptly, a slow smile spread across Annabelle's face as she spied the Marshal standing across the room.

Wesley looked puzzled as Annabelle Walsh glided toward him. He had never met the woman, but he was aware of her flawless beauty, and of the great wealth she controlled.

"Marshal Wesley," Annabelle said, extending her hand. "I don't believe we've ever been introduced."

"No," Clint replied, taking her hand. "Is there something I can do for you?"

"I was wondering if I might have a few minutes of your time?"

"Now?"

"Yes, if you don't mind."

"Not at all."

"Could we go outside, perhaps?"

"Sure," Clint said. Feeling like a serf escorting a queen, he took Annabelle's arm and guided her around the edge of the dance floor and out the side door.

Tyree let out a deep breath as he saw the two of them disappear into the shadows. There was trouble brewing, sure as death and hell, and Annabelle was the master brewer.

Outside, Annabelle smiled up at the Marshal as she took his hand in hers. "I have something to tell you," she said, her voice low and confiding. "Something important, but . . ." She looked over her shoulder, as if fearful of being watched.

"You can tell me," Clint assured her. "Don't be afraid."

Fluttering her lashes prettily, Annabelle stepped closer to the Marshal, as if his nearness gave her courage. "I have proof that Logan Tyree killed my brother."

"Proof!" Clint exclaimed. "Where? What kind of proof?"

"A signed confession."

"No shit! Excuse me, Miss Walsh. But where did you get such a thing?"

"I'm not at liberty to say," Annabelle murmured. "But it is quite genuine, I assure you."

Wesley grinned exuberantly. At last! He had Logan Tyree by the short hairs. A signed confession! It was too good to be true.

"This confession," he said eagerly. "Do you have it with you?"

"No. It's in my safe at the ranch." Annabelle smiled up at the Marshal. "But if you will come by tomorrow afternoon, I'll be glad to let you see it."

"I'll be there," Clint assured her. "You can count on that."

"About noon?" Annabelle asked.

"Noon," Clint said.

Hardly able to contain his excitement, Wesley escorted Annabelle back to the schoolhouse, then hurried toward his office. The circuit judge would be coming to town in less than two weeks. With Tyree's signed confession as evidence, the trial would be a mere formality, followed by a quick hanging. And then, at long last, Logan Tyree would be out of his life, and Rachel's, once and for all.

Chapter 19

*T*yree and Rachel lingered over a second cup of coffee the following morning. Tyree was wondering just what kind of mischief Annabelle had been stirring up with the Marshal when Rachel's voice interrupted his thoughts.

"What do you want to do after the wedding, Tyree?" she asked, smiling prettily.

"After?" He lifted one black brow. "The same as most couples do, I reckon."

Rachel blushed under his lusty gaze. "I didn't mean that. I mean, are you going to be happy staying on here? Would you rather go somewhere else and start a place of our own? Do you want children? Do you like beets?"

Tyree laughed softly. "Don't most women find out this kind of stuff before they say yes?"

"I guess so. But our courtship hasn't been exactly normal, you know."

Tyree nodded, his expression indulgent.

"I'd really like to know," Rachel said. "We've never talked about our future, never made any plans. Sometimes I feel as though I hardly know you."

"Getting cold feet?"

"Of course not."

Tyree's gaze drifted past Rachel to the window. He stared outside for a moment before returning his gaze to her face. "I've never spent much time making plans for the future. Guess I figured I probably didn't have one."

Rachel nodded. "I understand. But that's all changed now."

"Yeah."

Rachel cocked her head to one side. "You haven't answered my questions yet."

"I know, but let me ask you one. Do you want to leave here and start over somewhere else?"

"Not really. I love it here."

"I know you do. So if it's all right with your old man, let's just sit tight."

"I'd like that," Rachel said. She leaned across the table and squeezed Tyree's hand. "I don't think I could bear to leave the Lazy H. My whole life has been spent here."

"That's settled then. As for children," Tyree

said with a grin, "I guess I'd like nine or ten."

"Nine or ten!" Rachel exclaimed, blinking at him. "Are you kidding?"

"No, but I guess I'd settle for three or four. However many you want, as long as they're all girls as beautiful as their mother."

"I want boys," Rachel remarked. "Lots of boys with black hair and blue eyes."

"Boys are nothing but trouble," Tyree replied quietly. "I'm proof of that."

"Don't be silly. You're the best thing that ever happened to me."

"Am I?" Tyree's eyes probed hers and it occurred to Rachel that beneath all his arrogance there lurked a little boy after all, one who was looking for love and acceptance, a little boy who had been bad so long he couldn't believe anyone could love him.

"The very best thing," Rachel answered sincerely.

Tyree grinned at her. Then, rising to his feet, he lifted her from her chair and gave her a resounding kiss on the mouth.

"Got to go," he said briskly. "I'm a farmer, now. There's stock to feed out on the range, woman! There's fields to plow and harnesses to mend. But I'll be back for lunch."

So saying, he picked up his hat and ambled out the door, leaving Rachel to stare after him, her eyes dancing with amusement.

The next day, Tyree was sitting on the front porch of the Lazy H, mending a bridle for the gray, when Clint Wesley rode into the yard.

Rising, Tyree tossed the bridle aside and moved to stand near the steps as the Marshal swung out of the saddle.

"You're a long way from town," Tyree remarked.

"I've come to take you in," Wesley said, the words coming hard and fast, before his courage deserted him. "I have a warrant here, charging you with the murder of Job Walsh."

Tyree looked faintly amused. "That so?"

"Yes, that's so!"

"Seems I told you once I wasn't going back to jail."

"So you said."

"I haven't changed my mind."

"Be that as it may, I'm taking you in. Today."

"Suit yourself, kid," Tyree growled, no longer amused. "I'd just as soon kill you as look at you, so make your play or get the hell out of here."

For a moment, it looked like Wesley would back down; but then, with a suddenness that surprised both men, he reached for his gun.

Tyree reacted instinctively. His left-handed draw was smooth as silk and his Colt was out of the holster, the hammer cocked, the muzzle directed at Wesley's chest, before the Marshal's gun cleared leather.

Wesley's face went chalk white as he stared death in the face. The barrel of Tyree's Frontier Colt looked as big as a canyon, and Tyree's eyes, staring down at him, were as cold as the grave.

And then Rachel's voice cut across the heavy stillness. "Tyree! Don't!"

It was a near thing. Tyree's finger remained curled around the trigger, but the hammer didn't fall, and Wesley held his breath waiting, as Rachel ran out of the house and laid her hand on Tyree's arm.

"Please don't kill him," Rachel pleaded softly, and when Tyree failed to respond, she stepped purposefully into the line of fire.

Cursing himself for a fool, Tyree lowered his gun.

It was a chance Clint Wesley could not pass up. Taking a quick step to the right, he jerked his gun from the holster and lined it squarely on Tyree's chest as Rachel stepped out of the way.

"Drop it!" Clint commanded. There was a marked quiver in his voice, but his gun hand was steady as a rock.

"Clint, what are you doing?" Rachel demanded, shocked by the sudden turn of events.

"Stay out of this, Rachel," Wesley warned curtly. "He's a wanted man, and I'm taking him in."

Tyree stared at Wesley, weighing his chances of raising and firing his gun before the Marshal could pull the trigger. The odds were slim, but there was always a chance because Wesley was green as grass and not likely to expect such a desperate move. But even as Tyree considered it, he rejected the idea. He could not gun Wesley down in front of Rachel, could not abide seeing the love in her eyes turn to disgust as he killed a man she was fond of.

Nevertheless, he did not release his hold on the Colt, and his delay made Wesley nervous. Unconsciously, Clint tightened his finger on the trigger. He was as surprised as everyone else when his gun went off. The bullet went high, plowing a shallow furrow along the outside of Tyree's left arm.

Muttering an angry oath, Tyree dropped his gun as the Marshal's bullet raked his flesh.

For a moment, Wesley stared blankly at the blood dripping from Tyree's arm. And then he grinned hugely. By damn, he had done it! Logan Tyree was his prisoner.

Looking extraordinarily pleased with himself, Wesley fished a set of handcuffs out of his back pocket. "Get down here, Tyree," he ordered brusquely.

But the tall gunman refused to obey.

"Clint Wesley, I don't know what you think you're doing," Rachel scolded, "but I'll never forgive you for this. Never as long as I live!"

"I'm sorry you feel that way, Rachel," Clint said stolidly. "I'm just doing my job. Get down here, Tyree!"

"You want me, come up and get me," Tyree challenged, and some of the smugness went out of Wesley's expression.

Red-faced and wary, the Marshal climbed the porch stairs and locked the handcuffs in place, then he picked up Tyree's gun and shoved it in the waistband of his trousers. He heaved a sigh as he realized it was over. Tyree was unarmed, his hands cuffed behind his back.

Moments later, the two men were riding toward Yellow Creek. Rachel stared after them, utterly shocked by what had happened. Slowly, she began to smile. Who would have thought that Clint would actually summon the nerve to arrest Tyree? "Well, Mr. Wesley," she mused, "you have him now, but you won't have him for long."

The Yellow Creek Jail was a red brick building sandwiched between Wong's Chinese Laundry and the newspaper office. It was a long, low building, with two narrow windows facing the street, and a stout oak door.

Inside, Wesley motioned Tyree into the cellblock, opened the door to the first cell. With a grimace, Tyree stepped into the cell, shuddered imperceptibly as the iron-barred door closed behind him.

Clint Wesley turned the key, removed Tyree's handcuffs, then heaved a sigh of relief. The job was done and, by damn, he had done it! He was whistling a cheerful tune as he stepped out of the cellblock and closed the door that separated the Marshal's Office from the jail.

Tyree stared out the tiny barred window set

high in the rear wall of his cell while memories of the Yuma pen flitted across his mind: the high gray wall, the drab cell, the mean-spirited guards, the twang of the whip striking cowering, cringing flesh. The long days and longer nights. The unpalatable food, the tepid water green with slime.

He began to pace the tiny cell, unconsciously padding back and forth like a tiger in a cage. Damn Annabelle Walsh! He could see her fine hand in all this. And damn his own stupidity. He should have known she would make good on her threat. Obviously, she had given that damn confession he had signed to the Marshal. No doubt she would be the first one at the hanging, the last one to leave. He could see her now, standing right in the front row so she could watch him kick!

Swearing softly, he came to an abrupt halt. Pacing endlessly back and forth would get him nowhere, and he stretched out on the narrow cot that filled most of the cell, only to rise moments later to pace again.

A doctor came to dress his wound. It would heal nicely in a few weeks, the sawbones said. Wesley smiled, and Tyree scowled. If Wesley had his way, Tyree would not have a few weeks.

Tyree was pacing his cell again sometime later when the cellblock door swung open, and Clint Wesley stumbled into view. The Marshal's face was drained of color; his hands, held high above his head, trembled visibly.

Behind Clint, armed with sawed-off shotguns, stood Jorges and Nacho Arango, two of Annabelle's most ruthless killers.

Jorges shoved Wesley into an empty cell, jabbed his shotgun into the Marshal's chest while he looked askance at his brother.

Wesley held his breath and closed his eyes as he waited for Nacho to give the word that would scatter him all over the jailhouse wall.

But Nacho shook his head, and Jorges had to content himself with knocking the Marshal unconscious before backing out of the cell and locking the door.

Tyree stood in the middle of his cell, also waiting, feeling his stomach knot as Jorges unlocked the cell door. Nacho stepped inside, his cocked shotgun buried in Tyree's gut, while Jorges handcuffed Tyree's hands behind his back, then shoved Tyree out of the cell.

The gray stud was waiting outside, along with a dun gelding and a black Morgan mare. Jorges hustled Tyree into the saddle, took the gray's reins, and then they were riding out of Yellow Creek toward Coyote Butte at a brisk trot.

Sometime later, Jorges and Nacho slowed the horses to a walk. The streets of Yellow Creek had been deserted when they left the jail. Likely, no one had yet discovered that the Marshal was unconscious, his prisoner gone.

Tyree glanced at his captors. The Arango brothers were short, stocky men. He recalled seeing them at the Slash W. Neither could speak because they had run afoul of a couple of Apache warriors who had cut out their tongues and left them in the desert to die. Rumor had it that Job Walsh had saved their lives, and they'd been riding for the brand ever since.

It was full dark when they reached Coyote Butte. Jorges dismounted and pulled Tyree from the saddle while Nacho drove an iron spike deep into the hard ground, and then lashed Tyree's ankles together. That done, Nacho pulled a length of rawhide from his pocket, pushed Tyree to the ground, and tied his ankles and wrists together behind his back. Lastly, Nacho dropped a loop over Tyree's head, jerked it snug around his neck, then secured the loose end to the iron spike.

That done, Jorges and Nacho prepared a quick meal of beans and hard biscuits, then rolled into their blankets and were quickly asleep.

Wide awake and trussed up like a Christmas turkey, Tyree stared up at the stars, wondering what the hell Annabelle was up to. Apparently, she had decided not to settle for anything as quick as a hanging, unless she meant to tie the knot herself. He glanced at the lone cottonwood some twenty feet away, swore softly as the rope around his neck suddenly seemed to grow tight. Hanging was a bad way to die. The Apache feared it as nothing else, believing that a man's soul left his body with the last breath. When a man was hung, his soul was forever trapped within his corpse.

Tyree shifted uncomfortably. It was not a pleasant way to spend the night, lying on his side in the dirt with his arms and legs drawn together behind his back and a rope around his neck. There was no way to get comfortable and before long, his muscles began to knot up on him.

The moon was on the wane when he finally fell asleep courting thoughts of vengeance.

Rachel was still furious with Clint Wesley when she rode into town late that night. But mingled with her anger was a grudging admiration for his nerve. Who would have thought that Clint would actually try and arrest Tyree? The fool! She could not help wondering if it had occurred to him yet that, but for her timely interference, he would be laid out in Buckman's Funeral Parlor right now. Instead, thanks to her intervention, Clint was alive and well and Tyree was in jail, wounded and facing the prospect of a speedy trail and a hanging that was likely long overdue.

Patting her skirt pocket, Rachel felt a measure of comfort as her hand touched the derringer nestled inside. She had gotten Tyree into jail, and now she meant to get him out. Clint would be madder than hell when she insisted, at gun point, that he release Tyree. And her father would be appalled when he discovered she had broken a man out of jail.

But it could not be helped. She could not stand quietly by and let Tyree hang.

Yellow Creek was asleep under a pale yellow moon when Rachel turned the buggy down the main street. Reining the horse to a halt in front of the jailhouse, she drew a deep breath as she stepped carefully from the buggy. The gun was cold in her hand as she climbed the steps to the Marshal's Office and she stifled a nervous giggle as she opened the door, thinking how surprised Clint would be to see her wielding a gun and demanding Tyree's immediate release.

Closing the door softly behind her, Rachel hoped, fervently, that Clint would accede to her demands. If he refused, all would be lost, because there was no way on God's earth she could shoot Clint.

The Marshal's office was empty, quiet as death. A lamp, turned low, sent long shadows dancing on the walls as she glanced around the room. Clint's coat was hanging from a nail in the wall, his hat was on the top of his desk. Knowing he usually slept on a cot in one of the empty cells when he had a prisoner, Rachel tiptoed into the cellblock, thinking that, if she were lucky, Clint would be sound asleep and she could free Tyree with no one being the wiser.

But the keys to the cells were missing from the hook inside the cellblock door, and all the cells were empty.

She was puzzling over the whereabouts of

the Marshal and the gunman when a hoarse groan broke the eerie stillness. Rachel's first instinct was to run, but a second groan, louder than the first, sent her to investigate and she found Clint sprawled on the floor of the last cell, his hands pressed against the back of his head.

"Good heavens!" Rachel gasped, kneeling outside the cell. "What happened? Did Tyree . . . ?"

"No. Two of Annabelle's thugs buffaloed me. I guess they took Tyree."

Wesley rose unsteadily to his feet. "Extra key," he rasped. "Bottom desk drawer."

Rachel flew on winged feet into the office, muttering under her breath about the awful clutter in the bottom drawer as she rummaged around for the key to the cell. Apparently Clint never threw anything away, and she was forced to paw through papers, a set of handcuffs, a pair of fur-lined gloves, several socks that did not match, and an old wanted poster with Tyree's picture on it, before she found the extra keys.

Hurrying back to the cellblock, she unlocked the door and stepped into the cell. "Are you all right?" she queried anxiously, not liking the wan expression on his face, or the amount of blood matted in his hair. "Can you walk?"

"Of course I can walk," Clint retorted irritably, but his steps were none too steady as he made his way down the narrow corridor to the office. With a sigh, he eased down into the big leather chair behind the desk, sat back, very carefully, and closed his eyes.

Rachel whisked around the office, heating water in a pan on the pot-bellied stove, tidying up the top of the desk while she waited for the water to get hot, sweeping the floor because she was too agitated to sit still. When the water was warm, she took a handkerchief from her skirt pocket and dipped it in the pan, then began to sponge the blood from the gash in Clint's head. He winced as the warm water dribbled into the cut above his left ear, cussed aloud when she washed the wound with whiskey she found in one of the other desk drawers.

"Don't waste it all on my head," Wesley admonished, reaching for the bottle. "It'll do a lot more good on the inside."

Rachel frowned as he took a long drink from the bottle. She did not hold with strong drink, but she had to admit his color quickly improved after a swallow or two.

"What are you doing in town this late?" Clint asked, corking the bottle. "Nice young ladies don't generally come calling in the middle of the night. Especially at the jail."

"I came to break Tyree out," Rachel admitted sheepishly.

Clint Wesley could not have been more surprised if she had suddenly stripped naked and thrown herself across his lap.

"Break him out of jail!" Wesley exclaimed. "How'd you intend to do that?"

"With this," Rachel said, taking the derringer from her skirt pocket.

Clint stared at her, speechless. She was the most wonderful, unpredictable woman he had ever known, and he loved her more than words could say. Words, he mused bitterly. If only he had told her how he felt sooner, when it mattered, perhaps she would not now be engaged to a no-good drifter like Logan Tyree.

"I couldn't let Tyree kill you," Rachel explained. "And I couldn't let you hang him, so . . ." She shrugged. "It seemed like a good idea at the time."

"You're the beatenest woman I've ever known," Clint muttered. "How about helping me over to my place and fixing me something to eat? I'm starved."

"Your place? I thought you stayed here?"

"Not any more. I bought the old Miller place."

"Oh, I've always loved that old house. It's so romantic, with all those turrets and stained glass windows. And that wonderful balcony that overlooks the town."

"Yeah, I knew you liked it," Clint said. He had bought the house a few days before Rachel had announced her engagement to Tyree. "I bought it because I hoped that you, that is, that we . . ." Clint coughed and looked away, a flush spreading over his cheeks.

"Dammit, Rachel, I bought the place for you. For us."

"But I'm engaged to Tyree."

"I know," Clint said gruffly. "But, dammit, Rachel, honey, Tyree's a wanted man in practically every part of the country. What kind of life can you have with a drifter like that? He's no good for you, Rachel. He never will be. Sooner or later, somebody's gonna hold onto him long enough to give him the hanging he deserves, and then where will you be? I love you," he declared passionately. "I know I should have said something sooner, but I thought you knew. Everybody else does. I'd make you a good husband, Rachel, or die trying."

He finished abruptly, his eyes begging her to accept his proposal, to admit he was right about Tyree.

Momentarily taken aback, Rachel could only stand there, her eyes wide with surprise at the unexpected force of Clint's words, and the fervent love shining in his mild blue eyes.

"But, Clint," she stammered after a long moment. "I told you before. I don't love you. Not the way you deserve. I'm in love with Tyree."

"Tyree!" The name spewed from Wesley's mouth as if it were poison. "Dammit, Rachel, the man's not fit to wipe the dust from your shoes. He's a drifter, a hired killer! Hell, he'd probably gun you down if the price was right."

"Once, maybe, but not any more. He's changed."

"Sure," Clint said skeptically.

"It's true! He wants to settle down, have a family . . ."

"For how long?" Clint interrupted. "He's a loner, a man with itchy feet. He'll never settle down in one place."

"Clint, please."

"Rachel." His love for her vibrated in his voice. For once, he threw propriety to the wind, and took her boldly in his arms. His kiss was filled with longing and desire and yet, for all that, it was a chaste kiss, lacking the fire and promise that made Tyree's kisses so tantalizingly seductive.

With a sigh, Clint dropped his arms to his sides and took a step backward. There was a sadly haunted expression in his eyes, a note of despair in his voice when he spoke.

"He's wrong for you. Can't you see that?" He laughed suddenly, harshly, bitterly. "Hell, we're probably arguing over nothing."

"What do you mean?"

"Tyree is probably heading for the border with Annabelle right now."

"No!"

Wesley shrugged. "Then he's dead."

"Dead?" Rachel frowned. "I don't understand."

"Annabelle showed me a confession, signed by Tyree, a couple of days ago. It said that Tyree killed Job Walsh. Annabelle wouldn't tell me where she got it, or how, but when she told me about it, I figured she wanted Tyree out of the way for one reason or another and was using the law to get rid of him for her, all nice and legal. But then two of her men broke him out of jail. Why? Either she's decided to forgive Tyree for whatever he did to displease her, which I doubt, or . . ." Clint spread his hands in a gesture that spoke louder than words.

"Or Annabelle decided to exact her revenge herself."

"Exactly."

Rachel chewed on the inside of her lower lip. What Clint said made good sense. Annabelle had wanted to see Tyree hang and then, for some reason, she had changed her mind. But why?

Wesley reached for his hat, set it carefully on his head. It had been a hell of a night, but some good had come of it. Tyree was out of the way at last. Maybe, in time, Rachel would forget him. Maybe, in time, Clint could win her love. But for now, he just wanted to be alone.

"Go on home, Rachel," he said wearily.

"I can't leave you alone, not when you're hurt."

"I'll be fine," Clint said roughly. "Go on home."

With a sigh of resignation, Rachel murmured a subdued farewell and walked out of the Marshal's Office. She knew she had hurt

Clint, hurt him deeply. But she could not marry a man she didn't love just to spare his feelings.

Outside, Rachel gazed into the darkness. Where was Tyree? Confused and sick at heart, she climbed into the buggy and turned the horse toward home.

Chapter 20

*T*yree woke just after dawn. Nacho and Jorges were gone. But he was not alone. A six-foot rattlesnake lay coiled against his right side, its ugly, triangular-shaped head less than a foot from his own. An involuntary gasp brought a warning buzz from the disturbed reptile.

A long sixty seconds followed, with the snake staring, unblinking, at Tyree, and Tyree staring back. He had seen a man die from a snake bite once. It had not been a pretty sight: the man's leg swollen and turning black, his eyes wide with terror, the fever that shook him from head to toe as the poison spread through his system, convulsions . . . .

Another minute slid quietly into eternity.

Tyree's shirt was soaked with sweat. Perspiration dripped into his eyes, but he dared not blink it away. He knew a moment of gut-wrenching fear as the snake uncoiled and slithered slowly over his chest, its forked tongue darting in and out.

Holding his breath, Tyree slowly raised his head. Risking a look over his shoulder, he breathed an audible sigh of relief as he watched the snake disappear into a shady spot beneath a squat cactus some eight yards away.

Weak with relief, Tyree wriggled around on the hard ground, seeking a more comfortable position. It was then he saw the big blue bowl filled to the brim with water. Water that sparkled and shimmered in the early morning sunlight. He stared at the bowl, unable to believe it was real and not a mirage born out of his thirst.

It was hard work, inching his way toward the bowl. His wounded arm throbbed with each movement, but he struggled forward, his eyes fixed on the bowl and the promise it held.

He cursed with all the bitter rage of a man betrayed when the tether around his neck pulled him up a mere twelve inches short of his goal. He cursed until his throat was raw and his voice was reduced to a harsh rasp.

When his anger cooled, he turned his back to the sun and closed his eyes. The hours crawled by on leaded feet. The air, hot and dry, covered him like a heavy blanket. Sweat poured out of him, soaking his clothing, stinging his eyes. Flies came to torment him, crawling over his wounded arm. His lips cracked and bled, and he sucked the salty moisture, desperate for any trace of wetness to ease his horrible thirst. His tongue grew thick in his mouth, his throat felt tight and swollen.

Knowing it was useless, he pulled against his tether in a vain attempt to reach the beautiful blue bowl of crystal water that shimmered like liquid diamonds in the sunshine.

But straining against the hangman's rope only drew the noose tighter around his neck. Only a few inches, he mused ruefully. It might as well have been a mile. A wry grin turned down the corners of his mouth as he contemplated dying in the desert. He had always thought to meet his end quickly, from a bullet fired by that one gunman whose draw would be that fatal fraction of a second faster than his own. Or at the end of a rope. He had never imagined he would die an inch at a time under a blistering sun because he had walked out on a slut.

And still the minutes moved slowly onward and the sun climbed higher in the sky, beating down on his unprotected head, burning into his brain. He closed his eyes against the blinding glare and distorted images from his past crowded his mind. He frowned as people long forgotten paraded through the mists of time. So much killing, so much death. He heard the Reverend Jenkens' voice echo in his ears: "He who lives by the sword shall die by the sword . . ." and he laughed out loud. The Reverend was sure as hell wrong about that. He would have welcomed a bullet to the torture he now faced.

He shook his head from side to side, seeking relief from the bitter memories that plagued him and suddenly Rachel's image materialized before him. The other ghosts faded away and she stood alone in his memory.

Rachel. Warm, loving, caring.

Rachel. More beautiful than life.

Rachel. Perhaps he had loved her from the moment he first saw her bending over him. Why had he been so reluctant to admit it?

The hours and minutes they had spent together swirled together in his mind. Always, when he needed her, she had been there. Her tender care had saved his life. She had nursed his hurts, bandaged his wounds, made him realize the value of life. But, more importantly, she had healed the wounds he had carried inside, made him realize he was more than just a worthless saddle tramp, more than a hired gun.

"Rachel." He sobbed her name aloud, grieving for what might have been.

With a start, Tyree opened his eyes and the first thing he saw was the pretty blue bowl. No matter how many times he looked away, no matter how many times he cursed Annabelle, sooner or later his eyes were drawn back to the bowl and its precious, life-sustaining contents.

Once, he surged forward with all his might, ignoring the pains that raced through his limbs, ignoring the noose that cut ever deeper into his neck, choking off his breath. He strained forward, straining until the world went black and he fell into a fathomless void.

When he regained consciousness, the setting sun was turning the western horizon to flame. Great splashes of crimson and gold and orange stained the pale blue sky, gradually fading to lavender and then to gray as the sun dropped behind the mountains.

Tyree let out a long breath, shuddered convulsively as his whole body screamed for relief.

A soft mocking laugh drew his attention and he glanced over his shoulder to find Annabelle Walsh staring down at him. She was wearing a blue silk shirt, tight black pants, and black calfskin boots. Even now, when he was wracked with pain and unbearable thirst, he could not help thinking she was the most blatantly beautiful woman he had ever known. The most beautiful, and the most vindictive.

"Thirsty, Tyree?" Annabelle purred wickedly. "Hungry? Do your limbs ache from that dreadful position?" Her laugh was low and decidedly cruel. "You should never strike a lady, you know."

"I never have," Tyree retorted hoarsely, and knew a faint moment of satisfaction as Annabelle's green eyes grew dark with anger.

"Still full of fire, I see," Annabelle mused aloud. She dragged a hand through the thick mane of her red hair. "But that fire will be out by tomorrow. Before the day is out, the vultures will be fighting over your carcass."

"You gonna stay and watch?"

"Perhaps."

Annabelle's eyes moved slowly over Tyree's body, lingering on the taut muscles in his arms, the broad expanse of his chest, his long powerful legs. A melancholy expression softened the anger in her eyes. She had never wanted a man as much as she had wanted Logan Tyree. Why, of all the men she had desired, had he been the one to elude her grasp? No other man had ever been able to resist her feminine charm. Always, in the past, she had dominated the men in her life. But she had never been able to dominate Tyree. Always, he had been the master. Almost, she regretted her decision to kill him. Almost, she reached down to loosen his bonds.

But then the memory of his hand striking her flesh intruded on the thought of what might have been, shattering her wistful reverie. A nasty smile twitched at the corners of her mouth as an involuntary shudder of pain wracked Tyree's body. His pain pleased her, soothing her injured vanity. She was the master now.

A flat rock provided a place to sit, and Annabelle curled her legs under her, deciding she would stay and watch Tyree die. It gave her a sense of power, knowing she held his life in her hands. She could kill him now, quickly, or let him die slowly. She wondered what it would be like to see the life drain out of his body; wondered, absently, if his cool self-control would shatter in the end. It would be immensely satisfying, she mused, to see him break, to hear him whine and beg for mercy.

With greatly exaggerated gestures, she uncorked the canteen she had brought with her and took a long swallow. She was aware of Tyree's eyes watching her every move. Out of pure cussedness, she shook the canteen under Tyree's nose. The water sloshed inside, sounding delightfully cool and wet and refreshing, and Annabelle watched Tyree, waiting for him to beg her for a drink. It would be such fun to hear him beg. She might even give him a tiny swallow.

But Tyree did not beg. He licked his lips as he watched Annabelle take a long drink. But he did not beg.

When he remained mute, Annabelle poured a small amount into her hands and wiped her face and neck. Her sigh of pleasure was long and loud.

"Would you like a drink, Tyree?" she asked, shaking the canteen under his nose again. "It's so hot, and I know you must be *dying* for a drink."

It was in his mind to say yes, to beg her for just one swallow, but he knew her too well; knew she would only laugh in his face.

"Damn you," he rasped, hating her as he had never hated anyone in his life. "I hope you fry in hell."

The sound of approaching horses stifled Annabelle's reply, and she stood up, peering into the darkness.

Glancing past Annabelle, Tyree saw six men riding toward them. A sudden coldness engulfed Tyree as he recognized Joaquin Montoya riding in the lead. Montoya. Dealer in human flesh.

Montoya drew rein near Annabelle. Gallantly, he removed his sombrero and bowed from the waist.

"Ah, Senorita Walsh," he said jovially. "Disposing of that troublesome gunfighter, I see."

"Montoya," Annabelle said warmly. "How nice to see you again." Her eyes sparkled with approval. Montoya was a handsome man, with laughing black eyes and a sweeping black moustache. They were much alike, she mused. Perhaps that was why they got on so well together.

"The pleasure is all mine, chiquita," Montoya replied. He gestured at Tyree. "He looks about done for."

"There's life in him yet," Annabelle remarked. "He will wish for death many times before it comes."

Montoya studied Tyree for a long moment.

Then, dismounting, he squatted on his heels beside the gunman and ran a slender brown hand over Tyree's arms and legs, grunting softly.

"Why not sell him to me?" the bandit asked, rising to stand beside Annabelle.

"Whatever for?"

"I can sell him to the mines. They pay much for big men with strong backs. And this one, I think he could do the work of two men."

"No," Annabelle said, shaking her head. "He must die. Slowly."

"As you wish," Montoya conceded with a shrug. "But you can only kill him once. In the mine, he will die a little each day."

Annabelle regarded Tyree through thoughtful eyes. Montoya was right. You could only kill a man once. And for Tyree, death would come as a welcome release from the pain and thirst and suffering. But the mines . . . to be constantly underground, chained like a beast of burden, driven by the whip . . . ah, there was lasting punishment indeed, worse, in its own way, than death itself. The mine would humble him once and for all. Truly, he would rue the day he had left her.

"You will see he works hard?" Annabelle asked, lifting her gaze to Montoya's face.

"Si, very hard."

"And when he can no longer work?"

Montoya shrugged. "He will be driven out into the desert to die. So you see, in a way, his end will be the same."

"Very well," Annabelle said decisively. She dug into her pants pocket and withdrew the key to Tyree's handcuffs. "He is yours," she said, passing the key to Montoya.

Logan Tyree's eyes never left Annabelle's face. Not when one of Montoya's men cut the rope from his neck, not when they placed him on a horse, not when they tied his feet to the stirrups.

It was spooky, Annabelle thought, the way Tyree stared at her, his yellow eyes cold and unblinking, like a snake's. It was quite unsettling, and she turned away, shivering, as though someone had just walked over her grave.

"Annabelle."

Tyree's voice, raspy and harsh, reached out to her. Slowly, like one mesmerized, she pivoted to face him.

"I'll kill you for this," Tyree vowed. "Some night, you'll wake up to find my hands around your throat."

"You dare threaten me?" Annabelle asked in amazement. "Even now, when I hold your life in my hands?"

"Damn you!" Tyree hurled the words at her. "If you want my life, take it and be done with it!"

Annabelle frowned as she stared at Tyree, bemused by the faint glimmer of fear lurking deep in his eyes. He was not afraid of dying. She knew that. Of what, then, was he afraid?

"It is the loss of his freedom he fears,"

Montoya explained, reading the question in her eyes. "Life is cheap to a man who sells his gun to the highest bidder. But freedom, ah, freedom is much to be prized."

Head cocked to one side, Annabelle looked up at Tyree, and saw the truth of Montoya's words mirrored in Tyree's eyes. Her smile was cruel as she said, with finality, "There will be no death for you this night, Tyree, or for many days and nights to come. Only the rattle of chains on your feet, and the song of the whip on your back. Remember me, every time you pray for death. Montoya, take him away!"

It took six days to reach the silver mine located in a green valley in Mexico. Tyree spent most of that time dozing on the back of a horse, his hands cuffed behind his back, his feet lashed to the stirrups. Nights, when the outlaws made camp, he was shackled to a tree, or to one of the outlaws.

Montoya and his men spent their nights around a comfortable fire, eating, drinking, laughing. Looking forward to the time when they would be rid of Tyree and back home with their women.

Tyree had hoped that, somehow, he would find a way to escape before they reached Mexico, but Montoya was an expert in handling prisoners. He took no chances, made no mistakes, and there was no opportunity to make a break for it.

Tyree had recovered from his ordeal in the

desert when Montoya handed him over to Pedro Diaz, the mine boss.

Diaz was a grossly fat, ugly man with a bald pate, wide-set black eyes, and a mouth full of rotten teeth. He examined Tyree thoroughly.

"Not bad," Diaz muttered. "Not bad. I will give you two hundred for him."

Montoya looked hurt. "Two hundred? Really, Pedro, I think even a blind man could see he is worth more than that."

"No. Look, he has a bad right hand."

"Two seventy-five," Montoya argued. "He is worth at least that much."

"Let us say two fifty and part friends," Diaz countered.

"You drive a hard bargain, amigo," Montoya said with a wry smile.

The fat man's paunch shook like jelly as he laughingly reached into his pocket and withdrew a roll of bills. "You wanted two fifty all the time," Diaz remarked as he counted out the correct amount, "and we both know it. Come, let us drink to a bargain well made."

It was then that Tyree's nightmare began. He was issued a pair of worn white cotton breeches, a threadbare cotton shirt, and a pair of thick leather sandals. When he was dressed, a beetle-browed guard shoved a rifle barrel in his spine and marched him down a dirt path that led to a row of square cages constructed of tin and thick wire mesh.

It took three burly men to wrestle Tyree

into the cage; he shuddered as the door was locked behind him.

Like an animal, he paced the small cage. Three short strides took him from one end of the cage to the other. There was nothing to block his way, no bed, no chair, not even a chamber pot. Back and forth, back and forth, he paced, the tension growing in him all the while. The sun beat down on the tin roof and sweat poured down Tyree's face and neck and back. And still he prowled restlessly to and fro, driven by his anger, and by a virulent hatred for Annabelle Walsh that grew and thrived like a malignant tumor feeding upon itself.

It was just after sunset when the other prisoners emerged from the dark bowels of the mine. They walked with heavy steps and downcast eyes, faces devoid of all expression. The long line of men drew to a halt, and each man stepped into one of the cages. The doors closed. The locks were secured. The work day was over.

Tyree did not sleep that night. The cage was too small to allow for much movement and its sides seemed to close in on him, growing even smaller and more confining.

Worse things were waiting for him the next day. His hands and feet were fitted with shackles, and he was herded into one of the shafts along with a dozen other slaves. The shaft was long and narrow, dimly lit by lanterns strung from the sagging beams that shored up the tunnel. One of the guards ordered him toward a narrow vein of silver and told him to dig until the vein ran out. It was back-breaking work. The air was stale. His hands blistered. His hatred for Annabelle grew with each stroke of the axe.

In a week, his life had settled into a dreary routine far worse than anything he had ever imagined. He rose with the dawn. Ate a bowl of cornmeal mush. Relieved himself. And then it was time to go into the mine. Four hours later, a skinny Indian boy brought him a hunk of black bread and a cup of lukewarm water. At dusk, he was back in his cage. An hour later, a fat Mexican woman brought him his dinner. It was the highlight of his day, the only meal fit to eat. At dawn, the whole routine began again.

Tyree had thought life behind the dreary walls of Yuma was surely the worst thing that a man could endure. But he had been wrong. His cell in prison had been a mansion compared to the tiny mesh cage. The dusty prison yard looked like the Garden of Eden when compared to the mine shaft. And the guards at Yuma, hell, they had been saints compared to the guards in the mine.

Tyree had endured two weeks of hell when the guard known as Lobo stopped at his cage.

"Gringo," the guard called softly. "Are you awake?"

"Yeah."

"Luis tells me you are a famous gunfighter. Es verdad?"

"Yeah, es verdad."

Lobo thrumbed his chest proudly. "I, too, have the desire to be a gunfighter."

"Congratulations," Tyree muttered sarcastically.

"Tomorrow, you will teach me."

"Get lost, Lobo."

"You will teach me, gringo pig," Lobo said confidently. "Because it is the only way to avoid the mine. Tomorrow, you will work in the barn. I will meet you there."

"Whatever you say," Tyree remarked indifferently. But he felt a quick flutter of hope. Anything would be better than the mine.

Lobo was as good as his word, and the next morning Tyree found himself shoveling horseshit. It was hot, smelly work, but it was better than working in the dark bowels of the earth. He filled his nostrils with the scent of hay and leather and horseflesh. The barn reminded him of the Lazy H, and he thought briefly of Rachel.

He was wondering what she was doing, and what she thought of his disappearance from jail, when Lobo called him outside.

"Now, gringo," the guard ordered cockily. "Teach me."

"Can you use that hogleg?" Tyree asked, gesturing at the Colt's Dragoon holstered on the guard's right hip.

For his answer, Lobo drew and fired at a

bottle he had earlier placed on a fence post.

Tyree shook his head in disgust. "Is that the best you can do?"

"I hit it, did I not?" Lobo boasted, thumping his chest.

"You hit it all right, but I could have put six slugs in your gut while you drew your piece. Your draw has to be all one motion. You can't draw your weapon, cock it, raise it to fire, aim, and pull the trigger. It should all be one continuous move."

Lobo looked skeptical. "Show me," he demanded, handing Tyree an unloaded pistol and a holster.

Tyree strapped the holster in place, then held up his bound wrists. "You'll have to remove these chains."

Lobo hesitated for a moment, then removed the shackles from Tyree's wrists. "Show me," the guard said. "And if you are thinking of trying anything foolish, remember, I did hit the bottle. I will not miss anything so big as you."

Tyree grinned as he slid the gun into the holster. "Like this," Tyree said. "You've got to thumb back the hammer as the gun comes out of your holster. Know where you want your shot to go before you draw your gun and then put it there."

Lobo watched carefully as Tyree drew his gun, thumbing back the hammer as the old .44 cleared leather, coming up smooth and fast, the barrel aimed at a bird perched on a bush some ten yards away. There was a soft click as Tyree squeezed the trigger.

With a nod, Lobo holstered his gun, drew and fired a second time. This time his speed was better, but he missed his target.

An hour went by before Lobo called it quits. "Tomorrow, gringo," he called over his shoulder. "Same time."

"You're the boss," Tyree muttered laconically, and returned to the stable.

It was rather pleasant there, with just the horses for company. Lobo came in to check on him once in a while; other than that, he was left pretty much on his own. He cleaned the stalls, curried the horses, and thought about escape.

A week slid by. For Tyree, it was seven days of relatively easy work. Lobo grew more and more cocky as his draw improved. Tyree could tell the man spent long hours practicing, for his speed and accuracy seemed to increase daily.

"I heard you were the best," Lobo remarked one afternoon. "Even here, we have heard of your reputation."

"You heard right," Tyree admitted. "Give me a loaded gun, and I'll show you."

"You have given me an idea!" Lobo exclaimed, hitting his forehead with his flat palm. "El Patron has a bodyguard who is rumored to be the fastest gun in all of Mexico. I think it would amuse El Patron to see you and Paulo face each other."

"I think you're out of your mind."

"No, no. It is a great idea. I will give you a week to practice."

"And if I refuse?"

"I think maybe you will meet with a little accident in the mine. Maybe tomorrow. You comprende?"

"Yeah," Tyree drawled. "I comprende."

The shoot-out between Paulo and Logan Tyree was a big success. El Patron and his guards turned out in force to cheer the Mexican gunman. Bets were made, tequila was passed around, and there was much laughing and joking as the two gunmen stood face to face across six feet of sun-bleached ground.

Paulo was a slight young man with a dark olive complexion, straight black hair, and the cold, unblinking eyes of a born killer. He was dressed in tight black pants and a white linen shirt. His gunbelt was hand-tooled leather, all done in fancy scrollwork. His gun was a new, ivory-handled Colt .45.

Tyree looked ridiculous in contrast to the Mexican. His pants and shirt were coarse and ill-fitting. His gunbelt was scarred and worn, his gun an ill-cared for Smith & Wesson.

Both guns were empty because this was a contest for speed only.

Still, there was a decided air of tension between the two gunmen. No blood would be shed, no life hung in the balance, but a man's pride was just as dear as life itself.

Tyree stood easy beneath the blazing sun, his hands loose at his sides, a faint grin on his lips as he contemplated drawing against the younger man. The gun on his left hip was a welcome, familiar weight. His hands, temporarily freed of their restricting shackles, felt as light as air.

When all was ready, El Patron and his men fell silent. Lobo stepped forward to give the signal. Tyree's muscles tensed, though there was no outward change in his expression or his stance.

The signal was given, and Paulo made his move. He was like a snake, smooth and swift, all coiled energy and economy of movement. But Tyree was faster, smoother, more sure of himself. His gun cleared leather and he dry-fired the weapon as Paulo's gun cleared leather.

There was an audible sigh of defeat from El Patron and his cronies; a few quiet cheers from the handful of guards who had backed the gringo gunfighter.

Minutes after the match was over, Tyree's shackles were back in place and he was in his cage again. His vacation was over. The following morning he was back in the mine, back into the bowels of the earth to toil from dawn to dark. He saw men tortured to death, saw them starved and whipped and abused in ways that made the Mescalero look like amateurs.

Sometimes, at night, he could hear the anguished screams of the poor unfortunate wretches who had foolishly angered one of the guards, or broken a rule. But Tyree felt nothing for the men who labored beside him in the mine. They shared his pain. They shared his misery. They shared his dreams of freedom, but he was a man alone. He did not join in on those rare occasions when the prisoners were permitted to talk to each other, nor did he make any effort to get acquainted with the man in the cage next to his. He had always been a loner, and he felt no need to lament his fate with the other prisoners.

But one thing they all shared in common was a dream of freedom. Tyree spent many hours in the dark of night dreaming of the time when he would be free again, when his life would be his own. It was a hope that kept him going, that made his life worth living.

Sometimes, at night, when the wind was right, the haunting strains of a Spanish guitar drifted down to the cages, reminding Tyree of the night he had danced with Rachel in the yard of the Lazy H. The music, always bittersweet, filled Tyree with a deep sadness as he listened to the other prisoners reminisce about their wives and sweethearts and children.

Lying on his back in the cramped cage, Tyree stared up at the indigo sky and thought about Rachel. If his crude calendar was correct, it was May the 24th. Tomorrow would have been his wedding day. Closing his eyes, he envisioned Rachel clad in a gown of spotless white. Likely, she'd marry Wesley now, he mused bitterly, but maybe it was for the best. The Marshal would make a fine husband, a good father . . . He mouthed an obscenity as he pictured Rachel married to another man, and he put the thought out of his mind and instead imagined Rachel moving about the sunlit kitchen back at the Lazy H, her golden hair cascading down her back, a song on her lips. He remembered the taste and the touch and the womanly scent of her, and the memory aroused such a fierce longing in his heart he thought he would go mad.

But yearning for Rachel was not the worst torture because, even worse than his yearning for a woman was the gradual realization that only death would free him from the misery of the mine.

It was a fact he had always known, deep down. And yet, for the first few months, there lingered a faint unacknowledged hope that he would miraculously win his freedom; that he would once again be the master of his own fate, free to follow the sun, to chase the wind across the prairie, to love a woman with tawny hair and sky blue eyes.

It was a hope that died hard, but in time it was crushed beneath a burden of misery and despair that grew too heavy to bear as, seven days a week, he toiled in the mine, never seeing the sun. His hair grew long and matted, his body was layered with filth. He grew thin, thinner. His hands blistered, bled, scabbed over, and blistered again, until they became hard and calloused. His ruined right hand did not keep him from working in the mine or affect his work in any way. Indeed, the constant hard work and the long hours spent swinging a pick and shovel restored much of the strength to his right hand. With grim-faced amusement, he thought that, if he ever managed to escape from the mine, he would have to thank Annabelle for the increased dexterity of his broken hand. Thank her, and then kill her.

The days and weeks passed with incredible slowness. Like a dumb beast, Tyree moved obediently to the familiar tune of the whip across his back, silently cursing Annabelle Walsh each time the lash bit into his flesh.

As the weeks became months, Rachel ceased to exist for Tyree, as did everything else in the outside world. There was no room in his life for thoughts of a golden-haired girl with sweet lips and honeyed flesh. There was only room for hatred. Hate for Annabelle, for Montoya, for the guards who ruled his every waking moment. There was no place for memories of happier times. There was only room for hate, and for impotent dreams of vengeance.

Chapter 21

The days that passed so slowly for Logan Tyree passed slowly for Rachel, as well. She refused to believe he was dead. Perhaps Annabelle had nothing to do with the two men who had freed Tyree from jail. Perhaps Tyree had somehow gotten word to those men that he was in jail and needed help. Perhaps Annabelle had regretted her decision to be avenged on Tyree and that was why she sent her men to break Tyree out of jail.

A dozen times a day, she looked out the window, or went to the front door, eyes searching the horizon for some sign of a tall, dark-haired man riding toward her. Nightly, she lay awake in her bed, praying he would come for her. She would do anything he wanted, go anywhere he desired. Anywhere. Even if it meant going to live with the Indians where he had once known happiness.

But Tyree did not come, and as the days became weeks, Rachel stopped waiting for him and resigned herself to the fact that he was not coming—ever. The tears she had been holding back came then—hot, bitter tears that somehow helped to ease the dreadful ache in her heart.

The twenty-fifth of May was the worst day of her life. She spent most of the afternoon in her room, alone, staring out the window. Where was Tyree? Fighting tears, she went to her closet and ran her hand over the dress that was to have been her bridal gown. With a strangled sob, she snatched the dress from the hanger and began to tear at the fabric with her hands and when the material refused to give way, she grabbed a pair of scissors and slashed the dress to ribbons.

"I hate you, Tyree!" she screamed. "Hate you, hate you, hate you!"

Tears streamed from her eyes and she sank to the floor, her face buried in the soft white material of the ruined gown.

Clint Wesley came to see her almost daily. At first, Rachel was cold, almost rude, blaming him for what had happened to Tyree. But as time passed, her anger turned to apathy,

and then tolerance. Clint told her frequently
that he loved her, that he had always loved her.
And when he kissed her, it was the kiss of a
man who knew his own mind, and not the kiss
of a shy boy. He brought her flowers and
candy, courting her in earnest, determined to
make her love him. He took her to church
every Sunday, escorted her to social functions, took her for walks and picnics, anything
to cheer her and bring a smile to her face.

For Wesley, it was a time of waiting: waiting
for Rachel to forget Tyree, waiting for her
affection to turn to the love he so desired,
waiting for the day she would agree to be his
wife. He wooed her with kind words and
tender kisses, never pushing, never demanding, but the waiting was hard.

He sought Rachel's advice in decorating the
old Miller place, painted the rooms in the
colors she preferred, bought furniture she
liked, arranged it as she thought best, always
hoping that someday she would share the
house with him.

Once Rachel had convinced herself that she
would never see Tyree again, she tried to love
Clint, tried to convince herself that she was
better off without Logan Tyree who had been
nothing but an outlaw and a hired gun, after
all, while Clint Wesley was a fine honorable
man whose thoughts and actions were sincere
and above reproach. Clint loved her dearly
and proved it in every way possible. But no

matter how she tried, she could not persuade her stubborn heart to forsake the love she felt for Tyree.

Once, she tried to explain to Clint how she felt, but he kissed her to silence, declaring he did not give a damn how she felt about Logan Tyree.

"I love you," Clint had said firmly, "and I won't give up on us until the day you marry someone else. And if that man turns out to be Tyree, then I'll dance at your wedding and wish you all the best. But until then, I aim to keep trying to win your love."

John Halloran looked favorably upon Clint Wesley and the possibility of having him as a son-in-law. Clint was a good man. He would be good for Rachel if she would just give him half a chance. And perhaps Clint would be good for the Lazy H, as well. Perhaps, with a lawman in the family, Annabelle Walsh would stop trying to take over the ranch. Since Tyree's disappearance, Halloran cattle were being stolen from the new herd, fences were being cut, crops were destroyed in the fields.

Often, Halloran wondered why Annabelle did not have him killed out of hand the way she had killed others who opposed her. But no attempts were made on his life, or Rachel's. There was only a constant fight to survive. It was not until Slash W cattle began filtering into his grazing land that he realized Annabelle no longer considered him a threat.

Contemptuously, she allowed him to remain alive, knowing there was nothing he could do to hurt her. Still, seeing Slash W cattle on his range was like a slap in the face, but he could not fight, and he would not run.

In July, Rachel's mare gave birth to a long-legged bay filly.

Rachel watched in wonder as the filly entered the world: first two dainty hoofs, then a silky muzzle, followed by the head, body and hindquarters. Morgana had an easy time delivering her first foal and Rachel felt tears prick her eyes as the mare whickered softly to her foal, then licked the filly's face and ears. Within minutes, the filly was trying to stand. Rachel did not interfere, knowing the foal needed to learn to control her long spindly legs, knowing there was strength in struggling. Finally, after several attempts, the foal managed to gain her feet. Morgana blew softly, and then she began to lick the filly dry.

Rachel grinned as the filly began to root around the mare's underbelly, looking for nourishment. Her thoughts were no longer on the miracle of birth, but on a warm night in August when the gray mustang had sired the filly. The night she had spent in Tyree's arms. It was a night she would never forget. Tyree had been like a stallion himself that night, wild and untamed, bending her to his will, dominating her as the gray stud had dominated Morgana. And she had reveled in it, had gloried in his strength as she surrendered to him, totally and completely.

Tyree, Tyree. Would she never be free of him? He was there, wherever she looked. She thought of the night he made love to her before the fire, the night he had danced her around the yard, the day they had spent at the box social, the time he had saved Amy from harm, the hours he had spent taming the gray stallion. Every room in the house held a memory of Tyree.

In August, John Halloran surprised everyone by proposing to Claire Whiting, and she accepted. The wedding was held a week later at the church in town. Claire was an attractive, middle-aged woman, and she made a lovely bride.

Rachel wept quietly as the Reverend Jenkins pronounced Claire and her father man and wife. The lovely ceremony, the timeless words that united a man and a woman into one flesh, all seemed to mock the loneliness in Rachel's heart. She had been so certain Tyree would come back to her if he could. So certain. It was hard to admit she would never see him again, harder still because she was certain he was still alive. Somehow, she knew she would feel it if he were no longer alive. Better to think of him alive and well in some Mexican border town, even if it meant she would never see him again, than to picture him dead, his vitality forever stilled. No matter what the future held for her, no matter what man she eventually married, if she married at all, she knew Tyree would always have a place in her heart.

She smiled wistfully as her father kissed his bride. She recalled asking her father if he thought it wise to marry when they were having so much trouble with Annabelle.

"If I don't marry Claire now," her father had replied, giving her chin a squeeze, "I may never get the chance. Claire knows what I'm up against, and she wants to share it with me."

Fresh tears came then. If only Tyree were here to share their troubles. She had never been afraid when Tyree was near. He had always been so self-assured, so certain of what to do in a crisis.

Clint Wesley smiled indulgently as he handed his handkerchief to Rachel. Women. They were so emotional, always crying at weddings.

The reception, which was held in the schoolhouse, was lively and well-attended, for John Halloran and his bride were well thought of by their friends and neighbors in Yellow Creek.

Rachel sighed as her father and Claire danced the first dance. Her father's wedding had been everything she had hoped hers would be.

When the music ended, John Halloran claimed Rachel for the next dance.

"Well, daughter, what do you think?" he asked as he twirled her around the room.

"I think you've married a wonderful woman," Rachel said sincerely. "I think you'll be good for each other."

"Thank you, child. Now, what about you? Why don't you give in and marry Clint? Don't you think he's courted you long enough?"

"What's the matter, Pa?" Rachel asked, only partly kidding, "Can't you wait to be rid of me now that you've got another woman to look after you?"

"Rachel!"

"I'm sorry," Rachel said, ashamed. "I didn't mean it. Maybe you're right. Maybe I should marry Clint, but—"

"It's Tyree, isn't it? You're still hoping he'll come back."

"Yes."

"Once I thought he would make a good husband for you, honey, but maybe I was wrong. I don't know if he's dead or alive, but I do know that some men are like wild horses. No matter how you try and gentle them, that wild streak persists. You can't beat it out of them, and you can't love it out. It's ingrained too deep. Perhaps that's the way it is with Tyree."

"Perhaps." Rachel gave her father a hug. "Stop worrying about me, Pa. I'll be fine."

John Halloran kissed his daughter's cheek as the dance ended and Clint Wesley came to

claim her. Wesley had matured in the last
year, Halloran thought. There was a new air of
self-confidence about the man, an air of assurance that had been heretofore lacking in his
character. He had turned into a damned
handsome man, too, Halloran mused, and
tonight he looked mighty fine in a brown suit
and tie. He glanced at Rachel and saw that
she, too, was aware of the change in the
Marshal. Maybe there would be another wedding in the family before too long, after all.

"Take good care of my girl," Halloran said
to Clint. "She's the best there is."

"Yes, sir," Wesley agreed heartily. "The very
best." And the most beautiful, Clint thought to
himself. She looked incredibly lovely tonight
in a full-skirted cream-colored gown with
long billowy sleeves and a square neck edged
in ecru lace. Her hair, as gold as a new-minted
coin, was held away from her face with a wide
satin ribbon tied in a big bow. She looked
young and vivacious and so desirable, it made
him ache with longing just to look at her.

"Let's get some air," Clint suggested, and
taking Rachel's arm, he steered her out the
side door into the schoolyard.

It was a lovely night. The sky was a dark,
dark blue. Countless stars played hide and
seek with a few drifting powderpuff clouds,
while the air was sweet with the scent of
honeysuckle.

"They look happy together," Clint remarked as they strolled around the yard, "your father and Claire."

"Yes. She'll be good for Pa. He's lived alone too long."

"So have I," Clint said huskily. Taking her in his arms, he bent down and kissed her, a deeply passionate kiss that clearly revealed his longing for the woman in his arms.

Clint's mouth was warm, firm, demanding, touching a deep chord within Rachel that left her feeling shaky and confused. Clint's kisses had never aroused her before. Was she so hungry for a man that any man's kiss would do?

"Rachel, Rachel," Clint groaned. "Honey, please don't put me off any longer. I love you so damn much I'm going crazy."

"Clint, don't—"

"Marry me," he urged, kissing her again. "Tonight, tomorrow, just name the day."

"I can't."

"For God's sake, why not?"

"I don't know," Rachel said evasively. "I just can't. Not now."

"It's still Tyree, isn't it?" Clint rasped angrily. "It's always Tyree. What is there about that bastard that has you so starry-eyed you can't see straight?"

"I don't know," Rachel answered in a small voice. "I only know I can't marry you." Tears sparkled in her eyes. "I know this isn't fair to you, Clint. I wouldn't blame you if you never wanted to see me again. But I can't marry you until I'm sure it's right, and I can't promise you that it will ever be right."

Clint nodded, his eyes warm and loving as he took Rachel in his arms and held her close. He murmured soft words to her while she cried, and all the while he silently cursed Logan Tyree for causing her pain.

When Rachel's tears subsided, Clint took her back inside and kissed her goodnight.

"I'll wait," Clint murmured as he watched Rachel leave the schoolhouse with her father and Claire. "I'll wait until hell freezes over if I have to."

It was after midnight when the Hallorans started for home. The back of the buggy was piled high with wedding gifts. A huge sign, tied to the back of the buggy, proclaimed, *"Just Married"* in large red letters.

Rachel drove the team while her father and Claire sat together, holding hands and making plans for the future. Claire owned a small house in town and they decided to keep it for the time being, perhaps rent it out.

Rachel drove automatically, her thoughts turned inward. If Tyree had not come into her life, she would have married Clint and considered herself a lucky woman. But Tyree had come, and everything had turned upside down. She thought of Clint, and of Tyree, and she frowned. Maybe what she felt for Tyree wasn't love at all. Maybe she had been confusing lust with love. Maybe she should just marry Clint and settle down and raise a family. Perhaps she was being foolish to keep hoping that Tyree would come back to her. What if Clint got tired of waiting for her to say yes and he found someone else; she would wind up as a lonely old maid with no one to love, and no one to love her.

Lifting her head, she stared into the distance. What was she going to do? She shook her head, wishing she knew her own mind. It was then she saw the smoke.

"Oh, my God," she gasped. "The ranch is on fire!"

"Walsh!" Halloran hissed. Grabbing the reins from Rachel, he slapped the ends across the lead horse's rump. "Move, Rusty!" he hollered, and the team broke into a gallop.

When they reached the house, it was beyond saving. The roof had already collapsed and the whole structure was in flames.

The next hour was sheer hell. Racing to the barn, they grabbed feed buckets and began dousing the roof and walls with water. Fortunately, there was no wind to carry sparks to the outbuildings, but it seemed like the wisest thing, to wet down the barn and bunkhouse, just in case.

When that was done, there was nothing to do but watch as the fire gradually burned itself out. Rachel wept as she thought of the photo album that had been consumed in the flames, for it had held a faded photograph of her mother and father on their wedding day, as well as a cherished picture of her brother, Tommy. So many irreplaceable treasures, all gone, she lamented. Her mother's wedding dress. The family Bible that traced the Halloran births and deaths and marriages back to the year 1795. The delicately embroidered lace tablecloth her grandmother had made. The tiny white dress Tommy had been baptized in.

They spent the night in the bunkhouse, and the next morning, after feeding the stock, they drove back to Yellow Creek.

"At least we're not homeless," Claire said, trying to inject a note of cheer. "We've still got a house to live in."

John Halloran mustered a smile for his bride, but Rachel could not. Everything she loved was gone.

When news of the fire got around, their friends and neighbors came, bringing food and kind words of sympathy and offers to help rebuild when they were ready.

Wesley rode out to the Lazy H to see if he could find some clue as to who might have set the fire, but he found nothing.

John Halloran put on a brave front for Claire, but later, alone with Rachel, he admitted he was beat.

"She's won," he said dispiritedly. "Annabelle Walsh has won at last. I don't have the money, or the heart, to rebuild the ranch. We'll round up what cattle we have left and sell them. I'll see if I can get some work here in town."

"Pa—"

"I'm through fighting," Halloran said. "But I'll be damned if I'll sell the land! She can run her cattle on it, she can build on it, but it will never be hers. Not so long as I live!"

Chapter 22

*I*t was fall, Rachel's favorite season of the year, but she found no joy in the clear crisp air or in the glorious riot of red and gold leaves that clothed the trees. Though she hated to admit it, she knew her lassitude was because of Tyree. Try as she might, she could not put him out of her mind. She still loved him as much as ever, still clung to the hope that he would come back to her even though she knew, deep inside, that she was kidding herself. He had never really cared for her. He would never come back.

Clint continued to court her as sweetly and patiently as ever a man courted a woman. He never mentioned marriage, and yet Rachel knew she had only to say the word and he would marry her in a minute. But she would never be happy with Clint. Her heart belonged to Tyree and though he would never come to claim it, she could not give it to another. It was time to be totally honest with Clint, time to tell him she could never marry him. It would be the hardest thing she had ever done, but it was time to let Clint go and stand on her own two feet. Time for Clint to accept the fact that she would never be his. Maybe then Clint would find a woman worthy of him. Carol Ann came quickly to mind. They would be perfect for each other, Rachel knew. Just perfect.

Rachel was thinking about the Halloween party Carol Ann was giving and how she could manage a little matchmaking between Clint and Carol Ann in town later that day. Surely there was some way to bring the two of them together. She was puzzling over the best method when she turned the corner onto Main Street and came face to face with Annabelle Walsh. For a moment, the two women stared at each other. Annabelle was as beautiful as ever, Rachel thought grudgingly. Her flaming hair was swept high on her head, giving her a regal appearance, her full figure was fashionably clad in the latest Paris original.

Annabelle regarded Rachel with open hostility. What was there about this snit of a girl that had so charmed a man like Tyree? Her hair was long and tawny, her figure passable, her face quite pretty, but Annabelle knew without doubt that she, herself, was the more striking of the two. She had wealth and power, she had offered herself to Tyree, and yet he had left her for some country girl.

Rachel lifted her chin proudly under Annabelle's glacial green gaze. Even at this late date, she felt a surge of jealousy when she remembered that Tyree had once lived under Annabelle's roof. Tyree . . .

"Where is he?" Rachel blurted the words, not intending, until that instant, to speak to Annabelle at all.

Annabelle looked momentarily taken aback and Rachel knew intuitively that Annabelle was the key to the mystery of Tyree's whereabouts.

"You mean Tyree, of course," Annabelle answered with a knowing grin. "He was an interesting man, wasn't he? Wild, unpredictable. Rather like a stallion waiting to be tamed." Annabelle laughed softly, a decidedly nasty laugh. "Neither of us were able to accomplish that, were we?"

Rachel swallowed hard, trying to quell the fear rising in her heart. Annabelle spoke of Tyree in the past tense, as if he were dead.

She shook the thought from her mind. "You know where he is," Rachel said with conviction. "I know you do. Tell me. Please." She almost choked on the last word. How hard it was to humble herself before this woman who had ruined her life and destroyed the only home she had ever known. Yet she knew she would go down on her knees, if necessary, if only Annabelle would tell her where to find Tyree.

"You love him, don't you?" Annabelle said, amused.

"Yes."

"And were you foolish enough to believe he loved you in return?"

"No." The admission was barely audible.

"Tyree and his kind are incapable of love," Annabelle said, a faint note of sadness in her voice.

"So are women like you," Rachel said, and could have bit off her tongue. She had not meant to say the words aloud. Angering Annabelle was the last thing she wanted to do.

"You're a perceptive little bitch," Annabelle said haughtily. "Good day."

"Annabelle, please!"

"He's gone," Annabelle said curtly. "I sold him."

"Sold him?" Rachel repeated, certain she had misunderstood.

"Yes, to an old friend who sells men into slavery south of the border. Save your tears. He's probably dead by now. Or wishes he were. Whatever his condition, I'm sure our friend, Tyree, has no use for a woman. Any woman."

Tyree, sold into slavery. It was too awful to be true. And yet, Rachel could see the truth of it shining in the depths of Annabelle's cold green eyes.

"How could you?" Rachel breathed. "How could you be so cruel, so vindictive?"

"No man walks out on me," Annabelle

replied with a proud toss of her head. "No man."

"You sold Tyree into slavery because he hurt your pride?" Rachel asked in disbelief. "What kind of a woman are you?"

"A rich one," Annabelle murmured with a spiteful grin. "Good day, Miss Halloran."

Rachel stared after Annabelle Walsh, her mind in turmoil. Tyree was a prisoner, a slave in a mine. All these months she had believed he didn't care. She had pictured him drinking and whoring, and all the while he had been a slave. She blinked back the tears welling in her eyes. Crying would not help Tyree.

Turning on her heel, she walked briskly to the livery stable at the end of town. Candido had been working there since her father let him go. Perhaps Candido could help her.

But Candido only shook his head. "You will never get him out, Miss Rachel. I have heard stories about the mines and the men who run them. You cannot get within a mile of the place without being seen. One time I heard one of the owners had all the prisoners killed and dumped the bodies in a mine shaft rather than get caught by the law."

"I've got to do something, Candido. Please help me."

"What does your father say?"

"He's not here. He took Claire to St. Louis. They won't be back until spring."

"I am sorry. I cannot help you."

"Then I'll go alone," Rachel said resolutely.

Candido heaved a huge sigh. "I have a cousin who works at the mine near Verde. Perhaps he can help us."

Days later, Rachel and Candido reached the small town of Verde. Candido's cousin, Lado, was an old man, perhaps sixty years old. He had been a doctor in his prime; then, due to a scandal involving a rich landowner's daughter and a Juarista, he was forced to give up his practice. Now he traveled from mine to mine, treating the prisoners for a few pesos and all the tequila he could drink.

Yes, he had seen the gringo called Tyree.

"The gunfighter," Lado said, nodding sagely. He took a drink from the bottle that was never far from his hand. "I was there the day of the contest between the gringo and Paulo. El Patron was very angry when the gringo won."

"Is he still alive?" Rachel asked anxiously.

Lado shrugged. "Quien sabe?"

Ten minutes later, Rachel had a map giving directions to the mine.

"Senorita, you cannot ride into the mine and demand Tyree's release, nor can you buy his freedom. If the mine owners suspect you know he is there, they will kill him, and perhaps the others, too."

"Well, I've got to do something. I can't just leave him there. I can't go on not knowing if he's dead or alive."

They rode in silence. Rachel's mind concocted and rejected a half dozen ways to free

Tyree, but she refused to give up. There had to be a way.

They were on their way back to Yellow Creek when they skirted the outer edge of Sunset Canyon. Rachel shuddered as she remembered that day: the heat, the Indians . . .

"That's it!" she exclaimed.

"Senorita?"

"The Apache," Rachel said excitedly. "I'll go to the Mescalero. Tyree is their friend. Surely they'll help him."

"No. It is madness."

"I'll need your help," Rachel went on, ignoring his objection. "You can speak a little Apache, can't you?"

"Si, senorita, but . . ."

"Good. If we keep riding, we should find their camp before nightfall."

"Or they will find us," Candido said. "Santa Maria, pray for us."

They did not find the Apache camp, but that night, just before dark, the Indians found them. Rachel gave a little cry of alarm as thirty warriors seemed to appear out of nowhere, their obsidian eyes alight with interest as they came upon two lone white people.

Despite her intention to find the Indians, now that they were here, Rachel was quite frightened. What if they could not communicate with the Apache? What if the Indians killed them before they had a chance to explain what they were doing on Indian land?

She felt a glimmer of hope as she recognized one of the warriors who had been at Sunset Canyon that dreadful day.

She raised her hand in the sign Tyree had told her meant peace. "Friend," she said, hoping the warrior could not detect the fear in her voice. She tapped her breast. "Tyree's woman."

Standing Buffalo stared at Rachel, then he smiled. Yes, he remembered Tyree's woman. His disappointment had been keen that day in Sunset Canyon when Tyree had come to her rescue.

Rachel smiled back at the warrior. He recognized her, she saw it in his eyes.

The warrior spoke to the other braves and they all dismounted. In minutes, a fire was blazing in a shallow pit. The warriors sat on their heels, their eyes on Rachel. Only a few of them spoke English.

"Woman of Tyree, why are you here?"

"Tyree is in trouble," Rachel said earnestly. "He told me that he had lived with the Mescalero, that you were his friends. I've come to you for help because I have no one else to turn to."

Standing Buffalo frowned. "What kind of trouble?"

Quickly, Rachel explained about the mine.

Standing Buffalo nodded. "Yes. Some of our warriors have been taken to that place. It is a bad thing, to keep men as slaves."

"Then you'll help me?"

"Yes. We will ride for Mexico at first light.

One of my warriors will see that you get home safely."

"No. I'm going, too."

"No."

"Yes. He's . . . he's my husband and I'm going with you."

Standing Buffalo smiled. Truly, the woman with the yellow hair had the heart of a mountain lion. Tyree had chosen his woman wisely.

"The Mexican cannot come," Standing Buffalo said flatly. "My people will not ride with him."

Rachel did not argue. The hostility between the Mexicans and the Apaches was well-known, and dated back to the time when the Mexicans paid a bounty for Apache scalps.

They started for Mexico early the following morning. Candido was reluctant to leave Rachel in the company of thirty Apache warriors, but there was little he could do other than beg her to reconsider. But she would not change her mind.

The Indians took no thought of having a woman in their midst. Apache women were strong; some were warriors, some were medicine women. They treated her as a warrior, and expected her to keep up. She was tense and on edge the whole day, knowing it was only the fact she was Tyree's woman that made her presence tolerable. She shuddered to think what would happen to her if she was not under the protection of Tyree's name. Many of the warriors looked at her with desire in their eyes, a few glared at her in a way that made her know that, under other circumstances, she would have been killed and scalped the same as any other enemy.

By day's end, she was sure she was going to die. She ached in every part of her body. Her red shirt felt glued to her skin, her tan riding skirt was dusty, the hem torn where she had snagged it on a spiny cactus. Her boots were covered with dust. Never could she recall feeling quite so dirty or so utterly bone weary. Muscles she had not known she possessed shrieked in protest every time she moved. She was certain her legs were permanently bowed from the hours she had spent in the saddle; the insides of her thighs felt raw.

Standing Buffalo handed her a strip of jerky, offered her a drink of water from a waterskin. "We will start again at first light," he said. His black eyes studied her carefully. She had not complained once during the long trek. Perhaps, if Tyree were dead, he would keep the woman for his own.

Rachel felt her cheeks turn pink under the warrior's continued gaze. What was he thinking? His eyes, as dark as the night sky, were unfathomable, his face impassive.

She took a long drink from the waterskin before returning it to Standing Buffalo. "Thank you," she said, and looked away, unable to meet his gaze any longer.

The next day was the same as the last. They rode for miles across a land populated by little more than sand and cactus and an occasional reptile. Sweat poured down Rachel's face and neck and back, making her feel sticky and uncomfortable. Her feet and hands swelled, and she found herself yearning for a bath as never before.

The Indians rode silently, oblivious to the heat and the long ride. They paused only once, shortly after noon, to eat and rest the horses.

Wearily, Rachel loosened the cinch on the saddle, gave her weary horse a pat on the neck. She was glad she had left Morgana at home. This horse, a sturdy buckskin gelding, was much better suited to long hours and scant feed. He was a range bred horse, part mustang, part Quarter horse.

All too soon, the Indians were mounting up again. With a sigh, Rachel tightened the cinch and climbed into the saddle. Never, in all her life, had she spent so many hours on the back of a horse.

Later that afternoon, a handful of warriors broke away from the main group to go hunting. They returned at dusk with a wild turkey and several rabbits. Rachel's mouth began to water as she looked forward to fresh meat for dinner that night.

And still they traveled across the land, heading due south. Across low hills covered with catclaw and paloverde, through deep gullies and narrow valleys, across a shallow river, and suddenly they were in Mexico.

Rachel had lost track of the days when one of the scouts rode into their night camp with the news that the mine was less than a day's ride away. Rachel's weariness vanished like snow beneath a blazing sun. Tomorrow she would see Tyree!

She could not sleep that night, not when they were so close. She closed her eyes and summoned Tyree's image to mind, still clear even after all these months—the length and breadth of him; eyes that were the color of amber glass; a mouth that could be by turns warm and tender or fierce and demanding; hair as black as sin. Every nerve ending in her body seemed to come alive, yearning for his touch.

She was still awake when the Indians began to stir. They were unusually quiet as they moved about the camp. They did not eat breakfast. Small clay pots appeared and the warriors began to paint their faces for war. For the first time, it occurred to Rachel that there was going to be a fight, that men would be killed. Until that moment, she had not thought of the cost, only the joy of seeing Tyree again. But of course there would be a fight. They could not just walk in and pluck Tyree from the mine. There would be guards, a warning cry, a battle. Tyree could be killed . . . .

She shook the thought from her mind. She had not come this far to fail.

She glanced at the warriors moving around

her, and was suddenly afraid. These men were savages, strangers. They were killers, delighting in butchery and torture. What was she doing here? Why had she trusted them? Even now, they might turn on her.

She uttered a small cry of fright as a hand dropped on her shoulder. Whirling around, she stared, wide-eyed at the warrior beside her, and then let out a sigh of relief. It was Standing Buffalo, his face hideously streaked with black paint.

"Will you wait here?"

"No."

He nodded, as if he had expected her to refuse.

Ten minutes later they were riding toward the mine. Rachel's nerves were taut. Time and again she patted the derringer in her skirt pocket. Would she have the nerve to shoot a man, if necessary? Could she bear to take a human life? Only time would tell.

It was dusk when they reached the valley that housed the mine. From her vantage point, Rachel stared at the wooden outbuildings that housed the guards, then swung her gaze to the big stone house where the mine owners lived. And then she saw a long row of cages. They were empty, she saw with dismay, but even as she watched, she saw dozens of men being herded toward the cages. She leaned forward, eyes straining, but she could not pick Tyree out of the line of shackled, bearded men. It was a pitiful sight, she thought, her heart aching. The guards herded the prisoners like sheep, whipping those who did not move fast enough.

Tyree, Tyree. She could not bear to think of him being in such a dreadful place, could not stand to think of him suffering as these men were obviously suffering.

And then Standing Buffalo gave the signal and she was swept down the hill toward the mine, her horse carried along with the others as the Indians urged their ponies down the gentle slope and across the barren ground in front of the mine. A shout went up from the guard tower, and then the Mexican pitched over the railing onto the ground, an arrow in his throat.

The war cries of thirty Apache warriors filled the air as the Indians swarmed over the main house and outbuildings. Two thirds of the Mexicans were killed in the first rush, taken completely by surprise.

The noise and the gunsmoke were overpowering, and Rachel felt as though she were living in a nightmare as she guided her horse toward the long row of cages, the derringer in her hand. Indians and Mexicans fought and died on all sides, but she rode through the midst of them, her eyes riveted on the cages ahead, a silent prayer in her heart that she would find Tyree.

Men called out to her as she rode past, screaming for her to let them out of the cages, but she did not hear them, so intent was she on finding Tyree. A Mexican in a dirty blue

shirt grabbed at her leg and she fired the
derringer in his face, felt her insides heave
with revulsion as his eyes and nose dissolved
in a sea of blood.

And still she rode on. And then, near the
end of the row, she saw him. He was standing
at the door of the cage, staring at the fire that
had started in one of the outbuildings some
fifty feet away.

Rachel screamed his name as she jumped
off her horse.

Tyree's head swung around, and his eyes
widened with stunned disbelief. "My God," he
thought, "I must be seeing things."

"Tyree, stand aside!" Rachel had to shout to
be heard above the gunfire and the roar of the
flames.

She was real. He whispered her name as he
stood to one side while she shot the lock off
the door. And then she was in his arms, her
sweet mouth pressed to his. But only for a
moment.

"Come on, we've got to get out of here,"
Rachel urged. "Get on my horse."

"I can't."

"Damn!" She had forgotten about the
shackles that hobbled his feet.

She was wondering what to do when Tyree
dragged her down the row of cages to where a
man lay face down in the dust. It was the man
Rachel had killed, and she turned away, fighting the urge to vomit as Tyree began to search
through the dead man's pockets. At last, he
found the key. Moments later, his hands and

feet were free, and he tossed the key ring to the prisoner in the nearest cage.

Rachel heard Tyree mutter, "Good luck," under his breath as he lifted her into the saddle of the buckskin and swung up behind her. She felt a surge of relief as they started out of the yard. Thank God, Tyree was safe.

She kicked the buckskin, urging the horse to go faster, wanting to get away from the mine and the misery it represented. She did not think about the men they had left behind, or the Indians who might have been killed, she thought only of Tyree, of his hands gripping her waist.

She was smiling to herself as they rode out of the yard, congratulating herself on a job well done, when the pain hit. Glancing down, she was horrified to see the side of her shirt was dark with blood. Feeling suddenly light-headed, she grasped the buckskin's mane with her free hand. They could not stop now, not until she was sure Tyree was out of danger. She could not lose him again.

Once, she glanced over her shoulder. The mine buildings were all ablaze. Prisoners were streaming out of the yard, running away from the flames. She saw a man rolling on the ground, his clothing aflame. And then the warriors came riding toward them, blocking everything else from sight.

She tried to smile at Tyree, but his face blurred before her eyes and she felt herself falling, falling, into nothingness.

Tyree swore under his breath as Rachel went limp in his arms. A sharp tug on the reins brought the buckskin to an abrupt halt. It was then Tyree saw the blood staining Rachel's shirt.

"My God." He breathed the words as he lifted her shirt. Blood oozed from a bullet wound just under her ribcage. With an oath, he pressed his hand over the ugly wound, felt her blood well between his fingers.

Taking Rachel in his arms, he dismounted and laid her gently on the ground. Only then was he aware of Standing Buffalo and the other Indians milling around.

"Is she dead?" The question came from Standing Buffalo.

"No. Get me some blankets and some water."

"We will camp here," Standing Buffalo informed the others. "Red Elk, see to the wounded. Five Bears, take some men and find us some meat."

With quiet efficiency, the Indians began to make camp for the night.

Tyree took the blanket Standing Buffalo offered and placed it under Rachel. Removing his shirt, he ripped off a piece and began wiping the blood from her side. There was only a single entry wound, indicating the bullet was still lodged somewhere in her side. Gently, he probed the wound with his finger, but he could not locate the slug.

Rachel's eyelids fluttered open. She smiled

weakly as she saw Tyree bending over her. "You're safe," she murmured.

Tyree nodded as his hand caressed her cheek. "You damn fool," he scolded gently. "What are you doing riding around the countryside with a bunch of savages?"

"I came to find you," Rachel said thickly. "And I did."

"Yes. Lie still now. Don't talk."

"Am I going to die?"

"No!"

Rachel smiled at him. Of course, he would lie to her, but it didn't matter. He was alive and well. She did not care if she died, so long as it was in his arms.

"I've got to take the bullet out," Tyree said.

"No."

"It's got to be done."

Rachel shook her head violently from side to side. "No. Please, Tyree."

"Hey, you've spent a lot of time looking after me. Now it's my turn to take care of you."

Rachel glanced up as Standing Buffalo came to stand beside Tyree. He had a waterskin in one hand, and a long-bladed knife in the other. Rachel stared at the knife in horror. She could not bear it, she thought frantically. She could not bear the pain of the knife probing her flesh.

"Take me home," she pleaded. "Take me to Yellow Creek, Tyree. I want a doctor."

"Yellow Creek is ten days ride from here," Tyree replied.

"I don't care."

"Trust me, Rachel. That bullet has got to come out. Now. It won't get any easier if you wait." He took her hand in his and gave it a squeeze. "Trust me, Rachel. Just this once."

She nodded, then shuddered as Tyree took the knife from Standing Buffalo.

Tyree stared at the long blade. How could he dig the bullet from Rachel's flesh? He knew the agony it would cause her, knew he would rather cut off his right arm than cause her pain. Just thinking about cutting into her tender flesh made his palms sweat.

"Do you want me to do it, my brother?" Standing Buffalo asked quietly.

"No!" Rachel grabbed Tyree's hand. "You do it," she cried. "I don't want anyone else to do it but you."

Tyree nodded. "Here." He wadded up a strip of cloth and handed it to her. "Bite on this. Standing Buffalo, hold her down so she doesn't move."

Rachel closed her eyes, her teeth biting hard on the rag in her mouth as Tyree began to probe the wound with the knife. Pain coursed through her side, worse than anything she had ever imagined. Blood flowed in the wake of the blade, hot and wet and sticky. She clenched her hands into tight fists, her nails digging into her palms. Her thoughts

431

became confused. Sometimes it was Tyree who held the knife, probing her flesh, causing her terrible pain, and sometimes she was back in the past, reliving the day she had cut the bullet from his side. How had he stood the pain? How could she? When would it end?

She opened her eyes and saw Tyree's face through a red haze of pain. His brow was furrowed, sheened with sweat, his jaw rigid. She groaned as the knife slipped deeper into her side, heard Tyree swear softly, and then everything went black.

"Thank God," Tyree muttered. "She's fainted."

A short time later, he removed the slug from her side. He looked at it for a long moment, then tossed it aside. A little higher, he thought bleakly, a little higher and she would have been dead.

He washed the wound as best he could, packed the hole with tree moss to stop the bleeding, bandaged it with what was left of his shirt.

"The Mescalero will be at their winter camp by now," Standing Buffalo remarked. "We can be there day after tomorrow."

Tyree nodded. Rachel had lost a good deal of blood. Likely, she would soon have a fever. The doctor at Yellow Creek was too far away to do them any good, but there was a medicine man at the Apache camp. And he wanted a shaman close by, just in case.

Chapter 23

She opened her eyes slowly, blinking as she glanced around. Where was she? A low fire burned at her feet, a domed roof covered her head. Frowning, she saw a war shield propped against the wall, a lance, several clay pots and jars.

Alarmed, she tried to sit up, only to fall back as a sharp pain lanced her side. It came back to her then, the ride to Mexico, the battle at the mine, Tyree. Where was Tyree?

A short time later, a withered old man dressed in fringed buckskin pants and a sleeveless vest entered the lodge. He gave Rachel a toothless grin as he gathered up several items from the back of the lodge.

Muttering something to her in guttural Apache, he hurried outside again.

She was fretting over her whereabouts and the awful ache in her side when Tyree stepped into the wickiup. Just seeing him made her feel better. He had shaved and washed and trimmed his hair, and she thought he had never looked better, or more welcome.

"Where are we?" she asked.

"A box canyon about seventy miles from the mine. The Mescalero come here for the winter." He sat cross-legged beside her. "How are you?"

"Fine, now that you're here."

Tyree smiled. It was good to see her awake and alert. She had been unconscious for two days, burning with fever, and only the medicine man's skill had saved her. He knew he would never have forgiven himself if she had died.

"How long have we been here?" Rachel asked. "When can we go home?"

"No questions now. You rest."

"I'm tired of resting. I feel fine, really."

"Never mind. You just stay put." Tyree grinned suddenly. "Do I have to take your clothes away to make sure you won't get up until I say it's all right?"

Rachel laughed, wincing as the movement sent a fresh shaft of pain through her side. "I'll be good," she promised.

For the next few days, she ate and slept and ate again. Thanks to the wizened old medicine man, her side healed quickly and she was on her feet again before the next week was out, although Tyree would not let her stay up too long. Still, it was wonderful to be able to sit outside and feel the sun on her face.

It was a unique experience, sitting outside the medicine man's lodge in the middle of the Apache camp. These were the people Tyree had grown up with, and she studied them carefully. The women were short and tended to be plump. Their hair was long and straight and black, their eyes dark, their skin the color of copper. They wore long doeskin tunics that reached their ankles, or cotton blouses and full swirling calico skirts. Rachel was surprised to discover that Indian women were not so different from white women. They cared for their loved ones, sewed and cooked and mended, laughed and cried, nursed their young, argued with their husbands. They tended small vegetable gardens and made beautiful baskets from willow rods. Sometimes strips of black devil's-claw were intertwined with the willow to create intricate designs.

The Apache men spent their time hunting or gambling or repairing their weapons. They played with their children, guided the young warriors along the path to manhood, protected the village. They wore clouts and knee-high moccasins and deerskin vests. Their hair was also long and black, frequently adorned with feathers or bits of fur.

The children were happy, bright-eyed and inquisitive. They stared at Rachel with unabashed curiosity, fascinated by her golden hair and sky-blue eyes. The little girls played with dolls made of corn husks or helped their mothers with chores and younger brothers and sisters; the boys played at hunting and making war.

They were a proud and fearsome people and Rachel shuddered when she remembered the tales of treachery she had heard. The Apaches were rumored to be the most vicious fighters in the Southwest. The Chiricahua chief, Cochise, had fought in a long and bloody war with the whites that had lasted ten years. Geronimo was still at war with the Army, though he was currently raiding and killing far to the south. It was said the Apache fought without mercy, that they delighted in the shedding of blood.

For all their fearsome ways, they were a highly superstitious people. The newly dead were to be avoided at all costs, the names of the deceased were never spoken aloud lest their spirits be called back to earth. The Apache did not eat the fish that thrived in the river because it was believed the fish was related to the snake and was therefore cursed.

Rachel glanced around the camp. The Apache called themselves Dineh, meaning the People, the chosen ones. The name Apache was a Zuni word meaning enemy.

Rachel smiled warmly at Tyree when he came to sit beside her.

"You okay?" he asked. The concern in his eyes warmed her heart.

"I'm fine."

"That was a brave thing you did, coming after me."

Rachel shrugged. "I couldn't just leave you there."

"You could have," Tyree said quietly. "How the hell did you know where to find me anyway?"

"I asked Annabelle."

"Annabelle!" Tyree swore profusely, his hands itching to sink a knife into the treacherous heart of the flaming-haired woman who had sold him into hell.

"If it weren't for Annabelle, I never would have found you," Rachel remarked matter-of-factly.

Tyree snorted. "Hell, if it weren't for Annabelle, you wouldn't have had to come looking for me. Which, by the way, was a damn fool thing to do."

"You're welcome," Rachel said dryly.

"You know what I mean. Standing Buffalo told me how he found you. Dammit, Rachel, you might have been killed."

"It was a chance I had to take. But if you're sorry I found you, just say so, and I'll take you back!"

"Hold on," Tyree said, laughing softly. "I

didn't mean to make you mad." He placed his hand over her arm, let his fingers slide up the smooth flesh to her shoulder, to her neck, to the gentle curve of her cheek. Her skin was soft, warm. He gazed into her eyes, as blue as the sky above, and thought how brave she had been to come after him. His nostrils filled with the scent of her, stirring his desire, and he wished she were well enough that he could carry her into the lodge and make love to her. He had yearned for her for so long, wanting her, needing her.

His eyes moved over her face and found it perfect. Slowly, his gaze settled on her lips. Her mouth was slightly open, looking warm and inviting. Again, he thought of all the days and nights he had longed for her, and he bent forward to kiss her.

A soft laugh sounded from nearby. Rachel quickly drew back, her cheeks flushing, as she looked over Tyree's shoulder and saw several Indian children watching them.

Tyree glanced over his shoulder and scowled. "Go on, get lost," he muttered irritably, and Rachel laughed out loud as the children scattered.

"Oh, Tyree," she murmured, "it's so good to be alive."

As Rachel's strength returned, they began to take long walks together, resting when she grew weary, sometimes napping in the shade of a windblown pine. Tyree looked wonderful in the buckskins he wore, Rachel thought proudly. His hair, uncut for the last six months, hung past his shoulders, emphasizing his Indian blood. His skin had regained its healthy color now that he no longer spent the daylight hours underground, and from a distance it was hard to distinguish Tyree from the other Indian men.

Despite the fact that she was surrounded by a savage people and living in a crudely built brush hut, despite the strange food and the harsh guttural language she could not understand, Rachel was happier than she had ever been in her life. Tyree was alive and well. His amber eyes glowed with longing when he looked at her, and she could hardly wait until she was well again, until she could show him how much she loved him.

The old medicine man moved out of his lodge, taking up residence with his sister for the duration of their stay so that Tyree and his woman could be alone. Sometimes Rachel felt as if they were the only two people in the world, especially late at night when the village was asleep and she lay wrapped in Tyree's arms, her head pillowed on his shoulder, his breath warm against her face.

The first night they made love was like something out of a dream. The fire cast eerie shadows on the walls of the lodge. The buffalo robe beneath her was soft and warm, primitive. Tyree lay naked beside her, his dark bronze skin kissed by the light of the flickering flames. His eyes glowed brighter than the fire as he lowered his body over hers, his mouth caressing every inch of her eagerly quivering flesh, his hands moving intimately over her body until she was aflame with desire. She whispered his name, her arms twining around his neck as her hips lifted to receive him. Their flesh merged and now, engulfing him, she felt whole, fulfilled. Together, they soared upward, ever upward, leaving the earth and its cares far behind . . . .

Many nights, after the evening meal had been eaten and the children were in bed, the Apaches gathered around a central campfire to dance and sing and tell stories.

Rachel watched, fascinated, as the warriors danced and postured around the fire, recounting tales of great battles, of enemies slain and coup counted. Their copper-hued skin glistened brightly in the flickering light of the flames. Their faces, hideously streaked with paint, were reminiscent of spirits escaped from the bowels of hell. The rhythmic beat of the drums, the high-pitched chanting of the drummers, the rapt faces of the women and old men, all combined to make Rachel feel as if she were caught up in a world that was not quite real.

One night, Tyree joined the men as they danced. Rachel stared at him in wonder. Now, for this moment, he was totally Indian. His shoulder-length hair was held from his face with a strip of red cloth. His skin, as swarthy as any of the Apaches, glowed in the firelight. He was clad only in a brief wolfskin clout and knee-high moccasins, and Rachel felt a queer churning in the pit of her stomach as she watched him dance. He belongs here, she thought absently. He's a part of this, a part of the People. He was so handsome, so male, she felt a sudden rush of desire as he passed before her, his amber eyes alight with the joy of the dance, his head thrown back as he uttered a shrill cry.

It was good, Tyree thought exultantly, good to dance the dances of the People, good to be a part of the whole instead of standing on the outside looking in. He laughed aloud, filled with the joy of being alive. How easy it was to shed the veneer of civilization, he mused. How easy it was to revert to the old ways, the ancient ways. He knew a sudden yearning to ride to war, to feel the wind in his face as he went out in search of scalps and glory.

His feet moved easily to the rhythm of the drum, the Apache words came readily to his lips as he joined in the song. The night was filled with stars, the air was heavy with the scent of sage and woodsmoke and tobacco. The firelight danced along the sides of the wickiups, creating shadow dancers who bobbed and swayed to the beat of the drum. His eyes sought Rachel's face and he felt the desire swell in his loins as she smiled at him. Her blue eyes were wide as she watched him dance, and he wondered what she was thinking. Did she find him frightening, disgusting, repulsive? His steps carried him nearer to where she sat with some of the other women, and he let out a wild cry as he read the expression in her eyes. She was not disgusted by what she saw. The drumming, the dancing, the sweat dripping down his torso had awakened a primal urge within the core of her being. He saw it in her eyes and was glad.

Later, alone in their borrowed lodge, he made love to her, possessing her wildly, fiercely, making her feel like some primitive, uncivilized female completely devoid of modesty or shame. Caught up in the moment, Rachel gave herself to Tyree with carefree abandon, holding nothing back, but gladly giving all she had to give.

She was embarrassed to face him the following morning. What would he think of her? No lady worthy of the name would have behaved in such an uninhibited fashion. She had touched him and fondled him as never before, boldly exploring his lean frame, finding new ways to excite him. It had all seemed so right under cover of darkness, but now she was not so sure. Perhaps she had gone too far. But when she found the courage to meet his eyes, she saw only tenderness there.

The days passed, one upon the other. They walked in the woods, swam in the icy river, made love beneath the bold blue sky.

One night Tyree pulled her into the circle of

dancing men and women. Rachel blushed, her awkwardness making her uncomfortable and self-conscious. But Tyree refused to let her quit. The steps were simple, few in number, and she quickly learned the dance. She smiled at Tyree, pleased with her success, letting herself sway in time to the soft beat of the drums, basking in the desire she read in his eyes.

They had been in the Indian camp about three weeks when several of the young girls reached puberty. This was, Rachel learned, a time of celebration. The girls were dressed in elaborately painted and beaded costumes and then they danced before the tribe. The ceremony lasted four days. Four, Tyree explained, was a magic number. There were four directions to the earth, four seasons in the year.

During the celebration, many ritual chants and dances were performed, punctuated with feasting, entertainment and gift-giving. Rachel stared in awe as four Apache warriors stepped into the firelight one evening. They were dressed in spectacular kilts, black masks, and wooden headdresses. Each carried a wooden sword. They were called Gans, Tyree said, and represented the mountain spirits. Usually they danced to ward off evil or to cure an illness, but on this night they danced only to entertain.

At the end of the four days, the girls returned to their lodges. It was strange, Rachel thought, that the Indians made such a fuss over a condition of nature that white women spoke of only in whispers.

It was January when Rachel began to think about going home. Pleasant as her stay with the Indians had been, she could not remain at the rancheria indefinitely. Soon, her father and Claire would return from St. Louis. She did not want her absence to cause her father to worry when there was nothing to worry about. Not only that, but she was beginning to miss the comforts she was accustomed to, things like a hot bath in a tub, clean sheets on a soft bed, a downy pillow, fresh milk and cheese and bread. She wanted to put on a clean dress and go shopping in town, buy a new hat, visit with Carol Ann, go to church, read her Bible . . . so many things to do, things she had never thought she would miss until they were out of reach.

Yes, it was time to go home. She voiced the idea to Tyree later that night when they were alone in their lodge.

"Home." Tyree stared into the coals. "For me, this is home. I hadn't realized how much I missed it all until now."

He slanted a glance in Rachel's direction, saw the dismay in her eyes. "Don't worry," he said with a wry grin. "I'll take you back to Yellow Creek." His voice grew harsh, his expression ominous. "I have a little unfinished business with a certain black-hearted bitch."

"Annabelle." Rachel breathed the name aloud, hardly aware that she had spoken.

"Yes," Tyree said flatly. "Annabelle."

"Tyree, I thought that we . . . that you and I . . . I mean." She looked at him helplessly. He had not mentioned loving her, had not mentioned marriage. And now, suddenly, neither could she. "You know what I mean?"

"I know. We'll talk about it later. Right now you'd better get some sleep. We'll leave first thing in the morning."

Chapter 24

They left the rancheria early the next morning. For Rachel, going home had lost some of its enchantment. Tyree had spoken of the Indian camp as home. Would he return to the Apache once he had delivered her safely to Yellow Creek and her father's house? She could not bear the thought of losing him again, yet she could not summon the courage to ask what his plans were. If he was going to leave her, she did not want to know it. Not yet.

They talked of inconsequential things as they rode across the prairie. Rachel spoke of her father and Claire, of how Annabelle had burned the Lazy H, how Slash W cattle were running on Halloran range. She spoke of the new mercantile, of the five new families that had moved into town. She did not ask Tyree about the six months he had spent in the mine, and he did not enlighten her. She knew, nevertheless, that it had been hard on him. There was a new tenseness about him, a new bitterness in his eyes. There was something else, too, an intangible something she could not quite put her finger on. Sometimes she caught a hint of it when he thought she wasn't looking at him, an odd look lurking in the back of his eyes. She worried over it for several days and then, late one night, she saw Tyree staring into the flames and she knew what was driving him. It was a deep-rooted need for vengeance against Annabelle Walsh.

Despite the heat of the fire, Rachel felt suddenly cold all over. Logan Tyree was a violent man, a dangerous man to run afoul of. She felt a sudden surge of pity for Annabelle.

It took ten days to reach Yellow Creek. Rachel breathed a sigh of relief as she rode into the side yard and stepped wearily from her horse. This place would never be home the way the Lazy H had been home, but just now it looked like a king's palace. She smiled at Tyree as he came up behind her and took the buckskin's reins.

"I'll put the horses away," he said.

Rachel nodded. "I'll put the coffee on," she remarked, and hurried inside, weak with happiness because he wasn't just going to drop her off and ride on.

Claire's house was not particularly large,

but compared to an Apache wickiup, it seemed huge. She bustled about, and all the while she was thinking of Tyree, wanting Tyree.

She felt a rush of anticipation as he entered the kitchen and closed the door.

"Would you like to wash up?" Rachel asked. "There's a tub on the porch. It will only take a few minutes to heat some water."

"Sounds good." He pulled a chair out from the table, threw a leg over the seat and rested his arms on the back.

Rachel poured him a cup of coffee, aware of Tyree's eyes following her every move. She filled several large kettles with water from the pump and set them on the stove to heat.

"How's Wesley?" Tyree asked after a lengthy silence.

"He's fine," Rachel answered, frowning. "Why?"

Tyree shrugged. "Just curious. He still hanging around?"

"Not so much."

"Does he still want to marry you?"

Rachel felt herself go cold all over. "Yes, he does."

Tyree nodded, his eyes thoughtful.

"Tyree—"

"That water hot yet?"

"Yes."

With fluid grace, he unfolded from the chair, brought the tub inside, emptied the steaming pots of water into the tub. He swung around to face her, one heavy brow raised in question. "You gonna watch?" he asked laconically. "Or join me?"

"Neither," Rachel said, unable to stay the color suffusing her cheeks. "I'll wait in the parlor."

She left the room quickly, her cheeks burning. With the Apache, they had been so close. They had talked and laughed and shared the most intimate moments she had ever known. But here, in this house, she felt shy and ill at ease.

In the parlor, she paced the floor, her thoughts chaotic. Why hadn't Tyree mentioned marriage? What would her father say when he came home and found Tyree in the house? What would she say to Clint? Even though she had told Clint she could not marry him, ever, she knew he felt it was only a matter of time before she changed her mind and said yes. What would she do if Tyree left in the morning? And what about Annabelle?

Her thoughts came to an abrupt end as she heard Tyree step out of the tub. The vision of him standing naked in the kitchen filled her veins with fire and before she quite knew what she was doing, she was through the door and in his arms.

Without a word, Tyree lifted her in his arms and carried her through the parlor and down the hall to the bedroom, his mouth pressed over hers. Rachel clung to him, her whole being conscious of his damp flesh, of his hands deftly unfastening her shirt. His mouth never left hers as he undressed her and then they were lying side by side on the bed, their bodies pressed together.

That night, Rachel poured her whole soul into her lovemaking, wanting Tyree to know that he was loved, that he need never be alone again.

Later, he fell asleep holding her in his arms, holding her as if he would never let her go. Rachel lay beside him, studying his face, loving every line, every curve. The tears came then, falling silently down her cheeks until she, too, fell asleep.

When she woke, she was alone.

Tyree's thoughts were filled with Rachel as he rode out of Yellow Creek. She was a hell of a woman, he mused. Bright, beautiful, full of spirit and fire. Damn, she had guts, too, going to the Apache, then riding into Mexico to rescue him from that damn mine. He had used her and abused her, and she still loved him. Not even Red Leaf had loved him with such an all-consuming, all-forgiving love.

He thought of Rachel nursing him when he had escaped from Yuma, thought of her standing at the foot of his bed, her bright blue eyes shooting sparks at him as she ordered him to stay put. He saw her spread-eagled between four Apache bucks in Sunset Canyon, her eyes filling with hope when she saw him. He saw her lovely face lined with real concern when he went to her after Annabelle's men had whipped him and destroyed his gun hand. He saw the hurt welling in her eyes when he broke his promise to marry her and went to work for Annabelle instead. No other woman had ever shed tears for him.

Rachel. She was too good to be true. When had he fallen in love with her? When had she stopped being just a warm desirable body and become a person? When had he started to care what she thought of him?

With an effort, he put Rachel out of his mind as he crossed the narrow winding river that marked the beginning of the Slash W spread. Eyes and ears alert, he guided the Indian pony across the sleeping land. A cow bawled a warning as he passed too close to her calf, but other than that, his passing disturbed neither man nor beast as he closed in on his destination: the Slash W storehouse. Annabelle had always been careful to keep extra supplies on hand in case of an emergency, and Tyree had need of everything from boots to hat.

An hour later, the building he sought loomed in the darkness. Dismounting some two hundred yards from the storehouse, Tyree pulled the saddle and bridle from the Apache pony and shooed the horse away. If all went as planned, he would be mounted on a better animal before the night was out. If his plans went awry, he would have no need for a horse, or anything else.

Padding forward on silent feet, knife in hand, Tyree approached the storehouse, tiptoed warily around the corner of the building. A tall silhouette moved in the shadows; the telltale glow of a cigarette arched through the air as the cowhand guarding the storehouse tossed a burning butt into the dirt.

Soundless as a stalking cat, Tyree crept up behind the unsuspecting wrangler. Once he would have killed the man without a qualm, Tyree mused. But that was before Rachel entered his life. With a wry grin, he picked up a good-sized rock and hit the man across the back of the head, rendering him unconscious.

The door to the storehouse opened on well-oiled hinges as Tyree dragged the sentry inside and closed the door behind him. Using the wrangler's kerchief, he tied the man's hands behind his back. A quick search of the man's pockets turned up a pack of matches and Tyree lit the lamp hanging inside the door. Turning the wick down low, Tyree moved through the storehouse, helping himself to a pair of black whipcord britches, a dark blue shirt. Picking through a pile of hats, he selected a black felt stetson with a flat crown and a wide brim. Boots came next, and then a red silk kerchief which he knotted loosely around his neck. He lingered over a choice of guns and finally picked a used Navy Colt in a plain leather holster, and a full cartridge belt.

Outside again, he ghosted toward the barn

where a second Slash W cowhand fell victim to a sharp blow on the head. The butt of the Colt split the man's scalp just behind his ear. Blood dripped on Tyree's hands as he dragged the man into the barn. The blood was warm and wet and strangely satisfying and Tyree stared at the crimson smear for several moments, a bemused expression on his swarthy face. The quick violence, the blood on his hands, had released much of the anger he had been carrying around for the past six months.

Much. But not all.

He quickly hogtied the unconscious cowhand, stuffed a rag into his mouth and deposited him, none too gently, inside a vacant stall.

The inside of the barn smelled of animals and manure and hay. Moving carefully in the velvet darkness, Tyree headed for the stall that housed Annabelle's own mount, a flashy paint stallion with a blaze face.

He was about to throw a bridle over the paint's head when a familiar whinny stayed his hand. Grinning with real pleasure, Tyree made his way to a stall at the far end of the barn.

The gray mustang whickered a second time as Tyree opened the stall door and stepped inside. How like Annabelle, Tyree mused as he saddled the stud, to keep his horse for herself. A reminder, no doubt, of her victory over a man who dared walk out on her.

With a final tug on the cinch, Tyree led the

gray outside. He tethered the horse to a near-by oak tree, then hunkered down on his heels in the shadows outside Annabelle's bedroom, his eyes focused on her window.

He sat there, quiet as the night surrounding him, waiting for her light to go out.

The time passed slowly, but Tyree possessed the patience of a warrior. As a youth, he had once crouched in a pit for two days, waiting for an eagle to alight on his hiding place so that he might grab the bird and help himself to three of the white-tipped feathers so prized by the Mescalero.

An owl sliced noiselessly through the sky, great wings outstretched, talons poised to strike should an unwary rabbit or mouse venture into the darkness. A cat moved sound-lessly through the shrubbery. A coyote yapped in the distance. But Tyree remained motion-less as a rock.

Memories drifted down the corridor of his mind. The sting of the whip across his back. The long months of endless darkness in the bowels of the earth, searching for silver that was not even there. The longing for fresh air and cool clear water, for the touch of the sun on his face.

Anger stirred within him, making him im-patient for the vengeance he had promised himself, and he thrust the memories aside. Briefly, he thought of Rachel, sleeping peace-fully in her father's house.

It was well after midnight when the light in Annabelle's room went out. And still Tyree waited. Five minutes. Ten. Twenty.

After thirty minutes had gone by, he rose quietly to his feet, carefully opened the window, and stepped over the sill. Annabelle was a dark shape on the bed. He watched her for a moment, glad she was alone. Striking a match, he lit the lamp on the rosewood table beside her bed and turned the wick down low. Then, moving light as a feather, he straddled Annabelle's hips. His hands closed gently around her throat.

Annabelle's eyes fluttered open and she stirred restlessly as she tried to dislodge the weight from her hips. She came instantly awake as she recognized Tyree. She stared up at him, unblinking, for a full thirty seconds before she whispered his name.

"Tyree."

"Yes, ma'am."

His hands tightened cruelly around her neck and she shuddered beneath him, her delectable body trembling with fear and apprehension. But she did not struggle, and she did not plead for mercy. She just lay there, passive, her luminous emerald eyes gazing up at him, her full breasts rising and falling, straining against the sheer pink fabric of her nightgown.

The scent of her perfume was strong in Tyree's nostrils, reminding him of the nights she had tried to lure him into her bed. He was glad now that he had never made love to her.

"I've missed you," Annabelle said as he loosened his grip on her throat. She raked her nails over the muscles in his arms, let her hands slide down to caress his thighs. "I still want you, Tyree.

Suddenly, he felt sorry for her. With a sigh, he took his hands from her throat.

Annabelle's smile was a trifle smug as she rubbed a hand across her throat. She gazed up at him through her lashes, then patted the pillow next to hers, inviting him to join her under the covers, certain he would not be able to refuse such an invitation.

Tyree took a deep breath. She looked warm and willing, lying there, her green eyes alight with desire, and yet she did not stir him at all. She was nothing compared to Rachel.

Rachel. He stared at Annabelle, bemused. Why was he wasting time here when he could be with Rachel?

"Tyree?"

"So long, Annabelle." He stood up, all thought of vengeance forgotten.

"Where are you going?"

"Home," he said in a voice filled with wonder. "Home to Rachel."

"If that's what you want," Annabelle said with a shrug. Carelessly, she raised her hand and let it slide under her pillow. Home, indeed! If she could not have Tyree, then no one would have him. She smiled seductively as her fingers closed over the derringer.

Tyree swore as he realized she was reaching for her gun. Quick as a cat, he grabbed her wrist. Annabelle screamed with rage, her free hand clawing at Tyree's face, her legs kicking wildly as she fought to keep hold of the gun.

Tyree dragged Annabelle off the bed and they struggled in taut silence for several moments. Once, catching sight of the hatred that twisted Annabelle's face, Tyree wondered why he had ever thought her beautiful.

He had almost succeeded in wresting the gun from her hand when Annabelle kicked him in the groin, hard. With a grunt, Tyree doubled over, striking Annabelle's shoulder and knocking her off balance so that she fell back on the bed, dragging Tyree with her. There was a muffled explosion as the gun, pinned between their bodies, went off.

Annabelle writhed violently, her arm knocking the oil lamp off the table beside the bed, her hand pushing against Tyree's chest. An expression of horror contorted her face as Tyree stood up and she saw the blood welling up from her left breast. Then a shudder convulsed her body and she lay still, her green eyes vacant of life.

For a moment, Tyree stared at Annabelle, unmindful of the flames caused by the spilled oil lamp. Somehow, he thought it fitting that Annabelle had died by her own hand. And her own hatred. Then, as the fire began to lick at the sides of the bed, he turned on his heel and vaulted out the window.

He lingered in the darkness, watching the flames spread, watching as the hired hands fought to put out the raging blaze.

It was after dawn when he started for Yellow Creek.

Chapter 25

*R*achel was sitting in the kitchen, staring into a cup of cold coffee, wondering . . . wondering if Tyree had left her for good. Wondering how he could leave without a word after the night they had shared. She would have sworn he loved her, would have staked her life on it even though he had never said the words. Now she was not so sure. Where was he?

A knock at the back door disturbed her thoughts and she hurried across the room, her heart beating fast. Perhaps Tyree had come back to her. Dear God, please let it be Tyree.

Her face mirrored her disappointment when she opened the door and saw Clint

Wesley standing there, his face a mask of concern.

"Morning, Clint," she said without much enthusiasm. "Come in."

"Rachel, you darn fool, I just got through talking to Candido. Are you out of your mind, running off into the desert like that? You might have been killed. Or worse."

"I'm fine," she replied dully. "Would you like some coffee?"

"No." Clint shoved his hands into his pants' pockets. "Did you find him?"

"Yes."

"Where is he?"

"I don't know."

Clint did not believe her, and he was about to say so when footsteps sounded in the hallway. He drew his gun as Logan Tyree stepped into the kitchen.

Too late, Rachel started to call out a warning. Then, with a shrug, she sat back in her chair, a sudden intuition admonishing her not to interfere between the two men this time.

Tyree did not seem surprised to find the Marshal standing in the kitchen with a gun in his hand. Calm as could be, he crossed to the stove and poured himself a cup of coffee. For the first time in his life, he knew exactly what he wanted. It was a good feeling.

He shifted his coffee cup to his right hand, smiled lazily. "Morning, Marshal," he drawled, his eyes fixed on the Colt .44 nestled in Wesley's hand.

"Keep your hand away from that gun," Clint warned curtly. "I don't want to have to kill you."

"No?"

"No. I want to see you hang for the murder of Job Walsh, among other things."

"I'd like to avoid that, if you don't mind."

"Shut up!" Wesley snapped. He cocked the Colt, his mild blue eyes alight with the force of his hatred. If it weren't for Logan Tyree, Rachel would have been his wife long ago.

Tyree stirred impatiently. "Wesley, I don't want to draw on you, but if you don't put that gun down, I'm gonna take it away from you."

Wesley snorted. "I may not be a fast gun, Tyree, but I think I can crank off a round or two before you can . . . damn!" He swore as Tyree's bullet slammed into his forearm, knocking the Colt from fingers gone suddenly numb.

"You talk too much," Tyree mused, holstering his weapon.

Without a word, Rachel picked up a tea towel and wrapped it around the shallow wound in Clint's arm.

"This doesn't solve anything," Clint said through clenched teeth. "I intend to see you hang if it's the last thing I ever do."

"Wesley, you're a damn fool," Tyree observed without rancor. "And you'll never amount to anything as a lawman if you don't wise up. When you've got the drop on a man, you don't stand around listening to him jaw.

You either take his gun from him, or you kill him."

"Thanks for the lesson," Wesley muttered sarcastically.

"No charge," Tyree replied with a grin. "As for killing Walsh, you've got no proof that I gunned him. No witnesses. No evidence."

"I've got proof," Clint said triumphantly. "I've got your signed confession."

"Really? I'd like to see it."

"It's out at the Slash W. Annabelle showed it to me months ago."

"Forget it, Marshal. The Slash W went up in smoke late last night."

Rachel and Clint stared at Tyree, mouths agape, and then Wesley sighed heavily.

"All right, Tyree," the Marshal said wearily. "You win." He glanced at Rachel, then swung around to face Tyree again. "You're no good for her!" he lashed out. "You told me so yourself."

"That's true," Tyree said soberly.

"I'd make her a better husband than you ever could."

"True again," Tyree agreed with a shrug.

"And I love her." Clint looked at Rachel, his eyes pleading with her. "I do love you," he said fervently.

"I think he means it," Tyree said. "Any fool can see he's crazy about you."

Clint smiled exuberantly. Things were going better than he had dared hope. "He's a drifter, Rachel. I'll bet he's never stayed in one place longer than a few months at most."

"All true," Tyree agreed, grinning broadly. "But you've left out one thing. I love Rachel. And she loves me."

"Yeah." Wesley sighed heavily. Anyone could see that Rachel loved Tyree. It was there in her happy smile, and in the warmth of her eyes when she looked at Tyree.

"Clint, I'm sorry—"

"It's alright, Rachel," Wesley said, forcing himself to smile. "Be happy." Picking up his gun, he shoved it in his holster and left the house. Somehow, in his heart, he had known Rachel would never be his.

"Well?" Tyree said, taking Rachel in his arms. "Say something."

"I love you."

"I know that," he growled. "Dammit, Rachel, I hope you know what you're getting yourself into."

"I know," she said quietly, and then she smiled up at him, her face radiant, her eyes glowing. "You were right all along," she said, laughing merrily. "The beautiful princess should always marry the dragon."

"Told you so," Tyree said, grinning at her. It wouldn't be easy, hanging up his gun, settling down in one place. But with Rachel by his side, he could do it. By damn, he could do anything!

For a moment, Rachel fretted over the way she had hurt Clint, and then she brightened. Carol Ann would be there to comfort Clint, to give him the love and support every man needed. They were perfect for each other.

And then Tyree was kissing her, kissing her as if he would never let her go, and there was no room in Rachel's heart or thoughts for any other man. Only Tyree, always Tyree . . .

RECKLESS DESIRE

MADELINE BAKER

**Winner Of The *Romantic Times*
Reviewers' Choice Award For Best Indian Series!**

Cloud Walker knows he has no right to love Mary, the daughter of the great Cheyenne warrior, Two Hawks Flying. Serenely beautiful, sweetly tempting, Mary is tied to a man who despises her for her Indian heritage. But that gives Cloud Walker no right to claim her soft lips, to brand her yearning body with his savage love. Yet try as he might, he finds it impossible to deny their passion, impossible to escape the scandal, the soaring ecstasy of their uncontrollable desire.

__3727-0 $4.99 US/$5.99 CAN

Dorchester Publishing Co., Inc.
P.O. Box 6640
Wayne, PA 19087-8640

Please add $1.75 for shipping and handling for the first book and $.50 for each book thereafter. NY, NYC, and PA residents, please add appropriate sales tax. No cash, stamps, or C.O.D.s. All orders shipped within 6 weeks via postal service book rate. Canadian orders require $2.00 extra postage and must be paid in U.S. dollars through a U.S. banking facility.

Name_____
Address_____
City_____ State_____ Zip_____
I have enclosed $_____ in payment for the checked book(s).
Payment <u>must</u> accompany all orders. ❑ Please send a free catalog.

MADELINE BAKER

Beneath A Midnight Moon

Winner Of The *Romantic Times* Reviewers Choice Award!

He comes to her in visions—the hard-muscled stranger who promises to save her from certain death. She never dares hope that her fantasy love will hold her in his arms until the virile and magnificent dream appears in the flesh.

A warrior valiant and true, he can overcome any obstacle, yet his yearning for the virginal beauty he's rescued overwhelms him. But no matter how his fevered body aches for her, he is betrothed to another.

Bound together by destiny, yet kept apart by circumstances, they brave untold perils and ruthless enemies—and find a passion that can never be rent asunder.

_3649-5 $4.99 US/$5.99 CAN

Dorchester Publishing Co., Inc.
P.O. Box 6640
Wayne, PA 19087-8640

Please add $1.75 for shipping and handling for the first book and $.50 for each book thereafter. NY, NYC, and PA residents, please add appropriate sales tax. No cash, stamps, or C.O.D.s. All orders shipped within 6 weeks via postal service book rate. Canadian orders require $2.00 extra postage and must be paid in U.S. dollars through a U.S. banking facility.

Name_____
Address_____
City_____ State_____ Zip_____
I have enclosed $_____ in payment for the checked book(s).
Payment <u>must</u> accompany all orders. ▢ Please send a free catalog.

RECKLESS LOVE

MADELINE BAKER

"Madeline Baker's Indian romances should not be missed!"
—Romantic Times

Joshua Berdeen is the cavalry soldier who has traveled the country in search of lovely Hannah Kincaid. Josh offers her a life of ease in New York City and all the finer things.

Two Hawks Flying is the Cheyenne warrior who has branded Hannah's body with his searing desire. Outlawed by the civilized world, he can offer her only the burning ecstasy of his love. But she wants no soft words of courtship when his hard lips take her to the edge of rapture...and beyond.

__3869-2 $5.99 US/$7.99 CAN

Dorchester Publishing Co., Inc.
P.O. Box 6640
Wayne, PA 19087-8640

Please add $1.75 for shipping and handling for the first book and $.50 for each book thereafter. NY, NYC, and PA residents, please add appropriate sales tax. No cash, stamps, or C.O.D.s. All orders shipped within 6 weeks via postal service book rate. Canadian orders require $2.00 extra postage and must be paid in U.S. dollars through a U.S. banking facility.

Name_____
Address_____
City_____State_____Zip_____
I have enclosed $_____ in payment for the checked book(s).
Payment <u>must</u> accompany all orders. ❑ Please send a free catalog.

THE ANGEL & THE OUTLAW

MADELINE BAKER

Bestselling Author Of *Lakota Renegade*

An outlaw, a horse thief, a man killer, J.T. Cutter isn't surprised when he is strung up for his crimes. What amazes him is the heavenly being who grants him one year to change his wicked ways. Yet when he returns to his old life, he hopes to cram a whole lot of hell-raising into those twelve months no matter what the future holds.

But even as J.T. heads back down the trail to damnation, a sharp-tongued beauty is making other plans for him. With the body of a temptress and the heart of a saint, Brandy is the only woman who can save J.T. And no matter what it takes, she'll prove to him that the road to redemption can lead to rapturous bliss.

_3931-1 $5.99 US/$7.99 CAN

Dorchester Publishing Co., Inc.
P.O. Box 6640
Wayne, PA 19087-8640

Please add $1.75 for shipping and handling for the first book and $.50 for each book thereafter. NY, NYC, and PA residents, please add appropriate sales tax. No cash, stamps, or C.O.D.s. All orders shipped within 6 weeks via postal service book rate. Canadian orders require $2.00 extra postage and must be paid in U.S. dollars through a U.S. banking facility.

Name_____
Address_____
City_____State_____Zip_____
I have enclosed $_____ in payment for the checked book(s).
Payment <u>must</u> accompany all orders. ❑ Please send a free catalog.

DON'T MISS THESE OTHER HISTORICAL ROMANCES BY MADELINE BAKER

Feather in the Wind. Black Wind gazes out over a land as vast and empty as the sky, praying for the strength to guide his people, and he sees her face. Susannah comes to him in a vision, a woman as mysterious as the new moon over the prairie, as tender as springtime in the Paha Sapa. And he knows his life is changed forever. To the writer in her he is an inspiration, but to the lonely woman within he is a dream come true who will lure her across the years to fulfill a love beyond time.
_4197-9 $5.99 US/$6.99 CAN

Lacey's Way. Lacey Montana is making a long trek across the plains, following her father's prison wagon, when Indians suddenly attack the wagon, kidnapping her father and leaving her helpless and alone. By helping the wounded Matt Drago, part Apache and part gambler, she finds someone to help her locate her father. Stranded in the burning desert, desperation turns to fierce passion as they struggle to stay alive on their dangerous journey.
_3956-7 $5.99 US/$6.99 CAN

Dorchester Publishing Co., Inc.
P.O. Box 6640
Wayne, PA 19087-8640

Please add $1.75 for shipping and handling for the first book and $.50 for each book thereafter. NY, NYC, and PA residents, please add appropriate sales tax. No cash, stamps, or C.O.D.s. All orders shipped within 6 weeks via postal service book rate. Canadian orders require $2.00 extra postage and must be paid in U.S. dollars through a U.S. banking facility.

Name_____
Address_____
City_____ State_____ Zip_____
I have enclosed $_____ in payment for the checked book(s).
Payment <u>must</u> accompany all orders. ❏ Please send a free catalog.

"Powerful, passionate, and action-packed, Madeline Baker's historical romances will keep readers on the edge of their seats!"

—*Romantic Times*

MADELINE BAKER

WARRIOR'S LADY

A creature of moonlight and quicksilver, Leyla rescues the mysterious man from unspeakable torture, then heals him body and soul. The radiant enchantress is all he wants in a woman—gentle, innocent, exquisitely lovely—but his enemies will do everything in their power to keep her from him. Only a passion born of desperate need can prevail against such hatred and unite two lovers against such odds.

___4305-X $5.99 US/$6.99 CAN

Dorchester Publishing Co., Inc.
P.O. Box 6640
Wayne, PA 19087-8640

Please add $1.75 for shipping and handling for the first book and $.50 for each book thereafter. NY, NYC, and PA residents, please add appropriate sales tax. No cash, stamps, or C.O.D.s. All orders shipped within 6 weeks via postal service book rate. Canadian orders require $2.00 extra postage and must be paid in U.S. dollars through a U.S. banking facility.

Name_____
Address_____
City_____State_____Zip_____
I have enclosed $_____ in payment for the checked book(s).
Payment <u>must</u> accompany all orders. ❏ Please send a free catalog.

Spirit's Song

MADELINE BAKER

She is a runaway wife, with a hefty reward posted for her return. And he is the best darn tracker in the territory. For the half-breed bounty hunter, it is an easy choice. His was a hard life, with little to show for it except his horse, his Colt, and his scars. The pampered, brown-eyed beauty will go back to her rich husband in San Francisco, and he will be ten thousand dollars richer. But somewhere along the trail out of the Black Hills everything changes. Now, he will give his life to protect her, to hold her forever in his embrace. Now the moonlight poetry of their loving reflects the fiery vision of the Sun Dance: She must be his spirit's song.

___4476-5 $5.99 US/$6.99 CAN

Dorchester Publishing Co., Inc.
P.O. Box 6640
Wayne, PA 19087-8640

Please add $1.75 for shipping and handling for the first book and $.50 for each book thereafter. NY, NYC, and PA residents, please add appropriate sales tax. No cash, stamps, or C.O.D.s. All orders shipped within 6 weeks via postal service book rate. Canadian orders require $2.00 extra postage and must be paid in U.S. dollars through a U.S. banking facility.

Name_____
Address_____
City_____State_____Zip_____
I have enclosed $_____ in payment for the checked book(s).
Payment <u>must</u> accompany all orders. ❑ Please send a free catalog.
CHECK OUT OUR WEBSITE! www.dorchesterpub.com

ATTENTION ROMANCE CUSTOMERS!

SPECIAL
TOLL-FREE NUMBER
1-800-481-9191

Call Monday through Friday
10 a.m. to 9 p.m.
Eastern Time
Get a free catalogue,
join the Romance Book Club,
and order books using your
Visa, MasterCard,
or Discover®.

Leisure
Books

GO ONLINE WITH US AT DORCHESTERPUB.COM

She could barely breathe

She had gone flying straight into the path of a speeding taxi. Somehow she managed to spin out of its way, though its mirror caught her in the side. If the driver noticed, he kept going, and Rae froze, stunned, as a bus screeched to a stop mere inches from where she stood.

"Are you all right?" a man asked. He picked up the floral arrangement she'd dropped in the fracas and handed it to her.

But Rae was already searching the crowd for a face she recognized. This had been no accident. She'd felt strong hands on her back shove her into the oncoming traffic.

She allowed herself to be swept along with the crowd, and only when she got to the other side of the street did she look down at the flowers she was holding.

They were crushed. Mangled. Just as she might have been.

Rae felt sick. A certainty enveloped her.

Someone wanted her dead.

D0681489

ABOUT THE AUTHOR

Patricia Rosemoor began creating romantic fantasies as a child, never guessing that someday she would be writing for Harlequin Books. Although writing demands a lot of time, Patricia can't think of another profession that would allow her to explore so many intriguing settings and subjects. She thinks of each new idea as a challenge, creating a story that will fascinate her readers.

Books by Patricia Rosemoor

HARLEQUIN INTRIGUE
  38–DOUBLE IMAGES
  55–DANGEROUS ILLUSIONS
  74–DEATH SPIRAL
  81–CRIMSON HOLIDAY
  95–AMBUSHED
113–DO UNTO OTHERS
161–PUSHED TO THE LIMIT*
163–SQUARING ACCOUNTS*
165–NO HOLDS BARRED*

*Quid Pro Quo trilogy

Don't miss any of our special offers. Write to us at the following address for information on our newest releases.

Harlequin Reader Service
P.O. Box 1397, Buffalo, NY 14240
Canadian address: P.O. Box 603,
Fort Erie, Ont. L2A 5X3

The Kiss of Death

Patricia Rosemoor

Harlequin Books

TORONTO • NEW YORK • LONDON
AMSTERDAM • PARIS • SYDNEY • HAMBURG
STOCKHOLM • ATHENS • TOKYO • MILAN
MADRID • WARSAW • BUDAPEST • AUCKLAND

If you purchased this book without a cover you should be aware that this book is stolen property. It was reported as "unsold and destroyed" to the publisher, and neither the author nor the publisher has received any payment for this "stripped book."

To Cathy Andorka and Ursula Cacelli
who share my delight in AMC

Harlequin Intrigue edition published October 1992

ISBN 0-373-22199-1

THE KISS OF DEATH

Copyright © 1992 Patricia Pinianski. All rights reserved. Except for use in any review, the reproduction or utilization of this work in whole or in part in any form by any electronic, mechanical or other means, now known or hereafter invented, including xerography, photocopying and recording, or in any information storage or retrieval system, is forbidden without the permission of the publisher, Harlequin Enterprises Limited, 225 Duncan Mill Road, Don Mills, Ontario, Canada M3B 3K9.

All the characters in this book have no existence outside the imagination of the author and have no relation whatsoever to anyone bearing the same name or names. They are not even distantly inspired by any individual known or unknown to the author, and all incidents are pure invention.

® are Trademarks registered in the United States Patent and Trademark Office and in other countries.

Printed in U.S.A.

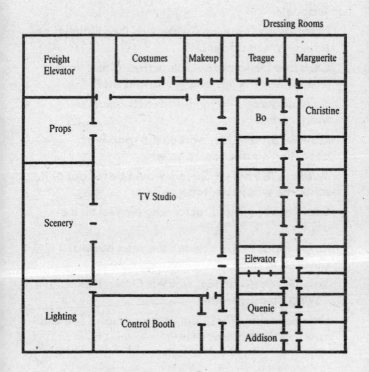

Dressing Rooms

Freight Elevator

Costumes

Makeup

Teague

Marguerite

Props

Bo

Christine

TV Studio

Scenery

Elevator

Lighting

Control Booth

Quenie

Addison

CAST OF CHARACTERS

Teague Slaughter—Women were dying to kiss him.

Rae Magill—She was in control . . . until her lips met Teague's.

Marguerite Lemmond—She was the villainess on-screen. What about off?

Christine Dellamore—This actress didn't have a jealous bone in her body . . . or did she?

Bo Hathaway—Why did this actor fear Marguerite?

Quenie Tovar—Her part on the soap was becoming smaller and smaller.

Addison Kilroe—If Quenie would be cut out of the script, he would be, too.

Saul Jacobi—The director who played all the angles.

Rufus Piggot—He dressed the stars but was devoted to one.

Yale Gordon—Whom was this network executive having an affair with?

Wilona Irwin—President of the "Rivals" fan club— how loyal a fan was she?

Chapter One

The Kiss of Death was back and sorely tempted to make heads roll! Rather, one head in particular.

Teague Slaughter pursued the amusing image as he stopped before the dressing room with its solid gold nameplate. As the new executive producer of the daytime soap opera "Rivals," he had the power to make it happen. He also had the responsibility to put the show before his private fantasies.

He'd no sooner touched knuckles to the door when the wood panel flew open to reveal Marguerite Lemond in a flame-red silk wrap rather than the costume she was supposed to be wearing. Dress rehearsal was scheduled to begin in fifteen minutes. Though barely topping five feet, the soap queen had the kind of presence that made itself felt, especially when her volatile emotions were in gear as they were now.

"It's about time!" she stated, green eyes shooting daggers at him, dark curls writhing around her shoulders like live snakes.

It wasn't that he had an overactive imagination. Teague merely knew her too well. He crossed his arms over his chest and raised a questioning brow. "I'm a busy man. What is it this time, Marguerite?" As if he couldn't guess she was still determined to make him change the new story line he'd created to boost the ratings.

With the blink of her fake lashes, the hard shell melted and Marguerite even managed to conjure re-alistic-looking tears, giving her eyes that luminous quality the camera loved. "You know what I want." She implied a wealth of meanings in the simple state-ment.

The actress whipped away from him and dramati-cally threw herself on the chaise lounge. Her robe slipped open, revealing a shapely thigh, which might belong to a woman who was twentysomething rather than fortysomething. She didn't bother to cover her-self, making Teague think she'd exposed her tanned flesh on purpose. Trying to seduce him?

Again?

Unmoved by the display, he stepped into the dress-ing room and propped himself against her makeup counter. If she kept this up, the only thing likely to rise was his temper . . . not that he would let it show. If the truth be known, her methods were predictable.

"The script stays as is," Teague told her.

They'd been going around and around the issue all week and he was weary of the debate.

"I could ask Yale to intercede," she threatened.

She was referring to Yale Gordon, the network rep-resentative to "Rivals," which was the Continental Broadcasting Corporation's longest running daytime drama—and the one with the poorest ratings. Teague knew how desperate Yale was to save the show, not to mention his own job. That the suave, silver-haired executive was probably under Marguerite's spell wouldn't count for much in this case.

"My guess is you've already approached Yale without any success," he speculated, and from Marguerite's chagrined expression knew he was correct. "Give it up, Marguerite. You can't win this one."

Her green eyes narrowed unattractively. "I can choose not to play. I could become ill, come down with laryngitis, unable to utter my lines."

If she wanted a game, two could play, Teague thought. And he was tougher than he had been the first time she'd sunk her fangs into him.

"Your not showing on the set this afternoon would go against you in contract negotiations."

"I knew it!" All pretense of amiability dissolved in an instant. Marguerite leapt from the chaise, her tone accusatory. "You want me off the show!"

"I never said that—"

"That's why my contract hasn't been renewed yet."

"*You* are responsible for the delay," he countered. "Demanding a ten-year contract with a guaranteed ongoing full salary even if the show is canceled is unreasonable."

"A star of my stature deserves special considerations. Your refusing to see that is just *your* way of throwing a wrench in the works." She stepped closer. "You want revenge, don't you?"

He certainly had enough reason to seek reciprocity. More than a dozen years before, Teague had gotten his start in daytime as an actor and had been doing quite well as a charismatic villain on "Rivals"...until Marguerite had chosen to vent her spite on him when he'd spurned her. Being her lover even for a short while had been hazardous duty and he'd wanted out of the affair almost as soon as it had begun.

"Actually, Marguerite, you did me a favor," he told her with a certain amount of detached pleasure. "It's somewhat ironic. If you hadn't had me fired I might not have gone on to another soap, another part, another career. If I hadn't gotten experience writing and producing, I might not be your boss now."

"And planning to kill me off!" Marguerite's voice rose loud enough to be heard on the set.

"You've seen next week's scripts—Dante Craven won't kill Faline Devereux." Teague referred to their television personae. He was reprising his villainous role for the current story line. "You'll merely be in a coma."

But Marguerite was obviously not willing to be reasoned with. Her pouty lips thinned as she spat, "Right, an indefinite coma...no doubt until my contract runs out. Then you can just write me off the show altogether. It's a devious plot to get rid of me. You want your pound of flesh. I know it!"

Having had enough of her histrionics, Teague towered over the actress. "Listen to me carefully. This new story was created with the audience share in mind, not to threaten you."

"And you weren't called The Kiss of Death, right?" Marguerite countered.

True, in the past, Dante Craven's leading ladies had had a limited life expectancy, thus the nickname. "But Faline is going to survive—and I'm thinking of the good of the show!"

Unfortunately that meant keeping the star in line and moderately happy, and Teague was at his wit's end as to how he could accomplish that. Though he might like to get rid of Marguerite—savor getting retribution for all the rotten things she'd done not only to him but to others in the industry—he had put his personal feelings on the back burner.

"Without me, there is no show!"

"Don't kid yourself. No one is indispensable." Trying to keep his temper from getting the best of him, Teague coldly said, "Now get your high-priced derriere dressed and out on the set pronto or—"

"Or what?"

"Or you'll be sorry you crossed me, lady."

HAVING HEARD the last interchange, Rae Magill stood frozen as Teague Slaughter swept out of Marguerite's dressing room and almost knocked her over. Rather than apologizing, he backed up and scowled at her, his normally vivid blue eyes icy, his handsome face shadowed with irritation. His thick brown hair shattered by golden highlights practically stood out around his chiseled features and brushed his wide, expensively sweatered shoulders, giving him the look of a lion whose mane had been seriously ruffled.

"Have you finished those changes in Act Five?" he asked.

"That's why I came to find you."

Rae straightened to her near six feet, the last couple of inches added by high-heeled sensible pumps. He was taller, able to stare down his blade of a nose at her—not that she was intimidated like the rest of the staff.

"The new pages are being copied now," she told him.

"Well, put a rush on it." Without so much as a by-your-leave, Teague stalked toward the hallway and elevator that would take him back up to the offices.

Rae glared after the broad back over which was stretched a vaguely southwestern design. Unusual sweaters were Teague Slaughter's personal trademark and no one wore them better. That she so much as noticed irritated her anew. Not having reason to be fond of the man, she avoided being around him any more than was necessary. Typically the head writer didn't spend much time on the set of a daytime drama, but having to deal with the script revisions at the last minute had forced the issue.

She reluctantly followed him toward the elevator but was stopped halfway there by Quenie Tovar and Addison Kilroe who were conferring in front of the woman's dressing room. The sixtyish couple playing Beatrice and Nigel Vanderlinde had both been with "Rivals" since its inception.

"The witch deserves whatever she gets," Quenie told Rae, sounding like the Grande Dame she now played. The original star of the show, she'd taken a back seat to Marguerite years ago.

"Yes, well..." Not wanting to backbite Marguerite, Rae tried to leave, but Quenie caught her by the arm.

"Now the shoe is on the other foot," the actress said gleefully, her pale blue eyes glittering with malice. "She's made all our lives miserable for years. Cutting the size of peoples' roles... getting them fired, for heaven's sake! There's no excuse for a viper like her."

"You are quite right, my dear." Addison was agreeable as always. He smoothed back his thinning gray hair and straightened his cravat. "But no need to worry anymore. With Teague in charge now, Marguerite won't be able to get away with any of her little tricks. He shall see to that."

Rae murmured noncommittally as she pulled her arm free and slipped away with a distracted smile. "See you on the set in a few minutes."

But Quenie was still ranting as Rae escaped toward the hallway. "It would serve Marguerite right if she couldn't escape The Kiss of Death!"

Teague was gone by the time Rae stopped before the elevator. She punched the call button and willed the car to hurry before she was embroiled in anyone else's grievances.

With feelings running high against the unlikable actress, Rae understood Marguerite's misplaced fear that she was being written out of the show. The Kiss of Death was not only the nickname bestowed on villain Dante Craven, whose leading ladies had all died on-screen through his machinations, if not always at his own hand. The moniker had stuck to Teague himself even though he'd changed careers long ago. Throughout the industry, he had a reputation for putting fear in others.

And for firing people who didn't tow the line, Rae thought sourly. Her friend Carol Flynn could attest to that fact.

A *ding* signaled the elevator's arrival. Rae took the car up one flight to her office where a clerk gave her several copies of the new pages.

Making a quick check on the changes, she had to hold the script toward a good light source and adjust its distance. Her sleek shoulder-length auburn hair slid along her cheek as she cocked her head and squinted her gray eyes in an attempt to focus. She normally used reading glasses that hung from a chain around her neck. But somehow she'd managed to misplace them after that morning's run-throughs. She hadn't been able to find the glasses when she'd returned from lunch.

"Seems to be all right to this blind person," she joked. "Deliver the other copies to the actors yourself," Rae instructed the young man.

Then she headed back downstairs.

Entering the dimly lit control room of Studio A, she handed the new scene to Director Saul Jacobi, whose dark brows pulled together as he quickly scanned the pages. Jacobi was wiry and sharp-featured, but attractive in an angular hard-edged way.

"Looks good, Rae." He sat down at the console next to his technical director and immediately integrated the pages into his script, then began making appropriate notes for camera directions in the columns. "You'd better stick around. No doubt Her Highness will demand changes. Have a seat."

"Right."

Though she figured Teague would be the only one to make any more changes from here on. Obviously out of sorts with Marguerite, he would no doubt counter any objections Her Highness might have to the reworked scene.

Careful to smooth her slim gray suit skirt over her knees, Rae took a raised chair toward the back of the large booth. Here she would be able to see while staying out of the way of the technical crew who dashed around adjusting lighting, sound and video quality.

She was watching Jacobi scribble his final notes when a peevish voice called, "Hey, anyone seen Slaughter?"

Rae glanced back to see Rufus Piggot pushing through the doorway. The property and costume supervisor looked downright disgusted, his shoulders appearing more rounded, his chest more caved-in, than usual.

"Did you check his office?" Rae asked.

"Dead end. He was supposed to be in makeup, but he's not there, either." Pulling a handkerchief from a pocket, he mopped the sweat from his bald pate. "It's been one helluva day. I'm too old to go chasing after people."

"Is there something I can help you with?" Rae asked.

"Nah, but thanks, cookie. Slaughter's the only one who can handle this one. That Marguerite Lemond is gonna get what she deserves sooner or later."

"What now?" Jacobi asked, looking up from his script.

"She saw the dress Christine was supposed to wear in the dinner-party scene and decided it was too sophisticated for Tempest. You know, the kinda trick she used to pull on Quenie whenever she got the chance."

Rufus had never hidden his devotion to the aging actress who had once been "Rivals'" leading lady. Rae thought his protectiveness of her sweet.

"What Marguerite meant was that she wanted the dress for herself," Rufus went on. "There was no changing her mind. Right now, wardrobe is going crazy trying to alter ten pounds of sequined material from a voluptuous size eight to a petite size four. And I'm afraid Christine is pretty upset."

"Christine is doing just fine, thank you."

Script in hand, Christine Dellamorte, the actress who played Tempest Vanderlinde Black, entered the control room, passed Rufus and stopped inches from Jacobi's shoulder. She glanced at the bank of monitors, each of which showed a different camera view or graphic display and nodded to herself in approval.

"Fighting with Marguerite is not worth the waste of energy." Christine flashed the costume supervisor a grateful smile. "Rufus found me another dress that's even more spectacular."

"You deserve it, cookie," Rufus said, a grin lightening his sour expression. "It'll be ready when you are." With that, he left the control room.

Jacobi was staring up at Christine, whose stylishly short blond hair glowed under the recessed lighting. "Are you really all right?"

"Of course. I'm used to Marguerite getting what I want or deserve, whether it be the best scenes or the most glamorous costumes or...anything." Her tone was light, yet Rae identified an underlying seriousness. "I just chalk it up to experience and go on."

"The consummate pro, as always," Jacobi said.

The pair exchanged a special smile that made Rae think they were on more than work-friendly terms.

"I try," Christine murmured. "One prima donna per set is enough, don't you think?" she asked, turning to Rae.

"Acting is a difficult job. Sometimes the stress gets to people," Rae said diplomatically.

"Stress." Christine sighed and her big blue eyes were filled with sympathy. "You're not exempt, either. You've had more than your share of grief since you joined us—all of two months ago? I wouldn't want to be in your shoes for anything. I admire the way you've taken over and improved the show in such a short time, despite the obstacles."

"You're going to make me blush," Rae said with a laugh.

Though in reality, she had nothing to laugh about. Her professional life had been one mini-disaster after another since she'd left the head-writing team of "Broken Hearts" where she'd done the day-by-day breakdowns to take the single head-writer slot at "Rivals."

She'd barely been at the more demanding job for a week when the writers' strike was announced. That had lasted nearly a month to be followed by a shake-up in the production staff. And when the former executive producer quit, Teague Slaughter had been hired to fill the slot. Had Rae realized she would find herself in the untenable position of working for The Kiss of Death, she would never have left her old job.

"Really. I think you're incredibly talented, Rae. No hype," Christine assured her.

"Thanks." The actress seemed sincere, but that was to be expected, Rae thought. Christine was as different from Marguerite as day was from night. "I only wish we could pull ahead with the scripts. This last-minute business is enough to give me an ulcer."

Because of the new story line—bringing Teague's character, Dante, back—added to the strike, the show was behind schedule, taping taking place one day ahead of airdate rather than a week.

"Things will come together. All the kinks are being ironed out nicely," Christine said. "I'd bet we'll be able to get back on schedule in the next week or so."

"I hope you're right."

"Then maybe you'll be able to take some time from your word processor to have a proper lunch with me."

"I'd like that," Rae said with a smile.

Jacobi hadn't been exaggerating when he'd called her the consummate professional. She always knew her lines, was on time, never made demands. And Christine was tactfully straightforward, never afraid to express her opinion. The young actress didn't like Marguerite, but she refused to let the leading lady make her lose her temper.

"Uh-oh, I forgot to feed Bonnie Blue and Ginny Green," Christine suddenly muttered. Everyone knew the birds were her "babies." "I'd better get back to my dressing room and give them something before they start complaining."

The director and his technical crew were busy with final setups—shading cameras, checking graphics, setting levels on background music and sound effects. Used to having a hubbub around her, Rae ignored the noise and glanced at the monitors. Marguerite was on the set, the focus of several cameras. The actress might be dressed and present as ordered, but she definitely wasn't happy. She was pacing and obviously spewing her complaints at Bo Hathaway.

The actor appeared unruffled by the tirade. Stopping her dead in her tracks, he took Marguerite's slender shoulders between firm hands and gazed down into her sharp-featured face. Chestnut hair crisply cut, brown eyes earnest, he looked every bit the leading man of "Rivals." If anyone could calm down the difficult actress, Rae figured Bo could. Although he and Marguerite didn't have an exclusive relationship, they often attended network public relations functions together and were usually on more than friendly terms.

But at the moment, the close-up on Camera Three brought home the flash of irritation in Marguerite's eyes and the tightness around her lips, both in response to whatever the actor was saying.

The sound engineer chose that moment to check the various studio microphones, including the boom mike placed near the couple.

"... could tell the press everything about you," Marguerite was saying, her low tone obviously meant for Bo's ears only.

"I don't take well to threats, Marguerite," the actor returned. "Remember the saying, 'He who is without secrets may cast the first verbal barrage.'"

"What do you mean by that?" the soap queen demanded as Bo whipped away from her and stormed off the set. "I'm not the one who's got anything to hide!"

"Ahh, blast! We don't have room for tantrums," Jacobi muttered. "We'll never get out of here tonight if we don't get started." The director threw a switch and spoke into a mike that was connected to studio speakers. "Time, boys and girls. Everyone should be on the set. Dress starts in two minutes with or without you. Una," he called the production assistant on the floor. "Round 'em up, sweetheart."

Una saluted and went charging toward the corridor leading to the dressing rooms.

Within minutes, the cast was assembled, the dress rehearsal in progress. Rae watched and listened avidly as they went from scene to scene, act to act. She so rarely had the chance to hear a polished performance of the script until the show was actually aired that she got completely caught up in the unfolding drama. Before she knew it, the finale of the dinner party to which Teague's character, Dante Craven, had invited all his old enemies was at hand. Before the last course was finished, Quenie as Beatrice Vanderlinde told Dante off in her spirited fashion and led the parade of guests from his mansion.

All but Faline, who Dante approached from behind. This was their big pseudo-romantic scene together. He would woo her into complacency so she wouldn't guess he was about to settle an old score with her by giving her a drugged drink.

Everything was going according to plan.

Yet Marguerite was visibly nervous as Teague poured two "cognacs" and handed her one. In truth, the liquid was merely tea. She would drink hers, while he was only supposed to pretend. Teague's close-up camera got a shot of the villain that sent a shiver up Rae's spine. Dressed in a black velvet Russian shirt, his hair slicked back, his expression a combination of seductiveness and cunning, Teague Slaughter had never looked so downright dangerous . . . or enticing.

Marquerite drank the amber liquid. She and Teague had barely exchanged a couple of lines when a peculiar expression crossed the actress's features. She faltered as if she'd forgotten what came next. Then she pulled away from Teague and faced the live camera directly.

"Saul, we've got to stop right now."

The director swore under his breath and flipped on the studio speaker. "Marguerite, this is dress rehearsal. We're not changing your lines. Keep going!"

"You don't understand," she complained, "I'm feeling kind of weird."

"The scene will be over in two minutes." Rae could tell Jacobi was barely holding on to his temper. "Then you can go to your dressing room and rest for a while. Now pick up where you left off!"

Marguerite appeared about to comply with his wishes when she put a hand to her stomach. Rae frowned. The soap queen really looked as if she weren't feeling well, though she *was* a good actress.

"I can't," Marguerite protested. "I'm feeling a little nauseous and my head hurts. I have to get to my dressing room now or I won't be able to tape."

With that pronouncement, she tottered off the set.

"Marguerite!" Teague yelled after her. "Get back here! Remember our discussion!"

But the actress kept going and Teague struck the side of the drink cart with a closed fist. The bottles and glasses jumped and clinked together. The rest of the cast and crew buzzed at his unusual behavior. Rae herself was surprised. Usually Teague Slaughter remained collected and very much in control. He could be the ultimate game player when he so chose. This was the second time in an hour—only the second time since she'd known him—that she'd seen him lose his cool.

"Do you believe this?" Jacobi demanded to no one in particular. Taking off his headsets, the director threw them down on the console, then flicked on the studio speakers. "I'll go see what's wrong with Her Highness this time," he said into his mike.

Teague waved at him in acknowledgment and edged the shadows of the set.

He had barely disappeared from monitor view when Rae decided she might as well stretch her legs. She wandered from the control room onto the studio floor just in time for the arrival of a frowsy woman wearing a ghastly flower-print dress and sensible oxfords.

"Oh, Bo, there you are!" cried the woman, puffing as if she'd been rushing around. Fake eyelashes that looked like caterpillars batted behind thick, horn-rimmed glasses, and she gazed at him with longing from under a fringe of limp brown bangs. "Heavens, I thought I'd never catch up to you."

The actor turned on his most charming smile. "Listen, Wilona, we're on a tight schedule today—"

"I know. I won't keep you. I was just wondering when you'd be able to autograph the photos I want to send out with the next set of newsletters."

Rae realized this must be Wilona Irwin, "Rivals" fan-club president. She wondered at the unusual policy of allowing a fan free rein in the studio, but if no one else objected, she certainly wasn't about to.

"Maybe I can do it sometime Monday if things get smoothed out around here," Bo was saying with little enthusiasm.

"Oh." Wilona's smile wilted. "Well, I guess that'll have to do."

"Sorry. I need to check on something," the actor said as he rushed off, his smile belying the fact that he seemed awfully anxious to get away from the woman.

Changing focus immediately, Wilona walked across the set without hesitation until she was face-to-face with Rae. "You're the new head writer."

Startled by the direct approach, Rae asked, "Can I do something for you?"

"You can give me an interview," Wilona said eagerly. She punched at her horn-rimmed glasses. "I was hoping to do an article on you—tie it in with the fabulous new story line you've created. Bringing Dante Craven back to the show was sheer genius."

Smart move, indeed, Rae thought, though it hadn't been hers. In the first week of his appearance, they'd already lured back thousands of old viewers whose loyalty to the show had waned over the years. Fan mail was pouring in by the bagful.

"You're giving me too much credit," Rae said. "I only wrote the new scenes. The idea for Teague Slaughter reprising his old role came from Yale Gordon, the network representative. And Teague himself thought of this particular story line. Maybe you should interview him."

Rae smiled smugly to herself when she imagined Teague's annoyance at being pestered by the overenthusiastic fan, as if he didn't have enough on his plate.

"If you think that's best," Wilona said, just as Jacobi led a wan-looking Marguerite back on the set. The fan-club president shifted and muttered, "Oh, dear, I do hope everything goes all right." Then, as abruptly as she'd appeared, she left.

Rae stared after the odd woman but didn't have much time to think about her behavior as Marguerite stepped up to the drink cart. By the time Rae followed Jacobi into the control room, Teague had reappeared, as well.

They finished rehearsing the Friday cliff-hanger scene, but not to Jacobi's satisfaction. "A little more enthusiasm when tape is rolling, boys and girls," he called out to the studio. "We don't have time for pickups today. Check makeup and hair quickly, please, and take your places."

TEAGUE WENT THROUGH his scenes with as much drama as he could muster considering all he'd had to deal with that day. Things couldn't get worse. He wanted this taping over with so he could go home, shower, eat a microwaved dinner and climb into bed early.

Some exciting prospect for a man who was known as The Kiss of Death!

When they got to the dinner-party scene, he mustered more enthusiasm than he'd thought was in him. His argument with Quenie went especially well. Then came his favorite part, the scene he'd been looking forward to doing all week. The scene Marguerite Lemond had been having fits over....

Teague's large hand engulfed her fragile sequined shoulder and he could feel her shudder at the touch. Little would viewers realize she was drawing on hatred rather than desire. The sexual tension seemed so palpable the audience would probably believe they'd taken up in their private lives where they'd left off a dozen years before.

"You'll stay for a drink," Teague said, nuzzling Marguerite's neck so the camera could get a good view of his mouth on her skin.

She threw back her head and protested. "I really should be going."

"But you don't want to, do you?" Teague asked in a low, throbbing voice that had once thrilled millions of women. "You want to stay with me, Faline...for as long as I'll let you."

"Let me?" she asked, her voice rising indignantly even as he let go of her to pour the fake cognacs. "Perhaps I should leave, after all."

"No."

Blocking her exit with his body, Teague handed Marguerite the drink and their gazes locked. If he weren't so exhausted, he might be amused by the spite glimmering from her eyes. Spite that would look like passion to the camera.

She lifted her drink. "To the unexpected," she ad-libbed, then drained the contents of the glass.

That was Marguerite. He wouldn't change the script so she did. A small ad lib wouldn't hurt. He only hoped she would stop there so they wouldn't have to tape the scene again.

"Do you have any idea of how beautiful you are?" he asked, fingers lifting her chin.

"You really think so, Dante?" A flush spread across her face as though she were blushing. "Tell me."

"Faline, I've never known you to be so modest." Teague slid his hand along her neck, which felt chilled and clammy—odd, considering the heat of the lights. Perhaps she really wasn't feeling well. "A man only has to look at you, and you can see what he thinks in his eyes."

"Ah!" Marguerite slid her arms around her midsection and winced convincingly. Spittle sprayed from her mouth as she demanded, "What's happening to me?" A slight change in line.

"You're tired, poor dear." Teague stepped back. "Why don't we find a place for you to lie down?" He indicated a couch several yards away. "You can sleep as long as you like."

But with the first step, Marguerite faltered, clutched her stomach and moaned. In character, Teague smiled a silky, evil smile. Marguerite looked up at him, her eyes round, her face now patchy red.

"Help me!" she begged, holding out an imploring hand to him. Another ad-lib. "Please. The drink . . ."

And then she slid to the floor at his feet exactly as planned.

"Perhaps I'll just let you sleep forever," Teague said with a cruel laugh that echoed through the studio and was meant to send chills up viewers' spines. "My very own Sleeping Beauty."

"Cut," came Jacobi's voice over the speakers. "That's a wrap. Great, both of you."

Teague allowed his shoulders to slump and rubbed the tension from the back of his neck as he started to leave.

Marguerite didn't move.

"You can get up now," Teague said.

"She's sleeping like you told her to." The cameraman chuckled as he looped his cable and pulled his camera back toward the wall.

"Ah, the influence of Dante Craven. Mayhaps you mesmerized her," the female floor director joked even as Marguerite lay frozen in a semi-fetal position.

Tempted to leave the actress to her dramatics, Teague hesitated. Something about the way she lay so still bothered him. He stooped over her, touched her shoulder.

"Marguerite, are you all right?"

"You gonna fall for that one?" asked Rufus Piggot, who was picking up the tray of drinks as his crew removed other props from the set. "She cries wolf when she can't get her own way."

Teague tugged at Marguerite until she rolled over on her back. Her skin was splotchy and a thin stream of saliva ran from the corner of her mouth. He grabbed her wrist and had a difficult time finding a faint thread of a pulse.

"Call the paramedics!" he shouted, even as he lifted one eyelid and noted the dilated pupil. Marguerite wasn't playing this time. "She's unconscious!"

Chapter Two

"*Dead.* Marguerite Lemond is dead," Addison Kilroe said. "I cannot reconcile myself with the fact."

Neither could anyone else, or so it seemed. Subdued cast and crew were huddled together mere yards from the paramedics who'd arrived only minutes after Jacobi had placed the call...yet too late to save the actress, Teague thought, wondering if she'd had any chance at all. As much as he'd disliked the woman, he hadn't wished her dead.

"The Kiss of Death struck for real this time," Addison added.

All eyes turned on Teague as if measuring whether or not he was taking pleasure in the tragedy. He clenched his jaw and glared at them, Addison in particular. The situation was too appalling for words, especially considering the woman had practically died in his arms. None of them had even taken Marguerite's cry for help seriously. Then one of the paramedics had said that Marguerite's symptoms indicated poisoning, though only an autopsy could confirm the hunch.

Not only dead, then, but murdered.

Teague felt as if he were orchestrating a nightmare.

"Is there a Teague Slaughter here?"

The query came from a middle-aged man whose seamed dusky face nearly matched his wrinkled brown suit. He was followed by two men and a woman.

"I'm Slaughter."

The leader flashed his badge. "Lieutenant Charlie Franklin, Homicide, N.Y.P.D."

"Thanks for getting here so fast."

"Unfortunately, my department never gets here fast enough," Franklin said, not without irony. His probing light brown eyes swept over the people assembled in the studio. "The deed is already done, isn't it? Nobody leaves until my technicians have a chance to go over the area, and my team gets a statement from each and every one of you."

Everyone groaned, including Teague who was beyond being bone tired. There was no helping it, he supposed, but he wished a full investigation could wait until morning.

"Before we start taking your individual statements, tell me what happened here tonight," Franklin said, flipping open a small notebook.

"We were wrapping up tomorrow's episode of 'Rivals,' taping the last scene," Teague told him. "Miss Lemond finished her drink and passed out on cue...only she didn't get up."

"Drink?"

"Yes, fake cognac that was supposedly drugged."

"And the paramedics suspect poison." Franklin clucked to himself as he continued scribbling. "Any indication that she wasn't feeling well prior to taping?"

"She ran off the set during dress rehearsal," Jacobi supplied. "We all thought she was faking illness because she hadn't gotten her own way about the scene, so I went to her dressing room to convince her that being 'sick' wasn't in her best interests.''

"And did you succeed?''

"Marguerite spent some time in her private bathroom, then said she was feeling better. She came back to the set with me, but she was flushed and tense and I suspected something really was wrong with her.'' Jacobi shrugged his shoulders. "Of course, her being poisoned never occurred to me. I figured she had a case of stomach flu.''

Guilt pricked Teague; he, of course, had assumed Marguerite was acting.

"So you did your taping and then what?'' Franklin asked.

"During the last scene, the one she ran out on during dress rehearsal,'' Teague said, "Marguerite clutched her stomach and flushed so realistically—''

Franklin interrupted. "At the same point she ran out the first time?''

"Right.'' Teague nodded. "After the drink.''

"Well, we have a place to start. If she was poisoned, that liquid is suspect,'' Franklin said. "Where is the glass and bottle?''

"Rufus Piggot, our property and costume supervisor, took the tray when his crew was cleaning up.''

"It's still sitting in the props room, drinks and all,'' Rufus volunteered, though he didn't sound thrilled at the attention being focused on him.

"We need to check out whatever Miss Lemond ingested.'' Franklin waved to one of his men to see to it.

"Tea,'' Rufus muttered while leading the way. "It was only tea. I fixed it myself.''

Franklin asked a few more questions to make certain he got the whole picture leading up to the death.

Teague explained how he'd recently been hired not only to produce the show but to act in it as well. He told the cop about the new story line and about Marguerite's objections. And he admitted that he had been the one to pour the drink.

If that drink had killed her, his fingerprints would be all over the bottle and glass...he only hoped his would be accompanied by those of the murderer!

While one of the evidence technicians checked the body and photographed the late actress, Lieutenant Franklin split cast and crew into two groups to be questioned by two police officers. He himself wanted to talk to those in charge of the production—Teague, Jacobi and Rae Magill.

Previously oblivious to Rae's presence, Teague was now acutely aware of the head writer who preceded him into the control room. From the moment he'd joined "Rivals," he'd sensed her dislike of him, but he had no idea of what he'd done to earn her enmity. They hadn't had a run-in. They hadn't yet had enough contact to warrant one.

So what was her problem?

Even now her brow was furrowed when she looked his way as if she disapproved of what she saw.

Though it was hardly the time to be noticing a woman, Teague liked what *he* saw, even if Rae Magill was too rigid by far. Her shiny russet hair begged to be touched, and a man could lose himself in those big gray eyes. As if she did so on purpose to make herself unapproachable, she stood too straight and tall, reminding him of a scarecrow with a steel pole for a spine. And her expression was equally stiff. A mask to cover her emotions?

He'd caught her smiling a couple of times—at an associate writer, an actor, or a secretary—and the expression had transformed her ordinary face into something of quiet beauty. But each time she'd become aware of his presence, she'd reverted to being a sourpuss. He didn't rate a smile or any other expression that smacked of approval.

Maybe she'd had a thing for Gary Noble, his predecessor, who Yale Gordon had fired. Whatever Rae's reasoning, Teague was determined to find out.

Once they'd all settled in, Franklin asked, "Anyone have reason to hate Marguerite Lemond?"

The question was a live bomb, one Teague didn't want to touch. Leaning back against the console, he crossed his arms over his chest and waited for Jacobi or Rae to field it.

Rae answered diplomatically, "Marguerite wasn't the most liked person on 'Rivals.'"

"Why not?"

"She was difficult," Jacobi said. "Difficult to please, difficult to work with."

"You, Mr. Slaughter." The querying light brown eyes settled on Teague, penetrating his skin, making him nervous though he had no reason to be. "Why didn't you like her?"

"I never said I didn't."

"You didn't interrupt Mr. Jacobi, either. So what did you have against the deceased?"

Knowing the cop would find out soon enough, Teague said, "She once had me fired from this show—*years* ago."

"But you never forgot it."

"No. But getting even isn't my style."

Rae started, then looked away. To his chagrin, Teague wasn't the only one who noticed.

Franklin addressed her. "Something wrong, Miss Magill?"

"No, nothing."

But her tone and obvious discomfort said otherwise. Franklin made another scribble in his notebook but didn't press the issue further. Teague wondered, however, if Rae's reaction hadn't been enough to damn him in the lieutenant's eyes.

He, Jacobi and Rae spent the next half hour answering the lieutenant's questions not only about them personally, but about Marguerite's relationships to other employees of the show. Teague sweated out every minute. He waited for Franklin to ask if any of them had a record—a history of arrest. What would he say then? Could he get away with denying it?

Teague Slaughter might not have a record, but Theodore Slavensky did.

When Franklin called the session to a halt without digging that deeply into any of their backgrounds, Teague sagged with relief. Still, the fact that Franklin had to consider him a prime suspect—he'd had both motive and opportunity—made Teague sweat. The lieutenant's digging into his past could seal his fate.

Back in the studio, the others milled about whispering among themselves. The air was thick with tension as the paramedics finally encased Marguerite in a body bag.

"My God, do you have to take her away in that...that thing?" Wilona Irwin wailed as if she and Marguerite had been personal friends.

Indeed, Marguerite had been responsible for getting Wilona free access to the set, or so Yale Gordon had told Teague. No wonder the fan-club president was overwrought, had been the moment he'd demanded someone call for help.

As the stretcher carrying Marguerite's remains was wheeled past them, Wilona sobbed and turned into Bo's chest. Looking helpless, the actor put his arms around her and patted her back soothingly.

Meanwhile, Franklin was checking with his staff. The preliminary questioning had been completed, the evidence gathered. The technician who'd been assigned to fetch the liquid from the prop room had several plastic Ziploc bags in hand. He spoke to the lieutenant in a low tone.

Taking one of the bags from the other man, Franklin announced, "You can all go home, folks, just don't leave town." As people started to turn away looking relieved, he added, "Just one thing." He held up a plastic bag containing a pair of tortoiseshell-rimmed glasses with a thin chain attached. "Who do these belong to?"

Silence stretched across the studio for a moment, before Rae Magill said, "Those are my reading glasses. I've been looking for them since lunch. Where did you find them?"

The evidence technician spoke up. "Tucked away in a cubbyhole where the drinks were prepared."

"What?" came Rae's horrified whisper.

Teague noted she grew visibly pale and thought she appeared shocked enough to faint. An interesting turn of events. Whether or not Rae Magill had reason to hate Marguerite, the discovery now threw the shadow of suspicion on the head writer, giving them something in common.

"I HOPE YOU CAN SEE without these, Miss Magill," Franklin said, indicating the glasses.

Rae took a deep breath, trying to calm her suddenly pounding pulse. "I have another pair at home, but—"

He cut her off. "Good." Then handed the bag containing her glasses back to his subordinate.

Not good. Bad with a capital B, Rae thought, her adrenaline pumping like mad. Everyone was looking at her as if she had something to hide.

"We're going to bring your glasses into the lab," Franklin added.

"For what?"

"So we can run a few tests."

Tempted to ask what kind of tests, Rae forced herself to remain silent. Tests that could pin the murder on her? For she did believe Marguerite had been murdered rather than dying of some mysterious natural causes. Plenty of her co-workers had reason to hate the actress—maybe enough to kill her—but she was not one of them! Sure, she'd had a few run-ins with the difficult woman, but nothing serious. Rae wanted to shout her denials, but she didn't want to dig herself in deeper by drawing more attention to herself.

She quelled the instinct to panic as the official investigative team finally left and the cast and crew dispersed, all talking in low tones among themselves.

Standing transfixed, Rae couldn't let go of an important fact that whirled through her mind: she hadn't been near the prop room all day, so she couldn't possibly have forgotten her glasses there!

That meant someone else had left them in the room, planting suspicion on an innocent person.

Rather her specifically, she realized, wondering who could dislike her enough to do so.

And how to prove it?

Before she could gather her wits about her, figure out what to do, Yale Gordon stormed into the studio, his gray suit impeccable, his silver hair practically bristling with his heightened mood. "Slaughter, Jacobi, Magill," the network executive said curtly. "In my office. Now."

A command rather than a request. Numb, Rae started forward, then practically tripped over her own feet from nerves. A strong hand steadied her.

"Thanks."

She met the vivid blue gaze of Teague Slaughter and her halfhearted smile faded. As did the open expression in his eyes. He let go of her, but she felt the lingering imprint of each finger in her flesh. Shivering, she rubbed her arm. Then she made for the elevator with the executive producer on her heels, the other two men behind him.

Rae didn't feel comfortable in the network representative's office, a sterile white environment except for the occasional framed black and white advertisement for "Rivals." Gordon led them to an alcove that made her momentarily claustrophobic. She, Teague and Jacobi sat at the small conference table, while Gordon stood at its head.

"Let's lay our cards on the table here," he began, leaning over and pressing his palms to the white laminate. "We all realize we have a major problem. Our star is dead and now we have to figure out where to go from here."

"And how to handle the media coverage," Teague said, leaning back in his white leather high-backed chair. "No doubt reporters will be pounding down our doors by morning."

"If they don't wake us in the middle of the night," Jacobi added grimly. "Think I'll take my phone off the hook."

"Don't you dare," Gordon ordered. "We can use every bit of publicity we can get."

Rae merely stared at the executive. A woman was dead and he was willing to take advantage of the tragedy—a crime—for the sake of publicity?

"If we don't get some sleep, we won't be worth a damn tomorrow," Jacobi grumbled.

Yale Gordon paced. "Then we'll use the weekend to play catch-up."

"The question is how to edit the story line," Teague said.

Rae added, "We can start by eliminating Faline from the dinner-party scene—"

"We're too far behind schedule as it is," Jacobi interrupted. He shook his dark head. "We don't have time for rewrites. We can't retape in time for tomorrow's airdate."

"Who said anything about retaping?" Gordon asked.

"Wait a minute," Rae objected. "The network can play some comedy reruns or game shows tomorrow in place of 'Rivals' while we regroup. Then we can spend the entire day figuring out how we can best write Marguerite's character out of the show."

"She *is* out," Gordon stated, his unwavering steely gaze meeting hers.

"But we can't use what we've got."

"We can, and we will."

Rae blinked and stared at the man, feeling incredibly naive as the truth hit her. "You can't mean to run what we just taped." Though she knew his answer before he gave it.

"Of course I do. I'm no fool. I can't afford to pass up a once-in-a-lifetime opportunity like this. Marguerite's death will hit the morning papers and be on every early newscast. 'Rivals' will have a bigger audience share tomorrow afternoon than ever before in the history of the show," the network executive said, sounding like the cat who'd swallowed the canary. "In the history of any daytime drama," he amended. "I guarantee it."

"But she was dying while we were taping!"

"Exactly."

Appalled, Rae looked to the other two men who sat opposite her. Jacobi seemed wired as if he agreed with her but was reluctant to voice his objections, while Teague calmly stared at Gordon, his face expressionless.

Gordon himself appeared to be on a high. And no wonder, Rae thought. He would use this tragedy to his own advantage. "Rivals" had been near cancellation when Gordon had hired her to inject new life into the show. He needed to save his butt with the network and he recognized Marguerite's death as his opportunity. He gave the word cutthroat new meaning.

Another thought made her uneasy: just what exactly was Yale Gordon capable of doing to boost the ratings?

RAE WAS STILL caught up over the network executive's ethics—or lack thereof—as she prepared to leave her office for the night a while later. Her head was spinning with all that had happened in a few short hours, including the fact that *she* might be considered a suspect.

No wonder she didn't realize she wasn't alone until a deep male voice interrupted her musings. "You don't by any chance have a car in a nearby lot?"

Teague Slaughter was slouched against the doorjamb. He was out of costume, wearing the sweater with the southwestern design that accentuated the breadth of his shoulders. She flicked her gaze back to the briefcase she was just closing so she wouldn't have to admire his potent masculinity, which had stirred her more than once that day.

"I don't own a car."

"Then I'll drive you home."

A pulse beat in her throat as she calmly said, "That won't be necessary."

"It's late. The streets aren't safe for an attractive woman this time of night."

Registering the compliment without recognizing it aloud, Rae said, "I'll take a taxi." She didn't want to have anything to do with the man if she could help it.

She hadn't the faintest idea of why he even wanted to bother with her...unless he was set on rehashing the evening's events. And she'd had more than enough of "Rivals" for one day. The morning with all its problems would come soon enough. She grabbed her taupe spring raincoat and fine leather briefcase and headed for the door, her determined pace making Teague back off into the hall. He seemed startled when she shouldered by him without stopping. The door clicked behind her and automatically locked.

Feeling oddly self-conscious, Rae headed for the reception area and the main elevators, separate from the one she'd used earlier when leaving the studio. Teague fell into step with her, and they both entered a waiting car. He pressed the button that would take them straight down to the lobby. The doors closed with a woosh, trapping her in a small space with the man she least wanted to be alone with in the entire world.

Against her better judgment, she asked, "So do you agree with Gordon?"

"That depends on which part of the discussion you mean. I'm not certain how I would have handled the story-line situation if it were solely up to me. Gordon was getting off on the publicity angle, but going with what we shot or killing the footage really was a difficult call at best. One way or another, people are going to know Marguerite's dead by tomorrow night," he said reasonably. "At any rate, my vote would merely count as a suggestion on this one, considering the network owns 'Rivals.'"

Teague stayed on Rae's heels as she left the elevator and signed out, said good-night to the guard and headed for the door the uniformed man would buzz open for them. Because she could see it was pouring outside, she stopped long enough to put on her raincoat—which gave Teague enough time to sign out and catch up to her.

"Gordon did have a point about the ratings," he continued as they stepped out into the wet night. "Our audience share certainly won't suffer. We're bound to be the most watched daytime drama until Marguerite's murderer is caught...or until the public gets tired of following the case."

Rae didn't like that answer. Too cut and dried. Cold. Something she would expect from a man with Teague's reputation as a hard nose.

Pausing below the underhang that was pounded by the rain, she thought of what might happen before the real murderer was caught. *If* the real murderer was caught. What if *she* were falsely accused merely because her reading glasses were found in the wrong place? A place she hadn't visited that day.

The very idea made her shiver.

"You're chilled," Teague said, grabbing her arm in a firm grip. "Come on. I'm not going to have my head writer get sick waiting for a taxi in the rain."

Rae didn't bother arguing; she was too tired to put up a fight.

Teague's gold Mercedes was parked at the curb mere yards away. Even so, water invaded the neck of her raincoat by the time he opened the door and urged her inside. She settled in, the delicious scent of leather assaulting her nose, reminding Rae of the differences between them. She was a working woman while he was a man of means—the reason, no doubt, for his callous attitude toward the little people who worked for him. Like her friend Carol.

A moment later, Teague slid behind the wheel and turned the key in the ignition. Water darkened his gold-shot brown hair and dripped from his face. His sweater sagged with the weight of the water it held. Rae figured he must be soaked to the skin but didn't say a word.

As they pulled away from the curb, the wheels of her mind were set in motion. She gave Teague her Chelsea-area address before asking, "Why are you going out of your way to take me home?"

"I told you—"

"The real reason."

"I didn't think you should be alone this late at night with a murderer on the loose."

Rae was startled into temporary silence by the unexpected answer. She didn't want to like Teague Slaughter, but she had to admit his being so protective of her was pretty nice of him, especially considering she'd been giving him the cold shoulder.

Then, again, maybe he'd never noticed.

Teague drove south for a few minutes before saying, "We're in the same boat, you know."

"What boat?"

"The one with the other suspects. I figure you and I are right out front at the helm. The cops know I had both motive and opportunity... and then they found your glasses where the tea was prepared."

Rae realized she'd only been thinking of herself when Teague was undoubtedly the prime suspect. "They don't even know for certain if Marguerite was poisoned," she said in attempt to soothe them both.

"Don't bury your head in the sand, Rae. Someone wanted Marguerite Lemond dead."

That *he* could be the murderer didn't escape Rae. He was known as The Kiss of Death, after all. But he could have made certain Marguerite's contract wasn't renewed if he really wanted to be rid of her. Common sense and instinct made Rae believe she had no reason to be scared of Teague...at least not afraid for her life.

That she was softening toward him in addition to finding him attractive unsettled her.

As if Teague could guess her tumultuous thoughts, he asked, "So what do you have against me?"

That pulse in her throat started acting up at his accusatory tone. "Whoever said I did?"

"Your actions speak for themselves."

Unwilling to address another unpleasant subject that night, she tried to make light of his observation. "Paranoia is symptomatic of a disturbed mind."

"Paranoia, huh?" Teague obviously didn't find that funny, because he sounded perfectly serious when he asked, "Then why do you get this prune-faced expression every time you're around me?"

Prune-faced? And he'd called her attractive only a short while ago! Rae stiffened in her seat and stared out at the hazy lights through the early May rain.

"You forced this ride on me," she said tersely. "Why? So you could insult me?"

"I just thought we had a few things to hash out to ease our working relationship for the future. Can't we be friends?"

Rae wasn't buying. "Look, Slaughter, just because I work for you doesn't mean I have to like you."

"Then you admit it."

"I'm not admitting anything. I'm tired." And cranky, she thought. "I just want to be left alone."

"Your request is my command."

With that, Teague whipped the car over to the curb. About to chastize him for leaving her off to slosh home in the pouring rain when she could have taken a taxi in the first place, Rae almost bit her tongue when she realized where they were—sitting in front of the four-story brownstone that housed her apartment.

"Thanks for the ride."

Pushing open the door against the wind and rain, Rae made good her escape. She sloshed through puddles and ran up the outside steps of the brownstone.

She was safely inside before the Mercedes pulled away from the curb. She stared out through the glass door until the taillights disappeared.

And for the first time since she'd moved to New York, Rae felt truly alone . . . and afraid.

Chapter Three

The next day was even more unsettling for Rae. That afternoon's episode of "Rivals" was hardly over before calls began pouring into the network offices. Viewers either praised or damned the show for airing Marguerite Lemond's death, with no one remaining neutral on the subject.

"I just listened to one of our more fanatical fans raving on and on," June Chin told Rae when she delivered a copy of scene changes to Teague's secretary. The Eurasian woman's exotic features pulled into a frown. "She threatened to blow up CBC if we didn't bring Faline Devereux back from the grave. As if we could."

"Great," Rae said. "Something more to worry about. Will any of us be safe leaving the building?"

"Teague wrote a memo to Yale Gordon about getting extra security, but you know how Gordon is."

June didn't have to add *cheap.*

As Rae started back for her own office, she muttered, "Who has time to worry about the crazies?"

Though ratings were up, a pall hung over the cast and crew—at least the members who had been present during taping the day before.

Even though Rae was somber, she had already managed to get through the rewrites for that day's taping. The altered scenes had been approved by Teague and Gordon without the usual back and forth interplay during which further changes were made. She'd even managed to go over the following week's scripts and mark each and every scene that would need revisions because of Marguerite's death. The three of them would have to come up with a new game plan, one they could all live with.

Thinking about the overwhelming amount of routine work still waiting for her, Rae headed for her office.

"Whoa, Rae, wait a minute."

Bo Hathaway determinedly cornered her. He seemed out of sorts. Tense. Expecting him to be the herald of more bad news, Rae asked, "What now?"

"Have you seen Wilona around here today?" When she stared at him without comprehension—she'd been certain he was going to tell her Lieutenant Franklin was looking for her—he clarified, "Wilona Irwin, president of the show's fan club. Oddly dressed woman with thick glasses—"

"Yes, I know who you mean, but no I haven't seen her. Is it something important?"

Taking a step back, Bo shoved his hands into his pants pockets. "Nah, not really. She's been after me to autograph some publicity photos, that's all."

"Right," Rae said, though she didn't believe him. He hadn't seemed thrilled about doing so at all the day before, and now she sensed the lie behind his too casual facade. "I heard Wilona ask you about it. Didn't you tell her you'd be available Monday?"

Bo's shrug seemed studied. "I have time now, but no big deal. Monday will be soon enough. You know how it is—I just wanted to get her off my back."

As Bo turned on his heel and headed for the elevator, his shoulders seemed weighted with worry. What in the world was wrong with him? Why was he so anxious to find Wilona? Not willing to waste her time speculating, Rae shook off the odd feeling and entered her office.

Finally she got to her regular duties, starting with going over the new batch of scripts that had arrived from her associate writers, these to be shot the week after next. She couldn't complete her rewrites or editing until after the special meeting with Teague and Gordon scheduled for the following day. No doubt they would spend the better part of Saturday morning hashing out the changes. Next, she went as far as she could breaking down the story lines that her writers would develop into scripts to be shot three weeks from now.

And beneath her professional exterior, which kept her working at a frenetic pace, Rae was frightened.

LATE THAT AFTERNOON, halfway through dress rehearsal, which was behind schedule because of the script changes, Lieutenant Charlie Franklin put in a solo appearance. Rae was called down to the studio where executives, cast and crew alike gathered to hear what the homicide detective had to say about the autopsy report. He was wearing the same brown suit, looking even more rumpled than he had the day before, but a glint in his pale brown eyes belied the sense of ineptitude presented by his unkempt appearance.

Though Rae would have liked to hide in the crowd, she stood in the front line, a reluctant couple of feet away from Teague Slaughter whose eyes slid over her with too much interest as people continued to gather around them. She refused to give him the satisfaction of returning his gaze, or worse, appearing embarrassed, but she was definitely relieved when Teague turned his attention toward Franklin as the lieutenant began.

"Marguerite Lemond *was* poisoned."

"So it was the tea?" Saul Jacobi asked.

"Right on the money."

"Then why didn't she die during rehearsal?"

"The amount ingested makes a difference as to the potency and reaction time," Franklin explained. "A smaller quantity might not have done the trick. A larger amount could have killed her sooner. Miss Lemond probably felt the effects during dress rehearsal, but didn't get enough of the poison in her system until after taking the second drink."

Rae's stomach turned and she flashed a look around the room for a potential murderer. These were people she knew, for heaven's sake. People she worked with.

"What exactly killed Marguerite?" Teague asked. "Cyanide?"

"Cyanide would have worked faster. The coroner identified the poison as a glycoside called convallatoxin, which is similar to digitalis."

"That's from a plant, isn't it?" a young actress asked. "Like foxglove?"

"Digitalis is from foxglove, but we're dealing with something even more common. This poison came from lily of the valley."

"Lily of the..." Quenie Tovar's voice trailed off and she grabbed onto Addison Kilroe. She seemed about to swoon. "Ooh!"

Franklin's gaze lit on the Grande Dame of "Rivals" instantly. "Do you know something about this, Miss Tovar?"

Quenie's eyes went round. "*Me?* You think *I* did it? That *I'm* the murderer?"

She appeared to be halfway between fainting and breaking Addison's arm, Rae thought.

"Now calm down, my dear," Her costar said with a grimace. "No one is accusing you of foul play."

"Well, they'd best not, because I'm not guilty!" Quenie was working herself up into hysteria. "I didn't do it, I tell you! I didn't poison Marguerite!"

"Someone care to tell me what's going on?" Franklin asked as Addison helped Quenie into a chair on the nearest set.

The older actor patted his costar's hand and said, "Yesterday morning, Quenie received a bouquet of lily of the valley."

Voices erupted from the crowd, over which Franklin demanded, "From who?"

Quenie's voice shook as she stated, "Teague Slaughter."

Everyone including Rae turned suspicious looks on the man they called The Kiss of Death.

"I didn't send anyone flowers, not yesterday, not since I've been here," Teague stated, his expression hard as granite.

"Yes, you did." Quenie lifted her quivering chin. "The flowers came with that card you signed."

Franklin approached the actress and helped her up from the chair. "Let's head for your dressing room so I can get a look at those flowers. And that card."

"I'm coming along," Teague growled, following directly on the lieutenant's heels.

Though she hadn't been invited, Rae traipsed after them, wondering if she might have been wrong about Teague Slaughter. *Was* he the murderer?

Surprisingly, as much as she wanted to think badly of him, the idea didn't sit well with her.

Rae was ambitious and a hard worker, a woman with midwestern values who hated the cutthroat part of the business she had chosen as her life's work. Ever since he'd fired her friend Carol, Rae had seen Teague as personifying that negative aspect. But now she was confused.

Her prejudice was neither stopping her from being attracted to the soap villain, nor making her believe Teague Slaughter could have plotted so foul a deed as murder.

TEAGUE TRAILED Franklin and Quenie inside the pink and mauve dressing room that was sparsely furnished with gilded antiques, its walls covered with framed photos of the soap queen at a younger age when she was a Hollywood glamour queen. He glanced over his shoulder to see Rae at the door, arms crossed over her chest. She was wearing her prune-faced expression, aiming it directly at him.

She wasn't alone.

The rest of the cast and crew had followed. Surrounding her, they formed a semicircle, their lowered voices humming with speculation, their eyes—all except Rae's—refusing to meet his.

Undoubtedly, they assumed he was guilty.

Teague turned away from the accusing expressions while Quenie went straight for a vase on a spindly-legged table next to a velvet-upholstered chaise. The container held a full spray of lily of the valley. Before reaching the bouquet, the actress stopped dead in her tracks, appearing reluctant to touch the white bell-shaped flowers as if they might poison her. Carefully, from beneath a gold ribbon wound around the vase itself, she slipped out the card and held it between the tips of her forefinger and thumb.

"Here it is."

Avoiding looking at Teague, she handed a cream-colored square to Franklin.

The lieutenant flipped the note open and read: "'Break a leg. Dante Craven.'" His brows shot up as he looked from Teague to Quenie.

"I thought you said the flowers were from Mr. Slaughter."

"Dante Craven is the villainous character I'm playing." Teague tried to keep the apprehension from his voice. He wanted to sound innocent rather than defensive, a major dramatic accomplishment as far as he was concerned. "Can I check that out for myself?"

Franklin shrugged and held out the card. Taking it from him, Teague noticed the embossed flowers entwined around the letters B-C. The logo was familiar, though he couldn't quite place it.

He quickly scanned the note inside. "I don't recognize the handwriting." And gave the card back to Franklin. "It certainly isn't mine."

"Well, who else would use the name 'Dante Craven'?" Quenie demanded. She was staring at him accusingly.

"Maybe someone who wants me to look guilty. Anyone could have signed that card."

Franklin's passive expression didn't change, so Teague couldn't tell what the cop was thinking.

"I'll need a professional opinion on that one." Franklin pulled the French-style telephone perched on the makeup table toward him. "I'm going to make a call, get one of my men over here to pick up the flowers and track down the shop that delivered these." He lifted the receiver. "Meanwhile, we'll go to your offices where we can find a memo or some other document with your handwriting. Something you wrote before you came under suspicion."

"And while we're at it," Teague added, "we can gather samples of handwriting belonging to everyone connected with the show."

A murmur swept through the small crowd outside the door. Protests? Teague realized cast and crew were avidly watching the drama being played out in the dressing room as if it were a scene from "Rivals." Even Rae was caught up, her expression more interested and less antagonistic than it usually was when he was around.

Franklin picked up the receiver and dialed as he addressed Teague. "On your toes, aren't you, Mr. Slaughter. You don't miss any little details."

"That's how I got to be an executive producer."

"I don't miss details, either," the detective said. "For example, even I know it isn't unusual for a florist to sign a card for a customer, especially if the order was phoned in." Obviously getting an answer on the line, he held up his hand to delay further argument. "Yeah, Franklin here. Send an evidence tech over to CBC to pick up a bunch of flowers." He listened for a second, then said, "No, I'm not pulling your leg. These blooms are deadly. And I want the shop that delivered them tracked down ASAP."

When the detective dropped the receiver in the cradle, Teague picked up the conversation. "And maybe the florist will be able to tell you who really bought that bouquet."

"Anything is possible."

"Lieutenant Franklin, surely you don't think I might have sent these to myself?" Quenie asked, sinking onto her chaise and clutching her heart.

"I don't know what to believe just yet, Miss Tovar."

"Oh, the room is whirling!" she wailed.

"Don't faint until we identify the shop." Shaking his head at the actress's histrionics, Franklin addressed Teague. "But first we're going to make a trip to the station."

"We?"

"Yeah, like you and me. Any objections?" When Teague gave him none, Franklin turned his gaze to Rae who still stood in the doorway. "And you, too, Miss Magill."

Starting out of her complacency, Rae said, "Me? Why?"

"Traces of the poison were found on your glasses." Franklin tucked the card into his breast pocket. "And only one set of prints, which I would bet will prove to be yours. As of this moment, you and Mr. Slaughter here are my prime suspects."

Rae paled visibly. "But the show—"

"Will just have to limp along on its own."

"Then we're under arrest?" she asked.

Teague recognized Rae's anxiety but nothing more incriminating in her manner. Not that he thought she was guilty. She hadn't been around long enough to get that fed up with Marguerite. Besides which, he didn't want her to be guilty, he realized with a start. Usually wary of women in the industry—he'd been used by several ambitious women during his early years in daytime drama—Teague was flabbergasted to find himself drawn to Rae Magill.

"I merely want to question you two in more detail," Franklin was saying. "At least for the moment."

The last sounded ominous, Teague thought, almost a threat. He didn't have to wonder if an innocent man could be railroaded into a jail cell. He knew for a fact that it could happen. Imagination was nothing compared to the reality of such a situation.

He'd promised himself never again....

TEAGUE PACED Lieutenant Charlie Franklin's dingy office, which smelled of old socks and leftover food, while Rae sat in an ancient pea-green vinyl-covered chair. Though a cop had just taken her fingerprints—the authorities wanted to check them against those on the glasses—she appeared composed, prim and proper, her camel-colored pencil-thin dress drawn down over her knees in a ladylike fashion. She hid behind the outfit and her calm expression as though they were a disguise.

Teague wasn't easily fooled. He suspected there was a lot more to Rae Magill than met the eye.

Thus far, she'd let him provide Franklin with all the answers that seemed innocuous enough. The cop had asked for general information about the workings of the show, professional relationships, lengths of time various people had worked for "Rivals." He'd made note of every answer in the small spiral notebook he carried.

But Franklin hadn't brought his number one suspects to the station to find out about other employees of CBC. Having been grilled by the authorities before, Teague was braced for the coming assault.

"So the two of you never met until you came to work for 'Rivals,' Mr. Slaughter." Franklin stopped jotting notes long enough to wave his pen at them. "Is that your story?"

"Not a story," Teague said, wondering where the cop was leading them. "The truth."

"Then why did the two of you leave CBC together last night?"

Franklin sat behind his desk like a cobra getting ready to strike. Wanting in the worst way to wipe the smug smile off the wiry man's face, Teague curled his hands into fists.

"You had someone watching the building?" Teague's edginess doubled.

"Answer the question."

And multiplied as he leaned toward Franklin, his fists on the man's desk. "Don't you cops have anything better to do than harrass innocent citizens?"

Franklin didn't even blink. "Innocent people aren't usually so defensive."

"I have a mind—"

"Mr. Slaughter was kind enough to give me a ride home because of the rain, Lieutenant Franklin," Rae interrupted, "as well as the late hour and the threat of a murderer lurking nearby. I accepted because I was tired and didn't want to argue with the man."

"Do the two of you argue often?"

Teague moved away from the desk. "We don't know each other well enough to argue."

And yet Rae disliked him. He felt a subtle hostility ooze from her pores even now, even as Franklin was hinting at some ridiculous conspiracy between them. Could that be why he was attracted to her? Teague wondered. Because she made herself unavailable to him?

"What was it you said you did before landing the role of Dante Craven the first time?" the cop asked, knocking the speculation right out of him.

"I didn't." Teague kept calm this time. He wasn't about to put his neck in a noose because of his past. He'd paid in spades for the stupidity of youth. He tried to steer Franklin away from the dangerous subject by asking, "What does that have to do with Marguerite Lemond's death?"

"That's what I'm trying to find out."

"Franklin, this is preposterous."

"Maybe...maybe not. I have before me my two main suspects. A little teamwork would have made the crime a piece of cake to pull off."

"But *I* didn't have a motive," Rae protested.

Teague clenched his jaw at the uncertain look she gave him and stared over her shoulder, at a grease stain on the wall. Did she really dislike him enough to think him capable of murder?

"Not unless you and Mr. Slaughter are close..." Franklin didn't say *lovers,* though his tone implied as much. "And you were trying to protect him."

"I've had enough of this," Rae said, standing. She didn't shout, didn't demand. Rather, she calmly said, "Either arrest us or let us go."

Teague had to give her credit. Her spine had that ramrod-straight look like she got when she was around him. He imagined she could be hard as nails when the going got tough—his kind of woman. And her matter-of-fact attitude might prove to their advantage if only she would cooperate.

"All right." Franklin dropped the pen and leaned back in his seat. "You can go back to the studio. But don't either of you leave town."

"We wouldn't think of it," Teague said, holding his own as the cop tried to stare him down. "We have a show to get on the air."

And a murderer to find, he added silently, for he knew he'd better convince Rae that they had to help themselves before false accusations landed them in matching jail cells.

RAE FELT AS TENSE as Teague looked when they left the station house and joined New York's rush-hour throng. The sidewalks were bursting with people.

Teague stared out into the sea of vehicles jamming the street. "Not a taxi to be had in Manhattan when you need one."

"At least it's not raining. We can walk."

It would be good to walk off the stress that was giving her a migraine. Good to walk off the indignity of being fingerprinted like some common criminal when she'd been brought up to respect hard work and unshakable ethics. What would her parents say if they knew? Glancing down at the ink smudges still staining the pads of her fingers propelled Rae into action. She started off without Teague, but his long-legged stride caught him up to her easily.

"Now you believe me, right?"

He didn't have to reiterate his being "stuck in the same boat" comment. She didn't answer, merely plunged into the throng of people crossing the street.

"So what are we going to do about it?" Teague asked, sheltering her within the curve of his arm from being rammed by an aggressive blonde headed straight for her.

Aware of the warmth radiating from him, Rae goose-stepped away, knocked into the woman who gave her a dirty look, and told herself she wasn't sorry when Teague let his arm drop to his side. "What can we do?"

"Prove we're innocent."

She flashed him an incredulous expression. "How?"

"By finding the real murderer."

"The police will do that."

"And if they don't?"

Rae was chilled by the thought.

"We'll have to work out a game plan," he said. "Maybe we should stop someplace, get a quick bite to eat and discuss what we can do and how to begin."

Rae didn't even break her stride as she protested. "Wait a minute, I didn't agree to play investigator."

"Would you rather do nothing until you land in jail for something you didn't do?"

As much as she disliked the thought of spending more time than she had to with The Kiss of Death, she hated the thought of spending any time at all behind bars even more.

When she didn't answer, he said, "I didn't think so."

Rae gave in as gracefully as she could manage. "Where do you suggest we start?"

"With the florist. If only I could remember where I've seen that logo. I suppose we could go through the yellow pages."

"What logo?"

"It was embossed on the florist's card. The letters B and C intertwined with flowers."

"Blooming Creations!" When he gave her a surprised look, she explained, "I'm certain I know the place. It's about a half mile from the studio. I pass the shop every day on my way to and from work."

Her upper arm was suddenly swallowed by Teague's steely fingers as he brought her to an abrupt halt. Almost running into them, a man veered off to the side, muttering under his breath.

"Where?" Teague demanded.

She pointed. "About three blocks from here."

"What are we waiting for?" Arm around her shoulders once more, Teague steered her toward the street before she had time to think.

As she was swept along, Rae could only hope she hadn't made a pact with the devil.

Chapter Four

Blooming Creations was everything its name implied
and more. Refrigeration units were filled not only with
simple bouquets from gladiolus to roses, but with
flowers already made up into spectacular baskets and
vases complete with ribbons. Trim materials and con-
tainers from the simple to the ornate filled a set of
shelves in the corner near the entrance to the back
room. Color photography beautifully framed and
hung on the wall opposite the counter showed off even
more elaborate concoctions for every conceivable occasion.

The tanned blond middle-aged man behind the sales
counter was something of an eye-catcher himself.
Wearing deep green trousers, pale pink shirt and rose-
colored jacket with a matching flower in his lapel, he
looked like one of the confections on display, Teague
thought wryly. The identification tag on his jacket
pocket identified him as Ernesto.

Rae wandered around the shop nervously, but
Teague stood fast opposite the counter while the other
man finished with a customer. He wondered what was
bugging Rae. The information they were about to get?
Or him? She didn't like having to work so closely with

him. He didn't have to be a genius to know that. He was more than a little annoyed by her attitude and was determined to get to the heart of the matter.

Then the customer left and the florist asked, "Can I help you?" He was looking from Teague to Rae as if trying to determine whether they were together.

Rae stopped at Teague's side as he said, "We'd like to speak to the owner."

"No *problemo*." The flamboyantly dressed man threw out his hands. "In person." His brow puckered and he flashed a neatly manicured finger at Teague. "Say, I know you. Aren't you The Kiss of Death, Dante Craven, himself?"

"Try Teague Slaughter."

"Yes, yes, of course. I never miss 'Rivals.'"

"I'm glad you enjoy our show," Rae said.

Teague noted she was hard-pressed to keep a grin in check. She seemed to want to smile at everyone but him.

"Our?" Ernesto focused on Rae. "I don't recognize you."

"Head writer Rae Magill."

The florist sighed. "Ah, the mind behind the drama. To be in the presence of such brilliance! What can I do for the two of you today? Another bouquet for one of the stars . . . ?" His tan turned ashen. "Oh, dear me. How can I be so *stupido*. I heard about Marguerite Lemond on 'Get Up, New York' this morning. You're here to order a tribute for the poor dear."

"Yes, of course," Teague said, giving Rae a quelling look when she seemed about to clarify.

They spent the next few moments picking out something appropriate for the funeral. A sober Teague realized their problems were nothing compared to the threat of death. While they were trying to extricate themselves from a bad situation, Marguerite would never have to worry about doing that—or anything else—again. He hadn't liked the woman but he hadn't wished her dead.

And he felt guilty that he hadn't thought about ordering the flowers himself. Rae seemed even more uneasy than she had earlier. Maybe she was feeling guilty, as well.

After Ernesto finished filling out the order, Teague handed over his credit card. "I'll have my secretary phone in the name and address of the funeral home as soon as we get back to the studio."

He was trying to figure out how he could tactfully turn the conversation around to the real reason they were there when the florist said, "I'm surprised you didn't send her in to place this order, too, though I suppose you must have been closer to Miss Lemond than to Miss Tovar."

"My secretary placed the order for the lily of the valley bouquet in person?"

"Yes, of course." Returning the credit card, Ernesto stared at him as if he were mad.

"What did she look like?" Rae asked.

"Pardon me?"

"I've never ordered flowers from this shop before," Teague admitted. "We'd like to know who did."

"You mean someone was playing a little joke on the Grande Dame of 'Rivals'?"

"Something like that," Teague agreed. A grisly joke for them all.

"Was she a Eurasian woman?" Rae asked.

"I wouldn't know. I didn't wait on her myself. My assistant took care of the order and made a point of telling me only because he knows I'm such a fan."

Teague latched on to that information. "Your assistant—is he in back?"

"My, no. He's out of town on a long-weekend tryst and won't return until early Monday morning. Rinaldo is scheduled to come in at eleven."

"We'd like to talk to him personally, but in the meantime," Rae said, "Maybe *you* can help us."

"If you want me to look up the order—"

"No, that wouldn't tell us anything new. We'd like to know about the flowers themselves. Lily of the valley," she clarified. "Are they really that poisonous?"

Ernesto's good humor evaporated and his face pulled into a frown. "Poisonous? You don't mean what I think you do?"

"Can you just answer the question," Teague urged, not wanting to go into details if they could be avoided.

The florist hesitated only a moment. "Yes, Mr. Slaughter, Lily of the valley is extremely poisonous."

"Which parts?" Rae asked.

"Everything, especially the leaves. Even the water in which the cut flowers are kept is poisonous. Depending on how much *she* ingested, a person could die."

Teague didn't miss the emphasis on the word "she" and figured Ernesto had guessed exactly why they were there. But the man had the good grace not to make an issue of the matter, and Teague only hoped the florist wouldn't start spreading rumors. Rae obviously was thinking the same.

"Ernesto," she said as a light tinkle signaled the entrance of a new customer. "I hope we can count on your discretion."

"Oh, my dear, don't worry, I'm not *loco*. Florists are like hairdressers—we know keeping confidences is smart business." With a broad smile, he handed Teague his credit card receipt. "I hope we'll be doing business again soon... for a more positive occasion, of course."

Teague left Blooming Creations feeling a little bit uneasy. Once on the street, he muttered, "Why do I feel as if I've just been blackmailed?"

"Perhaps because you have," Rae said. "In the very nicest of ways, of course."

Thoughtfully, they headed back for the studio, pushing their way through the rush-hour throng. They arrived at the "Rivals" offices just in time. June Chin was setting her desk in order, obviously getting ready to leave.

"Oh, boss, there you are," she said as she pulled her purse from a desk drawer. "I have a message for you from Yale Gordon. He wanted you to know that airing Marguerite's death was a stroke of genius—his words not mine—and that today's ratings soared even beyond his expectations. He figures there'll be follow-up stories in all the media."

Aware of Rae's stiffening beside him, Teague didn't respond directly to the information, because he could tell she was still angry over the issue.

"Thanks, June. Listen, I'm glad we were able to catch you before you left for the night."

"You want me to work overtime?" Though she looked disappointed, the secretary didn't argue.

"I merely wanted to ask you about something."

Relief brought back her smile. "So ask."

"Did you place an order at Blooming Creations the other day?"

"Blooming Creations?" Her dark eyes narrowed to slits. "What's that? Some kind of garden shop?"

"A florist." Of which she obviously knew nothing. "Never mind. Do you have the name of the funeral parlor—"

"Right here."

She held out a slip of paper with the information already written out for him. About to ask her to call Blooming Creations, Teague realized she was anxiously awaiting his dismissal. He could call the florist himself.

"You can go now."

June didn't hesitate to pick up her purse and immediately head for the elevator where she made her escape in the same car they'd arrived in. "You two try to have a good weekend," she called just before the doors closed.

Good weekend? How? Teague wondered as he strode into his office, Rae reluctantly following. With both a funeral to attend and a story line to edit, they weren't going to have much time for anything...not even solving a murder.

RAE PACED Teague's office while he made the call to the florist. This was a far cry from Yale Gordon's sterile environment. The walls were covered with an innovative crushed-looking material of bronze and copper, the floor covering an exquisite Serapi Oriental with a graphic design of intensely saturated reds and browns. The room reached out to her, no matter that she didn't want to like his office, didn't want to like anything about him. Just being closed in the same room with Teague Slaughter made her feel claustrophobic.

She resented having to work with the man on a professional basis. Having to depend on him personally was too much! But what else was she supposed to do? Whether or not she liked the fact, they were in this together.

No sooner did Teague end the call and the receiver touch the phone base than she jumped on him.

"What now?"

He remained steadfast in the face of her negative energy. "You really dislike me, don't you?"

"Don't be ridiculous." Avoiding a direct answer would be a lot more prudent than the truth. "We're just both on edge because of the circumstances."

"*You're* always on edge around me—and don't tell me I'm being ridiculous again."

She didn't deny it, merely said, "Look, personalities don't matter here."

"The hell they don't. I'd say Marguerite Lemond's personality instigated her own murder."

"You know what I mean."

"No, I don't."

He loomed closer. Close enough so she could pick out the gold-shot strands of his hair. Rae wondered if this was part of his intimidation technique. Well, it was working, but certainly not in the way he'd figured. Her knees were puddling beneath her and she leaned back into the support of the desk. And her traitorous pulse was racing. She gripped the desk ledge with both hands and looked The Kiss of Death in the eyes.

"I want to know what you're thinking, Rae, especially where I'm concerned."

She certainly couldn't tell him the truth—that dislike was all mixed up with a sexual attraction she couldn't control. Instead, she gave him a flippant yet basically honest answer. "I'm thinking you're wasting time."

He cursed under his breath and Rae was afraid he wouldn't let it be. She was wrong.

"All right," he said, backing off. "Then let's discuss personalities that clashed with Marguerite's. Who disliked her enough to do her in?"

Rae took a deep breath and let go of the desk. She'd been squeezing the wood so hard her fingers had almost gone numb. "Maybe you should rephrase that." At his querying look, she asked, "Who didn't want to see Marguerite get some just deserts?"

"I didn't want to see her dead."

She couldn't help being on the defensive. "I wasn't implying you did."

"But the thought occurred to you."

"No, actually, it hadn't."

That was the truth, at least. No matter her low opinion of the man, she really hadn't thought him capable of murder.

"Then why—never mind." He sounded exasperated, the same way she was feeling. "I'll start," he went on. "Quenie Tovar and Marguerite were at loggerheads forever. They've disliked and competed with each other from the beginning. At least since I came on to the show as a green actor."

"And not only has Quenie been losing ground to Marguerite," Rae said, thinking about the way the older actress's part had diminished as the younger's had expanded, "she had possession of the murder weapon."

"A bouquet of flowers supposedly ordered by my secretary. What if the woman was Quenie herself?"

"Not a chance," Rae stated emphatically. "Ernesto would have recognized her."

"Even if she disguised herself? She is an actress and has access to a large wardrobe and wig collection. Besides, he said he never saw the woman himself."

"Hmm. You've got a point there."

"You mean we're finally agreeing on something?"

His distrustful expression was so comical that she almost laughed. Not wanting to humanize him, she held herself in check. "We agree that Quenie is a ripe suspect. What about Addison Kilroe?"

"He never clashed directly with Marguerite to my memory."

"But whatever happens to Quenie directly affects him since they're a 'couple,'" Rae mused. "When Quenie's part diminished, so did his."

"And he might have been afraid of Marguerite succeeding in cutting Quenie out of the show altogether."

"Something else we agree on. I wonder if Christine had a similar fear."

"Not likely," Teague said. "She didn't care for Marguerite and made no bones about it, but she knows she's central to 'Rivals.' She doesn't have anything to worry about on that score."

Rae agreed with that fact. "Marguerite was pretty crummy to her in lots of little ways. I think we should check Christine out anyway."

Teague shrugged his agreement. "Bo Hathaway, too. Poor sucker might have realized Marguerite was just using him as she did every man she seduced."

Rae started at that. The rumor mill was still chewing on the fact that Teague had once had an affair with Marguerite and that he'd been fired from the show when she tired of him. Then she thought back to the last time she'd seen Bo and Marguerite together other than during the actual rehearsal and taping.

"She threatened Bo just before she died."

"What?"

"Something about telling the press everything about him."

"I don't remember your sharing this with Franklin."

Rae felt oddly guilty as she met Teague's accusing glare. "I forgot about the conversation until now."

"What else did they say?"

"It wasn't exactly a conversation. Bo turned the threat back on Marguerite, who said she wasn't the one who had anything to hide . . . but then she stalked off the set like maybe she did."

"Good God, is there anyone who isn't suspect?" Teague muttered.

"We're never going to figure this out."

"Not standing here talking, we're not."

Rae threw up her hands. "Where do you suggest we start?"

Rather than answering directly, Teague checked his watch, then picked up the telephone and punched an inner-office line. "Yeah, Slaughter here. How's taping going?"

His gaze connected with Rae as he listened, and she grew immediately uncomfortable. He seemed to be trying to get inside her, to figure her out again. Turning her back on him, she paced the length of the office and thought how lucky it was that Teague wasn't in Monday's show and so didn't have to be on the set himself. Then she projected to the weekend and realized they would probably be spending all their time together playing amateur sleuth when they weren't revising the following week's scripts.

Dear Lord, how was she going to stand being with him her every waking moment?

She had no answer by the time Teague said, "Uh–huh. Thanks." He hung up and, his expression impersonal once more, said, "Certain members of the cast are going to be tied up taping for another half hour minimum."

"So?"

"So it gives us time to search some dressing rooms."

"You're kidding, right?"

"How else are we going to get any answers?"

She'd never done anything really illegal in her life. Rae squirmed inside. The thought of going through someone else's personal property put the fear of God—and of being caught—in her.

"I don't know..."

"I thought we were in this together."

Rae wavered. They were. And deep down she knew if they were to clear themselves they had to take some chances. "I guess it's not like we'd be harming anyone, right? At least not anyone who's innocent."

"Marguerite had a way of corrupting innocence," Teague said, his handsome face tightening. "I don't condone murder, but I feel sorry for the poor sucker who killed her. No doubt the person was driven to the deed and in the end, Marguerite's going to have the last laugh when the person is punished.''

If only Teague hadn't said that! Rae hated that he'd sounded so compassionate. So caring.

So... human.

In spite of her prejudice, it made her like him just a little bit.

She was dwelling on the fact and only half listening to Teague's instructions as he pushed her out the door toward the studio elevator. He'd go through Quenie's and Addison's dressing rooms while she searched Bo's and Christine's. Within seconds, it seemed, they were on the lower floor, and she was about to commit her first criminal act.

Teague led the way, checking to make sure that no one was around to catch them at their skullduggery. Even so, Rae found herself looking over her shoulder.

Then Teague pushed her into Bo's dressing room. ''Be quiet and quick,'' he whispered. ''And don't dismiss anything as being unimportant.''

Oh, sure, she was supposed to be quick while inspecting every corner of the room and contemplating every item. She didn't bother to point out the fault of that logic to Teague, because he was already silently pulling the door closed.

She swallowed her scruples and began.

Bo Hathaway's dressing room was simple and neat with only a chair at the dressing table, a loveseat and a small filing cabinet as furniture. Painted a pale gray, the walls were adorned by a half-dozen black and white photographs mounted in silver frames. Each was a professional studio shot of Bo with a leading lady, covering the time he was first hired to the present. He and Marguerite made a convincing beautiful couple, appealing especially to middle-aged viewers who didn't want to think their sex lives were limited to the dull and predictable at fortysomething.

Rae sighed. She was a half decade away from forty and her own sex life had been nil for far too long. Maybe that's why she was responding so out of character to a man who had no ethics. She thought again of Teague's pitying the killer who would be brought to justice, giving Marguerite the last laugh. That just didn't fit with her preconceived notion of him.

Telling herself she should be concentrating on her search, she started with the bathroom. But for a few toiletries and a set of fresh towels, the tiny room was barren. Certainly nothing there to make her suspicious.

Bo's dressing table and drawers revealed nothing, nor did the corner of the room where a rack held both street clothes and a few garments worn by his character, Leopold Roman. Rae quickly went over the day's script in her mind, but she had no idea of what act cast and crew might be taping, or whether or not Bo might return to his dressing room for a needed costume change.

She hurried through the two-drawer filing cabinet, which was filled with press releases, newspaper clippings and photos. Everything was neatly organized by date. Among the most recent batch of folders, she found a bunch of contact sheets—miniature photos printed by directly laying negatives on the paper— shots taken by one of the network photographers.

Most were publicity stills of Bo alone or with Marguerite. Rae found the one he'd had blown up to hang on the wall. Others combined various cast members in

group photos. A few were of Bo and Christine Dellamorte, not posed like the friends they were supposed
to be on the show, but as if they were lovers.

Rae's brow furrowed. They looked fabulous together and there was a chemistry she'd never before
noted. In a word, they were hot. But, even though
she'd worked for "Rivals" only a few months, she
knew the story lines going back for years. The two had
never been paired together.

How odd.

Reluctantly she set the contact sheets back, thinking she'd better mention this to Teague. Maybe he
would know what to make of it.

With an ear to the door, Rae listened for any noise
in the hall. All quiet. She carefully opened the door a
crack and when she still heard and saw no one, she left
Bo's dressing room and made for Christine's.

Just in case . . . she knocked.

No response.

Slipping inside, she wondered how Teague was doing, whether or not he'd finished going through
Quenie's things. She checked her watch and realized
she'd taken longer in Bo's dressing room than she'd
imagined. She couldn't spare Teague a thought, not
when taping could wind up any minute.

Christine's dressing room was more personalized,
starting with the wall covering that made the area look
like a tiny jungle. The few pieces of furniture were
rattan. Despite the fact that the room had no windows, the actress had brought in a couple of plants,
which she'd placed under a special grow light. And in
the corner, resting on a two-foot base was a four-foot-
high bird cage. Bonnie Blue pecked at the bars and
squawked at her.

"Pretty bird, pretty bird."

"Who, you or me?" Rae whispered.

"Squ-u-a-a-wk!" Bonnie Blue indignantly replied.

Rae chuckled, but soon forgot about the bird in her frustrating search.

Nothing!

The only personal item of possible interest was a well-worn brown leather scrapbook bursting with mementos of Christine's career. Quite a contrast to Bo's careful organization.

Rae sat in one of the cushioned rattan chairs, slipped on her reading glasses, then opened to the beginning of Christine's love affair with acting. High school productions. College plays. Community theater. Some ads. An off-off Broadway production. She noted the eight-year-old clipping from the *Village Voice*, which included a photo of Christine and her co-star Hunt Harris. Though his name was familiar, she didn't recognize him. But the look he and Christine were giving each other was smoldering, hot enough to set the paper on fire.

First the shots of Christine with Bo, now this. Rae recognized Christine was wasted on the good-girl role in which she'd been cast. The realization gave her some interesting possibilities for future story lines, but further speculation ended when she heard footsteps outside the door.

Ditching the scrapbook, she popped out of the chair and panicked! Where to hide? The only conceivable place was behind the clothes rack, which was wedged next to the bird cage. Thank God Christine seemed to keep half her wardrobe at the studio—the rack was bulging with garments. Rae only prayed that Christine wouldn't pull one of the outfits from the rack and discover her!

She'd barely sheltered herself when the door opened.

Rae's heartbeat accelerated double-time as Christine entered. She was going to be caught! She knew it! She never should have let Teague talk her into doing this. Not alone. What excuse could she use for being in the actress's dressing room?

With bated breath, Rae awaited discovery. She couldn't see a thing from where she hid. The light footsteps stopped nearby, making her grimace. But Christine continued moving around the room, hesitating, moving again. At least Rae assumed the footsteps belonged to Christine. Oddly enough, they sounded muffled, as if someone were walking on tiptoe. And then they faded altogether and the door clicked closed!

Rae was about to sink down the wall in relief when Bonnie Blue croaked, "Pretty lady, pretty lady!" and made her jump and hiccup simultaneously.

"Trying to give me a heart attack, are you?" she scolded the bird.

As she wrestled with the clothes to leave her hiding place, she took a closer look at the cage and realized Bonnie Blue was alone. No Ginny Green. Not that she could ask about the other bird without revealing her own duplicity!

Wanting nothing more than to be somewhere safe, somewhere she could breathe easily, Rae opened the door...and almost fainted when she came face-to-face with a person on the other side!

Chapter Five

"Missus, you scare me!" The moon-faced woman put a hand to her ample bosom spread beneath a T-shirt and drew in a loud gulp of air.

"Bernice, I'm sorry." Rae laughed with relief that she'd been intercepted by none other than the cleaning lady. She'd been hiding from Bernice, for heaven's sake! "I was looking for Miss Dellamorte," she fibbed, hoping the cleaning woman would think she'd been in Christine's bathroom rather than hiding. "I thought she might be in her dressing room. You haven't seen her, have you?"

Her hurried speech was wasted, for Bernice merely stared wide-eyed, then bobbed her babushka-covered head and indicated the dressing room. "I clean now?"

"Yes, clean."

So she hadn't understood, after all. No explanations necessary.

Rae sighed with relief and moved out of the woman's way and around her cleaning cart. For once she was glad Bernice knew so little English, even if, as usual, she wondered how the Polish woman had made it in New York City for the five years she'd lived here without learning the language.

Hurrying down the hall toward Quenie and Addison's dressing rooms to find Teague, Rae had the distinct sensation of being watched. Surely Bernice wasn't suspicious, after all. She forced a smile to her lips and turned to wave at the cleaning woman. But Bernice was nowhere in sight, obviously already hard at work in Christine's dressing room since her cart was wedged in the doorway.

Though Rae thought she saw movement from the shadowy far corner of the hallway, she couldn't be certain. The very idea of someone spying on her—of guessing what she was up to—was enough to give her the creeps. Even as she told herself she was imagining things, that her guilty conscience was prickling her, she quickly passed up the older couple's dressing rooms and sped on toward the elevator that would take her back up to the executive floor.

Teague could just catch up to her there!

But she'd no sooner hit the call button, than he appeared at her side. "Going my way?"

"Wasn't that a movie?"

He raised his brows at her attempted humor. "Next thing I know you'll be smiling at me."

"Maybe if there's ever something to smile about."

He gave her a questioning look but she refused to say another word until they were on the floor above and back in his office. She sank into one of the cushioned chairs away from his desk. Her bones felt like putty that had gone soft in the summer sun.

His expression concerned, Teague stood over her. "You're white as a ghost. What happened?"

Because she felt so foolish, Rae wasn't willing to tell him about hiding from the cleaning lady or about imagining someone watching her.

"I illicitly ransacked two dressing rooms and rummaged through peoples' personal things without permission!" she snapped. "Isn't that enough?"

She thought he was going to press the issue until a curious expression flicked over his features. He settled one hip against the chair opposite and asked, "So was the dreadful experience worthwhile?"

"You mean did I find anything? Not really." Then she remembered she meant to mention the contact sheets. "I don't know. Maybe."

"Tell me."

Rae sucked in a deep breath. She was feeling better now. Safer. "You've seen Bo's dressing room, right? The photos on his wall?"

Teague nodded. "Bo posed romantically with each of his leading ladies."

"Well, he keeps contact sheets of all his publicity photo sessions," Rae said. "I found several sheets of him with Christine."

"So?"

"So these weren't just shots of a man and a woman who are supposed to be friends like they are on the show. They were hot—you know, like the two of them made a couple. Only they never have been as far as I know." The way Teague was looking at her, Rae was beginning to feel foolish again. "I'm sure it doesn't mean anything."

"We won't know unless we ask."

"Ask who?"

"The source."

"Bo Hathaway?" Rae stared, her face pulling into a frown. "Are you crazy?"

"There you go again."

She frowned even harder. "Go where?"

"You look like you've just sucked on a lemon and don't like it one bit."

"I don't like anything about this stupid situation!" she stated, ignoring the sourpuss reference. "I don't like someone being murdered. I don't like being a suspect. I don't like sneaking around ransacking peoples' dressing rooms."

"And, most of all, you don't like me."

Rae shot up and drew herself to her full height. "Give it a rest, Slaughter, or—"

"Or what?"

His lips were twitching, as though he were amused. A responding flush quickly spread through her body, thoroughly aggrieving Rae. Teague's grin widened.

"I'm getting my things and going home," she said stiffly. "I have a lot of work to do this weekend."

"*We've* got a lot of work to do. Together." He scribbled a notation on a pad of paper, tore the sheet off and handed it to her. "Be at my place at nine."

She checked the Central Park West address. "Marguerite's funeral is tomorrow morning." There would be no wake.

"I meant nine tonight. I'm going to convince Bo Hathaway to drop by for a drink after work."

Rae's pulse thudded as she thought about getting so directly involved with one of the suspects. "So you can grill him about those stills?"

"So we can find out exactly what he knew about Marguerite's enemies. He was closer to her than anyone else around here."

"And what if Bo is the killer?"

"I doubt he'll admit it," Teague said.

His tone certainly was more casual than Rae was feeling. Her imagination was starting to chew on unpleasant possibilities again. Her mouth suddenly went dry and she licked her lips nervously.

"But if we get too close..."

He moved in on her. "Don't worry," he said, his expression now serious. "I'll protect you."

Teague was too close, making Rae squirm. And he seemed about to touch her....

She forgot any dangers but him for the moment and grew hot under his penetrating gaze. She backed off and circled the man, placing herself at the door for a quick getaway. Her hand was on the knob before she realized he hadn't shared his discoveries.

Reluctantly she turned back to him.

"You never did tell me if you found anything to implicate Quenie or Addison."

"Not exactly." He propped himself against the desk. "Though the dart board was rather unusual."

"What dart board?"

"The one hanging on the back of Addison's dressing-room door," Teague explained. "I guess that's how he wiles away the time between rehearsal and taping. Anyway, something made me take a good look at it."

"And?"

"And I found a *Soap Suds Magazine* cover tacked to the other side. Marguerite was featured. Lots of holes square between her eyes. Addison's pretty good with a dart as a weapon."

Rae ignored the heavy sarcasm in his tone. "Do you think it means anything?"

Teague shrugged. "Only that he didn't like the woman."

"Which we already knew."

Still, the idea of Addison's using the villainess for target practice gave Rae the creeps. There was more to the older actor than was readily apparent. She wondered exactly how much he had hated Marguerite.

"I'll be at your apartment at nine o'clock," she said, finally opening the door.

"And don't be late."

Rae hurried back to her own office where she gathered her work and shoved it into a briefcase. Somehow, between trying to pry information out of Bo tonight and attending Marguerite's funeral early in the morning, she would have to find time to look over the materials—in addition to sleeping.

Maybe Bo wouldn't accept the invitation.

Of course, his not showing would create a whole new set of problems for her. Teague was far too interested in her opinion of him for her comfort. And the closer he got, the more her confusion grew.

As far as Rae was concerned, the most dangerous possibility of all was being alone with The Kiss of Death in the lion's own den.

SHE SHOULDN'T have spent the hour she took getting ready worrying. By the time she entered the luxury apartment on time as Teague had demanded, Bo Hathaway was already ensconced in the living room and was two sheets to the wind.

Rae recognized the money that had gone into the eleventh-floor apartment with its view of Central Park. The living-room walls were painted a brilliant yellow glazed with a more subdued green. The Heriz carpet was larger than the Serapi in Teague's office and equally unusual—a stylized composition of muted yellow and orange on a mellow ivory background. A mahogany shelving unit held a collection of pottery and other earthy objects of art. And a seemingly disparate collection of furniture both modern and antique drew the large room together in curious harmony.

Judging from her surroundings, Rae guessed Teague Slaughter had come from a very privileged background.

"There you are," Bo said as she entered the room. His smile smooth, the actor raised his glass of Scotch. "Now we can talk business."

Business? Rae wondered exactly what Teague had told the man to lure him there. She gave him a questioning look but his expression didn't change.

"Would you like a drink?" Teague asked as he moved to the bar, a modern portable affair near the double doors leading to the terrace overlooking Central Park.

"Something non-alcoholic."

Rae wanted to keep a clear head here. Teague filled both their glasses from the same bottle while she sat in a chair. Bo had sprawled out on the couch. His jacket was thrown over the back, his tie was askew and his hair was rumpled, careless behavior for a man who always seemed so perfectly put together. Rae wondered just when he'd started drinking.

And why.

Teague handed Rae her glass. "Peach-flavored selzer."

Before she could thank him, Bo spoke up. "So, do you two have plans for Leopold Roman in mind, or is this strictly a brainstorming session?"

He was looking to her and she drew a blank. She wasn't prepared for this game.

"Brainstorming," Teague said smoothly, taking the other chair, mere feet from hers. "We're going to be doing some fast rewrites and we need to figure out which direction you'll be taking. After all, Leopold is the one most affected by Faline's demise," he said of the soap characters.

Bo took a long slug of Scotch, then gazed at them both somewhat suspiciously. "This is kind of unusual, isn't it? Normally executive producers and head writers don't give actors the time of day when it comes to new story lines."

"Normally we're not faced with such unusual circumstances," Rae improvised. "We're both relatively new to the show. And our star was murdered. That's a first, too."

Bo frowned and muttered darkly, "I always knew someone was going to get even with Marguerite for all the crummy stuff she pulled on people."

"Any idea of who?" Teague urged.

Bo stared down into his glass. "Could've been anyone. Even you, Slaughter." With a broad sweep of his hand, he included Rae. "Or you." Then his visage grew dark and he weaved forward in his seat. "Wait a minute here. You don't think *I* killed her?"

"Of course not," Teague assured him. "You and Marguerite were so close."

That seemed to settle him back. "As familiar as she let anyone get, that is."

Rae asked, "Even though you and Marguerite were an item, you weren't close?"

"Us an item? Not hardly."

"Then Marguerite was seeing someone else."

"Sure. Why not? I had no objections," Bo stated. "We weren't exclusive. More like convenient." He suddenly grew nervous, as if realizing the liquor was making him too expansive. "I thought we were supposed to be talking business here. Are we going to discuss Leopold's future or not?"

"That's why I called the meeting," Teague lied smoothly. "Leopold and Faline were a hot item. It's going to be difficult to duplicate that kind of chemistry. Maybe Leopold needs to be alone for a while."

"Alone?" Bo looked appalled. "The women who watch 'Rivals' won't stand for that."

Seeing where Teague was headed, Rae supplied, "But he'll be so noble in his mourning that the fans will fall in love with him all over again."

"While someone else gets the press coverage!" Bo added indignantly. "Viewers' loyalties have been known to be fickle—and I'm not going to let some hotshot green kid steal my show!"

Rae glanced at Teague and could tell he was pleased with the way things were going. She turned back to the actor.

"What do you suggest, then?" she asked. "Another woman for Leopold?"

"As soon as possible!"

"Let's see who's available?" Teague mused. "Janet is too young. Sondra isn't really Leopold's type. And Tempest . . ." he drew out the reference to Christine's character " . . . no, that would never work."

"Why not?"

"Chemistry. Christine is a great actress but she's best at being noble," Teague said. "Besides, you two make great friends. No one would believe your becoming lovers."

"The hell they wouldn't!"

"Then why didn't anyone ever think of pairing the two of you together before?" Rae asked.

"There were plans for Christine and me being paired a while back. We would have made one sexy team!"

As Rae well knew from the contact sheets. "So what happened?"

"Marguerite Lemond happened," Bo said, downing the last of his drink. "The Leopold-Faline romance story line was created at her insistence. Yale Gordon agreed and Gary had no choice but to go along with his decision."

Rae knew he was referring to Gary Noble, the ex-executive producer who had walked off the show because of artistic differences, a catchall phrase in the entertainment industry. Since she'd been working for "Rivals" for little more than a month when he'd left the show, Rae hadn't know Gary well—but even she had been aware that he and network executive Yale Gordon had been at odds.

"Was Gary the only one upset by the decision to cast you opposite Marguerite instead of Christine?" she asked.

"Nah, everybody was pretty ticked off for a while. But then everything turned out fine anyway, didn't it?"

Except for Marguerite's death.

The discussion went on for more than another hour. They tried their best, but Bo Hathaway revealed no new information that might be of help. They were lucky they'd gotten anything at all out of him. Rae figured the Scotch had been talking rather than the very smart actor who dealt with members of the press on a regular basis.

That was the problem with people who worked in her professional world—they lived and breathed lies of various sorts.

Finally Teague escorted Bo to the front door and Rae gratefully let her head sink against the chair. She was exhausted. By the time she got home and in bed it would be close to midnight. Even assuming she fell asleep easily tonight, there would be no sleeping late this Saturday morning, not with a funeral to attend. And when was she going to go over her notes for revisions?

"So what do you think?" Teague asked as he returned to the living room.

"Other than Christine having another reason to resent Marguerite? I think I'm glad this is over."

And she was eager to end the evening for reasons that went beyond her weariness. She was too attracted to Teague for her own peace of mind. There was something very appealing about the lion in his den, just as she had feared. Wearing a black sweater with gold metallic design, he looked like one of his own artworks, worthy of display.

"I mean about Hathaway himself," Teague was saying.

She snapped back to reality. "We hit a nerve questioning him about his personal relationship with Marguerite. He was covering something."

"And acting a little too casual about their relationship."

"So you think he was jealous of her seeing other men?"

"Could be. Something punched his buttons."

Rae remembered the threat she'd overheard in the studio. "I wonder what Marguerite had on him that she could have exposed to the press."

"Or he about her."

The questions loomed unanswerable in her fatigued mind. "Forget it. I'm too pooped to figure it out. Besides, I wasn't cut out to be a private eye."

"I don't know." Arms folded across his broad sweatered chest, Teague loomed closer. "You can be pretty hard-boiled when you see fit."

He was zinging her again! Rae rose with all the dignity her poor tired bones could muster.

"Talking about who dislikes who!" she muttered.

"There you go, getting all stiff on me again."

His saying it made her spine straighten even as her insides softened to jelly. He really was too close for comfort, but Rae wasn't about to give away the fact. He had enough of an advantage over her as it was.

"Truce," she begged. "Please. I can't stand any more bickering tonight. I've got too many things to worry about."

"Truce," he agreed. "And I hope you mean it since we'll be working so closely together."

Did he have to remind her?

"I mean it if you do."

"Good. We need to get going on some ideas for those changes in story line."

"Right. We can go back to the studio to work on them after the funeral tomorrow."

"What's wrong with kicking over some ideas now?" he asked.

"It's late. I'm exhausted. And I've got to find a taxi before they all disappear for the night."

"I'll drive you home."

"I wouldn't think of putting you out."

Or of being alone with him any longer than necessary. It was becoming more and more difficult to keep in mind why she disliked Teague so. Her loyalty to Carol was being sorely tested.

Concentrating on the way he'd fired her friend made Rae angry all over again. While Teague Slaughter was certainly not a murderer, he didn't have the ethics she admired in a man—no doubt due to his wealthy background as attested to by his apartment. No doubt everything in life had come easy to him and he couldn't understand how hard other people struggled for success.

No doubt he was in the same league as Yale Gordon, to whom politics was more important than fairness.

"Are you awake or sleeping with your eyes open?" Teague asked, his face practically in hers.

Startled, she snapped to. "What?"

"I was saying the only thing that'll put me out is your running away after we just declared a truce."

She glared at him. "Is this going to take long?" But giving in seemed so much easier than fighting him at the moment. "All right." She flopped back down in the chair.

"Good. Want a drink?"

"I want to get started."

He ignored her petulant tone. "A real drink might relax you."

She almost asked if that was meant to be a crack but held herself in check before starting another argument she was in no shape to win.

"A glass of wine would be great . . . if it doesn't put me to sleep."

"I'll take that chance."

He was grinning at her again. Then his back was to her as he headed for the drink cart.

And Rae wondered if he really wanted to talk shop. Or did he just want to aggravate her?

As if he could read her thoughts, he said, "I've got an idea that might do double duty," as he opened a bottle of wine.

"I'm a captive audience."

She swore she heard a laugh muffled under the sound of pouring liquid. But Teague's features were straight when he handed her a half-filled stemmed cut-crystal glass. Her imagination at work again. She took a sip of the blush wine and was surprised when Teague didn't settle back in his chair. He seemed wound tight as a spring.

"What if we tailor the story line to make the various characters suspect by revealing motivations as we discover them?" he suggested as he paced the length of the room.

"You mean point out real reasons that cast members might have had for wanting Marguerite dead?"

"Exactly. Maybe we can make the killer nervous, and scared people make mistakes. We might be able to get the guilty one to show his or her hand."

"Clever idea," Rae admitted. "But... what if the killer wasn't one of the actors? What if one of the crew members murdered Marguerite? Rufus Piggot, for example, made no bones about hating her. And I don't think Saul Jacobi was too fond of her, either."

"True. But a few revealed truths should shake up the murderer and give him or her reason to suspect someone is looking closely at everyone."

"Yeah, and everyone will know that someone is me."

Rae took a long swallow of her wine. Teague stopped pacing mere inches from where she sat.

"You don't make story-line decisions alone. The killer won't know who to blame—you, me or Yale Gordon. The network rep has the last word, after all." He was making a convincing argument. "And in the meantime, using some real motivations will make our immediate work on revising the scripts easier. That'll give us more time to track down the guilty person."

"I see one tiny hitch here," Rae said. "What if Gordon doesn't go for it?"

He looked at her as if she were dim-witted. "We're not going to tell him what we're up to. And what choice does he have if he suspects? The show's in a bind. He's going to approve any decent solution we come up with to get us out of this fix. And he might even raise some enthusiasm if he thinks the ratings will benefit."

Aghast, Rae nearly choked on her wine. "Is that why you want to do this? Ratings?"

The thought horrified her . . . yet shouldn't surprise her, she realized. She'd seen too much of the downside of the entertainment industry to be surprised by much anymore. Still, she was disappointed—she had had that moment of liking Teague just a bit.

"Is that what you think of me?" he asked, glowering down at her.

Setting aside her glass, Rae rose to leave for the second time that evening. "I don't know what to think."

"Then let me be very explicit. I want to clear my name. And yours."

He set his glass down next to hers without taking his eyes from her face. Rae flushed under his close scrutiny. She was tired of her uncalled-for reactions to him, perhaps the reason her response was so sharp.

"I never got the idea you were too concerned about anyone but yourself!"

Rae started to move away but Teague caught her upper arm in a no-nonsense grip. Her heart thundered through her chest and she wanted to take flight, but she sensed she was stuck until he chose to release her.

"You have the wrong idea about me," he said quietly.

"I don't think so."

"Then you don't know as much as you think. I'm concerned about you, more than I care to be."

Before she could question his statement, he was demonstrating the very personal nature of his concern.

Rae found herself wrapped in Teague's arms, which banded her back like forged steel. She had been correct thinking she was stuck. She was strong . . . but he was stronger. Her struggle was futile and short-lived. The silent contest came to an abrupt halt when he dipped his head and took her mouth as firmly as he held her body against his.

At first she was startled and angry. Then she was appalled because whatever her will, her body responded to his persuasive prompting. Shamelessly. And then the reasons for fighting the sensations he stirred in her became muddled.

Her objections defused, she responded like a woman who hadn't been made love to in far too long...which in reality described her situation perfectly.

Stockpiled passion blasted through her, scorched her, melted the last of her resistance as she opened her mouth under his. He was no longer keeping her trapped. She was clinging to him, arms twining around him, kissing him back for all she was worth. She was floating on a cloud of desire.

Until her feet thudded back to earth in a jolt of reality when he untangled her arms from his neck and put her from him.

"Now why do I get the feeling you don't dislike me nearly as much as you think you do?" he asked.

Rattled by her own actions—not to mention the truth of his statement—Rae struck out, her hand making sharp contact with his cheek. Then she spun on her heel and ran for her life. This time she knew she wasn't imagining his laughter as she charged out of the apartment, slamming the hand-carved, brass-trimmed door behind her.

The elevator couldn't get her down to the street fast enough. Her mind was spinning. How could she have let herself get so out of control? This had never happened to her before. Never!

She laid blame for her insanity on Teague's own theory: he made her nervous, nervous people made mistakes, and boy, had she made a doozer!

Well, it wasn't going to happen again.

She had almost convinced herself of that by the time she hit the street and spotted the doorman.

"Could you signal a taxi for me?" she asked.

"Of course, Miss." The uniformed man stepped to the curb and blew his little whistle.

Shivering against the cool spring night, Rae realized she'd left Teague's apartment without her jacket or her purse. Luckily she'd stuffed her keys into her trousers' pocket. The driver would just have to wait for her to go up to her apartment for his money. Her ride home would be more expensive that way, but infinitely safer than if she had to go back upstairs to face that man.

The hairs on the back of her neck stood up and she whirled around, expecting Teague to have come after her with said jacket and purse. But the sidewalk behind her was as empty as the lobby of his building seemed to be.

Then why did she have the distinct impression that someone was watching her? The breath stilled in her throat and she froze until a light touch on her arm made her jump.

"Ah!"

"Very sorry, Miss." The doorman was giving her a strange look. "Your taxi is here."

"Yes, thank you," she said. "I—I'm afraid I don't have any money, but I'm certain Mr. Slaughter will repay you for your trouble."

The doorman merely bobbed his head and helped her into the cab. She gave the driver her address while staring out into the night, expecting some movement to betray the silent watcher. But as he pulled away from Teague's fancy apartment house, no one stirred. Even so, Rae was on guard, constantly looking out the rear window of the taxi as it sped along the street.

If anyone followed, she couldn't tell.

She wouldn't feel safe until she was in her fourth-floor walk-up, metal antiburglar bar thrown into place against the phantom murderer.

Chapter Six

Marguerite's funeral was an odd affair, Teague thought, swinging his car into the cemetery. He glanced at the directions he'd scribbled on a scrap of paper and took the road branching off to the left. Rather than a noisy wake the night before and a large audience in St. Patrick's Cathedral as might befit a woman of her renown, a modest service in the chapel of the Long Island cemetery was all that would precede the actual burial.

Not much time to play detective.

Tension rode with him into the small parking area fronting the building where a man who vaguely looked like Marguerite guarded the chapel door. A minute later, Teague was shaking the hand of the dead woman's only living relative, her brother Buddy Simpson, who had driven in from Ohio.

"Glad you could make it, Mr. Slaughter. My sister would have wanted you here."

"Nothing would have kept me away."

Buddy smiled sadly and turned to greet Addison Kilroe who'd arrived directly behind him. Teague experienced a twinge of guilt. He'd said the right thing for the wrong reason. His motivation for being at the event wasn't caring or even respect for the deceased. He was trying to find a murderer to save his own hide.

And Rae's, he added, spotting the russet-haired writer standing alone to one side of the sparsely populated chapel. Her fingers were twisted together in front of her, her spine even straighter than usual, if that were possible. And her expression was introspective. He approached her immediately and watched her face carefully for a reaction. He got none.

"I called you this morning to offer you a ride," he told her.

Certain she'd been in her apartment, Teague figured she'd been monitoring her answering machine and had chosen not to speak to him.

"I rented a car."

"Too bad. An unnecessary expense."

"One I don't regret."

She said that as though trying to tell him she did regret other things—like losing herself in that kiss, for instance.

Annoyance strengthened Teague's resolve to cut through the invisible barrier the frustrating woman continued setting up between them. Not privy to her reasons for putting him off, he had perversely kept Rae close to him longer than she had seen fit the night before by talking shop.

The memory of exactly how close they'd gotten still bothered him on a very basic, very male level, despite the time his hormones had had to cool off.

"Not many people came to pay their last respects," Rae commented sadly.

Teague took in the people who gathered in small groups here and there. Most were talking animatedly, some even laughing in low tones. The chapel was a shell without seating, and its focal point was the closed coffin covered and surrounded by flowers, which everyone seemed to be ignoring. So had the others come hoping for publicity? If so, they'd be sadly disappointed, for reporters had been kept out. Perhaps sheer curiosity had brought them to bury a woman they had disliked so much.

"Hmm, no one other than the cast and crew of 'Rivals' showed," Teague noted.

"Buddy said he didn't know who else to invite. He and Marguerite weren't very close."

"That doesn't surprise me."

For when they'd been lovers all those years before, he and Marguerite had never been more than physically intimate. Bo Hathaway had admitted practically the same thing the night before. Teague was beginning to feel sorry for the dead woman as he'd never been able to while she was alive.

"Even the people here don't seem to mourn her," Rae said. "Do you think Quenie will even bother to show for appearances' sake?"

Teague quickly glanced back over the small crowd. Sure enough, the older actress was nowhere to be seen. Buddy was leaving his post at the front door where Yale Gordon and his wife, Diane, had just entered. Teague's brows shot up when he noted the network executive's wife had chosen to wear a festive yellow and orange silk dress and a matching hat with an oversized veil that camouflaged her face.

When he realized Rae was waiting for his response, Teague said, "I don't know what Quenie might do. Maybe the Grande Dame of 'Rivals' plans to make an entrance."

He noted Gordon and his wife hung back near the door, Diane's stiff stance making her look anything but happy about being there. Perhaps her form of protest was wearing a dress that most people would consider inappropriate for a funeral.

"I want to thank you all for coming," Buddy said, his voice raised to be heard above the continuing din. "I would like to share a few thoughts about my sister before Reverend Potter takes over."

A hush fell within the chapel as Marguerite's brother approached the coffin and touched the metal surface with a hand that shook. He seemed to be gathering his courage. People moved in closer to him. When he looked up at them, tears filled his eyes.

"Maggie wasn't the easiest person to like," he began, "but she wasn't a bad person, just too self-absorbed."

As if on cue, the door banged open and all heads whipped around in the direction of the loud noise. No doubt the others also expected to see Quenie Tovar, just as Teague did. But, rather than the Grande Dame herself, Wilona Irwin stood in the chapel doorway.

Dressed in a dumpy navy dress with giant white polka dots, her nose red and her eyes swollen from crying, the "Rivals" fan-club president appeared to be a tragic figure. Hesitantly she shuffled forward, even while seeming as if she were trying to disappear into the woodwork.

"Sorry I'm late." She waved a hand filled with crumpled tissues. "Please go on."

Buddy cleared his throat nervously and did. "Maybe Maggie changed because our mother died when we were kids and our father was so busy getting drunk he didn't notice that we still existed. I guess that's when Maggie became an actress. She pretended everything was okay. She made life seem like an adventure, and she took me along for the ride.''

Teague felt Rae shift next to him. He glanced at her and realized that she, too, was touched by the man's words. A lump had settled in his own throat. These were things he should have known about a woman he'd slept with, but he hadn't.

''I remember when we were in high school,'' Buddy went on, ''a bunch of kids were giving her a hard time as usual about living in poverty and having a drunk for a father. That's when Maggie vowed she was going to be somebody. She was going to have everything we didn't. People were going to adore her. And once she got to the top, she would do whatever it took to stay there.'' Buddy paused to take a deep breath. ''That's the day Maggie Simpson became Marguerite Lemond. But to me, she'll always be Maggie, the sister who was good to me in her own way. The sister I never stopped loving.''

Teague noticed he wasn't the only one affected by Buddy's words about his sister. Addison's expression was grave and his chin was tucked into his chest. Bo looked like a man who had lost his best friend. Christine blinked rapidly and a few tears rolled down her cheeks. Jacobi's arms were crossed tightly over his chest and his jaw was clenched. But it was Wilona who cried freely, the sounds only partially muffled by the wadded tissues she put to her mouth.

Buddy's voice was choked as he asked, ''Reverend Potter, would you continue the service?''

The minister stepped up to the coffin. ''We are here today to bid farewell to our sister, Marguerite Lemond . . . er, Maggie Simpson. . . .''

A quarter of an hour later, the service came to an end. While most eyes were dry, the people present were far more subdued than when the service had begun. They spoke in whispers and it was no wonder the sounds most distinctly heard were the loud wails let out by Wilona.

It was as if she knew Marguerite well, Teague thought, as if she were losing a close personal friend.

Wilona seemed about to throw herself on the coffin as it was wheeled outside. Bo Hathaway broke from the knot of actors and stopped the fan-club president. He patted her shoulder awkwardly, but the woman seemed inconsolable as the coffin was lifted into the maw of the hearse that would transport it a hundred yards away to Marguerite's final resting place. Wilona wailed louder.

Rae leaned closer to Teague and whispered softly. "Goodness, do you think she's going to be all right?"

"Maybe," Teague said absently.

He was still wondering about the relationship between actress and fan. Could Wilona merely be so obsessed with the soap itself that she was really mourning Faline rather than Marguerite?

The chapel emptied and people followed the funeral car that crawled along the cemetery road. Teague and Rae were near the end of the small crowd, the last to pass the network executive and his wife who were off to the side arguing.

"I shall not stay another moment, Yale," Teague heard Diane say. "Take me home."

"Yes, of course, dear, as soon as—"

"This instant!"

Without another word, he escorted his wife to their Rolls.

"Isn't that an interesting little scenario," Rae commented in a low voice.

"Diane Gordon is near hysterics...although in a very different way than Wilona was."

Rae frowned. "Any idea of what Marguerite did to her?"

"Good question, one we might ask," Teague whispered as they continued following the funeral car and crowd. "Not that Gordon would give us a straight answer."

"Gordon." Rae sounded anxious. "Oh, Lord, he didn't say anything about when he wanted to go over the changes. Or did he discuss it with you?"

Teague shook his head. "He probably assumes I'll give him an update later. So where do we go to work when this is over—my place or yours?"

"Neither," Rae said. "The studio offices will do quite nicely."

He couldn't resist needling her. "Right. We'll have the whole place all to ourselves. Just you and me."

"About that..."

"What?" he asked innocently.

"Last night, I mean...what happened...that was a mistake."

"And that's a matter of opinion," he objected. "I don't happen to agree with you."

"You have nothing to say about it."

"Oh, don't I?"

Her furious scowl was definitely more intriguing than some faces she'd given him, Teague decided as Rae hurried to catch up to the small crowd now gathering around the funeral car that had halted at the grave site. Teague appreciatively watched the natural sway of her hips, emphasized by the narrow charcoal suit skirt. But then there were a lot of things he appreciated about the frustrating woman.

Like her talent.

Her drive.

And especially her straight-arrow ethics.

In an industry where people used one another at the drop of a hat to get ahead, Rae Magill was a breath of fresh air. Her reluctance to get involved with him had merely sparked Teague's interest, and he had always been a sucker for challenges. If she thought she could so easily put him off, Rae had another think coming. He was known for his relentless determination in pursuing his professional goals. How could he be any less attentive to his private life?

Only one catch, an annoying little voice reminded him. He had a prison record, one she didn't know about. He wondered what Straight Arrow Magill would have to say if she ever found out about his past. No matter that he'd been innocent, he hadn't been able to absolve himself in the eyes of the law, and he figured she was an even tougher nut to crack. He'd simply have to do everything in his power to make certain she never learned about his "vacation" in Joliet.

Catching up to her, he put such personal thoughts aside for the moment. As the coffin was lifted from the hearse and carried to the open grave, Teague found he did want to pay his last respects to Marguerite, after all. Buddy had managed to humanize her, and that's what he would remember rather than her faults.

He studied the somber faces around him and wondered if one of these people mistakenly thought he or she would be able to forever bury the secret reasons for Marguerite's death along with the woman.

"So WE MAKE IT look like Beatrice had reason to worry about Faline's driving her out of Hilldale's social set," Rae said, making quick notes about Quenie's character at her office computer terminal. They'd chosen to work on Quenie's motives first since she'd never shown up at the funeral. "Of course, we can then play up Nigel's devotion to Beatrice, make it obsessive, though in reality, I don't think Addison is all that devoted to Quenie."

"Only insofar as the demise of Quenie's story line affects him," Teague said. "Whether or not Addison works depends on her."

Rae kept her eyes glued to the terminal, but she didn't have to glance Teague's way to see him in her mind's eye. He almost looked as good in a navy pin-striped suit as he did in one of his designer sweaters. That was the problem—she didn't want to think about how good he looked.

"And so we make a parallel by playing up the fact that Nigel's social position is equally dependent on Beatrice," she said, forcing her attention on the work. Her fingers were flying over the computer keys as fast as she was talking. "And therefore we'll play up his need to protect her. Who next?"

"Bo's story line is the one most affected."

"But we still didn't come up with a motive."

"Why don't we stick to Leopold and Faline's personal relationship?"

Despite her resolve, Rae looked at Teague. He'd removed his jacket and had tossed it on her couch. The sleeves of his white-on-white shirt were rolled up, his tie was askew, and his hair was bristling like a lion's mane, as though he'd just brushed his hand through the golden-tipped mass.

Her pulse drummed as she remembered the way his hands had felt on her the night before.

"But Bo told us he didn't mind Marguerite's seeing other men," she said through gritted teeth.

She must have sounded odd, because Teague gave her an assessing look before asking, "But what if *she* minded? What if Bo had another lover and Marguerite was furious about how that would reflect on her?"

"I can buy that, but how does it give us a workable motive for his story line?"

"What if Faline knew some secret about Leopold—"

"As we know Marguerite did about Bo," Rae said, once more remembering what she'd overheard and making the parallel.

"And what if she threatened to reveal that secret unless he stopped seeing the other woman."

"Tempest!" Rae punched at her reading glasses and once more entered data furiously. "And her motive could be jealousy. That's all four of them. Great. This is all fitting together like the pieces of a jigsaw puzzle. It's so easy it's almost scary."

She saved the file and entered a request for a printout.

"There's nothing to be afraid of," Teague said. "Not if we play our cards close to the chest."

Her head whipped up and she met his vivid blue gaze. "Are you saying there might be something to fear?"

"Not as long as we're careful. No one has any reason to suspect we're playing amateur detective."

A chill shot through her and she went very still.

"Rae?"

The unease that had accompanied her home the night before returned. Still, she shook her head in denial. "Nothing."

"Tell me," he urged.

With a sigh, she removed the reading glasses and let them hang from the cord around her neck. Her office was comfortable, practical, and unlike Teague's bold personal statement, easy on the eye. The predominant gray of the furniture and carpeting was accented with touches of mauve and pale blue. Peaceful colors. But at the moment, she couldn't be more restless.

She got to her feet and moved to the window where she looked down on a typical Manhattan Saturday afternoon. People crawled the congested streets like ants far below.

"I had the feeling someone was watching me last night when I left your place."

Teague was at her side and looming over her in a flash. "Why didn't you tell me?"

"What? That my imagination was probably working overtime again?"

"Again?" he growled.

Now she'd gone and done it. Trying to bluff her way out of the admission—she was still embarrassed over the cleaning lady incident—she shouldered past him. "I'm a writer, remember? I've always had an overactive imagination."

She didn't get far before he gripped her upper arm and swung her around to face him. This was getting to be a habit, one she wasn't anxious to cultivate. The palm that had smacked his cheek itched.

"We're in this together," he reminded her. "That means holding nothing back."

His words put her more on edge and she waited for him to make a pass. He didn't. Even so, a curious energy snapped along her nerves.

"All right," she agreed. "From now on, I'll tell you everything." Suddenly his teeth looked very white and too large and her certainty about what he might or might not do fled. She backed away from the predatory smile and qualified, "I meant about our investigation."

"Why stop there?"

Heart hammering in her throat, she twisted her arm free and whipped away from him. That he let her was both a relief and disappointment. She had to give credit where credit was due: Teague Slaughter made her feel alive as no man before him ever had.

"Maybe we should get back to work," she suggested, retrieving the printouts of the notes they'd made. "Rather I should."

Teague was right behind her. "You can start actual rewrites later. It would be a shame to miss an opportunity like this."

She eyed him suspiciously. "What opportunity?"

He leaned in closer, backing her up against the desk. "To take up where we left off yesterday."

Rae shook the pages she was holding at him. "Now listen, Slaughter—"

"I meant finishing our search." He hesitated a beat and, his expression too innocent to be real, asked, "What did *you* mean?"

Rae's face flamed but she refused to show her embarrassment in any other tangible way. "The dressing rooms? We already looked through the obvious."

"Except for one."

"Whose?"

"Marguerite Lemond's."

TEAGUE'S RELENTLESS determination wasn't all bad, Rae thought once they were inside the dead woman's dressing room. The trait would probably save them both from being wrongly accused of murder. She merely wished he would stay focused on that goal and give her some breathing room. She didn't need to be any more confused than she already was. Nor did she need to experience a clash of wills every time she was around the man. The strain was taking its toll on her.

Yet she had to admit she felt far more at ease working side by side with the man than she did on her own looking for a murderer. Her firm resolve to dislike him was weakening.

"Do you honestly think we're going to learn anything the police didn't?" she asked, sizing up the mess left by the officials. "They did a pretty thorough job in here."

"That doesn't mean they would recognize something important if they saw it."

"They're professionals."

"But we knew Marguerite and how she thought."

"*You* knew Marguerite," Rae mumbled as she began sorting through the dead woman's clothing rack. "I was only witness to her theatrics."

She could feel Teague's eyes bore into her for a second before noises at the dressing table told her he was busy searching for some elusive clue. His unspoken response to her comment hung heavy between them, prompting her to seek some space.

"I'll check the bathroom."

But while the over-the-sink cabinet was filled with beauty products, the jars and bottles revealed only the secret of Marguerite's eternally youthful good looks.

"Nothing in there," Rae said as she stepped out. "What about you? Any luck?"

Teague was standing in front of the wall unit filled mostly with mementos and books. "Not yet. But maybe these will tell us something."

He lifted a huge stack of papers and set them down on the makeup table.

She stepped closer to take a better look. "Old scripts?"

"Marguerite had a habit of making notes to herself while she went over her lines. I thought maybe she'd have something interesting to say in one of these. Want to help?"

"Sure." Though Rae figured this was going to be a waste of time, she dragged a spare chair closer to the one he'd taken. "Give me half."

Dutifully Rae took her share, then went through each script one page at a time if not as thoroughly as Teague did. Marguerite had scrawled all kinds of notes in the margins—mostly about blocking or character motivation, but some reminding her of appointments or of things she needed to do. Boring reading as far as Rae was concerned. She tossed another script into the discard pile and realized that Teague was frowning as he stared down at a page.

"What?" she asked. "Did you find something?"

"I don't know."

"Let me see."

Teague handed her the script, and pointed at the note: "ask SJ about TIX for Sat."

"So she was reminding herself to check whether or not someone got tickets for what? The theater?" Rae guessed. "A concert? How is that important?"

"Not the event, the person. 'SJ'?"

"SJ—Saul Jacobi?" Rae wasn't surprised by a reference to the show's director. "So he was supposed to get her some kind of tickets."

"What if the tickets weren't for her alone but for *them?*" Teague suggested.

"Them? As in Jacobi being the other man in her life?"

"It works for me."

"Jacobi did have a way with Marguerite when she was in one of her moods," Rae said, thinking back to the fateful day. He'd been the one to coax the recalcitrant actress out of her dressing room when she'd left the set after complaining of not feeling well. "Even if they were seeing each other, that doesn't prove anything."

"Except maybe they wanted to keep the relationship a secret. Or one of them did."

"Hmm."

Thinking about the possibility, Rae went back to the few remaining copies that she searched even more diligently. Too bad she didn't find anything nearly as enlightening. When she was finished, she gathered all the scripts they'd gone through and headed for the wall unit where she returned the pile to its shelf. The top script slipped from the pile and went flying behind the others. Before she could catch the thing, it became wedged behind a couple of books one shelf down. She moved a few of the books to fish it out, and in doing so, noted another script had met the same fate.

"Here's one we missed."

But when she straightened, Rae realized what she was holding wasn't a script at all, but a copy of the long-range projection for "Rivals."

This particular projection covered three months of the show ending with episodes three weeks down the line. Rae had written it after intensive conferences with ex-executive producer Gary Noble, network executive Yale Gordon and sponsor representative Eldridge Banks. It detailed the immediate future for each of the story lines and each of the relationships—that is, when a major story would peak and which secondary story would move to the foreground. The actors were never supposed to see a long-range projection lest their characters' fates adversely affect their performances.

"Now how did she get her hot little hands on this?"

Reaching past her to return the last of his scripts to the pile, Teague asked, "What?"

She showed him the cover page.

"The long-range projection?" Teague shook his head. "That woman had her ways of knowing everything that was going on, didn't she?"

Marguerite could only have gotten it from one of five sources—herself, Teague, Noble, Gordon or Banks.

"I've had enough snooping for one day," Teague said. "What about you?"

Ray sighed her relief and hung on to the projection, which she intended to take with her. "I've had more than enough for today. Let's get out of here."

Teague flipped off the light and started to open the door, then froze. Rae ran into his broad back.

"What—"

"Sh-sh!" He closed the door most of the way, leaving it open only a crack. "I heard something," he whispered.

Rae stifled a chuckle when she thought about being caught by the cleaning lady a second time.

Teague, however, wasn't in the least amused. Tension vibrated from his taut body and, finally realizing how close she still was to him, Rae backed off. Then she, too, heard something—the sounds of someone who didn't want to be caught.

Who else had decided to make a special trip to the studio on a Saturday afternoon?

Chapter Seven

Rae stood tense and expectant in the dark. "Can you see anyone?" she whispered.

Teague was glued to the tiny crack in the door, leaving her no opportunity to look for herself.

"Someone's leaving Quenie's dressing room...."

"Who?"

Muffled footsteps and a door closing quietly was followed by Teague's soft exclamation. "Well, well, what is he doing sneaking around here?"

Teague pulled her in front of him so she could get up to the sliver of an opening between door and frame. He remained directly behind her, too close for comfort. She ignored the warmth that invaded her space. Eye pressed to the crack, Rae spied Rufus Piggot in front of Quenie's dressing room.

"Rufus?" They hadn't even considered the property and costume supervisor to be a suspect. "Maybe he's here for the same reason we are."

After glancing around furtively, Rufus patted his suit jacket as if he'd hidden something there, then slipped down the hall. Obviously he didn't want to be seen.

"Trying to unmask a murderer?" Teague asked, his lips next to her ear, "or to cover up for her?"

Too aware of him to relax, Rae still had the presence of mind to realize the "her" was Quenie Tovar.

"He's always seemed devoted to Quenie. I sometimes thought he might be in love with her." Rae shifted slightly, and although no part of Teague was touching her, she could feel his very presence in the dark. "I suppose he could be trying to protect her."

"Or trying to find something that would incriminate him," Teague added as Rufus turned the corner and disappeared from view. "We'll have to keep a vigilant eye on him."

Rae tried to move away from the door, intending to open it and escape the unwelcome effect Teague had on her. She found herself blocked by his unmovable body. His solid, very male, desirable body.

Her unbidden response was very instant, female and unacceptable.

"It's safe for us to leave now," she said breathlessly.

"Not yet."

Rae had the distinct feeling that Teague would enjoy himself if she revealed even the tiniest unease. Therefore she didn't argue, merely fumed in the dark and counted silently to ten. Distracting herself didn't work, didn't make the discomfort any easier to bear.

When she finished counting, she insisted, "He must be gone by now."

"But we can't be certain, can we?"

Teague still didn't move. He continued to surround her in the darkness and she suspected he was enjoying himself. He was keeping her off balance on purpose.

"If he sees us," she said, "he'll merely think we were in *your* dressing room."

"Doing what?"

Now he was definitely amused at her expense. In her mind's eye, she could see him grin. And she was getting irritated, not only at him but with herself. She landed a hard poke of her elbow in his solar plexus. That moved him just enough for a quick escape.

"Oh, sorry," Rae fibbed. She opened the door and stalked into the hallway. "Let him think what he likes."

Teague was on her heels in seconds. Together, they arrived at the elevator to the executive offices.

"The coast is clear," she observed, "but I didn't hear any elevator stop on this floor."

"Hmm, he must have used the fire stairs."

"Or he's still around somewhere." Looking for something or *someone?* Though Rae glanced over her shoulder, she had no sensation of being watched. "Maybe he went back to Props or Wardrobe."

Both departments were located on the same floor, adjoining the studio.

"Maybe," Teague agreed as their elevator car arrived.

A few minutes later, they were back in her office and Rae was packing up her briefcase with copies of the coming week's scripts and the revision notes they'd made earlier. At the last minute, she added the long-range projection that she'd found in Marguerite's dressing room. She might need a copy for reference while she was working at home.

"Maybe I should come with you," Teague suggested. "Together we can whip out new dialogue in no time at all."

"I need to think over the individual scenes," Rae insisted. Besides, she'd had enough. No way was she about to spend the rest of the day with the man. "You can add whatever you want after I write a first draft."

"If I didn't know better, I would think you're trying to avoid me."

Rae didn't try to deny it. "While I'm writing, you could be detecting."

"It wouldn't be the same without you."

"I'll bet." He wouldn't be able to trap her in an untenable position for his own amusement, she thought. "Just what do you see us doing next?"

"Other than manipulating the scripts to our advantage, all I can think of is keeping our eyes and ears open. Maybe something we've already learned will click."

"Thank goodness." Her sense of relief was overwhelming. She'd hated acting like some kind of thief. "I was afraid you might want to break into someone's apartment next. I don't have what it takes for this kind of excitement. Especially not what it would take to do hard time."

Teague flinched at the reference to prison, yet was quick on the uptake. "All the more reason for us to clear ourselves. If you think I'm treating this situation like a game, Rae, I'm not. The stakes are pretty high for both of us. And if someone's been watching you—"

"No doubt my imagination." She had herself half-convinced and didn't want Teague talking her back into a panic. "I was jumpy when I left your place last night."

"I remember," he said, both dark brows shooting up. "Rae, whatever you do, be careful, please. And if your imagination starts working overtime, let me know anyway. I promise I won't laugh."

"All right already. You've made your point." She was getting edgy again. "Can we go now?"

If she thought Teague was going to pursue the issue, she was pleasantly surprised. He didn't talk at all on the way down to the lobby. He took longer than necessary signing out at the guard's station. Rae waited for him by the door while he spoke to the guard himself, their voices too low for her to hear.

As they headed toward the garage where they'd left their cars, Teague let her in on what he'd learned.

"Rufus told the guard he had to make some costume and prop changes for Monday to go along with the revised script. A good excuse to anyone who doesn't know the changes haven't been made yet."

"Is he still in the building?" Rae asked.

"No. He left about five minutes ago, while we were in your office. He was in and out of the place in less than a half hour."

"Enough time to search Quenie's dressing room pretty well," Rae said thoughtfully. "Could he have found something you didn't?"

"I was pretty thorough . . . then, again, who knows what he was looking for."

The incident stayed in her mind the rest of the afternoon. And she called it forth later when she sat down to start the rewrite after taking an invigorating shower to refresh not only her body, but her mind. Improvising from what she and Teague had worked out earlier, she sketched a scene in which Nigel searched Beatrice's office where she planned her charity work. Not too subtle. Though not one of the actors, Rufus should get the parallel the moment he saw the new scene.

Rae continued working, planting doubts about each of the four suspects in the cast. When Monday's script was completely revised, she ate a late light dinner and crawled into bed. Exhaustion immediately claimed her.

The next morning, she woke feeling rested and ready to get back to work after eating a big breakfast. First order of business was to refresh her memory about everything that was supposed to happen in "Rivals" over the next three weeks. She reviewed the long-range projection she'd confiscated from Marguerite's office over a third cup of coffee. Wanting to identify any other story lines that might need fine-tuning to go along with the murder, she made notes as she read.

Everything was going smoothly until she came to the next-to-the-last page. Having read halfway through it, Rae couldn't believe her eyes. Someone had made a significant alteration! She went over the incriminating paragraph as if the words would transform once more. There was no mistake.

According to this projection, Faline Devereux had been scheduled to die!

Questions whirling in her mind, Rae called Teague immediately and told him of the newest development in their real-life plot.

"I have a few errands to run," he said, "but I can be there a little after noon."

"You want to come over? Why?"

"So I can see the projection for myself."

"You know what it says. I'll read it to you again."

He swept her objection away with a diversionary tactic. "Besides, I'd like to take a look at the revisions you made in Monday's script. I might want to make some additional changes myself.''

Gripping the receiver tightly, Rae fumed. She suspected that this was Teague's excuse to pursue her some more. Well, she might have been in a weakened state of mind the last two days, but now she was rested and ready for him.

"All right," she finally agreed. "I'll see you when you get here."

Truthful with herself, Rae couldn't help looking forward to another encounter with The Kiss of Death.

"Soon," Teague warned her.

Hanging up the telephone, Rae stared down at the truth she still held in her hand. The revised projection. Whoever had tampered with the story line must have given this copy to Marguerite.

But why? Merely to torture the actress?

Or had the motive indeed been more sinister?

No matter how she looked at it, Rae came to one conclusion: that Marguerite died the way Faline did in the revised story line was no coincidence.

Therefore, whoever tampered with the projection must be the murderer!

"NO WONDER she was so convinced we were lying," Teague said, papers in hand. "After seeing this, of course she wouldn't believe Faline was only going to be in a coma for a few weeks." He was actually feeling sorry for Marguerite—for the second time in two short days. "She must have gone crazy when she read her character was going to be killed off shortly. Marguerite never was the most secure person in the world to begin with."

"Could've fooled me."

Rae was curled up in a plush chair set in front of the bay windows of what should have been the living room. Teague had been surprised by the modest size and simplicity of her walk-up apartment. She certainly could afford something more elaborate now that she drew a head writer's salary. Instead, she seemed content with a few interesting pieces of expensive artwork, a comfortable if small seating arrangement and an elaborate work area with a state-of-the-art computer and laser printer. That told him how she spent most of her time when at home. It also said something about her confidence in herself—that she didn't feel she had something to prove to the rest of the world.

"But then you knew Marguerite far better than I did," Rae was saying.

He heard a hint of what in her voice? Sarcasm, yes, but something more. Certainly not jealousy. Though Teague was beginning to think he might not mind such an emotion coming from Rae Magill.

"I haven't known Marguerite in the biblical sense for many years, Rae. Even then I never could get inside her head. I think Marguerite was always playing some role, no matter who she was with."

"Sometimes that's safer."

"Than what?" Teague asked.

"Than putting your real self on the line."

Was Rae saying *she* was playing a role? She was a challenge, that was for certain. Even more important, he was beginning to think that she was a prize that went beyond her professional talents.

When she wasn't hiding in her straight-spined disguise, that was. Like now. While she wasn't exactly relaxed, she wasn't in the least rigid. She wore loose purple pants and a purple and turquoise top that fell becomingly off one shoulder. With equally colorful barrettes pulling her auburn hair back from her face, she looked like a completely different person.

The change in her was startling, a real revelation as far as Teague was concerned. For the first time, he was getting more than a brief glimpse at the real woman. And he liked what he saw. A more vivid if softer personality hid beneath the competent facade she presented at work, a fact Teague would like to explore more thoroughly.

His thoughts must have been readable, for Rae flushed and shifted uncomfortably. That's the way he liked her best—off balance.

"So what are we going to do about my discovery?" she asked, indicating the sheaf of papers he still held.

Not having the faintest idea at the moment, Teague joked, "We could line up all our suspects in the studio and ask which one of them stole the projection and revised it."

"And I'm certain the guilty party would confess immediately. Come on, Teague, be serious. Do you think we should let Lieutenant Franklin in on this?"

No way did Teague want to deal with the cop. "Let's not involve him yet. This may mean nothing."

"You don't believe that any more than I do." Her expression was puzzled. "But I suppose you're not any more eager to get involved with the authorities than I am, either. So we'll wait and see. What can he do to us if he finds out we withheld information? Put us in jail?"

Teague winced. That's exactly what could happen, though he wasn't about to say so. "How about giving me a look at Monday's script," he suggested instead.

Rae unfolded her legs and crossed to her workstation, an ornate system of wall units, bookshelves, desk and printer stand. "Actually, I worked on Tuesday while I was waiting for you. It's still a little rough, but you'll get the idea." She handed him two separate printouts.

While he read, she busied herself at the computer, entering more changes she'd made in Tuesday's script. No rest for the compulsive, he guessed. He made a few notes in the margins, but all in all, Teague realized Rae had done a remarkable job in so short a time.

"I'm impressed but not particularly surprised," he said when he finished reading.

She looked up from the computer and removed her reading glasses. "Think it'll work?"

"We'll have the murderer shaking in his or her boots."

"If one of our suspects is guilty."

He could tell uncertainty was making her question the validity of the work she'd done. "The world is filled with 'what ifs,'" Teague said. "Let's go with our instincts and believe we'll get the best return possible for our efforts. If nothing else, you have an introduction to a dynamite story line here." And if he didn't do something, she might work nonstop until she finished the entire week. "Listen, even intrepid investigators have to eat. What do you say to taking a walk down to Greenwich Village?"

"I've got too much work left to do," she said. "I don't think—"

He cut off her objection. "Please. It's a beautiful spring day and I wouldn't enjoy a walk without company. Besides, you need a reward for working so hard.

We can go French, Italian, Spanish . . . anything you like.''

In the end she let him choose.

As they walked to The Troika, a Slavic restaurant serving Russian, Ukrainian and Polish food, they kept to safe subjects, discussing neither the murder nor anything too personal. Teague learned Rae liked to eat—the reason she'd agreed to an outing with him, no doubt—and she indulged herself in all of the visual and performing arts, from special museum exhibits to bad movies.

A good start since he liked all of the above, as well. But start for what? Though her attitude toward him had softened, Rae gave no indication that she wanted more from him than a professional relationship. Except for that kiss, of course. His cheek twinged just a little, reminding him how that incident had ended.

But he saw her crack by the time their appetizers of pierogies had arrived. Maybe it was the wine, or maybe the romantic atmosphere. They'd passed the ethnic antique-laden interior and had opted for garden seating—a giant old-fashioned gazebo overflowing with perfumed flowers and strung with tiny white Italian lights that lit up the dusk. She sat back, utterly relaxed, and made sounds of contentment.

"Mmm, wonderful. And not just because I was so famished."

She had a smear of white at the corner of her mouth. Unable to help himself, Teague reached out and wiped it from her soft skin with his thumb. Though she seemed startled, she didn't pull her head away. "Sour cream," he explained.

"Oh." She blinked rapidly and sounded a bit breathless. "So, Slaughter isn't exactly ethnic. Where did you pick up your love of Slavic food?"

Teague toyed with admitting he was born Theodore Slavensky but quickly reconsidered. The fewer people who could connect him with his state-sponsored stay at Joliet prison, the better. He'd been Teague Slaughter for so long, no one in the business knew him as anyone else.

"My grandmother was half Ukrainian, half Polish," he said truthfully. "Most Sundays we had dinner at her house." He ate half a potato-filled pierogi. "These are delicious but the dough isn't quite as delicate as the stuff she used to make. The woman could have been a chef herself."

"You were lucky. Coming from a small town in the midwest, I grew up on pretty bland country cooking. I don't regret my childhood, but being a kid in New York must have been so much more exciting."

Teague winced at her assumption and covered by lifting his wine glass and sipping. She thought he was from New York. If he told her differently, she might start asking all kinds of questions he didn't want to answer about life in a rough Chicago neighborhood.

"Tell me about your childhood," he prompted, beating her to the punch.

"Oh, I grew up in Greenhill, a small town near Lafayette, Indiana. Our parents instilled the Great American Work Ethic in my brother and me. Live a clean, honest life, work hard, try to be successful, but don't be too disappointed if you don't get everything you dreamed of. Be happy with what God gave you, that sort of thing."

"It seems as though you followed their advice."

"They were happy. It worked for them for the most part. Life—and people—aren't always fair." She seemed uncomfortable explaining. "Dad had a boss who was a real hard nose. And who did whatever was politically expedient when it came to things like handing out promotions. Or firing people."

"He fired your father?"

She nodded. "When Dad was in his mid-forties. It was hell for him to get another job, especially considering his age. Anyway, my brother and I both managed to take a big step beyond what our parents accomplished. Matt is a successful architect in Indianapolis. Our parents are very proud of us. What about you?"

"I think you've done well, too."

"That's not what I meant. I was talking about your parents and how they feel about their famous son."

"My father died when I was ten. Mom's not impressed by much. She's pretty down to earth. She had to be to raise four kids by herself."

And it was the lack of a male influence that probably got him into trouble . . . if all those psychological studies confirming such facts could be trusted. Drawing on personal experience, Teague suspected they could.

"I'm sure your mother is proud of you."

"She is, but then she's too proud in general."

"What do you mean?"

"I'd like to give her a much better life. I certainly can afford it. But she insists on staying in the old neighborhood. I don't know what she does with the money I force on her—probably gives it to needy people. I worry about her living alone in the old house sometimes, but as she keeps reminding me, I'm her kid who will never know as much as she does.''

Laughter bubbled from Rae. ''Parents are all the same, aren't they?''

It was the first time Teague had really seen her laugh. Relaxed, she was far more approachable than usual. And prettier. Her features had softened and her skin glowed in the low light. Teague found he was a little bit smitten. Good thing that, despite herself, Rae was warming up to him, or he'd never have the opportunity to find out exactly how far this attraction could go. She was staring at him, her expression somewhat akin to awe, as if she'd never considered he was human or something.

They spent the rest of the meal talking amiably, Teague making certain the conversation stayed focused on her. Childhood anecdotes with the pickled herring. Teenage insecurities with the kulebiaka, a salmon-filled baked pastry. Adult aspirations with the raspberry kissel, a sweetened fruit puree.

And when they walked back to her place, it was hand in hand. Comfortable yet with the promise of excitement slowly building between them. Teague remembered the bedroom he'd gotten a glimpse of earlier—surprisingly frilly for a woman who usually appeared streamlined and efficient—and his thoughts strayed to more intimate speculation.

By the time they arrived at her stoop, he knew he wouldn't be content to let her go inside alone.

''Not in a hurry, are you?''

''I'd like to finish Tuesday's script tonight—''

He cut her off the simplest way he knew how. The kiss wasn't bold and heated as the one they'd shared in his apartment, but an exploration more hesitant.

Gentler. Even so, they were both breathing heavily when their lips separated. Rae was wide-eyed. And definitely nervous. Teague was on fire. Still, he restrained himself and waited to see what she would do.

"Maybe I can even start Wednesday's revisions," she babbled softly.

Another kiss made her move in closer to him, yet Teague didn't engulf her as his body urged him to. He kept it short and sweet and followed with an innocuous-enough suggestion.

"Now that you have the flow of the new story line, I could help with the dialogue."

Rae actually seemed to consider it for a moment—or perhaps she was trying to decipher his real intent. The latter, probably, and successfully, too, because she backed off.

"No, I'll get more done working alone."

That, he was certain, was true. "Then I'll walk you up to your apartment."

"That won't be necessary."

"I insist."

He held the downstairs door open for her. She entered the vestibule and unlocked the inner door. She glanced back at him as if she planned on protesting his presence yet again, but in the end, she merely led the way silently up the four flights. On the top landing, she turned to him quickly before he could get all the way up the last leg of stairs.

"My apartment. You can go on home."

"As soon as you're safely inside."

She backed away again and her shoe contacted something solid that almost tripped her. A small package. She picked up what really was a protective envelope, its sides bulging. Her name had been printed badly across the front with a bold black felt tip.

"What in the world . . . ? Who got up here without a key to the bottom door?"

Rae was breathing heavy again, but not from the climb and not from the kisses. She was frightened. Her face looked pasty under the dim hall light. Teague tried to reassure her momentarily.

"Maybe a neighbor dropped that off."

"You've got to be kidding. Do you actually know *your* neighbors?"

"Point taken," Teague said, keeping his own voice calmer than hers. Now she was starting to alarm him. "So open it up and solve the mystery."

She was ripping the end even as he said it. She spilled out the contents—a black rectangle fell into her hand.

"An unlabeled videotape." And checked inside the envelope. "But no note. What could this be?"

"Only one way to find out." He'd never thought of getting back in her apartment like this. "Let's watch some video."

Chapter Eight

"Maybe it's some actor's audition tape," Rae said as she loaded the videotape into the recorder.

Teague didn't believe that and he was certain Rae didn't, either. He could tell she was trying to keep her perspective, trying hard not to panic. That she was upset would be clear to anyone who got a good look at her. The murder and their consequent involvement had put a great strain on her. On them both, Teague amended, but she'd never before had experience dealing with the cops or being treated as if she were guilty of a crime as he had.

Wielding the controller to start the tape, Rae said, "Well, I'm ready for anything."

Not that Teague believed her. Even *he* wasn't ready for what they did see. Not quite.

"Oh, my God." She stood frozen in shock. "Someone sent me a porno tape."

There on the screen, big as life, a naked couple writhed on an ornate bed of pillows.

"This isn't just any porno tape," Teague said. "This is a personal statement."

"You mean a home video? If this is someone's idea of a joke, it's disgusting."

Rae's face flamed as if she'd belatedly remembered Teague's presence. She aimed the controller to click off the machine, but he prevented her from doing so. Her hand felt warm under his as if her whole body were burning with embarrassment. But he couldn't let her stop the tape just yet, not when he recognized one of the participants.

"Take a better look at the stars of this extravaganza," he suggested.

"Good Lord, that's Marguerite! But who's the man?"

She watched, her expression aghast as the man moved over Marguerite's body. Teague thought the silver head pressed to Marguerite's breast looked familiar. Suddenly the lovers flipped so that the woman was on top and there was a clear shot of the man's face.

"Yale Gordon," Teague said. "I thought so!" He pried the controller free from Rae's fingers and stopped the tape. Then he made her sit down to catch her breath. "That's enough for the moment."

"That's all I *ever* care to see."

"There might be something else important on this tape. We won't know for sure unless we watch it, will we?"

Rae swallowed hard. Teague realized the last thing in the world she wanted to do was to watch this kind of home video with him. That his former lover was one of the stars no doubt added insult to injury.

"Who would have sent this to me and why?" she asked.

"Maybe someone is trying to tell you something."

"About the murder? You think someone is trying to implicate Yale Gordon?"

"Makes sense. He was having an affair with Marguerite, one I'm certain he didn't want his wife to know about."

"But it seemed as if she knew something at the funeral," Rae reminded him. "Remember, she insisted on leaving."

"She might have suspected, but that's not the same as knowing for certain."

"It doesn't make sense that he would have done, uh, his thing on tape, not if he didn't want Diane to know about the relationship."

"He may not have been aware he was being taped."

"You mean Marguerite might have done this without his ever knowing?"

"She always was a little kinky," Teague admitted. He could tell all kinds of thoughts raced through Rae's head—like exactly what kinds of experiences he himself had shared with the late actress. "I wonder if she wanted more than an affair this time."

"Her threatening to show this tape to Diane would infuriate Gordon, but enough to kill her?"

"Murders have been committed over less."

"There's another thing," Rae said. "Blackmail. What if Marguerite didn't want to marry Gordon but was using the tape to get something else from him?"

"Like having her story lines changed the way she wanted to play them?" Teague suggested.

"Exactly."

"Gordon didn't back her up last time, though," Teague remembered. "He'd approved her going into a coma and for once she couldn't change his mind."

"Because he was plotting to get rid of her even then?" Rae suggested.

"Hmm, I guess we'll have to work together to revise Tuesday's script a bit more," Teague said.

"Together?" She gave him a suspicious look. "Why?"

"To weave in the blackmail angle, of course."

They spent the next hour discussing how best to do that. Rae couldn't hide her relief when he volunteered to take the videotape off her hands and to check it out himself at home.

The job was distasteful—he felt like a voyeur considering he knew both participants—and turned out to be fruitless. They'd gotten all the sender had meant them to know by watching the first few minutes.

Whoever had delivered the tape to Rae's door had to know things about Marguerite's death that they didn't. While the contents made Yale Gordon suspect, it didn't actually prove he'd killed the woman. The sender might be trying to throw them off the real trail. He or she might be the guilty party or could be trying to protect someone else.

He thought about Saul Jacobi's personal relationship with the late actress. If he really were involved with Marguerite as they suspected from finding the reference to the tickets on one of her scripts, the show's director would have had the opportunity to find the tape. Had Jacobi had reason to deliver it to Rae?

Quenie, Addison, Christine, Bo, Rufus, Gordon and now Jacobi. The list of suspects was growing, the situation getting more complicated by the moment.

"GOOD JOB." Yale Gordon closed the second script he'd just finished and sat back in his chair. "Really good," he enthused, his effusive approval of Rae's and Teague's revisions going beyond Rae's expectations. He was beaming so hard he practically lit up his office. "Throwing suspicion on all the main characters was a stroke of genius. Which of you is responsible for that idea?"

Rae looked to Teague who smoothly said, "Both. We came up with the new twists to the plot together."

"I knew you were the right person to head the show when Gary Noble left," Gordon said. "And the two of you make quite a team. You'll create ratings history together!"

"So you're giving your stamp of approval to all the directions we've chosen to take?" Rae asked pointedly.

"I don't see any problems. Jealousy, self-sacrifice, illicit affairs, blackmail—audiences eat that stuff up. The ratings are going to soar!"

He and Rae were hardly out of the office and out of earshot of the network executive before she said, "Ratings—that's all that man thinks of! He'd probably sell himself down the river if it meant a bigger audience share. Can you believe he went for the blackmail angle without showing a crack?"

"Maybe he wasn't being blackmailed."

Teague quickly related his ambivalence about the matter, and his new suspicions about Jacobi.

"But our intimating a videotape is involved should have pricked Gordon."

"Maybe it did, Rae. I wouldn't be surprised if he's learned a thing or two about acting in all his years with 'Rivals.'"

If the session with the network executive had been a bust, the cast read-through of Monday's script gave them more input than was possible to digest all at once.

"I can't believe you would single me out like this, Rae!" Quenie was the first to voice her objections. "Imagine Beatrice killing Faline over a little social rivalry. Nothing could be more ludicrous."

"I beg to differ with you, my dear," Addison objected. "Nigel's protecting Beatrice by murdering her arch rival is nonsense. What a preposterous premise!"

"We had to create several suspects," Rae reminded them. "Given the short notice and the lack of any ground setting ahead of time, we did what we could."

The show's leading cast members all seemed upset, Teague thought as he closely examined their expressions.

Christine spoke up. "Intimating Tempest was having an affair with Leopold . . . that's going to ruin the fabric of her character. Tempest has always been honest and aboveboard."

"But at least it will make your character more interesting for one," Quenie put in. Seemingly over her own snit, she said, "You should be grateful you're being given the wonderful opportunity to stretch yourself before it's too late and you bore the audience to death."

Teague had never heard Quenie aim so vicious an insult on anyone but Marguerite. He wondered if the women didn't get along and he'd missed the clues or if Quenie merely saw Christine as her newest real-life rival for exciting story lines.

"Well, I'm not at all grateful!" the blonde stated.

Teague had never heard her react so vehemently to anything before. He was beginning to think he and Rae had created a monster.

But Christine wasn't finished. "I'm going on record as saying I want this revision scrapped."

"C'mon. Christine, the change will be good for you," Bo said. "Leopold, on the other hand, has been known to play around before. It makes no sense that he would suddenly think he had to resort to murder to end an affair."

"We'll come up with a good rationale," Teague assured the leading man. He thought about the blackmail twist they'd worked into the next day's script and doubted either Christine or Bo was going to be pleased.

"It would make a lot more sense to place blame on The Kiss of Death himself," Bo said, staring daggers at Teague.

"That goes without saying, but it's too obvious," Teague returned.

The read-through over, the cast broke into small groups where they would go over lines until it was time to block for the cameras. Teague and Rae went into their own huddle outside the rehearsal hall.

"How do you think it's going?" she asked anxiously.

"Too well. We have too many nervous people in there."

"That's what I thought. This whole thing is going to backfire," she predicted.

"Not necessarily. It's too early to be so negative. A little pressure applied to the right points may make the murderer careless. Listen, I've got to get back in there to rehearse."

"And I've got to get back to my computer. I'm almost finished with Wednesday's script and want to look over the next half-dozen shows now that we have a handle on the new direction we're taking. I need to talk to my associate writers and get them started on reworking next week's scripts."

"Good," Teague said. "Later I was planning on talking to Jacobi about playing catch-up. We need to make up the time we lost due to the writers' strike. He'll have to push the shooting schedule. By the end of next week, I want to be three episodes ahead of airdate instead of one."

Rae was giving him an odd look, but she didn't say anything and he didn't have time to worry about it.

"We'll talk later," he promised.

Teague spent the rest of the morning blocking, going through a dry run and dress rehearsal of the day's episode with the rest of the cast. It wasn't until lunchtime that he had the opportunity to breathe and to think about the way he and Rae were working together both officially and undercover. They did make a great team as Gordon had said, and Rae even seemed to be warming up to him.

He touched up his foundation—he always saw to his own makeup needs, unlike most of the other men in the show—and traded the sanctity of his dressing room for the activity of the studio. Crews were making last-minute adjustments in lighting and set arrangements. He was headed for the control booth where he'd have that chat with the director.

Here and there, actors sat off by themselves or in two's going over their scenes. Bo was pacing the length of the studio, script in hand. His brow was furrowed in concentration, his lips moving as he silently rehearsed. He came to suddenly, and Teague realized the actor was scanning the studio floor as if he were looking for someone. His anxious expression made Teague curious enough to approach him.

"What's up, Bo?"

The actor jumped. "You startled me."

"Looking for anyone in particular?"

"Wilona Irwin. Have you seen her?"

"Not since the funeral service," Teague said. "Why? What's our fan-club president up to?"

"That's what I'd like to know. She was supposed to be here today. She wanted me to autograph publicity photos to go out with the newsletter."

"Maybe she forgot."

"Wilona? Are you kidding? That woman is like a vulture. She pins her sights on something and goes for it. She didn't forget." As if remembering they were about to start shooting, he glanced down at his script and hefted it. "I'd better go over the new scenes a few more times."

Taking that as a dismissal, Teague left the actor on his own and went in search of the director. But at the back of his mind, a question lurked: Why hadn't Wilona shown?

Something in his gut warned him that either something dire had happened to the woman . . . or that one more suspect had just been added to the list.

"SO I EXPECT TO SEE the new scripts by Thursday morning," Rae told Norman Parrish, her top associate writer, who was responsible for completing two episodes per week. Rae heard a long sigh through the receiver.

"You want to burn me out, or what, Rae?" he complained. "I've been working my butt off trying to start an extra episode like you asked."

"We all have to pitch in here," Rae said, annoyance making her snap. "No one asked for this situation, but we all have to live with it and do the best we can. Reworking next week's scripts is priority."

"All right, all right, don't let your girdle choke you. You're the boss lady. You command, I obey."

The girdle comment rankled. Norman was always making not-so-subtle references to her sex. If he weren't such a good and fast writer, Rae would be tempted to find his replacement immediately.

"Thursday morning," she reiterated, then hung up.

The annoyance drained out of her in a rush the moment the telephone was out of her hands. The stress was getting to her, no doubt about it. She wasn't usually so quick to anger. Or so harsh.

The way she was acting reminded her a little of Teague!

He was the one who fired people. He was the one who'd insisted on pushing the shooting schedule...and heaven help the person who foiled him. Given the circumstances, making up one day in two weeks would be an accomplishment. Two was near impossible. She'd almost forgotten how cold-blooded he could be, especially when it came to his job.

When Teague had expressed his concern over his mother the day before, she'd seen his human side, had actually started to like him. A mistake.

She'd almost forgotten about Teague Slaughter being The Kiss of Death.

No fool, she wouldn't forget again, Rae promised herself. She would temper her tendency to have warm personal feelings for the man with what she knew about him as an industry shark.

Rae got to work herself for the next hour or so, but as she was finishing up a rough draft of Thursday's changes, the murder intruded. More and more she felt Marguerite herself was the key, the most important clue to examine more carefully. But other than break into the dead woman's apartment—a criminal act Rae wasn't yet willing to contemplate—they'd done everything they could do to check her out, hadn't they?

Not quite.

Thinking about it, Rae realized that while they'd ransacked Marguerite's dressing room, they hadn't checked the costumes she'd worn or the props she'd handled during her last few days of shooting. She glanced at her watch. The cast and crew would be busy with the day's taping.

Too busy, she hoped, to worry about her nefarious activities.

Indeed, she took the stairs down one floor and edged the studio without anyone noticing her. Everyone was too busy with last-minute preparations for the next sequence to be videotaped to pay attention to a lone employee slipping into wardrobe. Rae stopped short as she realized the room wasn't empty. One of the costumers was frantically going through drawers holding accessories.

Rae stepped back behind a rack of clothing just as the woman muttered to herself, "Here it is!"

Clutching a necklace Quenie should have been wearing to keep continuity, the young woman rushed out the doors without ever noticing another presence in the shadows.

Rae waited only a moment before acting. She went directly to Marguerite's costume racks, the most extensive and expensive collection in the room. Most items were designer markdowns, but a very few had been purchased at full price at the actress's insistence. Her affair with Yale Gordon had no doubt given Marguerite the edge necessary to have her demands met.

She thought hard about what costumes the actress had worn the week before. The dinner-party gown, of course, was missing. She'd been wearing it when she'd been carted away in the body bag. But everything else was there, mostly a collection of colorful suits. Even while rummaging through every pocket, Rae felt odd. Stupid. What in the world did she expect to find? A blackmail note? A communication for an assignation? An object belonging to the murderer?

What she found was absolutely nothing, every pocket empty.

Though discouraged, she moved directly to the accessory area labeled Faline, whose drawers were coded so the wardrobe people would know what accessories went with which outfits. She continued her search, checking the assortment of paste jewels, expensive scarves and tiny beaded handbags. Still nothing.

About to leave, Rae hesitated. She remembered Marguerite using a big free-form purse the day she died. She looked through the drawers once more before thinking the bag might be too large to fit. Checking the shelves above, she was disappointed when she didn't spot the black leather immediately. A stool gave her the height necessary to search behind the front row. And upon further investigation she realized the black purse had been stuffed beneath them. With a sense of excitement, she retrieved and opened it. Empty!

And yet she hesitated returning the purse to the shelf. Checking the small inner pockets revealed no more than a stick of gum. Disgusted, she ran her hand along the soft bottom and felt a tear in the lining. She stuck her fingers through the ragged gap and fished around, coming up with nothing more exciting than a lipstick and a slightly used tissue. About to give up, she caught a flash of pink at the tear. Plunging back into the bag, Rae retrieved a slip of folded paper and immediately flattened it out.

Whatever she'd been expecting, it hadn't been this— a receipt from Blooming Creations! She quickly scanned the contents. The customer was listed as Teague Slaughter and the order was for a lily of the valley bouquet to be delivered to Quenie Tower!

An odd sensation washed over her. What was the receipt for the murder weapon doing in the dead woman's possession? Had someone purposely planted the receipt in the bag so more evidence against Teague would be found? Or had someone sent it to Marguerite as a macabre joke...like the altered long-range proposal?

One thing was perfectly clear. She had to figure out who that "someone" was!

Remembering the Blooming Creations employee who'd taken the order was to have returned from his weekend tryst that very morning, Rae decided an immediate trip to the florist was imperative.

She shoved the bag back into place on its shelf and folded the receipt. When she turned to leave the costume department, however, she was startled into stopping cold. Rufus Piggot was standing in the doorway, shoulders rounded, chest caved-in, expression unreadable. But his skin was ashen and he mopped a sheen of sweat from his bald pate with a handkerchief.

"Can I help you, cookie?"

No smile touched his thin mouth. His watery blue eyes narrowed. He was staring at the hand that tucked the folded receipt into her jacket pocket.

Rae thought quickly. "I was looking for you. I wanted to make certain you got the new scripts for tomorrow and Wednesday."

"I got 'em, but I haven't cracked the covers yet. So there's changes I should know about?"

"Most were dialogue, but we have added a few new scenes. I wanted to alert you."

He hesitated only a fraction of a second before saying, "I consider myself warned."

And a chill shot through Rae. Should she, too, feel warned? Had he learned that she and Teague had been in the building Saturday afternoon—and had he guessed that they'd seen him coming from Quenie's dressing room? What had he been looking for? The receipt she'd just found?

Knowing Rufus wasn't about to tell her even if she asked, Rae moved past him with a breezy, "Catch you later," and felt his stare follow.

A little unnerved, she sped through the studio just as Jacobi called a half-hour break. Something about a problem with the lighting. She considered telling Teague what she was up to, but decided finding him would only delay her. She'd catch him up on the details later. After collecting her purse, she headed out of the building. Rush hour had begun and flagging a taxi would be an exercise in futility, so she walked the few blocks to Blooming Creations.

As she entered the shop, Ernesto was handing a customer change. The transaction finished, the man left, roses tucked under one arm, and the florist spotted her.

"Ah, the very talented Rae Magill returns," he said, straightening his vivid yellow bow tie against his deep purple shirt. "What can I do for you this afternoon? Flowers to brighten your office? Or did you need something to cheer up your home?"

Realizing she was going to have to make a purchase to get what she wanted, Rae said, "I was looking for something very simple...as well as the opportunity to speak to Rinaldo."

Ernesto didn't miss a beat. "Rinaldo is filling out an order in back. He'll only be a little *momento*. In the meantime, we'll find something suitable for you." The florist led the way to the refrigeration unit where he chose a simple—and undoubtedly expensive—arrangement from the case. "I think you'll like this one."

"Yes, perfect," she said without checking the price.

Only when he had her credit card in hand did he shout, "Rinaldo, come out, *pronto*. You have company."

A dark-haired young man dressed in black but for the blood-red rosebud pinned to his jacket lapel stepped into the shop proper. When he saw her, he seemed puzzled.

"This is Rae Magill, writer extraordinaire," Ernesto explained as he rang up her forced purchase. "You remember, I told you about her this morning."

The antithesis of his employer, Rinaldo spoke in tones as subdued as his clothing. "You're here about the bouquet sent to Miss Tovar."

"I'm here to figure out who ordered it," she agreed.

"As I told Ernesto...she claimed to be Mr. Slaughter's secretary."

Could June Chin have lied? Rae wondered. "Then she was Eurasian?"

"No, no. One hundred percent Anglo."

"What did she look like?"

"Actually, she didn't look like a secretary at all," Rinaldo said, "at least not one who would be employed in this part of Manhattan. She dressed outlandishly."

"Punk?"

"Quite the opposite. Imminently forgettable. She was wearing some tiny flower print thing and those clunky shoes one usually spots on older women."

When Rinaldo frowned and seemed hesitant to go on, Ernesto encouraged him. "Just tell Miss Magill what you thought. Don't worry, she won't accuse you of being catty."

"Please," Rae urged.

"Well, I hate stereotyping anyone, but she looked like an old-fashioned librarian."

Rae was getting the feeling she knew exactly who had placed the order. "She wore glasses?"

Rinaldo nodded. "Horn-rimmed. And she had mousy brown hair and wispy bangs that hid half her face."

Wilona Irwin. Rae had no doubts. Rinaldo had described the fan-club president perfectly. One more suspect to add to their list!

"Thank you. You've been a great help."

"Lieutenant Franklin thought so, too," Ernesto said, handing her the flowers.

"The authorities were here today?"

"A few hours ago," Rinaldo said. "I told you everything I told them."

Rae stared at her credit card receipt. She'd gotten the information, all right, but not before she had bought an outrageously expensive floral arrangement she neither wanted nor needed!

"Thanks a lot," she said, unable to keep the note of irony from her voice.

"We'll see you again," Ernesto cheerfully called after her.

"In a pig's eye," Rae muttered to herself.

The rush-hour crowd had grown in size during the few minutes she'd been in the shop. Immersed in thought, Rae barely noticed. She went with the flow and headed back to the office on automatic.

Wilona Irwin! A person she never would have suspected. As far as Rae knew, the fan-club president had adored Marguerite. She'd sobbed her heart out at the funeral and had practically thrown herself on the woman's coffin, for heaven's sake! All an act? Or guilt?

The crowd stopped at a corner for a red light. Rae stood directly at the curb, wondering if Lieutenant Franklin had been able to identify the newest suspect. And hoping that Teague would be able to make more sense of this new information than she did.

Impatiently she looked up at the light. Still red. Honks made her glance to her left where a taxi careened around a bus. And as she stood slightly off balance, she was jostled from behind. Hard.

Rae went flying directly into the path of the speeding taxi!

Somehow she managed to spin out of the vehicle's direct line, though the taxi's mirror caught her in the side. If the driver noticed, he kept going, and Rae froze as the bus screeched to a stop mere inches from where she stood.

"Lady, whaddya doing in the street?" the bus driver yelled.

The near miss stunned Rae for a moment. She could barely breathe, no less answer.

"Are you all right?" a man asked.

"I—I guess," she said, ignoring the pain in her side.

"Get the hell outta there!" the bus driver yelled again.

The man took her arm, and guided her back to the curb, picking up the floral arrangement she'd dropped in the fracas on the way.

"Close call. Thank goodness you didn't get hurt."

"Thanks," she said as he handed her the flowers.

She was already searching the crowd for a face she recognized. This had been no near accident. She'd felt strong hands on her back shove her into the oncoming taxi's path. But no familiar face popped from the now moving crowd.

Rae allowed herself to be swept along, and only when she got to the other side of the street did she look down at the flowers she was holding.

They were crushed. Mangled. Just as she might have been.

Rae felt sick. A certainty enveloped her.

Someone wanted her dead.

Chapter Nine

"Someone shoved you in front of that taxi?" Teague repeated in a low voice, even though they were tucked in a corner of the hallway, away from the other actors and crew members. Rae was pale and serious, but she seemed steady enough. "Are you certain?"

"Positive. Someone must have followed me when I left CBC."

"And I still don't understand why you went alone without so much as telling me."

She didn't quite meet his gaze when she said, "I didn't want the shop to close before I got there."

"Or you didn't want me to interfere."

"You couldn't have stopped me."

"I could have tried," he argued.

"And wasted valuable time."

The first thing she'd done upon returning to the studio was to relate the events of the last hour, starting with the florist's receipt she'd found in Faline's purse and progressing to the conversation at the shop. She'd saved the taxi incident for last.

"So you went ahead and almost got yourself killed," he ground out more gruffly than he intended.

"Well, I'm alive and I got us another lead, didn't I?"

Rae's voice sounded strained. Teague decided to let up on her. She'd been through enough.

Still, for her own good he had to suggest, "You really should inform the authorities."

Rae's eyes were wide and disbelieving. "If I told Lieutenant Franklin someone tried to kill me, I'd have to tell him why, wouldn't I? Then we'd have to give up our own investigation. No doubt he'd place a guard on me...or he might think I was lying to take the heat off myself."

"You've got a point," Teague conceded more easily than he knew he should. "Wilona Irwin involved in a murder plot." He still couldn't believe the fanclub president was deeper than she seemed. "Bo was looking for her earlier."

"Right. She wanted him to sign some photographs. Then she could have followed me."

"Except she didn't show."

"That we know of," Rae returned. "Of course Rufus could have been the one. Or any of our other suspects."

"They all had opportunity since we were on extended break. But what do we really have on any of them? Marguerite's vague threat to Bo the day she died? Addison's dart board? Jacobi seeing Marguerite on the sly?"

"Don't forget the videotape of Marguerite and Gordon. That seems to be the most incriminating, but—"

"All right, boys and girls, places in five minutes," Jacobi announced over the intercom.

The proposed thirty minutes had drawn closer to sixty and the lighting crew was still on the set.

"Finally," Teague said.

"How long do you think you'll be taping?" Rae asked.

"Another hour or so if we don't have any more technical problems."

"When you're done, we should pay our fan-club president a surprise visit."

Just what he had been thinking. "In the meantime, stay out of trouble."

"Don't worry. I'll be holed up in my office burning up my keyboard."

"I'd rather you weren't alone, Rae."

"What you'd 'rather' doesn't count."

His temper surfaced at that. "The hell it doesn't!"

"Okay, look. You want to coddle me, walk me up to my office and I'll lock myself in," Rae suggested. "Though I don't really see the point."

"The point is," he said, calming himself, "I want you safe."

Obviously she couldn't argue with that. But as he escorted her to the elevator, she stated, "Maybe this isn't necessary. You're wanted on the set."

"I'm the director's boss."

And hers, he'd like to say, though pulling rank would only raise her hackles. Better to act the concerned investigative partner, which indeed he was. He couldn't fathom someone's need to threaten her very life. Obviously they'd stumbled onto something hot.

"Listen, Teague," she said at her office door. "Watch your own back. Okay?"

"Is that concern I hear in your lovely voice?"

"You bet. I don't want to be in this alone."

Her attempt at nonchalance wasn't a good one. He read the concern in her soft gray eyes. He couldn't believe it—she was the one who'd been threatened, but her worry was for him.

"Don't open up to anyone but me."

"How do I explain that?" she asked.

"Don't. Pretend you've gone home."

He threaded a hand through her shiny russet hair and planted a quick kiss on her forehead when he really wanted to take her in his arms and savor the very life force that had almost been taken away. Her surprise was reflected in her expression, and, as he moved away, her regret that he was leaving.

Teague smiled and sauntered away, reminding her, "Lock that door!"

The smile quickly disappeared as the gravity of the situation intruded. Someone was after Rae because she was—or they were—too close to the truth. They must have found something incriminating.

But what was so obvious that it would instigate the murderer into trying again, and in broad daylight with dozens of witnesses? Maybe the person panicked and had seized an opportunity not clearly thought out. Rae couldn't bring in the police, but she'd been correct. Too much explaining and they'd lose their obvious edge.

And he might be viewing the world on the wrong side of the bars yet again.

It was a miracle he could concentrate on the show, but somehow he managed to lose himself in the character of Dante Craven. The moment taping was over, he was off, not for his dressing room where he would get out of costume and makeup, but on his way to the executive floor to make sure a certain woman was all right.

Rae Magill was fast becoming an important part of his life. He only wondered if she would say the same about him.

RAE USED A FLASHLIGHT to check the street map of Queens. Security had had Wilona's address on file, but neither she nor Teague were familiar with the borough.

"Two more blocks and make a right," she said.

Rae kept her mind on the present and on the prospect that the nightmare would soon be over. She didn't want to think about her near miss with the taxi or about probable future attempts to silence her.

But about what? If only she knew for certain perhaps they could make some headway.

Teague made the required turn. "Where to now?"

"Left at the corner and then about halfway down the block, I guess."

They were in a true neighborhood—lots of small houses intermingled with the occasional larger apartment buildings. After circling a few times, Teague was even able to park on the next block.

Her gaze swept the addresses she could see dimly illuminated by porch lights. "It must be that one," she said, pointing to the outline of a small frame house that sat in the dark. "Do you think Wilona goes to bed this early?"

"Either that or she's already flown the coop."

Instinct made Rae believe in Wilona's innocence of Marguerite's actual murder. She was certain the woman was an unwitting accomplice. Wilona knew too much, that was for certain. Rae only hoped it wasn't enough to make her a second victim. Fear niggled at her insides as they approached the darkened house on foot.

"I'd say we're on a wild goose chase," Teague mused, even as he rang the bell insistently.

The dog next door barked furiously and another farther down sent up a like clamor.

He opened the screen and resorted to banging on the front door hard enough to shake the glass insets. No answer from inside.

Rae shifted nervously. "Teague, you don't think—"

But she never finished her morbid speculation before a strident voice cut through the night.

"Hey, what's all the racket about over there?" demanded a woman from the next porch. Hair in curlers, she hugged the edges of a bathrobe close to her neck. The barking dog stood next to her, its stance protective. "Knock it off or I'll call the cops."

"We're not here to start trouble." Rae kept her tone friendly and casual. "We're looking for Wilona Irwin. Have you seen her today?"

"Who wants to know?" the woman returned, the question laced with suspicion.

Before Rae could answer, Teague identified himself. "Teague Slaughter."

The woman's demeanor instantly changed. "Teague...yes, that voice, I recognize it!" She smoothed her hand over her curlers as if she were primping. "I can't believe I'm actually talking to Dante Craven! Wilona and I have been watching you since you came back to our show."

A fan. Thank God. "So you watched today's episode together?" Rae asked.

"Well, no, not today."

"We're worried about Wilona," Teague said in his best Dante voice. "She was supposed to be at the studio, but she never showed up. Since we were in the neighborhood, we decided to check on her. You know, to make certain everything was all right."

"My, Wilona never said you were so close." The woman was patting her curlers again. "She's not here. She went to her sister's Saturday, right after the funeral. What a tragedy about Faline—"

"Does her sister live nearby?" Teague interrupted.

"No, in New Jersey. Said she needed to get away for a while."

"Are you certain nothing was wrong?" Rae probed. "This doesn't sound like Wilona. Usually she's so full of energy. So committed."

"True. But she was real upset, you know."

"Maybe we could give her a call at her sister's to make her feel better," Teague suggested. "You wouldn't have the phone number, would you?"

"Sorry, she never gave it to me. All I know is Ellie lives in Easthaven, near Atlantic City."

"Ellie Irwin?"

"No. Her last name's . . . let's see. Sharpy. Shapey. Something like that."

"Oh, well, thanks anyway," Teague said. "If you see or hear from Wilona, tell her to get in touch with me as soon as possible."

"I'll do that, Dante, don't you worry."

Rae was continually amazed at how some fans couldn't keep soap stars separate from their characters.

On the way back to the car, she asked, "You don't really mean to give up so easily, do you?"

"Not by a long shot. We're heading for New Jersey to find Wilona."

"Do you even know where Easthaven is?"

"I know my way to Atlantic City."

"That's a good couple hours' drive," Rae complained.

"Got anything better to do?"

"Sleep."

"And you'll feel safe in your own bed tonight, right?"

He had a point. She really didn't want to be alone. And other than agreeing with his plan, what choice did she have? "Let's get going."

They stopped at a nearby gas station, and while Teague filled the tank, Rae bought a New Jersey map, found Easthaven and called directory assistance. Actually she called several times, each time trying a different version of the last name similar to those the neighbor had suggested. Finally, the operator found a number and an address for an Elinor Shapley.

"Got it." She waved the slip of paper with the information in triumph as she slid into the passenger seat. "We make a pretty good team."

"I've been thinking the same thing myself."

Teague's intimate tone lathered her insides with a warmth she'd rather not be feeling. Getting too close to the man was dangerous as she well knew. Then again, being too far away from him could prove potentially deadly as the afternoon's experience had shown. She was gratified when, without any more implied personal references, he drove out of the g station.

It wasn't until they were on the interstate that he renewed their discussion of motives. "So if Wilona isn't our murderer, why did she order those flowers? Why pretend to be my secretary?''

''Maybe someone convinced her to go along with what was supposed to be a joke.''

''A bad one for her, considering she must know the identity of the murderer.''

Having experienced firsthand how deadly even a little clue could be, Rae shivered. ''You think whoever killed Marguerite thought no one would figure out the lily of the valley connection?''

''That doesn't make sense,'' Teague countered. ''I'm certain the guilty one was trying to place the blame directly on me. And it worked.''

'''Whoever' spread the blame around. My glasses didn't get in the props area by themselves,'' she reminded him. ''Wilona must realize she's in danger. That's why she's hiding out. It's amazing she even came to the funeral.''

Sinking back into her seat, Rae allowed the last tiny bit of her energy to go on reserve. They drove in virtual silence, stopping only once to get coffee so Teague wouldn't fall asleep at the wheel. Rae had a cup as well and the caffeine jolted her mind into speculation about the things they'd found or learned over the past few days.

Marguerite's picture as a makeshift dart board. An altered long-range projection. Indication that Marguerite was seeing Saul Jacobi. A video that proved she was sleeping with Yale Gordon. The floral receipt in Marguerite's possession. Was it possible all these pieces fit together?

Arriving in Easthaven well after eleven, they pulled into a gas station that was about to lock up. Teague asked the owner for directions. Because the town was small, they didn't have far to go, but anticipation drained from Rae as quickly as it had swelled.

Elinor Shapley's house was as dark as Wilona's had been.

"I don't believe it," Rae moaned. "Do you think they've flown the coop together?"

"Maybe they're just out for the evening. Atlantic City's less than a half hour down the road."

"You think she'd be in the mood to gamble?"

"She'd be in the mood to be distracted," Teague said.

"Surely you're not thinking of going on to Atlantic City to look for them."

"I'm thinking we'll settle down right here and wait."

An hour's silence stretched between them. Exhaustion claimed Rae and she could hardly keep her eyes open. When Teague's large body jerked and he caught the steering wheel with both hands and yawned, she realized he'd been falling asleep.

"I think we'd better pack it in," Rae said.

"Did you notice any motels nearby?"

"I was talking about going back to Manhattan."

"I guess you can keep me awake long enough if you keep talking. But if we stay here overnight," he said reasonably, "we can check back early in the morning before going on to the city. Maybe we'll catch up with Wilona yet."

Rae was not thrilled, but neither did she want Teague to fall asleep at the wheel. She considered driving herself, then thought better of it. Alone in her fourth-floor walk-up with no security to speak of, she wouldn't get any sleep at all.

"We'll stay. We might as well try our luck with Wilona one more time," she agreed.

A low ramshackle building at the end of town provided their only option. The neon sign flashed, Ea t aven Mot in green, and below in smaller red letters, Va ncy. Teague left her in the car while he buzzed the office. Taking in the peeling paint and the bags of garbage piled up around the trash bins at one end of the building, Rae had visions of furry creatures already occupying the rooms. Perhaps sleeping on top of the bedding, wearing not only her clothes but her shoes, was a sterling idea. She was fond of all ten of her toes and wanted them accounted for in the morning.

A yellow pool of light flooded the stoop in front of the office. A wiry elderly man opened the door wearing a white T-shirt and suspendered pants. He shook his head and pointed, and obviously the two men struck a deal. A moment later, Teague was back in the car, key in hand.

"We got the bridal suite," he said, his voice filled with repressed laughter.

Rae started. "The what?"

"The only vacant room in the place," he amended.

The furry creatures were seeming more appealing than her proposed human roommate, but Rae didn't argue. She was too tired. *They* were too tired, she told herself, and in their mutual exhaustion, they would be oblivious to each other. She would be safe. Once they hit their separate beds, they would both be out in seconds.

Only there were no separate beds in the musty, dusty and far too intimate room.

One king-sized monstrosity—a water bed, yet—filled most of the "suite," effectively blocking any footpath to the bathroom. They would not only have to share the bed, but if the person on the outside needed the facility, he or she would have to crawl over the other to get to it. And on a water bed, they could hardly avoid personal contact.

Rae groaned inwardly.

What had she gotten herself into by agreeing to stay the night?

"You want to use the bathroom first or shall I?" Teague asked.

He was sucking back a smirk. She could see it trying to curl the edges of his lips. "You first," she said.

Waiting only until he closed the door behind him, she tested out the bed—and promptly rolled to the middle. This was worse than she'd thought—simply avoiding Teague as she slept was going to be near impossible! She could imagine herself on her side, hanging onto the edge of the bedframe all night!

Rae wasted moments fuming about how she'd gotten herself into such an untenable situation. She heard every movement Teague made in the bathroom, every squeak of a faucet and every spray of water. Eventually she calmed herself and vowed to make the best of things.

They were both adults, after all. They could control themselves.

With that reassurance in mind, she was crawling back to the edge of the bed when the door opened and Teague re-entered the room. His hair was damp and slicked back from his face. He reminded her of villain Dante Craven except he was wearing a marvelous sweater that was a waterfall of blues, each shade designed to enhance his eyes, which glowed as he stared down at her in the dim light.

"Time to trade places," he said, sucking back that smile once more.

With a smooth movement, Teague was straddling her, his body large and looming. The bed swayed. Rae's heart pounded. Her hormones raced. It took little imagination to picture him in that very same position, sans everything. The bed pulsated in an imitation of other rhythms. The heat between them grew.

"Ah..."

The helpless little cry Rae released mortified her, especially when, with seemingly no effort, Teague rolled over completely and landed on her other side without ever having actually touched her. The bed undulated vigorously, the lapping water gurgling at her in inanimate laughter. She burned, both with embarrassment and with a desire that was thoroughly unacceptable.

And apparently inevitable.

"Don't wait up," she muttered as she heaved herself over the padded frame.

The effect was that of a catapult, and she practically flew into the bathroom where she slammed the door behind her. She swore she heard a choked sound coming from the other side. The damnable man was laughing at her!

Now what?

How long could she stall washing her hands and face? More important, how could she fall asleep next to a man who made her pulse with sexual vibrations?

A bath—that always made her sleepy. But the moment she got a gander at the tub, Rae knew she wasn't going to sink against the filthy surface. And there were no cleaning tools to be found. But warm water would relax her, she was certain of it. A shower would have to do. Locking the door, she undressed quickly, hanging each item of her professional uniform on the single hook provided. She stripped off her pantyhose only to slip each foot back into a shoe before her toes could touch the grimy carpeting.

And when it came to stepping into the tub under the fitful shower spray, she couldn't bear to remove her shoes. She tried not to think about how quickly that very expensive kidskin would be ruined. Soaping and rinsing, letting the warmth of the water soothe her, Rae felt infinitely better by the time she left the tub. Eyes heavy, she patted herself dry and redressed in everything but suit jacket and pantyhose.

Then, after turning off the light, she carefully opened the door to the now darkened bedroom and moved cautiously toward the bed.

Her shoes made squishing sounds loud enough to wake the dead, but Rae was unwilling to remove them until she gripped the bedframe and slid onto the padded side. Ears straining, she listened to Teague's even breathing but couldn't decide whether or not he was asleep. She rolled onto the moving mattress carefully, never giving up her hold until she was certain that she could remain in that position without a death grip on the bedframe. As she let go and snuggled down into the covering, her sigh of relief was audible.

A corresponding snort preceded a sharp movement from the bed's other occupant. As Teague rolled, so did she, right into the middle of the bed, her shoulder and thigh smack up against his.

"Pleasant dreams," he whispered, laughter heavy in his words.

And Rae knew then she wouldn't have any dreams at all—fantasies, perhaps—because she wasn't going to get one wink of sleep lying close enough to Teague Slaughter to taste him!

Chapter Ten

Teague prayed for morning like nothing he'd ever wished for. After a short fitful sleep, he'd awakened to find Rae not only curled against him, but with a bare thigh thrown over his legs and an arm wound across his chest.

God help him, he was only a mere mortal, no matter his reputation. He quickened with Rae's every movement and each little sleepy sigh. This was torture, downright and damnable, and he guessed he deserved a dose for being amused at her expense the night before. Well, now it was his turn to suffer.

He wanted nothing more than to take Rae up on her unconscious offer and make love to her as her body was urging him to do. But he wouldn't, not when she would only accuse him of taking advantage of her afterward. She wanted him physically—he was very aware of that—just as he knew she didn't want him mentally. Some unspoken problem lay between them. He desired all of her with no regrets to follow.

She stirred as morning's first light poked through the dingy curtains.

"Mmm."

The murmur vibrated through Teague, stirring him to more urgent life. He gritted his teeth and closed his eyes, deepened his breathing, pretended sleep.

Rae moved her hand across his chest and her thigh climbed higher.

Torture. Sheer torture.

Still half-asleep, she rubbed against him, shifted and stretched with a serious early morning yawn. Then, as if realizing her close proximity to him, she practically jumped to the other side of the bed...not that Teague was laughing this time.

"Great!" she muttered softly. Then, "Teague? Are you awake?"

"Huh?" He feigned his own awakening, opening one eye to peer out at her. He yawned, long and loud, for effect. "It's morning already?"

She was already half off the bed, undoubtedly unaware of the way her slim, prim skirt rode up her thighs and molded her buttocks.

Teague groaned.

"What?" she asked suspiciously.

He couldn't resist. "I'm just so stiff...like something was parked on top of me all night."

"Waterbeds are overrated," she mumbled, quickly disappearing into the bathroom, no doubt to retrieve her composure in addition to her pantyhose.

He stretched out across the bed and peered over her side. Her shoes lay there...wet. Like she'd been out in the rain. Then he remembered the squishing sound he'd heard when she'd stumbled out of the bathroom in the dark. He didn't have to be a genius to realize what she'd done.

The image of Rae in the shower, naked but for a pair of black high heels, was enough to make him nuts. He lunged off the bed, paced the small area between it and the outside door, and prayed for the second time in one day.

Prayed for her to hurry so they could get the hell out of there! When he'd suggested staying the night, he hadn't known how big a sacrifice he'd be making.

At least the torture had been worth his while, he learned a quarter of an hour later when he banged at Elinor Shapley's front door a second time. A too-thin version of Wilona Irwin answered promptly. Through horn-rimmed glasses exactly like her sister's, she peered out suspiciously from the safe side of the screen door.

"Do I know you?"

"Only if you watch 'Rivals,'" Teague said smoothly. "We're looking for Wilona. May we come in?"

He had the screen door open before she could protest. He pushed Rae inside, then followed.

"Well make yourself at home, for Pete's sake," Ellie muttered darkly as they entered the old-fashioned, slightly dusty living room. Its owner was wearing an equally old-fashioned flower-print dust coat. "I'll fetch my sister." She was barely in the hall before yelling, "Wilona, you've got company!"

"She's here!" Rae whispered. "Now we'll get somewhere!"

"If we can trick her into talking," Teague returned in an equally low tone.

Ellie came back into the room, Wilona shuffling behind her. The fan-club president stopped dead in the doorway. "Mr. Slaughter, Miss Magill." Her face drained of color but for the two bright pink spots high on her cheeks. She stared at them wide-eyed. "You're the last people in the world I expected to see here."

"Who were you expecting?" Rae asked.

"No one."

"You're certain of that?" Teague wanted to jolt her into an admission. "Not even someone making a flower delivery?"

The woman's mouth opened and closed like a gaping fish and without preamble, she broke down in heart-wrenching sobs. Whatever he'd expected, it hadn't been this intense a reaction.

"It's all my fault," Wilona cried.

"Now, sister, you know that's not true." Ellie put her arm around the other woman's shoulders.

"Yes, it is. If it weren't for me, Marguerite Lemond would still be alive!"

A confession? Teague hadn't actually believed the odd woman was capable of murder.

"Then you admit you killed Marguerite?" he asked.

"Killed? No. No! Of course not. But I should have stopped her." Taking a tissue from her dust coat, identical to her sister's but for the color, she blew loudly. "Marguerite was so worried about losing her job and all when she asked me to help with that stupid publicity stunt. I could hardly refuse, now could I?"

"Sister does have such a sense of responsibility," Ellie confirmed. "She raised me when Mama took ill."

"Publicity?" Rae echoed belatedly. "What are you talking about?"

"Marguerite had this crazy idea to save her job—"

"But her job was never in jeopardy," Rae said.

"You mean her death was for nothing?" Wilona wailed even harder.

"Now, sister, I've told you over and over it's not your fault," Ellie said.

"Please, sit down and compose yourself."

Teague was acting, hiding his impatience. They had to keep Wilona Irwin calm if they were going to get the whole truth from her. He helped her to the couch where she plunked down like a sack of potatoes with all the starch drained from her. Ellie set herself next to Wilona and put a protective arm around her sister's shoulders. The fan-club president blew her nose hard and visibly got herself under control.

"Now, why don't you tell us everything," Teague urged, "and start from the beginning."

"A–all right. Marguerite was c–convinced that Faline Devereux was supposed to d–die after being in a coma for a while."

"Did she explain why she didn't believe us when we told her differently?" Rae asked gently.

Wilona shook her head. "She insisted everyone was l–lying to her, that she'd gotten her information from an impeccable source, and s–so s–she . . ."

The woman's voice faded off and she stared down at the crumpled tissues in her hand. Teague felt sorry for her. Under Marguerite's warped influence, she'd gotten herself into something darker than she'd ever bargained for.

"Marguerite what?" he asked, sounding more patient than he was feeling. "Go on, please."

Her expression stricken, Wilona looked up at him. "She said she wasn't going to take it lying down. She was going to fight for her role and for the show she made into the hottest daytime soap on television."

Teague didn't bother to correct her. At one time "Rivals" had been hot, but the show had slowly sunk nearly into oblivion the past few years. That's why Yale Gordon had felt it so necessary to get The Kiss of Death back.

"You referred to her getting publicity," Rae reminded Wilona. "Exactly what are we talking about?"

"The scene where Dante drugged Faline." The fan-club president swallowed hard. "Marguerite thought if she really were drugged—p–poisoned, actually—that there would be so much publicity the ratings would soar and all her old fans would rally around her."

Teague met Rae's gaze which reflected his own shock. "You mean she got some crazy idea to poison herself?" he managed to ask.

Wilona sniffed into her tissue and mumbled, "She figured if she got enough publicity and support from her fans, the network wouldn't get rid of her."

"How is a dead woman supposed to reap the benefits of a killer publicity stunt?" Rae demanded.

"That's just it. She wasn't supposed to be dead."

"She was supposed to recover," Ellie piped up. Teague was wondering if she'd been in on the scam, as well, when she volunteered, "If only I had known what Miss Lemond was asking Wilona to do, I could have stopped it."

Wilona started crying again. "I don't understand what went wrong."

Determined to get the entire story out of her before she became a basket case once more, Teague prompted her. "So Marguerite convinced you to place the lily of the valley order for her?"

"Well, she couldn't very well have done it herself," Wilona said defensively. "She's so famous, she would have been recognized."

"And you saw nothing wrong with helping her do something so dangerous?" Rae asked.

"She told me she knew what she was doing, that she would only put enough of the poisoned water into the drink bottle to make herself ill. I never thought she would misjudge how much to use." Wilona sobbed, "I—I never thought she would d–die."

"And what about using my name to send the flowers?" Teague asked. "Even if Marguerite had lived, I would have been charged with attempted murder and if found guilty, would have gone to prison."

Any remaining color drained from Wilona's face and she fell back against the cushions. "I never thought about that at all!" she wailed.

"Well, it's about time you did, isn't it?" Teague demanded, barely holding his temper in check. "Where do you get off playing with people's lives . . . ?"

A tight grip and sharp nails on his upper arm made him stop his tirade. Rae's expression was concerned and she was trying to convey a silent message to him. She wanted him to cool it, to let her take over.

"Marguerite inadvertently committed suicide," she said, and Teague could hear the note of relief in her voice that echoed his own. They were off the hook! "She may have taken her own life, but we will have to call the authorities and let them handle the situation as they see fit," Rae cautioned.

"I know," Wilona said. "I should have done it myself. I'm so ashamed I let the two of you be put under suspicion."

"Sister wanted to go to the police, but she was afraid. No one in our family has ever been in jail before."

"I'm sure that won't happen."

Rae looked from the two women to Teague for confirmation.

He didn't say a word. How could he when he'd done hard time for a crime he'd never committed? As far as he was concerned, there were no guarantees of justice when dealing with the legal system.

A sobbing Wilona said, "Don't try to soften the blow, please. I know I'm going to be arrested. It's no use pretending otherwise. I guess you're going to make me go back with you to face the music."

She appeared such a pitiful shell of her former self that Teague couldn't do it. "We're not the authorities, Wilona. We'll tell Lieutenant Franklin everything. In the meantime, you get yourself together and turn yourself in before he comes looking for you with a warrant. Cooperation should count in your favor."

Should. But would it?

Cooperate, his court-appointed lawyer had told him. *You're a seventeen-year-old kid, a minor, and this is your first serious offense. The judge will go easy on you.*

But his lawyer had been wrong. The judge hadn't wanted his cooperation. The judge had wanted him to lie, to admit to things he hadn't done. Old memories continued to haunt Teague as he and Rae drove back to the city where he would take the responsibility of dealing with Franklin first thing, no matter his own history.

Twenty years before, a member of an opposing gang had almost died after a fight in a back alley. He'd been blamed because he'd been the one to find the kid lying in his own blood, his gut split open by a knife. He'd been holding Henry Ortega, trying to stop the bleeding, trying to keep his archenemy from dying, when the police had arrived.

In gratitude for his worthless life, Henry had gotten his revenge for a dozen petty high-school skirmishes between the Latin Lords and the Polish Princes by naming Theodore Slavensky as his attacker. And the judge who'd passed sentence had received another commendation for curbing gang violence, which had been on the rise in Chicago even in those days.

Teague only hoped Wilona wouldn't be railroaded into a jail cell as easily as he had been. Not when the blame rested on a dead woman's insecurities.

"You're so quiet," Rae said as they approached the city limits. "What are you thinking about?"

If he told her, she would be revolted, would never want him to touch her again. And if he were smart, he wouldn't anyway. If he had any brains, he'd stay the hell away from Straight Arrow Magill.

He glanced at her. The way she was staring at him made his stomach tighten. Her expression held an intimacy he'd never before had the pleasure of seeing. In the past days, something had changed for Rae as well as for him, and Teague knew he wouldn't pass up the opportunity to take whatever she was willing to give him.

Even if she despised him for it afterward.

Even if he hated himself.

And maybe that meant he didn't have any smarts at all.

Arriving at the CBC building, they went straight up to the executive floor where Teague intended to call

Lieutenant Franklin first thing. He wanted the truth off his chest and the threat of exposure off his back.

"There you are," June Chin said the moment they stepped out of the elevator. Her slender black brows shot up as her glance turned from him to Rae. "Everyone has been looking for you, from Yale Gordon to—"

"Later," he said, cutting her off. He led the way into his office. "Close the door, would you?" he asked Rae. "I don't want rumors flying before the authorities have time to act on this."

Rae chuckled. "Plenty of rumors are going to be flying anyway. Did you see that look June gave us because we came in late and were together?"

Teague's hand froze on the telephone receiver. "Does what she thinks bother you?"

She shrugged. "Not particularly."

Relieved to hear it, he made the call.

Luckily Lieutenant Franklin was in his office and picked up the phone immediately. Steeling himself against the cop's reaction, Teague related every detail of his and Rae's investigation that led to Wilona and her confession. Sat silent while Franklin berated him for taking police matters into his own hands. Watched Rae pace and twist her fingers together.

Teague moved the receiver from his ear slightly as Franklin continued to shout at him. "I'm damned ticked two private citizens put their lives in danger instead of leaving the investigation to the professionals!"

Teague couldn't tell Franklin he'd left things up to the professionals once before and had regretted it for an eighteen-month enforced vacation with hardened criminals.

"I guess you'll just have to be ticked, then. But Rae Magill and I are off the hook."

"If Wilona Irwin backs your story."

"She will."

Teague had no doubts in that department. Wilona had been carrying around a load of guilt. She'd be glad to rid herself of the burden to the proper authorities. He only hoped Franklin had plenty of tissues on hand. The woman was a regular waterworks.

"Get back to me after you talk to your new witness, Lieutenant," Teague said. "You might want to give her a chance to come in herself."

Though from personal experience, he doubted the cop would do any such thing. He and his men would be all over Ellie's place like ticks on a dog.

He'd no sooner hung up than Rae attacked. "So what's the scoop?"

"He maybe believes us."

"He's *got* to believe us. Rather Wilona."

Rae's gray eyes looked like molten steel when she was angry, Teague thought. He kind of liked the heat and wondered if that's the way she'd look under him in bed.

"Franklin seems to think she might get cold feet," he said.

"Rinaldo can identify her," Rae reminded him. "And Franklin already knows it from his visit to Blooming Creations. Wilona will have to talk. In the meantime, we wait some more."

"You have plenty to do to keep that pretty head of yours occupied."

"Pretty?" She seemed startled. And suspicious. "I've been hearing other, less flattering descriptions from you in the past few days."

"I think you're more than pretty," Teague said, rising. He ran a thumb along her hairline and resisted the temptation to tangle his fingers in the shiny russet. "How about if I tell you how much tonight, over a late supper."

"After taping?" Her gaze didn't leave his for a second. "I'm not sure I want to hear any such thing."

About to kiss her, Teague remembered the way his morning had started and backed off. "Sometimes we have to suffer and hear the truth even when we don't want to."

TEAGUE'S FLATTERING statement kept echoing through Rae's head as she worked away morning and afternoon in her office. Though he'd been teasing her, there'd been an underlying seriousness to his words. He wanted her, but for what? Well, she knew the simple answer to that. She guessed what she really wanted to know was how much and for how long.

And she wondered how she could have forgotten Carol Flynn. Her friend had been so distraught, so bitter, so anti-Teague Slaughter when she'd been fired that Rae had taken on the other writer's feelings as her own. But that was before she'd even met Teague, no less gotten to know him. And shouldn't her own personally formed opinion count more than one she'd gleaned secondhand?

Again she'd experienced his kindness and consideration for someone else when Wilona had been half-hysterical. He hadn't insisted on the woman's returning to the city with them but had given her the chance to turn herself in. Those hadn't been the actions of an unconscionable man. She wished she could talk to Carol now, probe deeper into the other woman's story, but her friend was in L.A. and virtually impossible to reach.

Rae forced her concentration back on her work and kept plugging at the dialogue until early evening. Satisfied that she wouldn't get more accomplished that day, Rae wandered down to the studio where taping was in progress. She stood at the edge of a set not in use where other actors waited.

"Come to watch?" Christine whispered.

"Why not? Writing can be lonely."

Besides, she was hoping to get a few minutes with Teague to make plans. Unfortunately he was the central character in the scene being taped, so all she could do was watch him stalk around the set in character—he looked magnificent in a deep blue satin shirt—and wonder how the evening would end. A thrill shot through her at the speculation. There was something about Dante Craven—villain or not—that got to a woman.

"Acting can be pretty lonely, too, if you don't have real friends," Christine was saying. "What about that lunch I mentioned? Think you can squeeze it into your schedule next week?"

"I'm getting caught up. Sure," Rae agreed. "Maybe toward the middle of the week. So how do you feel about your new story line?"

"All right. Better than I did at first. I guess the character switch works," Christine admitted. "Who killed Faline, anyway?"

"Not I," Quenie muttered, drawing closer as she prepared to make an entrance.

"We haven't decided yet," Rae said. "Maybe Faline will have committed suicide."

"That would be a terrible waste of dramatic interplay." Addison stated as he walked toward the set.

And not necessarily the truth.

Rae had assumed everything was falling into place so neatly. The revisions, the relationship with Teague, the solution to Marguerite's death . . .

She thought hard about the last. About a woman so desperate to keep what she had that she'd mistakenly committed suicide.

Or had she?

Despite Wilona's story, something had been bothering Rae: the solution was too easy. She and Teague had been so eager to accept an end to the uncertainty, so eager to be off the hook, that they hadn't really thought it through.

Of all the things they'd learned surrounding Marguerite's death, most could be explained away as coincidence, but not the long-range projection. Someone had tampered with the story line so that Marguerite would suffer, maybe do something desperate. Of course, that didn't make the person a murderer. And perhaps the sequence of events had happened exactly as Wilona claimed.

Then why had someone tried to kill *her?* Rae wondered.

Until that very moment, she'd forgotten about her close encounter with a taxi. Had forgotten the feel of those hands on her back . . .

Pushing her . . .

"All right, boys and girls, good job. You deserve a break today," came Jacobi's voice over the intercom. "Take five."

Her troubled thoughts must have been written on her face, because when Teague found her, the first thing out of his mouth was, "What's wrong? Franklin hasn't been after you, has he?"

"No. Nothing's wrong. I haven't heard a peep from the Lieutenant. I'm tired, I guess."

Rae didn't want to worry Teague at the moment. She could be way off base. She could have imagined the hands on her back. Why take a chance on ruining not only his mood but his evening's performance? And, more important, their evening together. This discussion could wait until later. Much later.

"You want to cancel dinner?" he asked.

She could tell he didn't like that idea. Good. Feeling someone staring, she glanced over her shoulder. Bo, Christine and Jacobi stood nearby, pretending for all the world like they weren't interested.

"Actually, I was looking for you to make plans. My brain is fried already. I could go home and relax." She was making this up as she went along. She hadn't had anything specific in mind when she'd wandered down to the set but watching. Now she was too jumpy. "When you're done shooting, call me and I can—"

"I'll come pick you up," he interrupted. "Or if you'd rather, I could bring dinner and we can relax together. How do you feel about Chinese?"

"Sounds like a great idea."

The relaxing part, that was. She could take or leave the Chinese. Eating in the intimacy of her apartment wasn't as safe as a public restaurant.

Part of her was counting on that.

"I'd better get back," Teague said, indicating his set, his eyes on her lips like he wanted to do something about the silly grin plastered there.

"I'll be waiting."

Rae watched him stroll away, already becoming his character. He picked up a copy of the script and silently went over his next scene, and she left not only the studio but the building. Walking home along half-deserted streets, all she could think about was being alone with Teague Slaughter with a new if unspoken understanding between them. But her romantic fantasies seemed foolish when she got the creepy feeling that someone was invading her solitude.

That someone was following her!

She twirled, all movement around her a blur. The few other people on the street seemed intent on their own purposes. No one was paying her any mind. Her gaze shifted quickly to the nearby buildings. A door slowly closed behind the person who had entered. Someone she knew?

Suddenly the tautness that held her in its grip released as Rae realized she was being foolish. It was over, she told herself. Over. Marguerite had accidently committed suicide. No murderer was on the loose fearing discovery. Even so, she signaled a taxi and stared out through the rear window all the way home. And she was still looking around as she entered her building. Foolish, she chanted as she raced up the stairs, slowing only at the landing beneath her own.

And then came the moment she didn't feel so very ridiculous. Fear replaced her self-deprecation the moment her feet hit her fourth-floor landing. The moment she noticed her apartment door was cracked open.

Heart pounding, Rae stood frozen for a moment. Who had managed to open her door? And why? Was the person still inside?

The sensible part of her told her to run as fast as her legs would carry her back down the stairs. To find a phone and call the police. To let the professionals take care of this. But if someone were inside, he or she would have a chance to get away. She might never know who broke into her apartment. She might never know if Marguerite's death had been a suicide or not.

Somehow, she didn't think this break-in was a co-incidence.

She hefted the keyring in her hand and opened the small leather flap covering her mini-canister of tear gas. If someone were inside, she would be prepared!

Cautiously she reached out and pushed open the door without drawing closer. The kitchen was empty and as neat as she'd left it. No sign of an intruder. Slipping out of her heels, she entered on stockinged feet and listened intently. No untoward sounds. She slid down the hall. No one in the bedroom. She approached the living area.

A single lamp illuminated the room, and her eyes widened in shock. But even as she took in the superficial damage, the mess around her work area, she knew.

A quick search proved her correct: the long-range projection—the story-line narrative in which Faline's fate had been changed by another hand—was gone!

Chapter Eleven

"Are you certain you're all right?" Teague demanded as he burst into Rae's kitchen followed by Lieutenant Franklin. He took her in his arms and gave her a comforting squeeze.

"Now I am. Yes."

Her nerves had unraveled inch by inch as she'd waited for Teague to arrive. Luckily he'd been taping his last scene of the show when she'd placed the call. He, in turn, had alerted the authorities. Thank God he'd arrived before she'd fallen apart. The break-in was as much an unconscionable violation as an attack on her person. But Teague's very touch was soothing, righting her upside-down emotions.

Franklin was checking the doorframe. "How did the thief get in?"

"Through that door."

His dark brows shot up. "But there's no damage, no signs of forced entry."

"Whoever it was must have used my own keys." Rae flushed when she admitted, "I always keep a spare set in my desk at work. I'm afraid other people know about it because I had to use them once several weeks ago when I locked myself out. A messenger from the network delivered the set to me."

The policeman's look told her what he thought of that idea, though he didn't say anything. He merely locked the door and checked the inside bolts.

Teague let go of her and headed for the other room. "What a mess."

"The thief wasn't neat," Rae agreed, "but at least there's no permanent damage. The altered story line was obviously the target of the search."

"Are you certain?" Franklin asked. "Did you check your files carefully?"

"Both paper and computer files. I even checked my backup disks. As far as I can tell, nothing else is missing."

Franklin was making notes even as his piercing light eyes swept over the mess. "You're sure you brought this so-called long-range projection home?"

"You don't believe me?" Rae asked, her temper rising now that her nerves had steadied. "Who did all this, then? Me? You think I set up some fake robbery—for what purpose? So I could destroy Wilona Irwin's story?"

From her brief phone conversation with Teague, she knew the fan-club president had turned herself in and had confirmed their story to Franklin. Now that story was in question.

"You have a point." The lieutenant was unruffled by her anger. "And I never said I doubted you. I'm just trying to be thorough. For example, how would anyone know you had this altered projection?"

"I—I hadn't even thought of that." She remembered the feel of hands on her back, pushing her in the path of a runaway taxi. "Someone knew I was involved, though, and that I was trying to get at the truth.''

"Wilona knew," Teague said.

But Rae was certain Wilona hadn't tried to kill her. "Someone else. The person who'd been watching me. That person"—she didn't say murderer—"must have searched Marguerite's dressing room for the projection, couldn't find it, and assumed I had."

Throughout her speculation, Franklin had been attentive if openly disapproving. "Miss Magill, I'm going to give you the same good advice I offered your cohort here. Stop putting your nose where it doesn't belong. Amateur detectives have a way of getting in hot water. Stop while you still have the opportunity."

He meant stop before she ended up dead like Marguerite!

He didn't have to say that Wilona's story was suspect, that she'd jumped to the wrong conclusion, that Marguerite hadn't committed accidental suicide, after all . . . and that the murderer was still on the loose. Rae was ahead of him. Hadn't she already begun questioning the facts herself earlier? And to come home to proof . . .

If Franklin thought she was going to give up now, he had another think coming!

Rae's back was up—she was mad and sure as hell going to do something about it—but she didn't have the chance to tell the detective what she thought of his advice.

His evidence technician chose that moment to arrive. He immediately got busy dusting for fingerprints. Rae figured he was wasting his time. The murderer was too clever not to have worn gloves. Indeed, the only prints the technician found matched the ones at the ends of her own fingers!

Relieved when the two men left, Rae told herself that now she could settle down.

"I wondered what I'd found that would make the murderer come after me," she said to Teague as she set her anti-burglar bar in place. "Now I know."

"Maybe."

His skeptical tone made her snap, "The projection is missing! What more proof do you need?"

Intending to straighten up the mess, she headed for the living room. He was right on her heels, breathing down her neck.

"You had something else, remember—another piece of physical evidence."

She stopped short and reeled when he whomped into her. "What?" she asked as he steadied her.

"The videotape. It's at my place, remember?"

"But that would mean...you suspect Yale Gordon?"

"He's one of the few people who had a long-range projection," Teague reminded her.

"He wouldn't have known about the tape." She freed herself and began picking up the papers strewn across the floor. "At least not that I supposedly had it. No, someone else left it to throw us off the track by implicating him."

"You've got a point. It's too bad our killer didn't wait until Wilona's confession became public knowledge." Teague picked up a couple of books that had landed on the floor. "He or she might have gotten away with murder."

"Now we know someone 'helped' Marguerite get the publicity she so desperately wanted."

"And you're in danger," he stated. "You can't stay here tonight."

She stacked the papers on her desk. "Of course I can stay here. This is my apartment."

"And the murderer already got in once with the set of keys you so carelessly provided."

Certain he meant stupidly, she spoke through gritted teeth. "So I'll get the locks changed first thing in the morning."

Teague was looming over her again, but Rae ignored the sexual tension that snapped like a rubber band between them. She was far too irritated. She'd had enough of being scared and was annoyed of being told what to do. But, as usual, Teague thought he was in charge.

"New locks in the morning won't help you tonight. You're staying at my place," he insisted.

"The hell I am!" Now her temper really was up. "I'm staying right here. I have my burglar bolt, and if I have to, I can barricade the door with every movable object in the place. Satisfied?"

"Not by a long shot. Look, you're not safe here. Not alone, anyway. Admit it. And that couch doesn't look so comfortable," he complained.

Not alone? "Well, you're not sleeping on my couch, and don't get any ideas about sharing my bed, either."

His voice lowered into a Dante Craven imitation. "You didn't object to sharing last night."

She fought the thrill that shot down to her toes and drew herself up to her full height. "Last night I didn't have a choice."

"Last night you didn't have steel for a spine."

That did it! The thrill gone, she punched him in the chest with a finger. "Another thing. I don't appreciate your so-called compliments on my finer points."

"Well, I don't appreciate your looking at me like I crawled out of the sewer," he returned with equal heat. "Now would you be sensible and come home with me? My apartment has an extra bedroom and bed."

"Good for your apartment." She started to turn away and he gripped her upper arm in a manner that seemed to be second nature to him. "Why don't you just go on back there," she suggested. "Now."

"Not until you're ready to come with me!"

"Guess what?" She wrested her arm free. "I'm not going anywhere!"

They were at a standoff. Teague looked as if he were controlling himself with difficulty. As if he were ready to throw her over his shoulder and carry her out of the place whether she would or no.

Well, let him try!

"You won't come with me?"

"No."

"Fine."

"Fine!"

Teague stalked to the kitchen and undid the bar. "Don't forget to barricade yourself."

"I won't!"

Rae slammed the door behind him and immediately secured it. For good measure, she hooked a chair under the handle. Only when she stood there staring at the thing, wondering if she should drag the table over in addition, did she realize how ridiculous she was being.

And had been with Teague.

And he with her.

Obviously he cared about her safety or he wouldn't have been so impossible. So why hadn't he told her? Why did he have to be such a jerk, ordering her around instead of holding her in his arms and sweet-talking her the way he should have.

As upset as she was by the break-in, Rae didn't look forward to sleeping alone, that was for certain, but Teague hadn't given her much choice. She disliked taking orders professionally, but in her personal life she had a choice.

Readying herself for bed, she tried to put all negative thoughts from mind. She was safe for the moment. No one could get through that door now. No one could get to her.

She slid into bed.

Alone.

She was tense, her stomach knotted. She jumped at every sound, and there were plenty of noises in an old building. Creaks...groans...Rae moaned and flipped over on her stomach, then covered her head with a pillow. She couldn't wait for morning to come.

When it did, she jerked awake and shot straight up, heart pounding, until she realized the intrusive sound that had shattered her nerves was nothing more than her electronic alarm. A slam of her hand took care of the obnoxious buzz and she rose to get ready for work.

She left the apartment almost an hour later, still jittery, aware of every sound, every movement, every influence on her immediate environment. Therefore, she could hardly miss the gold Mercedes parked at the curb next to the fireplug.

Frowning, she drew closer. Had Teague forgotten about his car and taken a taxi home? She peered inside. His sweater bunched, his gold-tipped mane of hair rumpled, he was fast asleep in the reclined driver's seat.

"Jerk," she muttered, her voice soft and filled with reluctant affection.

She tapped at the glass. He was instantly awake if completely disoriented. His window rolled down smoothly and silently. He was frowning at her as if he'd never seen her before.

"Did you forget where you were?" she asked.

"Hmm, I never made it home? Man, I must have been tired when I left last night."

He didn't sound confused, only like he was trying to. She responded with a modicum of sarcasm.

"Our argument wore you out so much that you fell asleep the instant you touched down, right?"

He gave her an irritated scowl, to which she smiled prettily.

"All right, so I staked out your place," he grumbled. "What of it?"

"It was a sweet thing to do," Rae admitted. "Ridiculous, too." Especially since she hadn't known she had his protection and had tossed and turned most of the night when she could have relaxed.

"Get in," he ordered, then changed his tone to add, "please."

Grinning, Rae circled the car and slid in beside him. She leaned over and, catching him by surprise, planted a quick kiss on his beard-stubbled cheek. He wasn't so confused that he didn't try to take immediate advantage. His hands snaked out to halt her retreat.

"Not so fast," he growled.

She was looking longingly at his lips when she said, "We're going to be late for work."

"I know the boss."

"Drive."

He raised a single brow and asked, "Is that an order?"

"A reluctant request."

A grin twitched his lips as he started the engine. "We're going to be late anyway. I can't walk into the studio looking like a depraved lunatic. I've worn this sweater the last two days in a row."

"Maybe you'd better drop me off on your way home," Rae said, laughing. "If we come in together two days in a row, tongues will wag for sure."

Teague's good humor evaporated instantly and Rae's laughter died in her throat. As he drove, his silence discomfited her, but she couldn't think of a way to repair the damage. As a matter of fact, she could hardly believe she'd hurt the feelings of a man who was used to stepping on other people to get where he was in the industry.

Then she reminded herself that had been Carol's opinion, not hers. One day she would have to ask Teague his side of that old story.

Pulling up to the corner a short block down from the CBC building, Teague broke his silence. "You probably should get out here. I wouldn't want anyone to see you leaving my car and getting ideas."

Feeling like a numbskull, Rae opened the door but didn't immediately alight. "Teague, thanks."

"No problem," he said, ignoring the horns honking behind him. "The studio was on the way home."

"Not the ride." She touched his arm so he would look at her. His muscles were tight with tension. "For staying to protect me, even after I was so rude to you.

You know, we never did have that dinner. I'd like a raincheck if you would.''

He softened a little under her hand, though he remained straight-faced. "You've got it. See you later."

Rae slid out of the car and watched him pull the Mercedes into the traffic pattern, then set off for the next block and the CBC building. As she approached, she realized a couple of reporters waited outside. Until now she'd avoided the press, but one of the women in the small knot knew her and wouldn't let her get away.

"Rae," the television reporter said. "I hear there's a break in the mystery surrounding Marguerite Lemond's death. Is it possible she wasn't murdered?"

Eyeing the microphone shoved in her face, aware of one man trying to record her and another taking notes, Rae phrased her answer carefully. "Lieutenant Charlie Franklin is handling the investigation. He can update you on the status of the case."

"But sources tell me you know what happened."

"I'm sorry," she said with as natural a smile as she could manage, "but your sources are wrong."

Rae swept into the building and the doorman prevented the reporters from following. If only she did know what happened, she wouldn't have to mistrust practically everyone she set eyes on throughout her workday.

She had one tough time. Beyond busy. Her attention was split in far too many directions—something she could usually handle, she admitted—but not on a couple of hours of sleep following an emotional trauma. Between calling her associate writers and checking on their progress with the following week's scripts and finishing revisions for Friday, she had to tend to demands coming from Yale Gordon. He wanted some scenes changed for the day's shooting, specifically to heat up the suspicion on Beatrice Vanderlinde.

She wondered what had prompted that and whether or not she should be suspicious of his motives.

But stuck in the office all day with more work than she could handle, she didn't have time to think about a murder any more than she did about her relationship with Teague. At least not until early afternoon when she delivered the revised scenes, first leaving one on Gordon's desk, then bringing the others to the studio personally only moments before the final walkthrough preceding dress rehearsal.

At this rate, she figured they were never going to gain those two shooting days by the following Friday as Teague had demanded. Una took a pile of changes from her and started handing them out to the cast and crew on the floor. Not seeing Teague at the moment, Rae headed for studio control and the soap's director.

Christine Dellamorte was quietly talking to Saul Jacobi when Rae entered. Again, she had the fleeting impression that the two were more than co-workers, perhaps more than personal friends. But Jacobi had been seeing Marguerite, hadn't he? At least that's what they'd assumed from the cryptic note about the tickets.

"Christine, what are you doing here?" Rae asked. "I thought this was your day off." Normally actors were only required to work three of five days unless they were shooting more than one episode a day as they would be doing the following week.

Christine smiled and moved away from Jacobi. "I couldn't stay away. I wanted to find out what would happen next since things seem to be changing by the hour."

"That's what you call real dedication," the director said, taking his copy from Rae.

"That's what I call a star." Rae turned to see Yale Gordon in the doorway. He was beaming at Christine. Then he turned his attention to Rae. "I just went over those changes. Good job."

"All right, boys and girls," Jacobi was saying over the intercom. "Let's get moving. We're an hour behind schedule."

"And I'd better get moving, too," Rae said.

"I think you ought to stay in case we have any last-minute problems," the network representative told her.

Though she had plenty of work to get back to, she didn't object. Gordon was the boss. So she sat and watched while cameras tracked actors going over new lines. But now that Teague was on the studio floor waiting for an entrance, she kept getting distracted watching him.

And wondering what it would be like being made love to by a man with split personalities. Would he be Teague one minute, Dante the next? The thought shot goose bumps down to her toes.

"Nigel, you mustn't think the worst of me, no matter what you learn," Quenie was saying from the studio floor. "Sometimes we do things against our better nature because we have no choice."

"My dear Beatrice," Addison said, patting her shoulder. "I believe in you and I'll always be by your side, no matter—"

"Matter?" Quenie shrieked, coming out of character and facing the control-room window. "There's something the matter with this script."

Teague moved closer to the set to ask, "What's the problem, Quenie?"

She turned to him and waved the pages in his face. "From this scene, I gather Beatrice is going to be found guilty of Faline's death."

"Not necessarily."

"Pardon me if I disagree. And I'm not going to do it!" the Grande Dame insisted. "I'm not going to be railroaded off the show when Beatrice is sentenced to prison for murder. I will not allow Marguerite Lemond to reach out from the grave to have the last laugh!"

With that she threw the pages at Teague and stalked off the set.

"Quenie, come back here," he ordered so coldly that Rae grew uneasy even in her removed perch in studio control.

The actress paused, her pose regal. "When the script is changed, I shall return," she said dramatically. "Not before."

"Don't pull a Marguerite on me, Quenie," he warned her. "We're behind as it is. I don't need this. If your histrionics get this show in any more of a bind, your contract won't be renewed."

"Don't threaten me, Teague Slaughter. I once *was* this show, and I *will be* again! You can't afford to lose both of your leading ladies at the same time!"

"Don't be too sure of that! There are other actresses who can carry 'Rivals,' and we have a few of them working for us right now!"

But Quenie didn't bother to respond, already sweeping off the set with all the grandeur of her character.

And Rae was horrified. Everything Carol had once told her came back to haunt her. Teague's relentless drive to succeed. His stepping on others to do so. His reputation as a hard nose when he thought he was right.

Of course he hadn't actually fired Quenie—he'd merely threatened her. And it wasn't as if the actress were being reasonable. She was magnifying the changes all out of proportion.

Unless . . .

"We don't need that kind of attitude on this set!" Gordon blasted his disapproval of the actress's behavior. "Not now, not when the ratings are skyrocketing beyond my wildest expectations!"

"Quenie's terribly upset," Christine said stiffly. "I don't blame her. We're all under too much pressure here after what happened to Marguerite." The blonde exchanged a private look with Jacobi and slipped off her stool. "I'll see what I can do to calm her down."

Christine left the control room, and the director opened the intercom mike.

"Let's keep going, folks. Una, read Quenie's lines until she gets back on the set."

If she came back. Rae wasn't certain what Christine could say to soothe the actress. Odd how, just as Marguerite had been convinced Faline would die, Quenie was convinced Beatrice was going to prison and she therefore would be written off the show, as well. The similarity of the situations disturbed her. And so, a few minutes later, when Quenie was escorted back to the set with Christine's comforting arm around her shoulders, Rae slipped out of the control room. While Christine stood at the edge of the studio, her back turned, Rae hurried down the hall to the older actress's dressing room.

It didn't take long to find what she was looking for. Quenie hadn't made any special efforts to hide what didn't belong in her hands. She'd merely dumped it in the wastebasket where she'd apparently thought it belonged.

Another copy of the long-range projection.

Rae fished the copy out of the wastebasket and flipped through the back end where she found an addendum, which she hadn't written. New pages that indicated Beatrice was tried and convicted of Faline's murder, that the Grande Dame was sentenced to a state prison.

What did this mean? Rae's pulse began to thud with the implications as she slipped the projection between copies of the scene changes she was still carrying with her. She had no way of telling whether this was merely another cruel joke . . . or a warning of some kind for Quenie.

Preoccupied with those thoughts, she left the dressing room without a sense of caution and ran straight into Bo Hathaway.

"Whoa," he said, steadying her shoulders. "What's the big hurry?"

"I've got to get back to the control room."

"Drive safely," he joked.

It wasn't until she was halfway to her destination that she realized this was Bo's day off. Two actors so dedicated to the good of the show—or actors up to no good? And then there was Yale Gordon. He'd been the one to demand further changes implicating Beatrice. He could have been responsible for the second altered projection.

Or for both.

Keeping an eye on the network executive in studio control, Rae was certain he was getting more than a ratings high out of the situation as the rehearsal progressed. Almost as though he had a personal vendetta against Quenie.

As soon as possible, she escaped back to her office. She had an idea of how to find out whether or not he was involved. Everyone's computer terminals were linked on an office-wide system. Although security was supposed to be a big deal, the codes usually consisted of the person's initials and a password having to do with the person's job. Using her own terminal, she could try to break into Gordon's subdirectories. And if he had copied the long-range projection from her only to alter the content, she would find that file!

She'd no sooner opened her office door than her empty stomach rumbled and her mouth watered. The room was filled with incredible aromas. And her desk was covered with a half-dozen white cartons.

Chinese carryout!

Teague must have had a messenger deliver the feast. The one they were to have shared the night before. His way of saying he was sorry about their fight.

Sitting at her desk and opening the first carton, she immediately softened toward him, gave him the benefit of the doubt in the Quenie situation. He had been provoked over and over in the past week. Anyone would be an ogre under the circumstances.

How long was she supposed to wait for Teague? She wondered if he meant to run up before dress rehearsal and have a quick meal with her. Surely he hadn't thought she could eat all of this herself. There was so much, she could try a few bites and leave the rest to share, Rae decided. She found a fork. Chopsticks had never been her forte.

A taste of each of three cartons satisfied the initial nagging hunger that had plagued her. She could work as she munched, slow down the process to give Teague a chance to join her. She began her attack on the terminal, taking small bites of food between commands.

After dozens of frustrating tries, Rae finally figured out Gordon's password, which was, amusingly enough, TYRANT. She quickly broke into his files. And she realized she was breaking into a sweat, as well. One of the dishes must have had those hot peppers she usually avoided. Ignoring the discomfort, she began scanning filenames in the first subdirectory. She opened PROJ but the contents had to do with advertising projections rather than story line. She closed the file and continued searching, but her head was starting to hurt and she was finding it difficult to concentrate.

She'd just opened REVISE when a quick tap at the door was followed by Teague's immediate entrance. He eyed the food splayed across her desk. "Hey, what's going on here? Having a party without me?"

"You should have told me to wait for you," she said irritably. She felt hot and flushed, totally out of sorts. And guilty for snapping at him. "Having the Chinese sent over was a great way of making amends for last night."

Too bad her stomach was cramping, and that she was slightly nauseous. That pepper really didn't agree with her!

And now Teague was looking at her as if she had two heads. "Are you feeling all right?"

"Not really. Something I ate—the pepper, I think."

He stared into her eyes. "My God, no." Grabbed one of her hands. "Your skin is clammy and cold." Circled her wrist with his fingers. "I can hardly find your pulse ... just like Marguerite."

His words were coming as if from across the room, but his touch was comforting. When he let go of her hand, Rae tried to protest, but she was too weak. She could hardly hold herself in the chair. Her eyes drooped shut and she felt as if she were sliding ... a thousand miles away.

From a great distance, she heard a thundering echo that must have been Teague's voice.

"...an ambulance over here quick...poisoned...too late ..."

Chapter Twelve

"She was lucky you were there to get her help so fast, Mr. Slaughter," the emergency-room doctor said. "We treated her with both stomach lavage and a dose of quinidine. That's a cardiac depressent to control her heart's rhythm," he explained, adjusting his glasses as he consulted the chart he held. "Her pupils and respiration have both returned to normal and she's resting comfortably."

"She's unconscious, then?" Teague asked, his shaky gut not appeased by a long shot.

"Sleeping. She should be able to leave the hospital sometime tomorrow, barring any unforeseen developments. She'll be moving a little slow—her body has had quite a shock—but she should be good as new."

"Thank God."

Teague sank back into the waiting-room chair. He was alone. The show had to go on, so he'd ordered Jacobi to take cast and crew through dress rehearsal with a stand-in, and to shoot around him if necessary. If he didn't make it to the studio in time, they would have to cancel the show and air some comedy rerun.

"Uh, Mr. Slaughter," the doctor said, "Miss Magill is asleep, so you might as well relax and go back to work."

"I'm not leaving until I see her."

He wanted to make certain for himself that Rae was all right. He'd felt a sense of panic and helplessness when he'd realized what had happened. He could hardly believe Rae had survived.

"If it'll ease your mind, I'll let you see Miss Magill for a moment, but she probably won't come around. Don't be too worried, will you?"

But Teague knew he was going to worry until the murderer was caught. Obviously Rae held the key to the person's identity or she wouldn't have been a target twice now.

Three times was the charm.

He had to make certain the killer didn't have a third chance at her.

His determination grew when he saw Rae in the hospital bed, looking so wan, vulnerable and completely helpless. No steel spine here. Just a woman who was, in the end, defenseless against the unknown.

He stroked her pale cheek with the back of his knuckles. She stirred, murmuring, "Teague?" as if she recognized his touch. Her eyes fluttered open, connecting with his only for an instant. She gave him a sweet smile before drifting off.

Something squeezed his chest. Hard. He recognized the feeling through it was brand new to him. He'd cared for his family, had been infatuated with a few women, but he'd never before felt this overwhelming need for someone. He realized he didn't merely desire Rae, he loved her.

"Mr. Slaughter, time's up," a young dark-haired nurse whispered. "And someone's in the waiting room for you."

With regret that he had to leave Rae's side, Teague went to meet the someone.

"Lieutenant."

"Mr. Slaughter, I hear Miss Magill is going to make it thanks to the way you so conveniently intervened before she took in too much of the poison."

Teague didn't like the way Franklin phrased that. But, "Thank God," was all he said.

"My evidence technicians have taken those cartons of food to the lab. I don't think the contents will be any surprise to either of us."

Teague's eyes narrowed. Franklin was playing with him. He sensed it with every fiber of his being. "Did you find out where the food came from?"

"Yes, Mr. Slaughter, I did." The cop paused for effect, then said, "The receptionist who accepted delivery did so in your name."

"What?"

"And if Wilona Irwin hadn't convinced me about the flowers, I might suspect you were a murderer."

Franklin's tone made Teague believe the statement was really a challenge, that he might believe it anyway.

"Get yourself another suspect, Lieutenant," he said coldly. "I have things to do."

Teague pushed past the smaller man and was surprised when the cop didn't call him to a halt. He strode out to the street where he signaled a taxi that took him back to the studio.

Once there, he updated the cast and crew with a powerful edge born of real life events rather than from acting techniques. The entire cast seemed equally sharp. Even Quenie behaved herself and played her scenes in rare form. Taping was finished in record time.

About to head for his dressing room to change, Teague was stopped by Saul Jacobi, who had rushed out of studio control to intercept him.

"Hey, Slaughter, want to go out and get a drink?" the director asked. "We could both use one, huh?"

Getting plowed was the last thing on his mind. "I need to keep a clear head."

"You think someone is after you, too?"

Teague's gaze narrowed and he studied Jacobi closely when he asked, "Now why would you assume that?"

The director backed off immediately. "No reason. But no reason for anyone to be after Rae, right?"

"No reason at all."

Teague couldn't help but wonder at the director's sudden friendliness and interest. Like paying a surprise visit to Gary Noble, ex-executive producer of "Rivals," who might give him further insight to their suspects. The man's resignation had never been explained as far as Teague was concerned. "Artistic differences" was a crock, a catchall phrase invented to cover a multitude of possibilities.

"WHEN AN ACTRESS has more say-so than the executive producer of the show," Gary said straight off, when Teague paid his predecessor an unannounced visit, "it's time to leave."

"Marguerite."

"Who else? The bitch had Yale Gordon so hot for her he was wrapped around her panties."

"I'd heard they were an item." Teague was playing it cool, hoping Noble would reveal something he didn't already know. "But then Marguerite seemed to be an item with half the men connected to 'Rivals.'"

"She was quite the busy queen bee."

And Teague wondered if Noble had been one of the drones. He wasn't Marguerite's type. In his mid-forties, Noble had medium brown hair and eyes and equally average looks. His apartment was well-located and decorated, but wasn't indicative of tremendous wealth. And obviously he didn't have the power Marguerite had found to be such an aphrodisiac.

"Maybe one of her lovers really had a thing for her," Teague went on. "Maybe someone she seduced, then dumped. Feelings run high in those directions," he admitted. "I would have sworn Marguerite was ready to kill me when I told her our personal relationship was over."

"Instead, she had you fired." At a window overlooking the river, Noble turned to face Teague and raised his glass. "I know all the gossip even if I wasn't working on the show then. Marguerite had a couple of other actors after you fired—the late lamented Hunt Harris and lucky Bradley Scott, now star of 'Friends and Enemies'—but that's ancient history, too."

Teague remembered some speculation surrounding Hunt's death, that his driving a car into a retaining wall might have been purposeful. He catalogued the information and asked, "What about a guy who was so jealous he would rather see her dead than with another man?"

"A trick like Marguerite isn't something you chance going to jail for...no less losing a rich wife over."

Noble's brows raised when he noted Teague's confusion. "I'm talking about your esteemed boss."

"I didn't know Diane was the one with the money."

But that might explain why Yale Gordon was so desperate for a high audience share. Teague realized the network executive had been afraid of losing both his job and his wife and therefore his rich and famous life-style.

Wanting to know for certain about the show's director, Teague asked, "What about Saul Jacobi?"

"Jacobi plays the odds in everything, including women. He was giving it to both Marguerite and Christine and keeping the relationships hush-hush," Noble stated "I doubt whether they ever found out about each other, though. I only did by accident."

Another surprise. Teague hadn't had a clue Jacobi and Christine had been getting it on, although he and Rae had linked him with Marguerite because of the note on the script.

"What about Bo Hathaway?"

Noble laughed. "You're kidding, right?"

"Am I?"

"You didn't know Marguerite was only a cover-up for Bo?"

"He's gay?"

"Impotent. An injury in Vietnam. He and Marguerite used each other as a front for publicity purposes, nothing more."

Noble had turned out to be a font of information and Teague considered his time well spent. His predecessor had revealed something new about each of the three men who were all suspects. Information Teague intended to share with Rae as soon as possible. He was keeping an open mind, trying not worry about her as the doctor advised him.

Unable to help himself, he checked on her condition by telephone twice more that night and once in the morning. If only he could talk to Rae herself. But the first two times she was sleeping though she had awakened several times. And he couldn't speak to her in the morning because she was in with the doctors who were checking her before issuing her release. At least she was able to talk to someone!

When he picked her up from the hospital early that afternoon, he was quickly relieved of his anxiety. She looked like the old Rae—a quieter version, perhaps, due to the drugs still in her system. As he helped her into the car, he thanked God no permanent damage had been done.

Pulling the Mercedes away from the hospital, he asked, "Do you have a friend you could stay with for a day or two?"

"I'm not an invalid. I don't have to be coddled."

"I meant someplace safe."

"Oh. Not really."

"Then I think we should stick together," he said cautiously, remembering the way she'd thrown him out on his ear the last time he'd tried to order her around.

"Okay."

Teague started when she didn't object. "Okay?"

"Hey, so I'm feeling a little vulnerable here, but don't push it."

"Okay."

"Although I don't know how you can keep an eye on me at work," she continued.

"I can if we both use the same office."

"Preferably yours?"

He tried to remain noncommittal so she could make that decision. "Mmm."

Rae laughed. "Stop walking on eggs or you'll make me think there's something wrong with you."

There was, but he didn't know how to tell her he was a lovesick fool, out of his depths in dealing with a woman he was terrified of losing.

She'd probably laugh at him again.

"Today's one of my days off the set. Other than one more meeting later this afternoon with the sponsor representative, I can help you play catch-up with any more revisions."

"Great. Did next week's rewrites come in from the associates?"

"Three did. Norman called and said he'd get another script in first thing in the morning."

"I'll track down number five if it hasn't arrived by the time we do," she said.

The last few blocks of the drive, Teague relayed the information he'd gotten from Gary Noble the night before.

"So Yale couldn't afford to lose a rich wife," he said. "And Bo's war injury must have been the secret Marguerite was threatening him with when you overheard their argument. But Jacobi's seeing both Marguerite and Christine...while interesting, I can't squeeze a motive out of that one."

"Gordon still seems the likeliest candidate. He had the most to lose."

"But Bo's career is everything to him," Rae murmured.

Teague wondered if Rae really was up to even a few hours in the office. When he glanced her way, how-

ever, she seemed more thoughtful than tired. He'd
hoped rehashing Noble's information with Rae would
sort out a few things, eliminate some of the suspects,
but the deeper they got into the case, the more questions needed answering.

He was beginning to think they were doomed to be
in the dark—and in danger—forever.

"YOU'RE CERTAIN you'll be all right alone?"

"Go to your meeting." Curled up in a chair, Rae
was going over the following Wednesday's script and
didn't need Teague or anyone else hovering over her.
She kept her patience, however, when she assured him,
"I'll be fine."

"If you need anything, just ask June."

"I promise."

Teague hadn't been gone for more than a few minutes before Rae set down the script, stood and
stretched. Touched by Teague's concern, she'd gone
along with his idea of her using his office. And,
truthful with herself, she was glad he'd made the suggestion—not that she would feel safe anywhere with a
killer on the loose.

Twice the guilty one had come after her. Being
struck by a taxi would have looked like an accident,
but poison? The killer was getting desperate and Rae
didn't look forward to a third go-round. She might not
be so lucky next time. But what was she supposed to
do, turn tail and run home to the midwest, back to the
safety of her family? Never!

Teague's office was as good a hiding place as she
could manage, that was for certain. She suspected
June had strict orders about playing guard dog. Rae
actually felt better for the fact. Though she'd tried not

to let Teague see it, she was more than a little frazzled.

She moved around the office, taking a better look at the objects that revealed various layers of Teague Slaughter. The style of the office reflected his vivid personality. The neatness of his desk and shelves showed the same meticulous care he used in his work. And the framed photograph on the credenza revealed a sentimental streak totally at odds with what she'd learned about the man from Carol.

She lifted the frame and studied the picture of Teague at a much younger age, maybe nineteen or twenty. He and two other guys were dressed in jeans, T-shirts and black leather jackets, bandanas around their foreheads. They were posed to look impossibly macho. His first acting job? She remembered hearing he'd been in commercials before being hired to spice up "Rivals."

Setting the photograph back in place, she slid into the chair behind his desk. Was it her imagination or did his warmth linger and surround her? She relaxed, head back, feeling for all the world like a woman in love. . . .

And then his computer came into focus. Rae blinked and snapped back to reality. Computer. Files. She had been about to look into Gordon's file REVISE when the poison had made her too ill to go on.

Rae immediately drew closer to the terminal, determined to take up the investigation where she'd left off. How could she have forgotten about the file and about the second altered long-range projection? She'd never had the chance to tell Teague about them, either!

Breaking back into Gordon's records was a snap since she'd already figured out his codes. She entered the first subdirectory and requested REVISE. In turn, the computer asked if she wanted to create a new file.

Rae frowned and scanned the list of file names, just in case she'd gotten the exact spelling wrong. But she found nothing similar. Could she be in the wrong subdirectory? She scrolled up and looked for the other filename she'd opened the day before, PROJ. Sure enough it was there. And opening the file revealed the same advertising projection.

REVISE was gone. Someone had erased it! Someone who'd seen it on her office terminal screen after the paramedics had taken her to the hospital?

Rae wondered if the altered projection still lay on her desk where she'd left it between copies of yesterday's scene changes. One way to find out.

The moment she set foot outside the office, June Chin popped up from the seat behind her desk. "Something I can get you, Rae?"

"No. I have to get it myself. I'll be right back." She started down the hall but realized the other woman was following on her heels. Afraid June would try to stop her, she said, "I'm just going to my office for a minute."

"Then I'll go with you."

"Teague's orders, right?"

The Eurasian woman flushed and hedged, "I could use a walk myself."

Glad for the company, Rae shortened her stride so the smaller woman could keep up.

Once in her office, she made a shambles of her desk. To no avail.

"What are you looking for?" June asked. "Maybe I can help."

Considering June had never been suspect, Rae saw no reason to keep the information from her. "An unauthorized copy of the long-range projection. I know it was here yesterday."

"Unauthorized?" June echoed.

"Yes, someone got hold of an extra copy somehow." No doubt by breaking her codes as she had done to Gordon's.

But June dispelled her of that assumption when she asked, "You're not talking about the one I made for Saul Jacobi?"

"Jacobi asked for one?"

"Yes, some time ago. Gary told me to to ahead and make an extra copy for him."

But the ex-executive producer had never informed her. "Do you know why?"

"He said something about Jacobi's wanting some creative input. Then Gary left and I haven't heard anything about the issue since."

Rae couldn't believe it. A breakthrough. She'd been tracking Gordon for nothing. Saul Jacobi was the one who'd been altering the projections.

Back in Teague's office, she tried to prove it by breaking into Saul's records. It took some time, but she finally managed to get in. Disappointment awaited her, however, when, after looking through dozens of files, she found nothing to indicate he'd ever made the changes.

"You look like you're sitting under a thundercloud," Teague said as he came through the door. "But I'm going to make your mood all better by ordering us both to leave this slave mill early." He drew closer and propped a hip on the edge of his desk. "We can go to my place and you can take me up on that raincheck for dinner."

"I thought you weren't going to order me around anymore," she reminded him.

"I thought you told me not to walk on eggshells."

He had a point. Besides, his bossiness didn't really bother her as much as it once had. "No Chinese."

"Nothing vaguely resembling oriental," he promised.

"Then you've got yourself a deal."

"And I hope you'll let me convince you to stay the night."

Rae's heart raced at the prospect, but was the suggestion merely for her own protection, or did he want her close for other reasons? Whichever, she couldn't read him. And she was thankful she wouldn't have to be alone.

Teague was looking at the terminal. "What have you been working on?"

Her thoughts veered away from the personal. "Trying to track down a murderer."

"Via computer?"

She nodded. "There's something I never got to tell you yesterday. I found a second altered long-range projection in Quenie's dressing room. New pages had been added to make her think Beatrice will indeed go to jail...and that she would, of course, be written off the show."

"No wonder she stalked off the set."

"I immediately suspected Gordon, and so began checking his files. I'd just opened REVISE when the special lunch someone left caught up with me. Someone erased that file after I was taken to the hospital."

"So it looks like Gordon—"

"Wait," she interrupted. "There's more. A little while ago, June told me someone had an extra projection, one that had been authorized by Gary Noble before he left the show."

"Who?"

"Saul Jacobi. But assuming he was the one who made the changes, he was too smart to leave evidence, at least not here at the office."

Teague indicated the terminal screen. "Those are his files?"

She nodded. "And I checked every one to no avail. Damn, this is frustrating!"

"Finding revisions in either man's files wouldn't prove he was the killer, anyway," Teague said. "But one thing's for certain—we'll have to keep a closer eye on both of them."

"Not too close, I hope."

Rae busied herself logging out on the terminal, but her mind was in a whirl thinking about the one man she hoped was going to get much closer.

And soon.

Chapter Thirteen

"You're sure this food is safe?" Rae asked half-jokingly as she looked over the Italian feast Teague had ordered from a nearby restaurant.

In the same spirit, he said, "I guarantee it. I trust Chef Giuseppe not only with my life, but with my palate." He uncovered the last of several mouth-watering dishes laid out between them. "To ease your mind, however, I'll try everything first."

"No, I didn't mean—"

"I'll bet even the Borgias had food tasters," he interrupted, taking a forkful of angel-hair pasta with pesto sauce.

Rae chuckled at the thought of the famous Renaissance family with a reputation for poisonings fearing their own weapon. Despite the tension that lay coiled below the surface, she relaxed and even took a moment to admire the view of Central Park afforded by their intimate dining table that sat next to a living room window. When she looked back at Teague, his handsome face was wreathed in ecstacy.

"So?" she prompted.

"Superb." He speared some calamari next. "I'll be happy to do all your food-tasting from now on."

"As long as you leave some for me," she said with a laugh.

Ladling a good-sized portion of the pasta onto her plate, Rae tried to forget why she was there under Teague's protection, tried to forget that, a mere twenty-four hours before, someone had, indeed, tried to poison her.

"Do you know all the local chefs on a first-name basis?" she asked.

"Only the best. A bachelor has to look out for himself." He added squid to both their plates, then a helping of sauteed zucchini and mushrooms. "Though I have to admit I did learn to cook simple meals in self-defense. Restaurants can get boring without the right dinner companion."

Because he was staring at her as if *she* might be the right person, Rae grew flustered.

"Have you even been married?" she asked before realizing he might misinterpret her interest.

Sure enough his brows shot up. "Nope. Have you?"

"I never had the inclination," she admitted.

"What? No nesting instincts? No biological clock ticking away?"

Having passed her thirty-fifth birthday, Rae was sensitive on that score, but she didn't let on. "No man I wanted to spend the rest of my life with."

Until now, she added to herself. For some foolish reason, she could see herself spending an unspecified amount of time with Teague. But of course the very idea was ridiculous. This was no courtship they were sharing, more like a partnership born of desperation. She was feeling grateful to Teague for having saved her life and protecting her so the killer couldn't get to her.

"What about you?" she asked between bites of food. "Why haven't you ever taken the plunge?"

"Until recently I never believed I would meet the woman of my dreams."

His piercing gaze shot a thrill through Rae right down to her toes, and she realized she'd been experiencing a lot of that lately. To cover, she tasted each of the several dishes on her plate.

"Wonderful food," she said. "You'll have to give Chef Giuseppe my compliments."

"Or you can do so yourself when I introduce you," he said, sounding as if that might be at any moment. "You'll like his place. Very romantic."

Rae felt flushed and delighted and confused. Was Teague intimating he wanted an ongoing personal relationship? Something that went beyond "Rivals" and sleuthing and a hot kiss or two instigated by the thrill of danger? Not willing to be direct enough to ask, she waited until she'd swallowed a mouthful of food, then changed the subject.

"I noticed that old photograph of you in your office. Black leather suits you."

She'd struck a nerve. The change in Teague was subtle, but she noticed. Almost as if she'd put him on guard.

"Not anymore," he said without missing a bite. "It did once, though."

"Wasn't that photo taken on a shoot?"

"It was taken in Chicago before I turned pro. Professional actor, that is," he clarified.

What other kind of pro was there? she wondered. But one question at a time. "Chicago? I thought you were from New York."

"There are lots of things we don't know about each other, Miss Straight Arrow Magill."

Annoyed, she stopped eating. "I wish you would stop giving me little zingers. It's not very flattering."

"That wasn't an insult. It was an observation—and one of many things I appreciate about you," he said seriously. "It's what sets you apart from the hundreds of show-business barracudas I've met over the past dozen years."

"You don't have a very high opinion of women in this industry."

"There are more Marguerite Lemonds than you would care to know about."

"I agree there are some, but there are plenty of male sharks in the business, as well." Remembering that she hadn't had a high opinion of him only days ago, had considered *him* another industry shark, she asked, "Are you certain your judgment isn't askew because Marguerite happened to you when you were young and vulnerable?"

"My judgment is quite healthy, thank you. And I'm older and wiser now. I recognize a user when I see one."

"Then I guess I should be flattered if you think I'm a 'straight arrow.'"

"You should be proud of yourself for maintaining your integrity."

The subject was making her uncomfortable, so she changed it once more. "Getting back to Chicago, to the photograph. Those other guys—were they your childhood buddies?"

"Other members of the Polish Princes. I belonged to a gang." He stared at her intently. "Does that shock you?"

Because she was certain her reaction was important to him, Rae choked back a laugh. "Actually, a gang named Polish Princes is kind of amusing."

"There was nothing funny about having to be part of a gang to survive."

The laughter died where it sat in her throat. "You're serious."

"You'd better believe it. I don't like having to think about those days, but it's part of my past and I can't change what I was. Does that bother you?"

Was he asking for her approval? "No, why, should it?"

"I was in and out of trouble every time I turned around. Everything that happened wasn't my fault—"

"But like you said, that's the past. Right?"

"I'm in some hot water now."

"We both are," she corrected him. "And neither one of us deserves to be."

"Sometimes fate deals us a hand that's not fair. Sometimes we're set up and there's nothing we can do about it."

Rae had the feeling his comment went deeper than she was able to discern. But if he were trying to tell her something, she couldn't imagine what.

"And sometimes the fates are good to us," she countered.

Teague nodded. "Like when a commercial producer spotted my friends and me mugging for that photograph."

"A he or she producer?"

"A she." He grinned. "I was offered a part in a commercial advertising Harleys, and the rest is history. My life was changed forever."

They spent a leisurely hour finishing their meal, during which Rae forgot all about work and danger and became absorbed by her interest in the man. Afterward Teague suggested he make cappuccino to go with dessert. Despite his objections, Rae helped him clear the table and, rather than setting the china in the automatic dishwasher, she washed the dishes by hand so she could stay close to him while he prepared the espresso coffee.

As they quietly worked side by side, she thought about his past. A tough kid, a gang member, always in trouble. And she'd assumed he was from wealth as indicated by his tasteful and very expensive surroundings. That only went to show her how much a person could change. And how wrong another person could be if she relied on assumptions and secondhand information. Again she thought of asking for his side of the story with Carol, but she neither wanted to break the fragile bond building between them nor spoil the intimate mood of the evening.

"Two cappuccinos and cannoli coming up," he said.

Rae followed him back to the living room where he balanced a tray with cups, plates and candles on the table's edge. She helped him empty the tray and more than once, their hands brushed as they reached for the same item.

The third time it happened, Teague took her hand in his and drew it to his lips.

The delicate feathering of his breath and lips along the inside of her wrist melted her bones so she swayed toward him for support. The tray clattered to the floor as he caught her and held her against him.

"Feeling weak?"

"Weak-kneed, Doc," she joked.

"Respiration?"

"Slightly shallow."

"Pulse?"

"Definitely fast."

"Good. Then we have the same symptoms."

He pulled her closer, found her mouth, nudged her lips apart. Her pulse wasn't merely fast, it was racing. At least this time, her system was going berserk from something other than fear or danger...rather, not the fatal kind.

Rae told herself she should be every bit as afraid of Teague Slaughter as she had been a week ago. But it was impossible when she felt so right in his arms. Of course, this couldn't last. Not the feeling. Not spiraling desire. Not the relationship. Over the past few days, divisions had seemed hazy. Lines had been blurred. But they were still there, and later she would be accountable for her actions.

But for the moment...

"I want you, Miss Straight Arrow Magill," he murmured against her hair.

"Steel rod spine, sourpuss and all?" she asked.

"Everything you are, everything you have to give."

And give she wanted. To him. She had for days. And not just because she hadn't been with a man for so long that she'd lost track. But because at this moment she found Teague Slaughter irresistible.

She told him so in the best of ways. Kissing his sensual mouth. Sliding her hands under his sweater. Touching the electric musculature of his back. Making intimate thigh-to-thigh contact that sent her soaring, even though they were both still fully clothed.

Teague groaned and moved in a sensual circle, not losing contact for a second. Their sexy little dance brought them quickly to the couch. Impatient, not wanting to go any farther—the bedroom seemed a million miles away—Rae lifted Teague's sweater. He helped her remove it. Then before she had the chance, he was unbuttoning her blouse. Unzipping her skirt. Stripping her of all garments, while seeming to touch every inch of her skin. He stepped out of his trousers and briefs and Rae was certain she'd never before seen such a beautiful man.

"Are you sure about this?" he whispered as he pressed her close and life stirred against her inner thigh. He found a breast and coaxed a nipple erect with his tongue.

Desire raged between them as she murmured, "Positive," and her hands tangled in his hair. She pulled his face up to hers for yet another hungry kiss.

The only thing she wasn't certain about were her feelings. Why she was so eager to make love with a man she hadn't even liked a few days before? As Teague lowered her to the couch cushions and entered her, she had herself convinced. If for no other reason, she needed his joining as a life-affirming celebration, a way to thank the fates—and Teague—that she was still alive.

And celebrating was so easy with this man who made her blood run thick with each touch, each stroke. In unison there was strength and together they would survive. The thought echoed over and over in her head as they partnered each other perfectly, giving and taking and coming together in a final frenzy that left them both breathing hard as if they had run a million miles.

Her heart was pounding, an ear-shattering sound, the reason why she wasn't certain of exactly what Teague whispered at the crucial moment. But she could have sworn "love" was among the jumble of words.

Afterward they lay together on the couch, limbs entwined, for what seemed to Rae like a blissful eternity.

His breathing finally steady, Teague said, "Dessert was definitely the best part of the meal."

Rae feigned shock. "We forget all about the cannoli and cappuccino."

"Are you sorry?"

"Greedy." She untangled herself from him. "We could have *two* desserts."

Teague bounded off the couch in one easy movement and drew her up with him. "Sounds good to me."

But when he started pulling her back to the window, she protested, "Wait a minute...my clothes."

"You look perfect now."

His eyes were on her, and even in dim light, Rae thought they looked darker, as if he were still excited. Her gaze dropped to a level that proved that theory.

Rae licked her lips. "I'm not exactly comfortable like this." When she reached for her undergarments, however, Teague stopped her.

"Let me help."

His idea of help was to touch as much of her as possible while fastening her bra and rebuttoning her blouse. Rae flushed and forgot her interest in the dessert on the table. She was certain Teague had had a hidden agenda all along when he pushed her back against the high couch arm, and insinuated a hand between her thighs.

Leaning over her, Teague made slow, exquisite love to her a second time. Rae curled her arms around his neck and her legs around his thighs and let him rock her to ecstacy.

This time when they untangled and he rescued her skirt from the floor, Rae grabbed the garment from him.

Laughing, she said, "I think I'd better do this my-self."

"Spoilsport," he muttered, fetching his own clothes.

But he was more relaxed than she'd ever seen him as he did his reverse strip, drawing on each garment in a provocative manner to make her smile.

Rae was enveloped by a welcome mood filled with excitement as they took their seats at the table. The cold cappuccino was refreshing, the room-temperature cannoli a delight on the tongue. But gradually, her keen physical awareness of everything she touched and tasted fought a losing battle to reality. What she and Teague had shared had been nothing more than a diversion. Making love hadn't erased their reason for being together.

And so Marguerite Lemond was allowed to intrude on their evening.

"Isn't it odd that the murderer used lily of the valley to poison first Marguerite and then me?" Rae suggested. She'd considered the fact several times during her waking moments at the hospital.

"I hadn't thought about it."

Especially when you consider using lily of the valley on herself was Marguerite's own idea. How would somebody plotting her murder have know about that.

"Hmm. Only if she told someone. Or if that someone passed on the information."

"Wilona!" they said simultaneously.

Teague moved to the telephone resting on an end table. "Why don't I give our fan-club president a call and find out?"

Rae headed in the opposite direction. "I'm going to listen in on the kitchen extension." By the time she picked up the receiver, the connection had been made.

"Irwin residence," came Wilona's shaky voice.

"This is Teague Slaughter."

The woman sounded stunned to hear his voice. "I— I'm so flattered you called."

"I wanted to make certain you were all right."

"As well as can be expected, considering . . ." She choked back a sob.

"At least you haven't been arrested."

"No, not yet." She sniffled before saying indignantly, "But that Lieutenant Franklin wanted to arrest me. I could tell."

"Franklin's a cop. It's his job to be suspicious of everyone," Teague assured her.

"He said I was an accessory, even though I told him Marguerite only intended to make herself sick, and that I had no idea that lily of the valley could be deadly. But I don't think *he* believed me."

Teague said, "I believe you and I'm certain others do, too, Wilona. By the way, did you ever tell anyone else about Marguerite's plans?"

"Well . . . um, no. . . ."

"But someone else knew?"

"I—I'm not sure. The day Marguerite told me, we were in her dressing room and she thought she heard someone in the hall. She looked out, but no one was there. Marguerite insisted another dressing-room door closed and that someone was hiding from her. I thought her nerves were on edge."

"Does Franklin know all this?"

"Should I have told him?"

"For everyone's sake, yes."

It was more than likely that someone else had known about Marguerite's plan and had used it against her—the information sent Rae's mind spinning. Teague gave the weepy woman some additional encouragement and signed off. Rae was at his side in a hurry.

"Can you believe it?" she asked. "Someone else knew but said nothing to the authorities, not even after you and I were named as suspects."

"The question is, was the person silent out of fear of being suspect, or because he or she used the information to murder Marguerite?"

"That someone gave Marguerite extra water from lily of the valley to drink, enough to kill her!" Rae exclaimed. "What about Jacobi—he went to Marguerite's dressing room supposedly to calm her down during rehearsal. But why?"

"What if Marguerite found out about Jacobi going after Christine and was planning on having Yale Gordon fire Jacobi?" Teague speculated. "She was good at disposing of men when she was through with them, as I can testify from personal experience. And Gary Noble said she had a few more notches at 'Rivals'— Hunt Harris and Bradley Scott—so this was a pattern for her."

Rae frowned. She knew Brad Scott, but she couldn't quite place Hunt Harris. Unfortunately talk of firings reminded her of Carol Flynn. She could no longer put off knowing his side of the story for her own peace of mind.

"Teague, when we first started working together, I'm sure you realized you weren't my favorite person."

"How could I have not noticed considering the looks you gave me. Your reason has something to do with Marguerite?"

"No. Another woman. Carol Flynn."

Teague tensed immediately at the mention of her friend's name. "What about Carol?"

"Why did you fire her?"

"Because she was a user," he said without hesitation.

"One of those barracudas?"

"Exactly. She slept with me because she thought I would promote her to a soon-to-be-vacated head writer's position, and I was—"

"You slept with her?"

Not knowing Carol had had a personal relationship with Teague, Rae was appalled. Carol had never told her that part of the story. She couldn't believe she'd just fallen into the same trap.

"A couple of times," he said tersely. "I thought we were mutually attracted to each other. I didn't realize Carol had an ulterior motive. When I talked to one of the head writers about promoting her, I found she wasn't even pulling her own weight as it was, but that people felt sorry for her and were covering. She thought a relationship with me would smooth things over. Well, it didn't work. Instead of promoting Carol, I fired her.''

Rae only half heard the explanation. The firing part. ''Are you sure you didn't fire Carol because you were tired of her? Or because she stopped wanting to sleep with you? Or because of some damn political reason that had nothing to do with anything? Are you any better than Marguerite?''

His eyes blazed like dark coals at the indictment. ''You obviously don't know the first thing about me. Not about who I am or how I operate.''

''I know enough.''

''Apparently you must to make such half-cocked accusations!'' he yelled, sounding ready to explode. ''Rae, I am not your father's boss!''

''What is that supposed to mean?''

''It means that, despite all your talk about ethics, work and otherwise, you have trouble believing they can get you where you want to go because of what happened to your father.''

''Leave my father out of this,'' Rae said furiously. ''You don't know anything about him!''

''Only what you told me. The night we had dinner, you talked about how the system worked for the most part. And how your father got fired at an age where it was difficult for him to find another job. He may have gotten a raw deal—''

''May have gotten?'' Her voice rose on each word.

''But don't judge everyone by what happened to him. I've never fired anyone indiscriminately or out of revenge or because they were inconvenient,'' Teague assured her. ''Your friend Carol was deadweight and not above using me to get what she wanted.''

''It all comes back to you, doesn't it?''

He was silent for a long moment before calmly asking, "If you suspect I was such a reprehensible person, then how could you have been attracted to me in the first place?"

"I haven't the faintest idea. I wish I hadn't been."

"I thought tonight meant something to you."

"It did—it was a great way of relieving tension," Rae said, then felt guilty when she saw the hurt she inflicted in his eyes. But she wouldn't take back the words.

"Think what you like, Miss Straight Arrow Magill. Don't bother listening to the facts. What's the truth compared to your misplaced sense of ethics?"

With that he stalked out of his own apartment.

And Rae was left dazed, wondering if she'd just made the biggest mistake of her life. Having just slept with her boss, would she now be fired?

Furious, she paced the living room for a while, waiting for Teague to return so she could hash it all out with him. If she was going to be pushed off of "Rivals" she might as well know now. But Teague didn't return. And exhaustion caught up with her until the only thing she could think of was to crawl into a nice comfortable bed and let her worries drift away.

Not *his* bed, though. She wouldn't be caught dead in Teague Slaughter's room.

And she might be found dead in the morning if she tried to crawl into her own.

A hotel! She would get out of this place and check into a hotel as soon as she could pull on her pantyhose and comb her disheveled hair. She crawled around the floor and had just found the pantyhose hiding under a chair when a banging at the door made her jump. No doubt Teague had stalked out of the place without his keys.

Working up enough steam to have it out with him, she whipped to her feet and to the door, then threw the heavy wooden panel open only to find Lieutenant Franklin and a uniformed policeman on the other side.

"Lieutenant."

"Miss Magill. Would you tell Mr. Slaughter I would like to see him."

Immediately uneasy, Rae said, "I don't know where Teague is at the moment. Why do you want to see him?"

Pulling a slip of paper from his breast pocket, Franklin said, "I have here a warrant for Teague Slaughter's—excuse me—a warrant for Theodore Slavensky's arrest."

"What?"

Franklin pushed past her. "Search the apartment," he told the officer.

"I told you he's not here," Rae said, alarmed when the officer pulled his gun. "Arrest for what?" Even as she asked, Rae knew the answer.

"For Marguerite Lemond's murder."

"He's no murderer!"

Teague might be a lot of things—shark and snake came readily to mind—but she didn't believe him capable of killing anyone.

When Rae caught her breath, she demanded an explanation. "What made you decide to arrest him now? Have you found new evidence?"

"I was suspicious when he avoided talking about his background, so I delved into his past. Once I found out his real name, the rest was easy. Did you know the man you're defending served hard time, Miss Magill?''

The talk of gangs and of doing what one had to and of fate playing tricks on a person came back to haunt her.

"For what?" she asked.

"A young man almost died because of Theodore Slavensky. Henry Ortega, the leader of a rival gang. And you want to know the motive, Miss Magill? Revenge." Glancing at the pantyhose wadded in her fist, Franklin said, "And maybe I was correct about other things, as well."

Rae didn't ask him to clarify. The detective thought she and Teague were in this together. Only he wasn't talking about arresting her, just Teague.

And then she would be left alone. . . .

A chill enveloped Rae as she realized she would be perfect prey for a murderer!

HIS MOOD AS BLACK as the night surrounding him, Teague drove like a madman the short distance to the CBC building.

Maybe he was crazy. He definitely should have his head examined for getting involved with yet another woman in the entertainment industry, that was for certain. He'd thought Rae was different.

Had she made him care about her and then slept with him out of some perverse sense of loyalty to Carol Flynn? Had she been trying to even the score for what she saw as an injustice to her friend?

In a business where sex was used often as another trading tool—one that Carol had used on him, no matter what Rae believed—he shouldn't be surprised. But he was. And disappointed.

He didn't want to add heartbroken....

He remembered Rae's last words to him, that their lovemaking was a great way of relieving tension. Surely she hadn't meant that.

But Teague feared that she had.

He parked the car and entered the CBC building lobby. All was quiet. The hour was late and he was sure the cast and crew of "Rivals" were long gone. He didn't even know why he was there, except that he hadn't been able to remain in his apartment—not with her around—for a single moment longer. That Rae might also leave occurred to him, and he worried that she would go back to her place and put herself in danger. No matter what her motives for getting involved with him, he couldn't turn off his feelings, couldn't stop caring.

But he also couldn't stop her from doing any damn thing she well pleased!

"Everything all right, Mr. Slaughter?" the security guard asked as he signed in.

Teague realized he was scowling. He forced his features to soften into a smile that prompted a like response from the guard. He'd always been a great actor.

"Just worried about the show, as usual. I thought I'd stop by to see how taping went."

"I heard it went smooth as glass. Everything's going to work out," the guard said. "You wait and see."

But Teague wasn't so certain that things would work out, not between him and Rae anyway. And as for the murderer... he had no intentions of waiting and seeing anything. If he hadn't had a purpose when he left his apartment for the studio, he had one now. On the chance that they might have overlooked something previously, he decided to investigate again, starting with the dressing rooms Rae had first searched. After all, how did he even know she'd told him everything she'd found.

Teague got into the elevator knowing that was pique talking. He didn't believe it for a moment. Nor did he really believe Rae had set him up. He couldn't think about their personal relationship now—assuming they still had one—or he would be too distracted.

When he got to the studio floor, Teague realized that while taping was indeed done for the night, the studio wasn't quite empty. He checked out the area from the shadows near the door to the dressing rooms.

Scattered workers were still around, members of the stage crew taking down the last of the sets not needed for the next day. Rufus Piggot was on the floor, but after giving one of the men instructions, the little man turned away and shuffled toward his office. Teague knew engineers would be in master control, and videotape editors would be in editing suites assembling the next day's episodes of the network's three soaps, inserting commercials between acts. But, if he were careful not to draw attention to himself, no one should pay him any mind.

He slipped out of the studio and down the hall to Bo's dressing room. To be safe, he knocked. No answer. The door was locked, but as executive producer, Teague had the master key. Once inside, he quietly closed the door and flicked on the light. After a cursory inspection of the room, he was drawn to Bo's files.

Everything was so neat and organized. Maybe he'd even find a folder labeled Murder. Now he was being ridiculous. If anything, the murderer was clever. What he did find was the contact sheets Rae had told him about. Sorting through them, he took a long look at the ones of Bo and Christine.

Rae had been correct about the sexual tension that jumped off the page. Remembering Noble had told him Bo was impotent, Teague knew the chemistry was strictly manufactured, making Bo Hathaway an even better actor than he'd ever realized. Was keeping that secret important enough to make the actor into a murderer?

He didn't want to think so, but neither could he see Christine or Jacobi in that role. And he'd discounted Quenie, Addison and Rufus altogether. Yale Gordon, however, was another story, one they hadn't checked closely enough. In Teague's mind, Gordon was unprincipled and greedy... and capable of anything.

He shoved the prints back into the file and left the dressing room. It was high time he searched the network representative's office. He didn't know why he hadn't done so before.

About to leave the area, Teague wavered. He might as well check one more soap star's dressing room as planned.

He opened the door and flipped on the light, gave the room a cursory once-over, but found nothing of interest until he hit on the scrapbook.

Teague settled in a cushioned wicker chair and flipped through the personal history of the star that began back in high school.

Paging through the memories automatically, he almost passed up the *Village Voice* review... until he glanced at the accompanying picture of a man who Teague instantly recognized!

Teague continued on, more carefully perusing pages filled with a combination of clippings and personal photographs that told a story of love won and lost. Of personal triumph and tragedy.

The truth unfolded before his very eyes.

The truth Rae must have seen but had not recognized....

Chapter Fourteen

Rae entered the CBC lobby with her stomach tied up in knots. First the argument with Teague, who'd walked out on her, albeit for good reason. Then her go-round with Franklin with his insinuations. Last but not least, the lieutenant's threat that she'd be seeing him very soon.

No doubt with a warrant for her own arrest!

"Miss Magill, you're here, too," the security guard said. "I don't know about you workaholics."

"Really," she said as pleasantly as she could manage. "How nice to hear others are as concerned as I am."

Signing in, she noted Teague had arrived a full twenty minutes before her. Well, she would just have to be careful and avoid him until he had a chance to cool off. Not that he would forgive her.

Getting into the elevator, Rae remembered how steamed she'd been when he'd brought her father into the argument. And how uneasy that what he'd been saying was true.

She'd always been proud of her ethics, of living up to her parent's standards. But deep inside she'd always wondered if having morals and ethics was enough to make a person happy, because of the way her father had been discarded when he should have been promoted. So what had she chosen as her profession but one of the toughest, most cutthroat businesses around.

And when Carol Flynn had sung a familiar song, Rae had believed her friend without doubt.

It was horrible to have to admit to being wrong, but that's exactly what she knew she was going to do. Everything she'd learned about Teague had told her he wasn't the monster Carol had made him out to be. And Carol had never admitted to sleeping with him. She had been protecting her own reputation.

As Rae had gotten to know Teague Slaughter, she'd warned herself to be fair, to listen to his side with an open mind. And then she'd done exactly the opposite, as if she hadn't wanted him to get too close.

And now she'd probably lost him for good.

But she couldn't let him go to prison for something he hadn't done. Not again. She, too, remembered things he'd told her. Or had tried to. She didn't believe he'd stabbed Henry Ortega any more than he had poisoned Marguerite.

Now to prove it!

Rae exited the elevator on the "Rivals" studio floor. Not that she even knew exactly what she was looking for. But they'd gone through neither Yale Gordon's nor Saul Jacobi's offices, and she intended to do both, starting with the director's work area, located next to studio control. Surely a writer could come up with a convincing tale so the security guard would unlock Jacobi's office for her and not mention it to the director the next day.

But when she reached the office area behind the studio, she found she wouldn't have to worry about making up a story, after all. The cleaning cart was wedged in the open doorway to Jacobi's office.

Rae approached the cart. "Bernice?"

Just inside the door, the cleaning lady jumped. "Missus, you scare me."

"Sorry. Are you almost finished in here?"

"Finished, yes."

"Good. I'll wait."

A moment later, Bernice piled her cart with cleaning supplies. "You go in now?"

"Yes, Bernice, thank you."

She started to do so until the cleaning woman put a hand on her arm and looked at her with worried eyes.

"Missus. I hear you sick." Bernice patted her stomach. "No good. Hospital."

"Yes. I was poisoned. But I'm all right . . . good . . . now."

Bernice shook her head solemnly. "Bad things, Missus. Bad things here." She crossed herself superstitiously. "Bird bad omen."

"Bird?"

"Bird dead. Missus Lemond dead. You hospital."

"What dead bird?" Rae had a sudden flash of Christine's bird cage and only Bonnie Blue inside. But she'd seen both birds since. "Miss Dellamorte's bird?"

Bernice nodded. "Missus Dellamorte, she cry. But new bird now, so Missus Dellamorte happy."

"How odd," Rae murmured. Then to Bernice, "Thank you for your concern."

"Yes, Missus," Bernice said, bobbing her head, but Rae wasn't quite convinced she understood.

The cleaning lady moved on and Rae was in Jacobi's office.

Her head whirled as she began her search. While the floor and seeable surfaces were clean, the place was a mess, things strewn everywhere, no order at all, making her wonder what the director's apartment must look like. She attacked a stack of papers that turned out to be mostly old scripts. Halfway down the pile, she found what she was looking for.

The long-range projection.

Hands trembling, she flipped to the end. Then went back in a few pages. This was *her* projection, not one that had been edited. Did that mean he had made another copy? She continued searching, going through every pile and checking under every surface and in every drawer, but she found no other version.

Perhaps someone else had made a copy of this projection without his knowledge.

Rae stopped for a moment. If only she could figure out who, she would know the identity of the murderer.

Leaving the office, Rae was on her way to the dressing rooms when she realized she wasn't alone. She whipped around. The hallway behind her was empty. No Bernice. Someone else. Someone was hiding from her. And waiting....

She slipped inside the pitch-black studio, moved carefully along the wall, behind one of the sets. She waited for her eyes to adjust. All she could see were the red emergency exit signs, greenish fluorescent light spilling in from the hallway, and a soft golden halo from equipment through the windows of studio control. She glanced back toward the hall in time to see a silhouette become one with the dark.

A murderer was in the studio with her and if she weren't very clever, she would be the next victim.

Other doors branched off the cavernous room leading to the various departments—makeup, wardrobe, sets and props. Perhaps the killer would assume she'd chosen one of them as her escape route.

Soft footfalls moved at random.

Away.

Closer.

And Rae could hardly breathe.

She waited for the killer to go off in another direction again, then seized her opportunity. First kicking off her shoes, she used the other person's footfalls as her cover. On silent bare feet, she ducked into the darkened control room and snugged herself next to the rack of equipment against the back wall. The footsteps seemed louder and quicker now and were coming in her direction.

They stopped outside the control-room door.

Rae's heart beat in her throat as she tried to hold her breath. She prayed the killer had vision and hearing no better than her own. But her prayer went unanswered.

"I know you're in there," came a calm, sexless whisper that drew ever closer.

A sharp metallic click sparked Rae's imagination. The safety of a gun. In her mind's eye, she could see it turning on her.

"Shall I turn on the light?" asked the killer, blocking the doorway now. Rae was certain the still-disguised voice was that of a woman. "Would that make you feel braver?"

Her breathing controlled so as not to betray her, Rae moved away from the equipment rack and toward the console, home to the camera switcher and special effects and audio controls. She was thinking fast, trying to figure out how to save herself. Teague was in the area somewhere. How close? Would he hear her if she screamed?

"I knew you knew," the killer said. "Why haven't you told the police?"

Only wishing that she did know for sure who the murderer was, and that the knowledge could somehow help her, Rae wedged a hip against the console, letting her left hand fall behind her, out of the killer's sight. Not that either of them could see much by the muted glow of lit switcher buttons. Two phantoms in the dark, only one armed. She could vaguely see the gun. It looked too small to be deadly, but she knew better. Rae felt carefully behind her, knowing what the correct switch looked like, what it would feel like. All she had to do was find it before the other woman figured out what she was up to.

"What did you think I knew?" Rae asked, triumphant when she felt the slender metal against her fingertip. "What exactly did you think I knew?"

Repeating her question to cover the metallic click, she threw on the switch and therefore the studio intercom . . . just as a woman said, "That I killed Marguerite."

Rae prayed that Teague—or anyone—was around the studio this late at night to hear their conversation over the speakers. Christine Dellamorte had killed Marguerite Lemond!

Stalling for time, Rae asked, "So why did you kill Marguerite, Christine? Was Saul Jacobi really that important to you?"

Christine let out a ragged cry. "Marguerite's sleeping with Saul was only the catalyst. I've hated that bitch for as long as I could remember. She never could keep her hands off any man, especially if he belonged to another woman. This wasn't the first time she took what belonged to me. She wanted Hunt Harris only because he was mine."

Teague had mentioned the man earlier, and now Rae knew why the name had been familiar. He'd been the actor in Christine's scrapbook, the costar with whom she'd had such an intense rapport. Rae should have placed the name when Teague had talked about Hunt Harris and Brad Scott being Marguerite's victims.

"So Marguerite stole Hunt from you," Rae said in an effort to stall the inevitable.

"He was my lover long before he got the role on 'Rivals.' We were happy together. Making plans to get married. Waiting until he hit the big one. Instead, Marguerite hit on him practically the moment he was hired." Christine hesitated, then whispered, "She seduced Hunt away from me."

Rae knew the other woman was crying. Not loudly and to great effect like Wilona, but silently like one who has suffered untold grief. Pity stirred in her against all reason. This woman had killed Marguerite and was going to kill her. Rae didn't know why the victim should feel sorry for her own potential murderer, but she did.

"Hunt was dazzled by Marguerite," Christine went on without prompting. "She made him forget everything we ever shared...all our bright plans for the future. When he finally came to his senses, she had him fired. I took him back, but it was no good. *We* were no good. His career...well, he couldn't get work." A single sob escaped Christine before she pulled herself back together to coolly finish, "Hunt needed work. It was killing him. His despair drove him to suicide."

"Oh, my God," Rae whispered.

She hadn't known Hunt Harris. But the tears that seared the back of her eyelids were for him. And for Christine, who had been destroyed as completely as the lover she had survived.

"You've been waiting all these years to get your revenge?" Rae asked.

"It wasn't like that, not really. I wanted to take everything Marguerite cared about away from her. But you know what?" The disembodied voice now spoke as if from an emotional distance. "She didn't care about anything or anyone but herself. I learned that quickly enough after I was hired to play Tempest."

Rae was getting anxious now. She didn't know how long she could keep Christine talking and distracted. While she felt sorry for the woman, she wasn't about to be her willing victim.

"You plotted to get on 'Rivals' so you could find a way to kill Marguerite?" Rae asked. She emphasized the last in case anyone was listening....

"I wanted the part on 'Rivals' because it was a good career move. When it came to taking something back from Marguerite, I felt helpless. She won every skirmish, whether it was over a costume or a scene or a story line."

"Is that why you changed the long-range projection?"

"I figured it was the only way I could get to the witch," Christine said. "She wasn't supposed to have the damn thing, so she could hardly go crying to Yale Gordon about it, could she? Marguerite went crazy when she thought Faline was being written out of the show and no one could convince her otherwise. And I enjoyed every minute of her misery.''

Rae kept the questions flowing. "She wasn't suspicious when you handed over the altered projection?''

"I conveniently left it where she could find it for herself. It was the first time I had the upper hand. And you know what? It felt good. So good. I hadn't actually thought about murder, not even when Wilona first confided in me about Marguerite's plans to get publicity. Then I caught the conniving bitch with Saul. I was furious... and devastated. She was simply amused.''

Only half-listening, Rae wondered if she could make a move on Christine without getting shot.

"That's when you decided to give Marguerite a deadly dose of lily of the valley.''

"Yes. I added more of the liquid to the stuff she had to drink on camera.''

The gun was pointed straight at Rae, the distance minimal. She didn't stand a chance unless she could get Christine off guard. "And you tested the poison on your bird?''

The questions were coming automatically now. But when would the other woman tire of sharing her victory? Rae suspected she was going to have to do something to trip the other woman up. She began inching her hip off the console.

"That was an accident," Christine was saying. "Ginny got out of her cage and drank the poisoned water when I wasn't looking. I loved that bird. Another thing *she* took from me.''

Rae wasn't going to argue that the pet bird's death was Christine's own fault. "I wondered about Ginny."

"I was so hoping you hadn't noticed she was gone the day I saw you go into my dressing room. I followed you inside to find out what you wanted and realized you were hiding behind the costume rack."

The information stunned Rae. All along, she'd thought Bernice had been in the room with her.

"You wouldn't have been trying to cover if you hadn't suspected me," Christine went on. "And then I saw the scrapbook out of place and feared you had the key to the whole thing." Her tone changed subtly, became more threatening. "I was hoping I was wrong, that you would leave the investigation to the police, but you didn't. I'm sorry about this, Rae, I really am. I like you."

That made Rae really nervous. She was running out of time. "You like me," she choked out, free at least of her seat on the console. "Is that why you tried to set me up?"

"I knew Teague would be under suspicion and I was merely trying to give the police some more suspects. Your interference distracted me or I would have implicated others."

"You would have let an innocent person take the rap for you?"

"I was hoping it wouldn't come to that. I thought if I created enough confusion, the case would go unsolved. Then no one who was innocent would get hurt."

"Really." Her limbs felt frozen and her mouth went dry. Rae knew her time was running out. She wiped her sweaty palms on her skirt. No one was coming to

her rescue. She was going to have to go for the gun.
"Is that why you've tried to kill me twice?"

"The first time was a warning. I was hoping to scare
you so you would keep your nose to yourself. But it
didn't do any good. I *had* to stop you to protect myself," Christine said.

And Rae had to do the same. She gathered strength
from somewhere....

"Don't you see that?" Christine demanded. "Poisoning you was an unfortunate necessity . . . as unfortunate as the accident you're about to have."

THE AMPLIFIED SHOT echoed through the studio and
was followed by a furious screech. Right outside the
door, Teague ran into the cavernous space and immediately became disoriented by the dark. It took him
a moment to spot the struggling silhouette in the control room. Before he could act, the single outline separated into two.

"Don't try that again, Rae!"

And Teague froze at the sound of Christine's voice.
He'd already figured out she was the murderer, but
he'd had no idea that Rae was in immediate danger.
He'd been on his way back to the apartment to tell
her....

"Why not? You're going to kill me, aren't you?"

"I don't want to, Rae. I told you I'm sorry. I don't
have any choice. Now let's get out of here, nice and
easy. Don't try anything," Christine warned her again.

Teague thought fast. If he let his presence be
known, the actress would probably shoot Rae on the
spot, then come after him. But if she was taking Rae
elsewhere, that would buy him some time. He hung
back and melded further into the dark as stumbling

sounds told him the women were coming out of the control booth.

"You don't have to do this, Christine. You already said you don't want to."

To an untrained ear, Rae might sound conversational, but Teague heard the underlying panic in her voice.

"I can't go to prison and be locked up like an animal because of *her*. I'd rather die first."

They passed into the light and Teague saw the gun pressed into Rae's back. The blonde steered her toward the elevator where a car waited.

The moment the elevator doors closed, Teague was off, out of the studio and taking the fire stairs two at a time. He arrived at the executive floor and looked through the window slot just in time to see Christine push Rae by him and toward the general elevators that went to the lobby.

And, he remembered as the car went up instead of down, to the roof!

Dear God, what did Christine plan for Rae?

He didn't need a divine answer to know. Another set of fire stairs would lead him up the two remaining flights to the roof, but the women had a good head start. With a burst of speed he didn't know he possessed, Teague was on his way, determined to stop the insane actress at any cost.

He couldn't let the woman he loved die, not even if he was meant to lose her to her own ethics! But no, he wouldn't lose her at all if he had to tie her up and make her listen to reason. He'd been too damn stubborn to stay and fight long enough to get the situation straightened out. Surely once she had time to think about it, she couldn't hold Carol Flynn's unconscionable actions against him.

But would she believe him about his more distant past? a little voice taunted him. He chose not to consider her reaction. Perhaps she would never have to know.

Sprinting to the top of the skyscraper left him short of breath and a little weak-kneed but no less driven. He cautiously opened the door to the roof and then cursed when a gust of wind tore it from his hand.

"What's that?" Christine asked as the door's hinges protested under the sudden pressure.

Teague ducked back into the stairwell and listened intently. Feeling as if a mile rather than a hundred feet or so separated them, he stood silent and frustrated. He'd gotten only a glimpse of Rae's horrified expression as she stood on the precipice of a no-win fall.

"YOUR GUILTY CONSCIENCE, Christine," Rae said, uneasily glancing over the side of the building, a hollow space that seemed to go on forever. Light headed, she decided she must have imagined the flash of movement near the stairwell. "You can't live with another death—the death of an *innocent person*—on your conscience."

"Hunt was innocent, too, and I've lived with the memory of his death and his pain for so many years that a little more won't make a difference."

Rae drew a shaky breath and took a good look around. This was all so unreal. Lights meant to warn low-flying aircraft of the skyscraper's existence illuminated and exaggerated the field of battle. The roof was flat but for the lights, elevator shafts, stairwells and a four-foot retaining wall skirting its perimeter.

And beyond lay the city, its sparkling necklace of brilliant lights surrounding them.

What irony! When she'd arrived in The Big Apple to seek her fortune in daytime television, she'd had dreams of having all of Manhattan at her feet some-day... only this wasn't exactly what she'd envisioned.

Standing near a stationary metal ladder that would take her up and over the edge, an eerie wind wailing through the building tops around her, Rae fought the queasiness that threatened to empty her stomach.

"You can't mean for me to jump," she went on. Anything to stall. "Why do you want me to die when you won't get away with it?"

"Everyone will think you committed suicide," the actress explained in a reasonable manner. And yet her voice was tight, her speech unnatural. "They'll believe you were guilty of Marguerite's death and couldn't live with yourself any longer. I think I'll leave a suicide note on your computer." Her laugh was odd, a little too bright. "I've already broken your access codes, so it won't be any problem, you see. You were looking in the wrong person's files for the revisions I made. You should have looked in your own."

So Christine had been the one to erase REVISE to make her suspect Gordon. Though the blonde's entire focus was on her, Rae kept looking back toward the stairwell surreptitiously. Her vigilance was rewarded when she saw another movement. A dark shadow separated from the structure.

Please, God, let it be Teague!

Hope renewed, she asked, "So you changed Quenie's story line, too?" in an effort to stall for time. Her nerves were stretched so tight she was afraid they would snap.

"I told you I was trying to create confusion," Christine said, suddenly terse. She waved the gun at Rae. "Enough talk. Get up that ladder."

Rae froze. The woman was serious. The moment of truth was at hand. And God knew, she was no heroine. Look how she'd bungled her attempt to get the gun away from Christine in studio control. But she couldn't just let it happen.

"I'm not going to jump to save you," Rae said, and, hoping to outbluff the other woman, added, "You'll have to shoot me!"

Christine laughed again, the sound more frenzied this time. "If I have to, I'll shoot you, put your fingerprints on the gun and throw your body over the side!"

"You'll have to do better than that!" came a male shout.

Teague! Rae was never so glad to see anyone in her life as he ran forward and into the light.

Christine turned—

"You'll have to shoot us both!" Teague warned her.

—and aimed her gun directly at him. The report echoed through upper Manhattan. Teague stopped cold as if he'd hit an invisible wall. He swayed and stumbled to his knees.

And Christine was raising her gun again!

Limbs suddenly unfrozen, Rae lunged forward and grabbed the other woman's hand. The actress shrieked and fought like a tiger, pummeling Rae with her free fist, then grabbing her hair. Rae used both hands to keep the gun pointed away from herself. A second later, a shot went wild.

"Rae!" Teague grunted.

From the corner of her eye she saw him rising unsteadily to his feet.

"I'm...all...right," she gritted out, still struggling.

Her scalp was on fire and her eyes teared as Christine ripped at her hair. Without slackening her grip, Rae slipped both thumbs down to Christine's wrist and using her sharp nails, applied as much pressure as she could to the tender area.

Christine screeched.

Rae felt the other woman's grip on the gun slacken and with desperation born of fear, gave Christine's arm a tremendous jerk. Held too loosely, the gun went flying and sailed right over the retaining wall and off the skyscraper.

And Rae was physically jerked from Christine, who looked like a wild woman, completely out of control. Rae came to a quick stop against Teague's chest where she felt something warm and sticky penetrate her blouse.

"Thank God you're all right," he said.

"You're the one who's bleeding—"

"Nothing ever goes right for me!" Christine wailed to herself. "Not since that bitch Marguerite got her hooks into Hunt. She's dead, but if I go to jail, she's won! Now what am I supposed to do?"

She wasn't even looking at them, didn't seem to know they existed. She's lost it, Rae thought, watching Christine glance around in a daze and crumple inside before Rae's pitying eyes.

"Turn yourself in," Teague said gently.

Christine's eyes lost the dazed look as they finally focused on the couple. "Never!"

"Explain everything that happened, starting with Hunt," he said. "The courts will go easy on you."

"They'll get you the help you need," Rae added, certain that a psychiatric evaluation was in order. The woman was having a nervous breakdown right before their eyes.

But Christine wasn't listening. She scrambled up the ladder to the top of the retaining wall. "I'd rather die before letting Marguerite win again!"

"Wait!" Rae yelled, lunging back out of Teague's arms as Christine turned unsteadily to face her chosen destiny.

He, too, flew forward, arms reaching, fingers grabbing . . . but not fast enough.

They were both left with nothing more than fistsful of the sporadic night wind as Christine Dellamorte let go of the ladder and leaned forward to seek release from her pain.

RAE'S STOMACH WAS STILL churning as the ambulance slid into the night carrying its misshapen cargo in a zipped plastic bag. Death wasn't a pretty sight.

That might have been her.

Them, she amended, eyes focusing on the temporary bandage on Teague's shoulder. He'd refused to go to the hospital with the paramedics, but had promised to do so on his own later, after everything was straightened out with the authorities. Rae thanked God that she'd stopped Christine from getting off another round. Obviously the woman had known how to handle a gun.

"I misjudged you," Lieutenant Franklin admitted. "I thought I had my man . . . and I was wrong. See you both tomorrow." The homicide detective headed for his unmarked car but paused long enough to say, "Next time, let the professionals handle it."

"God forbid there should be a next time," Rae muttered.

At least this case was solved to Franklin's satisfaction. He'd taken their depositions and had confiscated the scrapbook as evidence. Furthermore, Rufus Piggot had been in the property department and had entered the studio in time to hear Christine's threat before the gun had gone off. Because he'd had no desire to be a hero, he'd sneaked back to his office to call the police.

"I left that videotape of Gordon and Marguerite at Rae's door," Rufus was saying. "I knew Quenie stole it from Marguerite as an insurance policy against being written off the show."

"And you took it from her dressing room the day of the funeral, right?" Rae said.

"How'd you know, cookie?"

"We saw you," Teague said.

"Hmph, and I was so careful." Rufus shook his head. "I woulda sworn Gordon was guilty. He hated Quenie, too, 'cause she dropped hints about his playing around to Diane."

No wonder there'd been such animosity between the two. "Thanks for everything, Rufus," Rae said.

"For you, cookie, anytime." With a wave, Rufus headed down the street.

"Now it's time to get you to a doctor," she said, starting off toward the garage where Teague parked his car.

He grabbed her by the upper arm and swung her around to face him. "The doctor can wait."

Rae didn't meet his eyes. Tension snapped through her as she remembered all the nasty things she'd said to Teague earlier. Though he'd come to her rescue, she wasn't sure he would forgive her. "You've already waited too long as it is," she argued, wondering what she could say to keep the man she loved in more than her professional life.

"You sound worried."

"Damned straight I'm worried. You lost a lot of blood." She looked down at her ruined blouse. Anywhere but at him. "Most of it on me."

"I was hoping it would be more personal than that."

His hopeful tone made her meet his gaze, after all. "Teague, I..." The moment of truth had arrived, finding Rae with a mouth as dry as cotton. "I, uh, was as wrong as the Lieutenant."

"About?"

He wasn't exactly making this easy for her. Frowning, she shot him an annoyed look and figured he was thinking she was a sourpuss again.

"About Carol. You had some valid points. I didn't really want to hear your side of the story, I guess. I did some thinking after you left. About my ethical code. I guess I was defensive over what happened to Dad. I let my own rigidity get in the way of my happiness."

"Are you saying I made you happy?"

"Uh-huh."

"And that maybe you were looking for an excuse to drive me away?"

"I didn't say that," she quickly retorted. "I didn't do any such thing, not on purpose." Reluctantly she added, "Well, maybe subconsciously."

"Why?"

"I was afraid of getting too involved with you. You're so much stronger than I am."

Teague indicated his wounded shoulder. "Not at the moment."

"Not physically. I'm talking about our personalities. We're both strong-minded people. I like to be in charge. And when you're around," she admitted, "I don't know if I'm coming or going."

"That's what happens when you fall in love." Before she could respond to that, before she could demand to know if he loved her, too, Teague said, "But if a relationship is going to be successful, both people have to be honest. I haven't told you everything about me."

Relationship? Her pulse picked up in tempo. Then he did care. "You mean about Theodore Slavensky? I already know."

"Franklin." He spat out the detective's name. "Listen, I want to tell you my side of the story."

"I'd like to hear it." Though she understood now why he hadn't been open before.

"I grew up in a multi-ethnic, tough Chicago neighborhood. Being part of a gang was a fact of life for protection—not that I was a complete innocent."

"I never thought you were," Rae said blandly, but she wasn't referring to his youth.

"Okay, so I was involved in a few petty crimes." Now he was starting to sound defensive. "A rival gang started a war and threats of revenge went back and forth. One night, the leader of the other gang got caught alone in an alley and was knifed. I found Henry and saved his life. He was so grateful, he pointed the finger at me, Rae, but I swear I didn't do it."

"I believe you, Teague." To reassure him, she moved closer and slid her hand up his good arm. "I didn't believe Franklin when he told me."

"The jury didn't believe me. I spent eighteen months at Joliet for something I didn't do. That's why I insisted we had to save ourselves by solving Marguerite's murder."

"But it's in your past." She touched his cheek, let her hand drift down to his neck. "All that matters is the future."

His gaze was soft and filled with longing when he asked, "You don't hold it against me, Miss Straight Arrow Magill?"

Not in the least put out by the nickname this time, Rae shook her head. "I'm only sorry you had to go through such a horrible experience. But it's part of what made you who you are."

"Who am I?"

Emboldened by the fact that he was sharing so much with her, she moved closer and slid her hand around the back of his neck. "A man who is ethical and strong, but the kind of tough I respect."

"My past is what drew me to you." He wrapped an arm around her waist and firmly drew her to him. "I respect a woman with ethics. But when you brought up Carol, I was crazy enough to believe you used me to get even for her. I was wrong. You're everything you seemed and more."

He took her mouth with his, a farther reach than usual. Rae realized her feet were bare. Her shoes still lay on a set in the studio. His kiss was passionate and so full of promise, she ached with relief and wanted to protest when he ended it.

"I love you Rae Magill, and I really do hope you feel the same about me, because we're perfect for each other."

Rae grinned and pressed closer. "That's something I don't ever intend to argue about."

HARLEQUIN

I N T R I G U E®

A SPAULDING AND DARIEN MYSTERY

This month read the heart-stopping conclusion to the exciting four-book series of Spaulding and Darien mysteries, #197 WHEN SHE WAS BAD. An engaging pair of amateur sleuths—writer Jenny Spaulding and lawyer Peter Darien—were introduced to Harlequin Intrigue readers in three previous books. Be sure not to miss any books in this outstanding series:

#147 BUTTON, BUTTON: When Jenny and Peter first met, they had nothing in common—except a hunch that Jenny's father's death was not a suicide. But would they live long enough to prove it was murder?

#159 DOUBLE DARE: Jenny and Peter solve the disappearance of a popular TV sitcom star, unraveling the tangled web of Tinseltown's intrigues.

#171 ALL FALL DOWN: In an isolated storm-besieged inn, the guests are being murdered one by one. Jenny and Peter must find the killer before they become the next victims.

#197 WHEN SHE WAS BAD: Jenny and Peter are getting ready to walk down the aisle, but unless they can thwart a deadly enemy masquerading as a friend, there won't be a wedding. Or a bride.

You can order #147 *Button, Button,* #159 *Double Dare,* #171 *All Fall Down* and #197 *When She Was Bad* by sending your name, address, zip or postal code, along with a check or money order for $2.50 for book #147, $2.75 for book #159, $2.79 for book #171 or $2.89 for book #197, plus 75¢ postage and handling ($1.00 in Canada), payable to Harlequin Reader Service, to:

In the U.S.
3010 Walden Avenue
P.O. Box 1325
Buffalo, NY 14269-1325

In Canada
P.O. Box 609
Fort Erie, Ontario
L2A 5X3

Please specify book title(s) with your order.
Canadian residents add applicable federal and provincial taxes.

SDRE

HE CROSSED TIME FOR HER

Captain Richard Colter rode the high seas, brandished a sword and pillaged treasure ships. A swashbuckling privateer, he was a man with voracious appetites and a lust for living. And in the eighteenth century, any woman swooned at his feet for the favor of his wild passion. History had it that Captain Richard Colter went down with his ship, the *Black Cutter,* in a dazzling sea battle off the Florida coast in 1792.

Then what was he doing washed ashore on a Key West beach in 1992—alive?

MARGARET ST. GEORGE brings you an extraspecial love story next month, about an extraordinary man who would do anything for the woman he loved:

#462 THE PIRATE AND HIS LADY
by Margaret St. George
November 1992

When love is meant to be, nothing can stand in its way...not even time.

Don't miss American Romance
#462 THE PIRATE AND HIS LADY.
It's a love story you'll never forget.

PAL

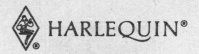 HARLEQUIN®

THE TAGGARTS OF TEXAS!

Harlequin's Ruth Jean Dale brings you
THE TAGGARTS OF TEXAS!

Those Taggart men—strong, sexy and hard to resist...

You've met Jesse James Taggart in FIREWORKS!
Harlequin Romance #3205 (July 1992)

Now meet Trey Smith—he's THE RED-BLOODED YANKEE!
Harlequin Temptation #413 (October 1992)

Then there's Daniel Boone Taggart in SHOWDOWN!
Harlequin Romance #3242 (January 1993)

And finally the Taggarts who started it all—in LEGEND!
Harlequin Historical #168 (April 1993)

Read all the Taggart romances!
Meet all the Taggart men!

Available wherever Harlequin books are sold.

If you missed *Fireworks!* (July 1992) and would like to order it, please send your name, address, zip or postal code, along with a check or money order for $2.89 (please do not send cash), plus 75¢ postage and handling ($1.00 in Canada) for each book ordered, payable to Harlequin Reader Service to:

In the U.S.	In Canada
3010 Walden Avenue	P.O. Box 609
P.O. Box 1325	Fort Erie, Ontario
Buffalo, NY 14269-1325	L2A 5X3

Please specify book title with your order.
Canadian residents add applicable federal and provincial taxes.

HARLEQUIN

AMERICAN ◆ ROMANCE®

A Calendar of Romance

American Romance's yearlong celebration continues.... Join your favorite authors as they celebrate love set against the special times each month throughout 1992.

Next month... Mix one man and one woman, two matchmaking moms, three young boys and 50,000 turkeys and you have a recipe for an uproarious Thanksgiving. It'll be a holiday that Luke, Darcy and the Calloway turkey farm will never forget!

NOVEMBER

#461
COUNT YOUR BLESSINGS
by Kathy Clark

S	M	T	W	T	F	S
1	2	3	4	5	6	7
8	9					
22	23	24	25	26	27	28
29	30					

Read all the Calendar of Romance titles!

If you missed any of the Calendar of Romance titles—#421 *Happy New Year, Darling*; #425 *Valentine Hearts and Flowers*; #429 *Flannery's Rainbow*; #433 *A Man for Easter*; #437 *Cinderella Mom*; #441 *Daddy's Girl*; #445 *Home Free*; #449 *Opposing Camps*; #455 *Sand Man* or #457 *Under His Spell*—and would like to order them, send your name, address, zip or postal code, along with a check or money order for $3.29 each for #421 and #425 or $3.39 each for #429, #433, #437, #441, #445, #449, #455 or #457, plus 75¢ postage and handling ($1.00 in Canada), payable to Harlequin Reader Service to:

In the U.S.

3010 Walden Avenue
P.O. Box 1325
Buffalo, NY 14269-1325

In Canada

P.O. Box 609
Fort Erie, Ontario
L2A 5X3

Please specify book title(s) with your order.
Canadian residents add applicable federal and provincial taxes.

COR11

HARLEQUIN HISTORICAL

CHRISTMAS

• STORIES • 1992 •

Capture the magic and romance of Christmas in the 1800s with HARLEQUIN HISTORICAL CHRISTMAS STORIES 1992—a collection of three stories by celebrated historical authors. The perfect Christmas gift!

Don't miss these heartwarming stories, available in November wherever Harlequin books are sold:

MISS MONTRACHET REQUESTS by Maura Seger
CHRISTMAS BOUNTY by Erin Yorke
A PROMISE KEPT by Bronwyn Williams

Plus, this Christmas you can also receive a FREE keepsake Christmas ornament. Watch for details in all November and December Harlequin books.

DISCOVER THE ROMANCE AND MAGIC OF THE HOLIDAY SEASON WITH HARLEQUIN HISTORICAL CHRISTMAS STORIES!

HX92R

HARLEQUIN®

I N T R I G U E®

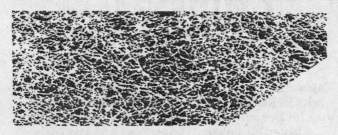

INTRIGUE IS CELEBRATING ITS 200TH BOOK!

Remember all those great adventures you had....

The SHADOW OF THE MOON spills across the stained carpet
and the NIGHTWIND howls. You're stuck in a HAUNTED
HOUSE in which HIDDEN SERPENTS slither. There's a CALL
AFTER MIDNIGHT. It's THE LATE GENTLEMAN ringing to
see if that FACE IN THE MIRROR is SUITABLE FOR
FRAMING. "What do you mean?" you scream wildly into the
phone. But the only reply is WHISPERS IN THE NIGHT.

And the suspense continues! Don't miss Intrigue #200
BREACH OF FAITH
by Aimée Thurlo

Two hundred escapes into suspense and danger with
mysterious men brave enough to stop your heart.

IF TRUTH BE KNOWN, a trip through a Harlequin Intrigue
can be STRANGER THAN FICTION!   HI200